Praise for *The Question of Red*

"A huge bestseller on its publication in Indonesia, *The Question of Red* signalled Laksmi Pamuntjak's bravery and scope as a writer, and may yet prove to be a landmark work of Southeast Asian writing."
—Tash Aw, author of *Harmony Silk Factory*, *Map of the Invisible World*, and *Five Star Billionaire*

"With this novel Laksmi Pamuntjak firmly establishes herself as one of the most eloquent writers of Indonesian history, intertwining scenes of great tension and reckless passion with sections of great historical interest . . ."
—Professor Saskia Wieringa, author of *Lubang Buaya*, writing in the *Jakarta Globe*

"In *The Question of Red*, Laksmi Pamuntjak masterfully weaves a web of narratives dealing with a dark, bloody chapter of Indonesia's history, the 1965–66 anti-Communist purge—a topic that remains controversial to this day. It is more than a love story or a historical novel, it is also an erudite reflection of the stunning amalgam of what Indonesia is: a Muslim-majority country influenced by both the modern West and its Hindu heritage."
—Yenni Kwok, journalist for *Time* and the *New York Times*

"What makes *The Question of Red* not merely a historical epic or a common love story is the stylishness of its prose, the psychological depth of its characters, its reflexivity and erudition, and the meticulous research that lies at its heart, which breathes life into the setting and all the life situations and existential dilemmas it encompasses."
—*Kompas* (Indonesia)

"This novel . . . comes to us indirectly 'at the point of forgetting.' [Here is] a disappeared person; to stress his absence, the novel presents only the few letters unearthed from beneath the tree in a corner of Buru Island. We get the voice of a person, Bhisma, who 'twinkles and fades.' *Amba* [*The Question of Red*] is one of a few novels that stress the sense of anxiety plaguing us in Indonesia these days: the anxiety that the terrifying 'events of 1965' will be lost, stripped from collective memory. We do not want to return to brutality."

—*Tempo Magazine*

"This is a richly textured, multilayered novel; an intricate weave of erased histories, living memories, and formative myths of war and peace. At the centre of the saga are the compelling figures of the doomed lovers, Amba and Bhisma, who attempt to undo an ancient legend with tragic consequences. With passion and exemplary commitment, Pamuntjak brings to life a forgotten era of turbulence, with its casualties, its victims, and its perpetrators. I was immersed in the novel's world for a week, and when I emerged I was spellbound for days."

—Aamer Hussein, author of *Cloud Messenger* and *Another Gulhomar Tree*, writing in the *Friday Times* (Pakistan)

"The most important Indonesian novel of this winter."

—Cornelia Zetszche, member of the 2015 Weltempfänger Best Fiction jury

The QUESTION of RED

The QUESTION *of* RED

A NOVEL

LAKSMI
PAMUNTJAK

Text copyright © 2013 Laksmi Pamuntjak
Translation copyright © 2014 Laksmi Pamuntjak

Previously published as *Amba* by Gramedia Pustaka Utama in Indonesia in 2013. Translated from Indonesian by the author.

Published by AmazonCrossing, Seattle

www.apub.com

Amazon, the Amazon logo, and AmazonCrossing are trademarks of Amazon.com, Inc., or its affiliates.

ISBN-13: 9781503936430
ISBN-10: 1503936430

Cover design by Rachel Adam

Printed in the United States of America

For those once incarcerated in Buru,
who have given me new eyes

For my parents, and for my daughter, Nadia

Contents

A Note on Buru

The Maluku Islands, part of what is commonly referred to as the Spice Islands in the Indonesian archipelago, sit east of Sulawesi (Celebes) and west of Papua.

Buru, the third largest island in the Maluku Islands, is largely mountainous, with a flat coastal plain where most of its 162,000 inhabitants live.

Rich in teak, sago, clove, and melaleuca oil, Buru became part of independent Indonesia in 1950. The population is evenly divided between followers of Sunni Islam and Christianity—about 40 percent each—and the rest still practice traditional forms of worship. About one third of the island's inhabitants are indigenous.

During President Suharto's administration (1965–1998), the island was the site of a large penal colony where more than 12,000 alleged Communists and Communist Party sympathizers were detained for more than a decade *without being formally charged or tried in court. Hundreds of prisoners died or were killed there.*

Even though the prisoners were officially liberated between 1978 and 1979, many chose to remain in Buru. Since then the island has remained a symbol of President Suharto's "New Order" repression.

Prologue

The Mahabharata *tells the story of a king who had three daughters as precious as diamonds: Amba, the eldest; and the twins, Ambika and Ambalika. Amba was bound in a pledge of marriage—as was the fate of most women—to King Salwa, a man she neither loved nor hated.*

One day a sudden blinding light engulfed the royal court. There was talk of a thief in a chariot, a ghostly presence. Amba and her sisters had been abducted, and the whole court was aflutter because none but the great warrior Bhisma could have managed such a feat. While the epic tells us that the fates were kind to Ambika and Ambalika, who went on to perpetuate the Bharata line through their sons Destarastra and Pandu, Amba's life took quite a different turn.

King Salwa sent an army to retrieve his betrothed, but his men were no match for Bhisma. By dawn the next day bones were broken, blood was coursing, and the heads of half the king's army were floating in the river. Meanwhile—and this is the part the book only ever hints at, and which we must flesh out—Amba had fallen in love with her captor, and he with her.

But the depth of this feeling frightened Amba: it was a feeling more powerful than any she'd ever felt. Overwhelmed, she entreated Bhisma to return her to Salwa. Bhisma recognized the longing in her eyes and, for fear of its repercussions, took no time in returning the princess to her designated suitor.

King Salwa, however, would not take Amba back. His pride was too immense, a mountain from which he ruled. He told her that she had dishonored him. She had worn her love for Bhisma like a mask; it had altered the contours of her face, and it was plain for all to see. Disgraced, the distraught princess had no other recourse but to return to Bhisma, her last hope of saving her honor. But how could she have known that Bhisma had taken a vow of celibacy long before they met? Devoted son that he was, Bhisma had sworn his chastity so his father could marry the woman he himself loved. Always quick to reward duty before self, the gods had granted Bhisma the power to choose his own death; until such time, he would be invincible. Invincibility, of course, meant nothing to a man in love; yet more than any man, Bhisma knew where man ended and history began. When Amba arrived to beg him to marry her, he shook his head and turned away. But even the trees and the birds could taste his grief.

As Amba was shuttled back and forth, eventually abandoned, alone, her heart turned to stone.

In the next life Amba returned as Srikandi, one of Prince Arjuna's many wives. In the Indian version of the epic, Srikandi is known as Sikhandin, a male warrior who had once been a woman. It was also foretold that she would be the one to bring down the indomitable Bhisma.

At the Battle of Kurusetra, the great conflict between the Kurawas and the Pandawas, Prince Arjuna was sure to have his warrior wife beside him. From her chariot Srikandi let fly scores of arrows, like a flock of birds set loose upon an island. In the Indonesian version of the epic, Srikandi's femaleness so disarmed the gallant Bhisma that he yielded, not even two fingers' breadth of his body left unpierced by her arrows. In both versions, Srikandi made the same choice, to kill Bhisma and save Arjuna, as though it never occurred to anybody there might have been another way, an outcome less brutal and more merciful, a solution that didn't so inextricably intertwine their fates like the red and white of the Indonesian flag—so heavy, so weighted with destiny.

∞

Now, it is important to understand that the Javanese are careful with the names they give their children. They understand all too well the great burden and history of a name. Either your life does your name justice or you might as well not have been born at all. The elders have a phrase for this: keberatan nama. It means a state of being burdened by a name too great, or too portentous.

And so, Amba killed Bhisma, thus ending the battle of all battles. The sheer glamor of which, surely, makes the princess ripe for eternal veneration: a heroine from antiquity, a role model for the feminist movement.

And yet this is not what happens. The name Amba, far from being heroic, still reminds folks of the worst of all fallen women, a woman twice spurned, a woman discarded by not one, but two noble men, and one whose legacy is not defined by her brains or by her skills or by the quality of her heart, but by her burning desire for revenge. And there is nothing more shameful than a woman who does not gracefully accept her fate, justified or otherwise.

Yet every so often people dare choose a culturally unpopular name for their offspring. They do so because they may have a different take on mythology's influence in human lives, or they are prepared to challenge the notion that a name makes a person. Sometimes it simply feels right, because no other name will do.

For is it not true that all stories exist to be written anew?

BOOK 1

Samuel and Amba

Buru Island, March 2006

1

Nightshade

Beyond Buru Island, the sea is deep and motherly. It knows how to wait. In the morning, in the green fields farther inland, dewdrops rest on the tips of grass like glass fans, and the breeze hovers a fraction longer, as if to chance upon a secret, or to find what rises to the surface after the rain. Yet the fields are silent. It is the night that will reveal what is obscured by daylight.

But every so often something happens on this island that is so singular, and so irreducible, that folks don't know how to talk about it other than in whispers.

Such is the story of Amba and Bhisma. Sweet and lethal, like nightshade.

※

March 2006

Three days ago, two women were brought to Waeapo Hospital. The first was a woman from Jakarta; the ID card in her wallet said her name was Amba Kinanti Eilers. It seemed that she had married a foreign man and adopted his family name. The ID card also said she was sixty-two years of age. She had been attacked by the other woman and was unconscious.

The other woman turned out to be Mukaburung, the adopted daughter of the chieftain of Kepala Air, in the headwater area of the River Waeapo. There were claims that Mukaburung had also hurt herself, but the details were hazier here. At any rate she was kept in the same hospital for a few days before she returned to her village. There was no denying that the two women were a spectacle, one that simultaneously displaced and fed the general stupor.

But in Buru, people are used to asking questions without receiving answers. And turning the other way.

It appeared that a code of silence had been forged between hospital management and the local leaders. During the staff meeting that followed the women's arrival, the eagerly awaited statement from the head of the hospital contained only three sentences: *Both women need tending. Everything is under control. Don't ask too many questions.*

Nothing was known of the woman from Jakarta. She was in all probability Javanese, yet something about her was also not wholly of Java.

She had an interesting face, hard edged and dignified, and could certainly pass for fifteen years younger than the stated sixty-two. She also had startling eyes, tender yet exacting, undeniably a mother's eyes. But there was something about her mouth, the stern yet sensuous curve of her lips, that suggested something guarded yet vulnerable, as though long trained to keep secrets. More vexing still was her behavior when she finally came back to consciousness. She kept insisting on visiting her husband in the ward at the other end of the corridor.

"He's there," she said repeatedly. "I swear. I've come all this way to see him."

No man in that ward fit the description she gave.

"We'd love to help," the head of the hospital told her, "but the only patients here are a few locals with minor injuries. Everyone knows each other around here."

"All this time, I've been married to a dead man," she said.

And then she slid into total silence, a kind of waking coma.

❧

Twenty-four hours later, a few details started to surface. The woman named Amba had been brought to the hospital after she'd been found in the pouring rain, covered in blood, hugging a grave on a hilly patch in the middle of the woods. Mukaburung was found not very far away. She was on her knees facing the same grave, as though in supplication, holding a bloodied knife in her hand. Not that there was anything unusual about these circumstances, apart from the knife and the blood, for the natives of Waeapo were used to coddling the dead as though they were the living.

When asked why she did what she did, Mukaburung said, "That stupid woman had no right to hug that grave."

The sight had made my blood boil, she later told others. *Didn't she know that the man in the grave was my husband, wedded to me by my adopted father, the chieftain himself?*

❧

There is a man sitting in the administration office. No one has ever seen him before. Once again, the hospital is aflutter.

Like Amba, he too seems to have fallen from the sky. What's more, he has come to claim her. The task of telling him what has happened, and of ensuring that he is who he claims to be, has fallen on the shoulders of Dr. Wasis, the most senior doctor in the hospital.

Dr. Wasis, a man most flat in all his aspects, which is to say his face, his comportment, even his voice, has been told by his staff that the visitor has "policemen friends." It goes without saying that these "policemen friends" must have been responsible for directing the stranger to the hospital. So everyone leaves it at that. On this island, you don't mess around with the police or with the military. Anyone already claimed by one of the two is best left alone.

What everyone in the hospital *can* and *does* gossip about, however, is who this visitor could be to the woman from Jakarta. He looks to be in his midforties . . . Her son? A friend or an associate? A younger lover? Nothing in the visitor's features suggests he is even remotely related to her. He is about as pin-downable as a bead from an ancient world, his skin a glossy caramel, his features vaguely Melanesian, his eyes a disconcerting milky green-gold. Then there is also that wiry, well-muscled frame, and the not-so-ordinary matter of his height. All of six foot, by local standards a giant. Listen to the nurses rustling in the background like bitches in heat.

There was once a time when only seafarers made their way to Buru, and some eventually settled down here. They were the people of Buton and Bugis: sturdy, direct, happiest at sea. But these days folks have stopped asking where other people come from. Even Buru, for all its slough and bile and resistance, is now a land of many colors.

The doctor is presently telling the visitor that it had taken two men and a woman to wrest Amba away from the grave. In addition to hugging the rain-soaked mound as if for dear life, she had also planted a rectangular object on the mound, something that, someone reported, had looked like a picture frame. It was from this she had strenuously resisted being parted.

"But you told me," says the visitor, visibly shaken, "that she was stabbed several times."

"Oh yes, she was. But I wouldn't say they were, you know, serious wounds," says the doctor. "Still. She was . . . glued to this object. Her hands were torn when they finally yanked it from her grip. It turned out to be a photo of a child. They told me the woman looked heartbroken when it was taken from her."

"Do you—do you know where it is now, that photo?"

"With the police, I would think. Taken as evidence, I mean."

"I see," the visitor says. "Thank you." He hesitates. "My name is Samuel, by the way."

"Ah."

"It's . . . Samuel Lawerissa."

"Ah."

Then, after a sheepish silence: "Well, thank you, Samuel, for coming to help us with this matter." Silence again, before the doctor says, his own nervousness barely concealed, "So, I take it you are *Ibu* Amba's relative?"

"No. A friend."

"A friend?"

"Yes."

"Perhaps you can tell me a little about her?"

The man named Samuel nods, his eyes polite, but he says nothing.

"What was he to her, the man whose grave she, er, clung to?"

Again, nothing. Of all the deep, difficult emotions, silent possessiveness isn't exactly the worst they've seen in Buru. The doctor is Javanese; he knows something about the many shades of wordlessness. Yet his brows are furrowed for a second.

"You let me know how I can help, yes?" he finally says to Samuel. "Come. I will walk you to her room."

❧

They are in her room. It is not quite noon and a slant of light cuts into a portion of the woman's face as she lies on her piss-scented mattress. Her eyes are wide and inanimate, her arm and fingers scarred, a mess; she appears sullied, sad, despite life's best effort to dignify.

And then it happens, the most extraordinary aspect yet about the visitor—how being in the presence of this woman alters his demeanor. When he first arrived, this man named Samuel, there was something petulant and fettered about him, as though his mind was being gnawed by something inside. But in this room, his face becomes something else. There is something about the sight of the woman that breaks him to pieces.

Suddenly the doctor feels his heart burst.

❧

"You told me they were shallow wounds," Samuel says, half accusingly.

"Yes," the doctor says. His tone falters just a bit. "And that's why she'll live. Give her ten more days or so."

"I'm sure you, or the chief, must have your reasons," Samuel says, trying not to sound too stricken. "But may I know why the woman who hurt my friend was brought to the hospital as well? It doesn't make sense to me that they have been kept close to each other."

"The woman who attacked your friend . . . she stabbed herself, too, you see. To her, it was some kind of purification, I think." The doctor sighs, as if fighting difficult memories. "Also, it was the wish—no, the express order—of her adopted father, the local chieftain. He seemed worried that Mukaburung might be taken into custody by the police. I guess he just wanted to prevent that from happening."

Samuel frowns for a second, but decides to let it go.

And because Samuel says nothing, the doctor asks him whether he knows what *nituro* means. He doesn't wait for Samuel to answer. "Dead soul," he says. "One who once haunted the coast in search of a lost love, a lover most likely, or a daughter. That's what it means."

They both look at the woman.

How perverse it is, Samuel thinks, to see her like this: those blistered shoulders, her hand faintly jaundiced like the onset of death, the skin with its tracery of bestial blues and reds and greens.

"She came to Buru to look for the love of her life. His name is Bhisma," he says at long last. "I traveled to Buru by chance with her and someone who, at her insistence, pretended to be her relative, a man who was also Bhisma's best friend. And then I lost her."

As he follows Dr. Wasis back to his office, Samuel tries not to check his own feelings, to see if he is holding up. Neither does he bother to look at his cell phone when it rings. It's no use to him; he doesn't want to talk to anyone. All he sees is the image of Amba the moment he first saw her, on board that shitty, stinking ship only a few weeks ago.

She is older, true, but it changes nothing. It never does. She had bewitched him, and it tore him apart then as it tears him apart now, this enchantment, this weighty, ravelled web. She was like this wounded but proud animal, looking for her lost cub. He simply wants to stay with her until she is back on her feet.

When they reach the doctor's office, on the first floor, Samuel sits down in the offered chair. To the doctor's surprise, he begins to talk.

"When I met her"—his voice surprising even to himself—"we were on the *Lambelu*. You know it, I'm sure, the big state ship that sails three times a week from Ambon to Buru?"

The doctor nods.

"She was not traveling alone. As I told you before, she was accompanied by a person who I thought at first was her relative, a slightly older man. They told me they were going to Buru looking for someone. I became friends with them and somehow fell into helping them in their search.

"We began as soon as we disembarked at Namlea, following leads, meeting people, old and new. But we came to a dead end. She was upset, yes, but she seemed to agree with her friend and me that there was little else we could do. That it was best to go home. Suddenly, on our last night in Buru, her friend announced he had to go back earlier, he had things to do. He asked me could I please take Ibu back home to Jakarta? With pleasure, I said. So I traveled back to Ambon with her on the express ferry. Then we stayed in Ambon one night in order to catch the flight to Jakarta the next day.

"We had agreed to meet in the lobby early in the morning and leave together for the airport. But when I came down the next morning, the receptionist told me that she had left earlier. I raced to the airport and searched the whole place like a madman. She was nowhere to be found. Eventually I realized that she had probably never intended to go to the airport. As my plane was due to leave I decided to board anyway. I mean, nothing good could come of lingering. Clearly she didn't want me to follow her. So what would be the point."

An hour later, Samuel is sitting on the porch of the hospital, dragging deeply on a cigarette. It is raining now, everything heavy and hostile. Leaves and canopies sag under the weight like an army of defeated slaves, while moss and gravel, those tiny, near-imperceptible things, are quietly swept by the current into another village, voiceless and shattered, like the stories of people without names.

There is something at once soothing and disabling about such rain: its swish and odor, its largesse and melancholy, its slow but savage way of bringing out unbidden memories. But Samuel can only feel dread and desperation in his already smoke-filled lungs. What can he possibly say to himself to make this feeling go away? The feeling of having failed, despite everything he's done to keep her safe. And now she lies there in her bed, conscious but refusing to even acknowledge him. If she chooses to punish him with her silence, what else can he do but sit it out?

Every now and then he leaves the porch to peer into her room. He wonders for the umpteenth time whether he has misread everything, misread *her*: whether all this time their friendship had been a ruse, a mere vessel for her to get to this point, *the* point at which she wanted her story to end. And whether she'd chosen him, out of all the men who were available to her, to bear the message of all heartbroken women: *that you, too, must suffer what it means to be left in the dark, alone and abandoned.*

He lights another cigarette and looks back at the rain, at its curtain of fineness, its quiet deceit.

The truth is, he is no stranger to this island. In fact he spent the later part of his childhood on this very soil, something he had deliberately kept from Amba until shortly before she ran away from him. Yet, absurdly, he now feels slighted for not having deserved her trust.

Indeed, it was Buru that had raised Samuel; it had taught him most things he knew. In 1950, after the Indonesian government defeated the Republic of South Moluccas, Samuel's parents, both Ambonese, were exiled to Holland, along with thousands of their compatriots. This made all of them fighting on the side of the Dutch that most bruising of things: traitors.

In 1966, when Samuel was eight, his parents sent him to Buru to live with a distant uncle. They thought he'd be safer anywhere outside the city of Ambon, where his parents had a history. Samuel remembers little of what life in Holland was like, except that they were always cold and hungry and that his parents were always at each other's throats. His father was a drunk and an inveterate gambler, and all he remembers of his mother was someone who was never not crying. It was clear that exile, with their five children, daily rations, and living on other people's good graces, had shocked them to the bone.

Whatever their motive for choosing to send Samuel away, and not one of their other children, was never clear. He was certain of only one thing: it wasn't his parents who raised him.

At the time, Samuel's uncle, also an Ambonese, was manning the State Oil company depot in Namlea, a small operation by any standard. Samuel didn't much care for him, or his wife. His uncle never had much interest in the lives of others. All he ever cared about was how he would fill his own time, recording everything and missing nothing, including how the indigenous people of Buru reacted when the government told them sometime in the '60s, in no uncertain terms, that a boatload of strangers was coming to the island.

Samuel was watching from afar the afternoon the first batch of political prisoners arrived, exhausted and mute in khaki uniforms. This was in 1969. He decided to follow them as they were marched to a mangrove area and a building known as the Transit Unit. At eleven he was long limbed and fleet footed: already a stealthy and seasoned tracker. He noted how the Transit Unit seemed like a godsend to these people, how it made them smile, how it made their eyes go wide. It delighted him, that a single alien structure, not the prettiest of places, could offer so much hope: the outdoor kitchen he knew so well, where he often went to steal matchboxes and coffee. The sight that would greet them once they went inside, through the side door: the broken chairs, the moldy pantry, the words "Ganyang PKI—Annihilate the Communist Party," written in red paint. The rush of stale air mixed with the smell of rat piss. But the strangers he watched seemed unfazed, because the larder held sugar, salt, and enough coffee for one night, and such things seemed to count as happiness.

Later, when he left Buru for the first time as a young man, he knew no other place that could teach him anything he had not already learned. Buru taught him about rain and drought, true and stirring things.

It was like that, too, with Amba. He felt that somehow he had established an innate understanding of her when he met her on the way back to Buru. And now he has come back to Buru for her.

A new nurse comes in. She has a different air from the others, who were all timidity and empty pleasantries. This one is all confidence and poise—with a face, Samuel thinks, that isn't half bad. He watches her greet Amba. There is less ceremony, that's true, yet there is still a TV commercial aspect to her tone, the high melodious lilt, as though she is speaking to an infant. The how-are-you-today, the isn't-it-a-lovely-morning, do-you-think-you-can-try-some-food-now routine.

To her credit, Amba says nothing, for she's no child. Yet Samuel sees the tension in her muscles slowly unknot. She is so painfully thin he can see everything happening underneath her skin. He gets up, wanting all of a sudden to touch her hand.

He watches quietly as the nurse tells Amba that the people at the hospital have made a mistake with her name. They thought her name was Am-ba-ra, but that was to be expected, because folks around here are generally mistrustful of two-syllable names beginning with *A*. It's like missing a certain vital essence, a certain conviction. "And don't you worry, I've set the record straight," she told Amba proudly. "I told them that your name comes from *The Mahabharata*, and that it is the name of a famous princess."

"Okay," Samuel says, hearing his own impatient voice fill the room. "You can go now. I will look after her."

13

Then, as though morphing back to her original character, the nurse says the next time she comes she will try to bring a radio for Amba. "Radio equals music equals healing," she says and giggles idiotically before going back to talking about food to encourage her patient's response. She mentions black-rice pudding, fried banana, sticky-rice cakes. The best breadfruit on the planet. "Would you like me to bring some? But only if you promise me to eat."

Samuel watches a few more minutes of this pointless fussing. Suddenly the nurse turns to him.

"That woman who attacked Ibu," she says sharply. "You want to know about her, don't you?"

Samuel returns her pointed stare. "No, not really." He frowns, then says, "Not right now, at any rate."

"Well, I'm telling you that we all know her. We all know her because she used to come here often."

"Okay. Thank you. But not right now."

"And because we know her, this woman, we know that her claim is true. The dead man, he really was her husband. Her husband was a doctor, you know. She was a gift to him, for being so indispensable in the village."

He feels the dawning of panic. *Shut up,* he wants to tell the stupid bitch. But how does it work here? To tell someone to shut up? He turns around, wishing for the first time she was really dead.

"That dead man in the grave," the nurse continues like a spoiled child, "you know what they called him?"

Stupid bitch.

"They called him the Wise Man from Waeapo," she says. "Nobody knows where he came from, and it's true—some of us have never seen him, including me. But rumor has it he was so tall and splendid looking that some say he was not of this world. Others say he was a political prisoner, a *tapol*, during the Suharto era. Imagine. A Communist!"

"Please," he hisses. "Can't you see that this woman doesn't need to hear all this?"

The nurse turns toward the door, and for a few seconds she looks almost beautiful. For one outrageous second, he thinks of asking for her number, but his thoughts return to earth as soon as he hears the nurse's parting words.

"It would have been nice to grow old with someone, don't you think?"

2

Rubble

A week is a long time to hang around an infirmary in some outpost of civilization. It brings neither joy nor retribution to Samuel, whose mornings are usually spent in injurious silence, watching Amba propped up like a lifeless doll against her saggy pillow. Sometimes the nurses wheel her to the terrace and leave her there with him. They all think alike—that she is his responsibility, after all.

At his insistence several days earlier, Amba's bed has been moved closer to the window in her room, away from the door, from everything that might happen outside it, and everything that it might usher in. Every time he drifts into sleep, he dreams of a woman, her features obscured by the darkness, sneaking into Amba's room with a large carving knife and slicing her neck like a pig, over and over until the whole room turns red.

As he stands gazing at Amba, he realizes her right arm and upper right chest are still weak from the blows she suffered at the native woman's hand. She can't even raise her hand to reach the glass of water; he has to hold it for her. Dr. Wasis said she would need a couple more weeks of antibiotics, followed by physical therapy. Samuel realizes the doctor could not even look him in the eye when he mentioned those two words. He tries not to think about how much he may have to shell out if he does have to take Amba to Ambon, say, on the fast boat, and into a major hospital for such treatment. He doesn't have a clue whether she has money for such expenses. If not, how spectacularly speedy his slide from a nobody to a pauper would be, at his pathetic age of forty-eight.

He tries not to think of death. He tries not to think of his life without this woman.

How does it come to this? A month ago, he had enlisted a policeman friend to assist him and Amba, before she ran away from him. A policeman so formidably ugly as to have earned the nickname "the Grotesque." Now the guy seems to have fallen off the face of the earth. Not only has he disappeared, but calls to Samuel's other contact, Hasan, his jerk of a friend at the police HQ, also draw a blank.

Outside, some people are arguing, their voices rising. He can smell exhaust from the parking lot. Funny how between that and the cloud of cigarette smoke there is so much here that can jeopardize a person's health. Again, he wonders how this place can possibly call itself a hospital, and suddenly, he is all choked up. He can't go on waiting. He has to have a plan.

The nurse reappears at the door. "I think the woman who attacked your friend wants to talk to you," she says, her face vexed, as though by a missed association.

As Samuel runs after her he barely feels his feet meet the floor.

It was love, not hate, that drove her to draw her dagger, so Mukaburung tells him. For it is possible that in the mud and sewage of one's life one finds a higher love. "My last husband," she says, "the man who is lying in that grave, he never touched me, not even once. He told me his heart belonged to another woman and that he must stay true to her. But I, Mukaburung, don't mind. I don't mind that he never touched me. It's because he never touched me that I believe he loved me the most out of all the men who thought and called me theirs."

Her arm is withered, a warrior's arm. Samuel places his hand on it, not trusting himself to speak.

"You're a friend, yes?" she inquires cheekily. And smiles.

But then, of course she knows the answer. She knows she has been forgiven.

Which is what he is explaining now to Amba.

There is a suspense-filled moment, like the one you wait for in a movie, then Samuel sees it: her tears.

The next morning, Samuel finds Amba propped up in her bed.

"Can you get me a glass of water?" she says weakly, as though she has woken from a long dream.

It is midnight, two days after Amba's release from the hospital. She and Samuel have been ensconced in this unfamiliar room—*Only for special guests,* the host told them proudly—since 10:00 p.m. It turns out to be the *pamali* room, a room for prayers and offerings.

Long tracts of awkward silence engulf them. Stifling the urge to light another cigarette, Samuel says, "We might be here a long time.

The ceremony at the grave could take another hour or so. But this is still the safest place for us to be for now."

Amba is barely there, her gaze faraway. But he knows she's listening.

"The villagers—you never know. I don't think they understand why you're here, who you are. Many are still suspicious of outsiders. That includes me. I may look like an Ambonese guy, but not quite. What business do I have in this village? So, as I said, we're probably safest here. That man, the one who spoke to us just now, the one ogling you all night at the grave, well, he's the *mauweng*. This is his house."

And because she still doesn't say anything, Samuel goes on. "Chieftain, leader of the clan, and witch doctor rolled into one. When the ceremony wraps up—if it ever does—the entire village will probably end up here."

She frowns. Then says, "If he's the chieftain, doesn't it mean he's the adoptive father of the woman who attacked me? I can't see how that makes me safe."

Finally.

"Relax. You see how he was to us," Samuel says. "Even village leadership, in the end, is about balancing the odds."

Silence, the length of the room. "I suspect your man was held in higher regard than even the mauweng himself," Samuel offers, after clearing his throat. "Had he been a native, he might have been made a *soa* chief, or even the ruler of a *negeri*."

Amba smiles. Relaxes. *You're sweet,* she seems to be saying, *for trying so hard.*

Earlier in the evening they, too, had been at the ceremony at the very grave Amba had, only a few weeks earlier, been found tethered to, and where they were both surprised to see no sign of Mukaburung. Citing Amba's condition, they stayed no more than an hour. The chieftain had been particularly attentive to her during the ceremony despite Amba having no clue who he was.

But yes, he was needlessly charming. *Tonight,* he told her, *we would commemorate the death of the Wise Man. Even though he often left us to tend to other villages, every year since his death we would celebrate his life by feasting on the fruits of our hunt. And you, Ibu, have every right to join us.*

Up to this point Amba and Samuel still had not been told how the Wise Man from Waeapo had met his end. From the edges and elbows of conversations among the villagers, it could be surmised that he left Waeapo in the second half of 1999. They couldn't remember which month; all they knew was that he went away to heal people in other soas. Then he was said to have died six years ago, in early 2000, somewhere outside the village, whereupon his body was returned to Kepala Air for proper burial.

At dawn, the morning after the ceremony, Samuel and Amba find themselves unexpectedly roused from sleep when a young policeman in plainclothes bursts in on them. It was Hasan, Samuel's contact at the police headquarters.

The police like to think it is they who own the island, not the military, and in many ways they do. Hasan was someone who knew what he was doing, how to let himself in. Even when people were milling outside, the usual vacant types too quickly dispatched to "safeguard" a place, all he needed to do was slip them each a *kretek* cigarette. Share a round, talk shop. Then find out the whereabouts of his quarry.

After Samuel introduces him to Amba, Hasan tells them that Mukaburung was taken to the police headquarters in Namlea the previous night, before the soa began the festivities. The native woman had gone with them quietly, without so much as a squeak.

"Probably as quietly as she entered the village many years before, like a chicken without its head," Hasan laughs, a little jarringly. He says the soa had decided, despite the chieftain's protestations, not to go out on a limb for her. Indeed, they hadn't even lifted a finger for her; instead, they would rather pity the woman who had come from afar, the woman Mukaburung had assaulted. They would rather Amba be given

Mukaburung's place, in exchange for the horrors she'd gone through. Such is this funny world.

Yes, Samuel thinks. *In Buru feelings change in a mere hour. Sometimes it doesn't even take that long.*

Meanwhile, morning brings in more people, including snoopy children who can't get enough of the strange looks of the "foreigners."

"What is going to happen to that woman who attacked me?" Amba asks with a sudden urgency, her voice raspy. She rises from her corner in that strange room, saying she can't stay, not when another woman's freedom hangs in the balance, and not, certainly, on her account.

Hasan tells her that Mukaburung will be charged. The order comes directly from the local chief of police. A prison sentence for assault is the most lenient they are looking at. Two, three years. Maybe more.

Samuel's heart lurches. A direct order from the chief of police means there is no arrest warrant. No legal process. Mukaburung's face flashes unbidden in his mind. How amazing she had looked, that day at the hospital, her canyon-wide grin, her black teeth, her bright, burning eyes.

Meanwhile. "Can't you see that I am not pressing charges?" says Amba, her gaze hard, unforgiving. "You should have been able to convince them."

The young policeman shrugs. "Sorry lady," he says. "But this isn't my problem."

In a cloud of silence they make their way into morning mists the color of concrete. Before they get into the young policeman's van, Samuel hesitates. An internal voice: *Don't allow yourself to be herded like some stupid sheep right into this corrupt system. You have to learn to keep the police out of your business, to trust your own instincts.* But he can't bring himself to do anything. And he knows Amba is watching him.

He lets the moment go and follows her into the van.

❧

There are four faces in the office Amba, Samuel, and Hasan have been directed to: a police officer sitting behind his desk and three junior policemen, all in plainclothes.

Samuel's lips are sealed. He pretends not to know any of them, and the policemen pretend they've never seen him. But the theatrics of concealment go several ways. Amba, who knows about Samuel's relationship with the Buru police, also feigns ignorance.

The police headquarters are brand new, swanky even by Jakarta's standards. Large and labyrinthine, with a roof that glitters in the sun. Inside: shiny walls, polished floors, the scent of new furniture.

"Unbelievable," says Amba.

For a moment Samuel feels that familiar sense of relief, the same relief he felt when he watched her enter the city of Ambon on the way to Buru for the first time, before he saw her again on the ferry, taking stock of the sleek new airport. There, it seemed she experienced the return of hope, as if that bright airport was a symbol of resurrection, a new beginning that could rise from the desperation of the Maluku Islands, where Muslims and Christians had only recently turned on each other for five years, hacking each other, family, friends, neighbors, colleagues, to death.

You can never tell, from the outsider's languorous view, the spleen and sleaze that go on behind the closed doors lining the sparkling corridors, the money being passed beneath and over however many tables.

He wonders where the Grotesque is, the only policeman he trusts. The one man he thought could help Amba find the man she loved, and whom he had introduced to her two days before she pulled that spectacular disappearing act. Now he has to focus, appear in control.

The officer behind the desk, a man in his fifties, with a thin mustache and a paunch, leads by addressing him first.

"How long have you been here, on Buru?"

"I got here around two weeks ago."

"Where from?"

"Ambon."

"And you sailed here?"

"Yes. On the *Lambelu*."

"On the *Lambelu*?"

Samuel nods.

"I see. And you checked in at the Namlea Hotel."

"Yes."

"Is this your first time here?"

"No."

Samuel knows how ridiculous it is, these stupid, pointless questions, and they're being directed to *him* of all people. Everybody in the police station knows him. He lets the interrogator shift his attention to Amba.

"Is this your first time here?"

"Yes."

"But our records show that you were in Buru five weeks ago."

"Yes, well, that would be true of me. But I can't speak for my companions."

"In our records you were listed as having checked in at the hostel in Savanajaya."

"Well, yes. But that was, as you rightly pointed out, five weeks ago."

"How did you even find the place? Who made the booking?"

"A relative."

"Who is this relative? Does he have a name?"

"He was a *warga*, a long time ago."

Samuel feels his heart stop. The word *warga* is the code name on Buru for a political prisoner. It is a word often used by the local army and police to avoid saying *tahanan politik*, or its official shorthand, tapol, which still carries, even now, the whiff of the political subversive in the minds of the average Indonesian. A word synonymous with someone who has been imprisoned for holding dissenting political views.

Besides, he knows what kind of people these men questioning them are—typical state apparatchiks, men between their early thirties and early fifties who have grown up with Suharto's anti-Communist paranoia: all those history textbook lies, that shitty propaganda movie schoolchildren had to watch every year, the absurd tales of bloodthirsty Communist women sawing off the genitals of respectable men. These are men who go into law enforcement because they are too stupid to do anything else. Men who've never read a book in their lives other than moronic police academy manuals. Who still cannot utter the acronym for the Indonesian Communist Party—PKI—without flinching, without feeling obliged to show disgust.

He hates these people. God, he hates these people. He hates them all the more because even he, Samuel from Ambon, who didn't even grow up in Ambon, isn't free from their grip.

He watches the interrogator stare at Amba. "Yes, he would have been, wouldn't he?" the man says snidely. "Metaphorically speaking, he couldn't have *not* been. Because no one who isn't from around here would have known that part of Savanajaya if he hadn't been a warga a long time ago."

Samuel holds back a laugh. The interrogator has marked himself as one of the breed of Indonesian bureaucrats too prone to saying *istilahnya*, "metaphorically speaking," as a way of filling a gap for thought, which is almost invariably followed by something very literal.

"Yes. Yes." Amba nods impatiently. "Of course."

"So what's his name, this relative of yours, this ex-warga?"

"Zulfikar. Zulfikar Hamsa."

The interrogator shoots a quick glance at Samuel, the meaning of which only he and Samuel and the policemen in that office understand.

"Why did he, this Zulfikar, take you there, to Savanajaya? Of course, we are aware that he was a warga. But that was then. What was his business here now?"

"I asked him to come with me. To accompany me to Buru, I mean. Obviously, I am . . ."

It is clear, at least to Samuel, that Amba doesn't want to add *a woman* because by saying it she would endorse a certain erroneous perception of women as the weaker sex, fearful of unknown places and incapable of traveling alone.

"Obviously, I needed assistance. I was looking for someone."

"Who were you looking for?"

"My husband."

"Well, isn't that interesting," the interrogator says. "Our records show that this relative of yours told one of our men that *he* was your husband."

Amba shrugs. "I guess it seemed expedient at the time for my relative to say that he was my husband."

"Well, he could have just said he was your relative, couldn't he?"

Silence.

"I mean, he could have told my men like it really was. He could have said he was your relative. Nothing could have been simpler."

"As I said, it seemed expedient to him at the time. I mean, three men stormed in on us one morning. They were big men. Big men with crew cuts and a military bearing. We weren't sure who they were. Their motives weren't clear. My relative acted on his instinct, an instinct I would have thought perfectly normal in men. To feel compelled to protect women of my, well, age by saying they are their husbands. Besides, we really thought these strangers wished to harm us."

"When you said *us*, who's *us*?"

"Myself, Zulfikar, and him," Amba says, nodding at Samuel.

Samuel can sense her frustration. Her eyes seem to be accusing him: *Aren't you supposed to be working off and on for the police? Should we even be having this conversation? Shouldn't we be here solely to plead for Mukaburung's freedom? Why the hell are you being so useless?*

"Look," Amba says. "We're actually here for something else. I want you to pardon the woman who attacked me."

But the interrogator won't have it, to be bullied in his own kingdom. Instead, he pushes a pen and a piece of paper across the desk. "Write down his name. Your *real* husband's name."

Amba hesitates before picking up the pen and jotting down a name. She pushes the paper back with no visible emotion on her face. The interrogator has a satisfied, slightly cruel look as he reads it.

"Sir," Samuel says, unable to hold back any longer. "This lady's husband is dead. What she found was his grave. You know all that, but still you ask all these questions."

And because this bureaucrat is so damn hard, so damn broken, what the hell. "The lady here only recently found out that her husband is dead," Samuel goes on. "The reason we're here today is because we want you to pardon the woman you arrested last night."

Still, there isn't a sliver of sympathy in the interrogator's face as he taps the tabletop with his pen, a grating noncommittal gesture. "The native woman?" he says at long last. "As far as we know she comes from a village in Waeapo, in the woods behind the estuary. Or is last known to have resided there." He keeps up his tapping display of power for some time, before looking up at a young officer standing behind them like a dog waiting to be unleashed. "Hey, you. You're familiar with the case?"

The young officer steps forward but stops in his tracks when he reaches Amba and Samuel's side, not wanting to walk past them.

"Yes, sir. We processed the woman last night. Mukaburung, that's her name. Not sure about her age, but she must be around fifty."

"Where is she now, this Mukaburung?"

"She's in the cell here, sir."

"How come I don't have a copy of the arrest warrant?" asks the interrogator, rummaging through his desk, at one point looking under it in a slightly deranged way. "How strange. Who was the arresting officer?"

The junior officer mumbles a name.

"What time was this?"

"I can't remember, but it's all in the report, sir."

"How come you have it? Where's the arresting officer?"

"He asked for leave, sir, just after the arrest. He had to go home, had a bit of a situation with the family. So he turned the report over to me to complete and file."

"On what charges was she brought here, this . . . this . . . Mukaburung woman? Holy shit, what a name." The questioner sits back, shakes his head and suddenly breaks into laughter. "I mean, can you believe it? Mukaburung. Bird Face. As in, *she has the face of a bird.*"

Something about this crudeness jolts Samuel. He tries not to think of that incredible beak-like nose, those small but intense bird eyes; a well-earned name, if irony is to reign.

"That of course won't be her real name," the interrogator drones on. "A warga must have given it to her a long time ago. Only a warga could have been so sick in the head, and in the—sorry." He points down between his trousers, to the organ Indonesians so often absurdly refer to as *burung*, "bird," clearly stifling a laugh on account of the lady in the room. "And God knows in exchange for what. Perhaps he taught her how to keep ducks, count money, make coffee, and in return she gave him . . . sorry, Bu," he says, glancing at Amba, his expression a smirk more than an apology. "You know. A disease. Ha ha ha."

"According to the report she tried to kill this lady here, sir," says the young officer, all red faced, trying also not to laugh.

Amba just sits there, her face turning dark.

The interrogator heaves an exaggerated sigh. "Now, if only I knew that being a policeman would amount to no more than managing a dating service, I could have been spared all that physical training in bad weather, all that training in forensics and investigation. Anyway, that's all moot now, isn't it." He looks up at Amba. "So, tell me, you're here to press charges?"

"No, on the contrary, I am here to *not* press charges."

"To drop the charges, you mean."

"I didn't press charges so how could I drop them?"

"Well, *somebody* did. You do remember that woman attacked you."

"I'm here to tell you that I don't give a shit about the attack, so you can just forget the whole thing ever happened. You have nothing without my testimony."

"There were witnesses."

"Then they saw it wrong. They don't know what really happened. So I demand that you drop the case."

"You can't tell me to do that. Only my boss, the chief of police, can have this case dropped."

"You have to drop the whole thing. Just ask Manalisa. He'll tell you the same thing."

Then, just like that, the interrogator's expression turns to stone. Suddenly he is no longer interested in playacting. "What do you know about Manalisa?"

"He's the man who led me to the grave."

In the silence that follows, it all seems almost too much: the officer's shock, Amba's quiet ruthlessness, Samuel's being completely overawed. In his years on Buru, Samuel himself has never met the legendary Manalisa. Yet anyone who has lived on the island more than a week knows that Manalisa, a native leader, is the real master of Buru. There is no stone he hasn't turned on this island, no path he hasn't trodden. He is a shaman and a warrior rolled into one. It is said that he can appear and disappear at will, and anyone who is of no interest to him can live his or her whole life on the island and never see him. •

Clearly he, Samuel goddamn Lawerissa, is one of those people. The stories are wild and vivid: How the man is said to be massive, erect of posture, deceptively athletic. How he roams around the island, alone, undaunted, timeless. How he is reputed to know things others don't: the location of a fabled Japanese treasure chest in a place where no one else dares to venture, the secret spot where the *jugun ianfu* used to go into hiding. Even the subject matter is raw and riveting: jugun ianfu—women, mostly from Java, who were forced to be the sexual slaves of Japanese soldiers stationed on Buru between 1942 and 1945, only to be abandoned on the island when Japan was defeated in the Second World War. Although the existence of these women continues to be debated, the thought that Manalisa has met them is enough to make it true.

"Where . . . How on earth did you meet Manalisa?" The interrogator's voice, echoing Samuel's thought, is suddenly less authoritative.

"Manalisa found me." Sweet triumph.

Suddenly, as if on cue in some third-rate TV sitcom, there is a pounding on the door, and a figure Samuel has only ever heard described, a figure so bulky and tall and enfolding, like a wild, overgrown tree, strides in. The man's face a riot of slash-and-burn, over whose soot-black naked torso hangs an imposing stone-and-feather necklace, and whose back-strapped spear is rusty with blood. He walks toward Amba with huge, engulfing steps. And stops.

In these brief seconds the entire sham of grit-coated police gall is completely thrown off track. For a moment, no one can breathe. Beyond the door, now left ajar, Samuel catches sight of his friend First Lieutenant Sabarudin, aka the Grotesque. The other Man of the Moment.

And now the giant raises his massive arm and points at the questioner, who is standing in some kind of salutary mode.

"Mukaburung is my niece," he says. "She goes home today, with me."

Samuel has never seen a man so reduced as the interrogator in his valiant effort to keep his cool. *Or a woman so rejuvenated*, he thinks, gazing at Amba with awe.

๛

Later, when Hasan brings back the van to collect them along with Manalisa and Mukaburung, Amba half runs to greet it, as if wanting to make sure it won't suddenly disappear on her. Before she gets in, she glances at her reflection in the side window and loosens her hair.

Gauche as the image is, Samuel feels his heart collapse.

3

The Wise Man of Waeapo

Ask an old warrior what is the oldest-known valor, and he will say duty. Duty before all else.

They have returned Mukaburung to her village, and Amba and Samuel have wasted no time in staying close to Manalisa. No pandering to the chieftain, no pleasantries with the villagers, no massaging of the police's egos.

The man is indeed remarkable: his physique, his great mystical age of one hundred, his scarlet betel-chewing mouth. The fact that he exists. Even more arresting is the way he holds on to his love and memory of Bhisma: as when he first utters the name of the fallen warrior. It is as though his voice, his memory, issues from an inner silence far deeper than Lake Rana. If with Zulfikar, Bhisma's other comrade, this love is magnified, brought into the sunlight, with Manalisa it seems deeper and darker, driven to the core of this man.

He insists on calling Bhisma his brother. He wants to start at the beginning.

❧

The man Manalisa came to know as Bhisma was in the third batch of political prisoners sent to the penal colony. He was different from the rest. To this man, a sense of duty was nothing to be overly impressed by; it was merely something one had to live with. Something akin to fate.

Now if the political prisoners' life on Buru had not been what it was, perhaps the question of fate would not have been as pertinent. For Manalisa, the beginning of his brotherhood with Bhisma was easy to mark. After many months of observing him from the shelter of the forest's fringe, months of witnessing how loosely guarded he was—tending to patients in the middle of the night, traveling from barracks to barracks, sometimes from unit to unit, often alone and unsupervised—Manalisa decided to step onto his path one day. His appearance, according to Manalisa, was such a shock to Bhisma that he fell back on his haunches. The moment Manalisa picked him up was the start of their friendship, that long, silent clinch of their fates.

Manalisa says he knew their regard was mutual, even though he soon returned into the depths of the forest and didn't see Bhisma again until a few months later. But from then on, each time they met Bhisma became more adept at sharing his innermost thoughts.

It started with the anger he felt toward the men in uniform manning the compounds. He told Manalisa how the political prisoners were utilized to transform this island, their forced labor turning virgin land into rice fields, planting vegetables to eat and sell, building roads. *Those who dumped us in this hellhole also want us to die here,* Bhisma had said. *They want to kill us slowly in nature's prison and bury us with no name on the headstone.*

Manalisa says that his brother possessed the tranquility of a beloved house cat, and this meant he knew how to remain quietly attentive to the life around him. He would always quarter his food lest someone was starving, he didn't bad-mouth, snitch, or gamble, and he was as loyal as a dog was to his master—only in this case his master was his fellow prisoner, and for that he was loved immensely. He says he heard whispers among Bhisma's comrades that he was the best Communist, for he never took anything for himself. To them, Bhisma was also the worst Communist, for he liked to write poems with a dark, doubting lyricism that bore no mission, no message to better the world, poems that did not serve the revolution.

One day, from nearby in the forest's shadows, Manalisa had watched Bhisma sitting with half a dozen of his fellow political prisoners. From under a tree after a day's hard slog, they were watching grass slowly boil under a snarling sun. Some drew the shifting shape of clouds with their fingers in the air. Mostly they ignored each other.

Then Manalisa heard Bhisma ask the man next to him the color of a bird that flew by. The man was Bhisma's buddy, someone Manalisa had earlier heard addressed as Zulfikar. Zulfikar replied, "Red and green." Bhisma had nodded slowly and leaned back against the tree. "Red and green," Manalisa heard him repeat those words with a sigh. "Funny, I thought it was just one color." It was then that Manalisa had suspected in his brother an inability to recognize colors.

"Of course," Manalisa says to Amba and Samuel, "in flapping its wings, a bird never indulges a man's vision. We are inferior to birds, and the birds know that. But how does it feel to live, literally, in a world without all colors? How did he cope?"

So Bhisma had suffered from a form of color-blindness, Samuel thinks. What are the odds. Perhaps he lived in a world where red and green were one and the same, or even one in pure black and white. Whatever it was, it must have been a devastating condition, to be on the verge of making the wrong call at any time, all your life, and of being found out. He would have had to fashion an instinctive camouflage,

33

and learn to keep people, and revealing words, at bay. He would have had to develop an arsenal of deception: phrases, remarks, bogus histories. Yet he had treated ills of all colors, and called them by their names. Perhaps he had survived, to an extent, by entering and making peace with that colorless world, by coloring his reading of an object through the descriptions of others.

"I told my friend I liked his name," the old warrior continues. "*Basudara, beta suka ose pung nama!* I liked the sound of it, his name. I asked him why he didn't call himself Bhismo. I thought Javanese people always pronounced the last syllable with an *o*. Bhis-mo. Ah, the Javanese. Always too complicated for me. All that—what do they call it—*unggah-ungguh*? All those masks and pleasantries? Anyway. To my surprise, Bhisma agreed with me. 'The Javanese are complicated,' he said.

"'I've been away from Indonesia too long,' he told me. 'My mother named me Bhisma with an *a* expressly in order not to call me Bhismo. Besides, I like to read names the way they are spelled. I mean, you're right. Why complicate things?'"

Manalisa describes how for several years the two continued their friendship through their meetings in the woods. "But then Bhisma who was not Bhismo was suddenly nowhere to be found. It was late '79, I think. They were taking down the prison camp. Suddenly I lost every trace of him. For a while I thought he had boarded the last ship, sailed away, and remade his life in Jakarta. But I had never lost anyone before—and I didn't become Manalisa *not* to know what happened or didn't happen."

There was good reason for the vanishing, for the retreat into the shadows, and it's coming back to Samuel, too. The fact that the camps were dismantled slowly, almost furtively, over a period of two years. In late '77, after the Suharto administration first announced plans to put an end to the prison camps, corvée was phased out, despite each unit still being required to deliver a mandatory amount of logs daily. Manalisa says during this time he had watched all that took place from afar. He saw Bhisma, his brother, examining prisoners, many of them now too sick and too old, and thus forced to stay. He helped decide who deserved to be released first, giving priority to the aged and the ailing.

Manalisa also witnessed how quickly life at the camp changed. Soon the prison resembled a new city unveiled. Guests from Jakarta descended in droves, mostly journalists with hungry eyes and snap-happy cameras. The soccer field turned, as if overnight, into a giant exhibition space, crammed with travelers' bags, and the ex-prisoners were busy exchanging goods, entrusting letters, buying and selling, giving away for free possessions long accumulated.

Even though he had left Buru by then, Samuel doesn't find it difficult to imagine how the prisoners must have felt at the prospect of their release. The air would have been thick with mixed feelings: elation at arriving at a new chapter in life most of them never dreamed of and fear that it was all but a dream, that at any moment the camp commander would announce that there'd been a change of plans, the government had revoked the order, and all had to be restored to what it once was.

Two Navy vessels had stood sentry at the port, big and booming, a gift from the heavens. For the first time the prisoners were allowed to rid themselves of the unit numbers on their uniforms. There were neither shouts nor reprimands, only white noise and chatter. The drama of freedom was in full production.

In no time, the Buru landscape changed radically, returning to an older time, a time that was part of Manalisa's history, free of the bells and wooden gongs in each of the camp's units. All the barbed fences surrounding the barracks were taken down. Guard posts were deserted, torn down, gone.

Manalisa watched every departing boat, looking for Bhisma. When the last batch of prisoners set sail on December 20, 1979, with Bhisma not among them, Manalisa finally conceded he had met his match. His brother had left the island, and he'd done so through magic.

The old warrior, quite the performer, suddenly slaps his thigh, shakes with laughter. "But no, I was wrong," he says. "I met him again, my brother, two or three years later. Another chance encounter in the mountains. This time he took *me* by surprise. He had changed. He was even thinner than before. All angles and edges. There was this new tightness to his cheeks, like so." Manalisa pulls his own cheeks in demonstration. "I found him sitting on a huge rock like this, like an ancient sage. Obviously, he was trying to look like me. Ha ha ha.

"Anyway, I climbed up and sat next to him. 'You disappeared,' I told him. 'But you never left. Why? Did you forget something?' Bhisma laughed and said, 'Come, brother. You must know me by now. There is nothing to reclaim. What was lost was never mine to begin with.'"

Astounding, Manalisa says, how the two of them fell into conversation easily, as naturally as the first time. Beneath his new beard, his new long mane, Bhisma was still a *saule*, Manalisa thought, not a bad-looking guy.

They shared stories: Bhisma told Manalisa about his prisoner friends, including one who refused to go home because his wife had remarried. There's nothing more shameful, Bhisma told the old warrior, than finding your wife fattened and festooned by another man.

"'And you? What's your story?' I asked him.

"'I have nothing, no one to go home to,' Bhisma said. 'No one I wouldn't shame to ruins. My parents despised anything to do with Communism.' Then he said softly, as if to himself, that if he wanted one thing it was for his parents and sisters, and for the woman he loved, to live the rest of their days in peace. But that only could be achieved if they thought he was dead."

Amba, who all this time has sat in blushing silence, suddenly lets out a cry. "That's untrue," she says, her voice catching. "That's just untrue. It's unbelievable that he would think that. That I could live my life happily, thinking he might be dead."

Manalisa pauses for a while, sensing a thaw. "After less than two years," he continues, "my brother took what few belongings he had to an area well away from the Transmigration Area, away from Suharto's bullshit largesse. He hated being in that area. He didn't think like the others, who had simply been grateful. So he chose to return to Waeapo, that cool, woody place where the prisoner camp had once stood. He told me he loved that place. It was close to his heart. It had a lot of trees and he loved trees. Only this time he decided to settle closer to the estuary. He had wanted to live with the sound of water."

Once Bhisma was a free man, and settled in the home of his own choosing, he and Manalisa began to meet more regularly, to collect each other's anecdotes. Bhisma told stories about his patients, the kinds of ailments he had learned to obliterate or to make peace with. Manalisa taught Bhisma how to hunt. Bhisma talked about blood and paranoia. Manalisa showed him one secret grave after another and told him the story behind each one.

They talked about life, about what made people the way they were.

"I pointed at Bhisma and said, 'You're not like the others. What made you different?' Bhisma told me, 'I've learned not to read humankind by racial characteristics. What, pray, is Javanese? Such a patchwork of a place. And an imaginary one, at that. Besides, I am part West Sumatran.'"

"Oh, he told you that?" Amba interjects, then pauses. Then: "That's lovely. So lovely."

There follows a prolonged silence. Too long and big-boned even for Manalisa to handle, because after a while he gazes at Amba and tells her he always recognized a deep ache in Bhisma, a loss so quiet and so crushing, and that for many months he waited for his brother to offer something about what this might be. Then one day Bhisma told him that somewhere out there was a woman, a Javanese woman, like his mother and also so unlike his mother, and so very different from the rest. And that this woman, too, ruled his planet. That she lived inside him, despite the years they had been apart. That she had lengthened his shadow everywhere he cast his gaze. Had become his duty. Had become his fate.

The next day, Manalisa says, his brother Bhisma took him to his meranti tree. It was a very old tree, sitting at the intersection of the areas that had been Unit XVI and Unit XV in the penal colony, left there after the prison camp was taken down. Bhisma had chosen his place well. He was blessed with a good place to return to. It was at the base of that tree that Bhisma had buried his letters over the years.

The old warrior's eyes look suspiciously moist as he adds, "Thus began my long wait for you, Ibu Amba. You are the woman my brother spoke to me about. And now here you are. You have returned to claim the letters that have been waiting for you."

"How did you and Manalisa meet?"

He's been dying to ask that question. Then he catches the glance they send each other, these improbable partners in crime in their brief moment of complicity. There follows another long silence before Amba reveals how, on the afternoon she arrived in Namlea, she had been met by Sabarudin, the Grotesque, who came with a car. Unbeknownst to Samuel, she had managed to get the policeman's cell phone number during their first meeting, and they had stayed in touch. When she told Sabarudin that she planned to come back to Buru alone to continue her search, this time without Samuel, he agreed to help. When they got into the car, the policeman told her he'd just been in contact with the healer from Banten, who had instructed him to take her to Kepala Air. *And then?* Amba had asked. *Then we wait,* Sabarudin said as they drove off.

At the Kepala Air intersection, he jammed on the brakes, and the car screeched to a halt. The Grotesque looked as though he'd seen a ghost, and Amba, following the direction of his stare, saw beside the road a figure unlike any she'd ever seen.

Manalisa, she heard Sabarudin whisper.

They both got out of the car, watching as the huge man lumbered toward them. Leaning down toward Amba, he said, *I've waited a long time for you. Now come with me. I'll take you to his grave.*

It is the afternoon. Amba and Samuel are sitting on the stone seats beneath an assembly of trees in a schoolyard in the village of Walgan. It is the same school Samuel had come to with Amba and Zulfikar in the beginning of their search for Bhisma. Before Zulfikar, that endearingly insufferable man, left. Before it was just Samuel and Amba and the ghost of that damn doctor.

He sees anew how pretty the school is. Banana trees line the outer walls, while inside, the courtyard is hedged by a row of duku and turi and a durian tree. The sense of prison has gone; now its fences and borders resemble nothing of the Buru that raised Samuel like the prodigal son. But at the back, where pinang, aren, and tall grass spill out uncontrollably far into idle land, the school suddenly looks endangered and vulnerable.

Manalisa stands erect on a bit of raised earth not far from where they are sitting. Samuel's attention switches between the two of them, Amba and Manalisa: a bleached soul and a ravishing voice, the engine of stories.

For a long time, no one speaks.

❧

History is like a long, twisted joke. You never know when the punch line will come. When Manalisa tells them that the tree shading the stone seats where they sit is Bhisma's meranti tree, there is again a brief silence, followed by a collective *Aaah*. They all look up. There it is, swaying sleepily to the lull of the wind, the guardian of Bhisma's secrets.

Manalisa reaches down to the bag at his feet and takes out a tied bundle of bamboo tubes. He holds it and says, "These are the tubes that have sheltered Bhisma's words. Yes, Ibu, these are for you. Twenty-two tubes. Letters, journals."

"This is all?"

"I wouldn't know. But whatever is here is yours."

Manalisa also hands to Amba a thin pile of official documents and police reports. He is less eloquent about these. He simply says, *whispers*, "They are important because they will tell you when and how he died. Of course, it wasn't easy, to hear that he died. It still isn't easy for me, after more than six years."

The light is fading around them. Amba seems to realize Manalisa will not tell her how Bhisma died. But she stays calm.

"My brother would have liked to see what became of the tree. He would be happy to know it has survived."

❧

They are entering Namlea now, and it is raining. Samuel is behind the wheel. Amba has not said a word since leaving the school in Walgan and parting with Manalisa. The tubes clatter against each other in her bag. Once or twice Samuel almost offered to stop somewhere for a meal; they have had nothing but peanuts and prawn crackers all day. But Amba looked so faint and seemed not to register his presence. Recognizing the look, he knew too well not to ignore it, not to intrude upon her silence.

As they enter the city his head is bursting with questions: *What will happen after this? Will they go back to Ambon, and then Jakarta? Alone, together, when? What will happen after that? Will they say good-bye at Jakarta Airport, shake each other's hands with awkward smiles? Will he dare ask for her phone number, which she has never offered (even though she must have given it to that damn Sabarudin)? If she does give it to him, how long will he have to wait—days, a week, a month—before he can text her:* Hey, Samuel here, how are you? Wanna meet for coffee somewhere? *Or will everything be brought to an end in a mere few days? Will they simply go back to their former lives, as people do?*

Earlier, Amba had invited Manalisa to join them on the trip to Namlea. He refused and insisted on saying good-bye in front of the school in Walgan.

"I'm going in the opposite direction, toward the mountain," he told her. "I have no need for Namlea. That city is wretched. It is not Buru."

Amba reached for his hand, and the old warrior held hers for a long time. A pang of jealousy on Samuel's part. It must have shown, because just before he started the engine, Amba suddenly said, "There is so much good in you, Samuel, yet you suffer because you're the jealous type."

He had swung around in disbelief.

"Don't be jealous. I mean it. That was what did me in with Bhisma. I didn't look for him hard enough when I had the chance because deep down I was insecure. I thought he was too good for me, that his love for me must have been a mistake, a momentary aberration, and that our separation was the gods' way of knocking some sense into him. Then came all the false pride, the woman warrior thing, thinking I didn't need his love. But I was always jealous of him. That's the sad, shattering truth. And jealous people are insecure people."

The remainder of the journey had passed in a darker, more difficult silence.

⁂

When they reach the hotel, Amba tells him she is tired. She wants to go to her room, to be happily, gloriously alone. Samuel senses the same stirrings of foreboding that a few weeks ago he had chosen not to heed and which landed him in such a fine mess.

So many things can happen in a day, he thinks.

This could be the last he will ever see of this woman. She could leave the hotel while he is watching television in his room in a beer-laced stupor.

She could go to the port, hire a van with a driver, go back inland, go back to the stupid grave and resolve to live there, as anything, as anyone, as long as she's near that stupid dead man, near his stupid rotting body. The same, blind way Mukaburung had changed her life on Bhisma's account, committed a crime on his behalf.

As he stands in the lobby looking down at Amba beside him, these crazy thoughts filling his head, Samuel wonders if it is possible that Amba has never intended to return to Jakarta, to that false life she began the day she lost Bhisma forever, more than forty years ago. Is it possible that she came here intending to die on this godforsaken island?

"Okay," he says. "But we still have to eat. No room service, last time I checked. So shall we meet here, tonight? Say, at eight? Go out, find a restaurant, beer, anything?"

"We'll see."

"You *have* to eat. You're not yet well."

"First I must read the documents," Amba says quietly. "After that, we'll see."

"All twenty-two tubes?"

"Well, there's too little time if we are meeting again at eight. Maybe only the documents pertaining to his death, then. And Bhisma's letters . . . I need more time for those."

"We'll never leave Buru that way," Samuel says, his voice shaking. "Or else you're hatching another plan. Something unbearable, something that doesn't involve me. I deserve—"

"God, Samuel, stop being such a child," Amba snaps. "Isn't this my hour? Have I not earned it?"

Samuel doesn't know what has come over him, but in the sweeping gust of feelings he suddenly takes her into his arms and holds her there. It isn't the first time, he realizes, for such a fire to erupt within him, and, as ever, the valor it is freighted with so disarms him that his undoing is rapid. He loses his nerve. One glance at her shows her blighted eyes, and he sees a depth so indecipherable, like a name in the dark.

He feels he has made her sin.

It is then he realizes that the woman he has fallen in love with, this woman fifteen years older than him, has nothing to give him. She has given her all to the man who now lies cold in his grave. There is nothing left to strive for, other than the love of her daughter, perhaps. Not even the foreigner who had been lucky to marry her. Samuel tries not to feel the weight of her body on his chest, the closeness of her breathing, her weak attempts at pushing him away. He tries not to look at her mouth, curled and confused and so achingly kissable. At the tears in her eyes even if her gaze is cold, as though she is trying to freeze and compress her pain into each eye socket. So there it is, perhaps, the confirmation Samuel has been waiting for. That she *does* care for him. Cares for him a little bit. Even if it is only because he has been her lifeline to her overriding hunger for the only man she's ever loved. For doesn't he have

Bhisma's height, his eyes, his scarred soul? Isn't that what she has told him, more than once, since they arrived in Buru? And isn't that why she thinks she has to let him go? Because, after all, you can't love the same man twice?

Samuel doesn't know whether the moment calls for magnanimity or something else. He knows his loss is complete, and with this comes a feeling of shame. He releases her and murmurs, "Why don't you go up to your room?"

But unexpectedly, Amba clings to Samuel longer. When she lets him go she gazes at him with a searching look and whispers, "You . . . you are so good. Do you know that?"

᠔᠒

At eight they meet for dinner as planned, and after a few minutes of leisurely strolling they find a welcoming restaurant not far from the hotel. The rain has stopped, and the city has suddenly lit up. Namlea comes alive at this time, and you can always tell whether a ship has just docked from the number of vehicles crowding the port's main parking lot. Samuel has lost count of how many times he has been part of that landscape and not really given a damn.

After dinner, they settle in for a nightcap in the hotel coffee shop.

"I think I now know what actually happened that day," she says after a sip of something fizzy and blue. "No. I now *definitely* know what actually happened that day."

"Which day? The day Bhisma died?"

"No. Long before that. The day Manalisa mentioned. In Yogyakarta, forty years ago, back in October 1965. The day we were wrested apart forever. What happened back then wasn't as bad as I thought, as I felt at the time—have felt all these years. Despite everything, he had—*he had*—loved me."

Samuel's throat constricts. "Of course he did," he says uselessly.

By now she has surely read some of Bhisma's letters. She may also have learned from the police reports how Bhisma died. He knows she won't want to talk about that, yet surely she needs to go back to the beginning now. He doesn't want to start with the account of how she lost her lover, but with how it all began, the story of Amba and Bhisma. Hasn't he earned by now the right to know the full story? Hasn't he finally earned her trust?

BOOK 2

Amba, Bhisma, and Salwa

1956–1965

4

The Self-Willed Bird

Kadipura, Central Java

When Amba was still the only child, she knew she would never be as pretty as her mother, but that was okay. Even at the age of two, she knew how to win hearts without relying on her looks; she'd squeal at the right moment, poke her father's nose when he was nuzzling her, do that clicking thing with her tongue that seemed to delight people to no end. A few months after the twins were born, she came to realize they were quite possibly the prettiest girls the planet had ever seen and that she would have to step up her charms. But that was okay, too.

Growing up, however, was not so okay. It could break even the toughest souls. Going about their town of two hundred thousand, with her mother and her sisters next to her, Amba often felt loose and form-less, like a spilled grocery bag. She couldn't help it. People would greet her warmly, sometimes even fondly, but her mother and sisters they would practically fete. They would often praise her bouncy big hair, or the fact that she'd grown a few inches taller, but her mother and the twins—they were *lovely*.

In time, Amba came to know she was not unlovely. She had a cat's eyes, piercing and disarmingly almond shaped, and all her power was in that pillowy, firecracker mouth. Besides, what was the use for self-pity? She always knew that beauty is more a curse than a blessing. It exalts and entraps.

On this subject she had plenty of evidence. Take her mother, who always felt she had to be nice to people just because they were generous with their praise. She was not just the town belle, she was the belle of belles. This meant she could be as choosy as she wanted. And yet, how quickly she accepted Amba's father's proposal for fear of hurting his feelings (not that *Bapak* didn't deserve her). The twins were champions at this sort of thing, too, this thing called involuntary self-sabotage. Beauty is a curse. Why need it? Why want it?

So began Amba's lifelong relationship with books.

It came as a surprise to no one, then, that at twelve she often sounded twice her age—the difficult themes she raised, the brutality of her observations. On her best days, she was crisp, a little cruel, quick on the draw. On her worst days, she could be obnoxious and shameless, saying the most vicious things, things that sometimes made her mother weep. And the thing with Amba was it wasn't an act, or a compensation for some lack of confidence—she just seemed to become that way.

Even if they didn't always agree on things, Amba relied on her sister Ambika for companionship, for a certain tolerance of her quirks, for the occasional complicity.

"I think school is overrated," Amba would declare, even though their father was the principal. "I think we should all tutor ourselves, like free-willed birds."

"You always say that," Ambika said. "But then you go to school, you study like hell, you turn in your homework one day—sometimes one week—early, then you come out top of the class."

Unlike her sister, Ambika had always worn the confidence of someone too pretty for her own good. Even at ten, it was clear that she would grow up into a woman over whom men would lose their minds. What was the point of using her brain too much, if at all? Why should she, when the mere sight of her already pleased so many? Why should she study as hard as Amba, or try so hard to sound older than she was? Life was already so hectic.

Day in, day out Ambika helped her older sister fetch water from the well, swept the floor, helped her mother cook, washed her own and her lazy twin sister's clothes. Every time she felt the angry nip of entitlement she would remember the part in *The Mahabharata* where it told of a pair of identical sisters too gorgeous for words, lusted over by all the princes of the land, kidnapped and fought over and handed to the king of kings in order to bear his children, children who would one day rule over the kingdom of kingdoms. Who cared whether the king in question was himself an imp, all of twelve and ailing? You can't turn your back on such stories. Not with her name, at any rate; even if she and her twin sister were far from identical, they were both destined to be queens. Granted, for Amba the story had taken a wildly different turn, but that was not Ambika's burden to bear.

And so no disagreement between them ever reached fever pitch. No ill feelings were allowed to brew or fester for too long. They were sisters, and living with a sister was like living with doubts—cranky and torturous things you nonetheless stuck to because they kept you honest.

When their father returned home, Amba and Ambika and their sister would sit down together on a woven mat on the front porch, listening to children's songs on the radio and enjoying the fried cassava and sweet tea their mother brought them. The tolerant afternoon breeze would bring a momentary truce to any bickering, and the sisters' minds would drift as their father ruminated on landscapes and seasons, on the sun and the moon, on the trees that stood witness to human lives, and on the importance of work. They would listen to their mother, too, who preferred to regale them with stories of food and local gossip. *Do you know that the daughter of our neighbor has just been made the lead singer of the Krida Beksa troupe? Now isn't that odd? I've always thought she was a much better dancer.*

Their differences aside, Ambika loved Amba fiercely and singularly, as any girl growing up in a small town loves an older, more worldly sister. They would walk the town, using their noses to track new scents. They sought out old buildings, trod on rickety floors, and stepped into sudden zones of shadow, courting danger. They shouted curse words into abandoned wells and reveled in the abundance of echoes.

They often left Ambalika, who had always been rather sickly, at home and *lived*. Whatever love was Ambalika's due was for their parents to give. It was an irrational feeling they couldn't explain, and they were too intent on their own fun to miss her.

Amba and Ambika understood this division of love as they understood the division of labor, each child expected to do certain chores. It was something natural, to be accepted, much in the way they learned not to panic when the cat fell from the roof—of course it would survive—or when they broke out in a rash—which would most likely be from a brush with a featherworm—because it would settle down of its own accord.

They were each other's eyes and ears; they were the co-discoverers of pimples, golden crabs, and secret caves. They witnessed each other's first menstruation and gawked at each other's nipples, marveling at how they could become so hard when poked, like cooked mung beans. They had special names for themselves, *putri wani* (brave princesses), as opposed to *putri malu* (shy princesses)—small leafy plants that wilted at the slightest touch. Whatever ideas they each formed about life couldn't have been attained without the other.

But Amba, as the older of the two, was the free-willed bird. There were things she just knew. And she knew things about her sister that her sister herself wasn't aware of.

Ambika liked boys. Liked them too much. Despite her age, despite her endearing ineloquence. And there it was, the main difference between these sisters. Ambika might have been only eleven years old, but she had no idea whatsoever of what it meant to keep a healthy distance from members of the opposite sex. Hers was a body that responded completely, effortlessly, to the male gaze. If an older boy who had a crush on her came to watch her at dance practice, her movements soared. If he suddenly stopped coming, she wilted like a flower and refused to dance for a month.

Amba, in contrast, had no patience for the obsession with physical beauty. She thought beauty the most overrated attribute in the catalog of human qualities, and couldn't understand the currency it held in the Javanese culture. Neither did she have time for feminine suffering.

Although she was only twelve, Amba knew a thing or two about being faithful. Her own mother was faithful, waking before sunup every morning and, talc dappled and fresh faced, serving her husband's first coffee of the day. She kept her house fragrant and untroubled even though times hadn't always been easy. She was the smile that sent her three girls away to school every morning.

Amba was told that her mother, when she was growing up, was considered the most accomplished girl in her village. She was multitalented, did well in school, and was exceptionally pleasing to the eye. Her parents had done all they could to safeguard her purity, for a flower so fair was so much more than a child—she was a duty. Her soulful face and dulcet voice had also made her one of her hometown's favorite *pesindens* (female singers) of the local shadow puppet troupe. In fact, so fond was she of singing that she learned many more old Javanese lyrics and more *keroncong* melodies in Dutch or Indonesian-Malay than she was ever taught at school.

The story of Amba's mother's encounter with the great performer Srimulat, the beautiful lead artiste of the Rose Flower Keroncong Orchestra, was the stuff of family legend, titillating not so much for how close she had been to being lured away by Srimulat and her troupe, but for the fact that she wasn't. Whenever her daughters asked her the reason why, their mother had only one answer: *Where was I to go? What was I to run from?*

Her parents, despite their strictness, had doted on her, and her loveliness was, to them, a source of pride. They had promised her a good match, a man who would show her the lasting joys of marriage. Who knows, they had murmured, maybe they would find her someone like Srimulat's husband, a man so gentle, so loving, a man who would speak to her soul. A man who would encourage her to sing and watch performances for the rest of her life, for by then she would be a respectable adult woman.

Amba's mother had accepted Amba's father's proposal three months later, and to him she had remained faithful. Only in the last ten months, after sixteen years of marriage, of tending to the needs of her family and of never earning her own money, had she been supplying local desserts to Rusmini's *warung*, the most popular local roadside eatery in town, a small but important way of having her own income.

Amba and her sisters had shown their support for their mother by not saying a word to their father and clocking extra hours heating palm sugar and coconut milk in the kitchen three days a week. It was that sticking-together thing again, writ large. Even though Amba's mother's income was modest, earning it had returned to her something akin to pride, a feeling she hadn't felt since the days when she had made some money from singing, or from winning a regency-level *macapat* competition. Amba's mother knew there was no need for her to earn her own income; her husband was not poor, despite money being scarce for most people in those days. The fact that it had taken her this long, sixteen years, to effect such a little change to family tradition, was itself a form of loyalty—to the idea that any man worth his salt could, and should, single-handedly look after the well-being of his entire family.

Yes, Amba's mother had certainly been faithful, and Amba had loved her in the way most daughters loved their mothers: as tutor, role model, caretaker, and someone who taught her to cook, clean, sew, and look after her sisters. But some days she didn't think of her mother at all. It was her father who taught her how to feel.

When Amba was eight, she suddenly discovered there was another way to see her father. He was her father, but he could also be her friend. At first, the revelation was startling. But Amba soon saw why it had made sense. Hadn't he given her half of the blood that coursed through her veins? Hadn't he given her part of her bones, her tissues, her cat's eyes? Didn't that make them soulmates, wedded to each other for as long as they lived? It made absolute sense that he would want to share with her things that really mattered to him. Things that were honest and true.

Some of the literature she read had taught her that there comes a time when a man stops talking to his wife and starts looking for other objects he can possess. Because of this a man needs the ear of someone he can absolutely trust. It was her father's luck that Amba was that person.

Later, when he had to account for why he had loved Amba more than his other daughters, he said it was because of something she asked him one day after she'd just turned eleven. It was as if he'd forgotten his first daughter in the joy of siring twins, and twins too beautiful at that. But on this day she bewitched him anew. This is what happened on the day Sudarminto fell in love with his eldest daughter.

He was returning some books to the shelf in his little study. He had a few loose sheets of paper in his hand, and when he thought nobody was watching, he bent down to shove them back into a cardboard box on the bottom shelf, like a dirty secret. But Amba was behind him all along, sitting on the living room chair with a textbook on her lap.

"What makes Centhini so important?"

Sudarminto swung around.

"I mean, Centhini is a woman. A servant, no less . . ."

"Have you read the book?"

"Just some parts."

Sudarminto paused. He thought about what he should say if Amba had indeed read the whole *Book of Centhini* and, worse, the parts she was not supposed to. Sudarminto looked at his daughter. He was almost certain that she had indeed read the entire story—the girl was a book freak, as other teachers had told him. Despite all the texts he had on explaining the unexplainable to children, he hadn't prepared himself for this unexplainable.

It came as a surprise to him, then, when his eleven-year-old daughter decided to save her father the embarrassment. She said, "I think I know the answer. Centhini is a servant, a person of a low caste, an outsider, someone who's paid not to have her own opinion, and because of that she can't possibly give advice to or pass judgments on others. And that she did is a wonderful thing."

So relieved was Sudarminto by this that he forgot those very words had once come from his own mouth: his daughter had recited them verbatim. For Amba, nothing about that moment pleased her more than realizing that, with intellect, she had staked her claim over her father.

The Book of Centhini isn't only one of Indonesia's oldest manuscripts. It is also an encyclopedia of life filled with poetry, song, and prophecies. What's more, it is named after a maid. Yes, a maid, a woman low on the pecking order, but one who held all the wisdom of the world. Sudarminto always thought it a rather gorgeous idea that such a lowly woman could rise so in respectability. But try telling this to thirty sniffly schoolchildren in a crammed classroom, most of whom were so poor they had not the faintest idea what having a maid even felt like. So he waited patiently for that moment, when one of them would ask, "Why Centhini? Why the maid? Why is the book not named after Centhini's mistress or her mistress's husband, whom the book is mostly about?"

At such a moment in the narrative, Sudarminto had learned to skirt the brink of the allowable; he would recite a livelier poem and scan his students' faces, one by one, searching for signs of appreciation. Out of such experiments came those rare moments when all childish voices were suspended, and it seemed the world softened to a hush.

Other men might have dreamed of winning a lottery, buying hectares of land and building grand houses; they might have hunted the strongest, most elusive prey and married off sons and daughters. But all Sudarminto wanted to do was to write down years of secret dreams.

In bed at night he would listen to the radio. But often sleep eluded him altogether. He would lie still for what seemed like an eternity, listening to the noises of the night and his wife's soft breathing next to him. Then, as if in an opium-induced trance, his thoughts would travel with Prince Jayengraga on his sexual escapades. Sometimes he had difficulties dampening his gasping breath.

Sometimes, to his immense shame, Sudarminto would linger on the vision of Jayengraga bedding three women in one night or the thought of the shepherd he raped after a frenzied orgy at the widow's house. There was also a certain illicit pleasure in imagining what it must feel like to ram your penis into a horse's ass.

Whatever his guilty night pleasures, the next morning he would wash them off with dawn prayer, in much the same way Jayengraga would rush to the mosque after a wildly erotic night.

All the while, young Amba was watching and taking notes. She instinctively realized her father secretly admired the randy prince. There was nothing sexier, she later learned, than a man who dared design his own destiny and who made no apologies for chasing pleasure. (That the prince happened to be handsome and virile was a bonus.) Even at the age of eleven, she understood how this sort of bravado, this confidence in life might have appealed to her father, who could hardly be considered in charge of, let alone the architect of, his own fate.

Despite his little secrets, Amba's father had been faithful, too. Not once did he ever betray the love of his wife, or the trust of his daughters. For he had an even larger kingdom to rule than his wife's and a bigger example to set.

Being a teacher made life easier for him in so many ways; it gave him respectability and trust. But it also made life difficult because it meant that he had the wisdom of many books and was as such permitted no error of judgment. To the town folk, knowledge and wisdom were not things he had to teach or train himself in; they were supposed to have come to him like a mandate from heaven. Knowledge was supposed to be part of him. Moreover, he was both a teacher and a member of the aristocracy—his father, a school principal, was also a *priyayi*, a man drawn straight from the administrative layers of the royal court of Yogyakarta—and this gave him a rather special status in town.

Although Amba's father called himself a Muslim, he was not a descendent of a religious person. Most Javanese are only partly Muslim, meaning they are also faithful to local traditions older than the fourteenth century, the time when traders from other parts of the world began to spread the Islamic faith. Like most Javanese, Amba's father held on to traces of Buddhism, Hinduism, and animism as if they were glorious sequins of the past.

Sudarminto felt he was first and foremost part of Kadipura. The small town was located at the foot of Mount Merapi, not far from the Central Javanese city of Klaten. It only took twenty minutes by bicycle to reach the main road linking Yogyakarta to Solo. The town's paddies, which supplied rice for the neighboring towns, possessed a sturdy irrigation system. Through the center of town stretched a shopping street and rows of solid stone houses, interspersed by colonial buildings left by the Dutch. The old missionary school, once the pride of the town, was suddenly no more; it had been replaced by new schools staffed by new teachers, who seemed to have sprung out from nowhere. These included the so-called instant teachers brought in to match the alarmingly fast-growing number of students.

Sudarminto was not among them. He was proud to call himself a "true teacher." And he was the truest among the true. How could he not be? His father was a school principal, and so was his grandfather. He also knew how to distinguish the instant from the true teachers at a glance, and he knew how to surround himself with his own kind.

But Kadipura had changed all too swiftly: its town hall, its mosques, and its schools suddenly found themselves overcrowded, and it had taken Sudarminto some time to notice that the true teachers were being fast outnumbered by the instant ones, quite a few from the neighboring towns. In time, like everybody else, they too became split into two camps. One called the other "that PNI person" or "that PKI person," "that Nationalist" or "that Communist." The rest, who weren't quite sure where they were in the ideological divide, stayed silent.

Sudarminto was a moderate man. He smoked in moderation, liked his coffee plain, such a contrast to the triple-sugared preference of his peers, and couldn't stand even the slightest hint of garlic or chili in his food. He had no visible hobbies other than those he felt compelled to show off every now and then—gardening, mainly, something soothing and entirely nonpolemical.

And yet, for all his middle-wayness he didn't know how to stay in the middle in matters religious. How to avoid tension, which was never there when he was growing up. Not to mention his dark secrets, which only Amba knew, a complicity that on Amba's part made her love her father more deeply, more fiercely, even though he wasn't aware of it.

But he was living and laboring in a changing universe; that much he knew.

And Amba didn't make matters easier.

❧

One afternoon in late 1956, Amba went looking for her father in his study. As she later remembered it, the air was hot and thick despite the settling of dusk, and all around was the familiar mix of incense, burnt grass, oil, and fermented prawn. She could hear the sound of footsteps and soft patter in the kitchen. Soon on the table there would be fried soybean cakes, a relish of grated coconut and spices, and mixed blanched vegetables served with steamed white rice and prawn crackers. And a few pieces of fried chicken, if Amba's mother was feeling generous.

Amba was clearly upset. Before her father could ask her what was wrong, she told him that her religion teacher had just reprimanded her for not reading the Qur'an.

"Is that true?"

"Well, I don't mind learning the Qur'an, but I find Arabic letters hard to pronounce," Amba said. "Mr. Baedowi said everyone has to be able to read the Qur'an properly, for that is the sign of faith. He told me I shouldn't become like those Kadipurans who love their *macapatan* but are strangers to their religion."

"Hmm."

Amba looked at her father.

"I guess your teacher may be right, Amba."

But deep down Sudarminto was just as upset as his daughter. This man named Baedowi was a newcomer in Kadipura. Sudarminto heard he was never seen attending any *tablikh*, nor was he ever invited to preside over sermons in private houses, as was increasingly the norm in those days. Was it possible that he was a free agent, a religious teacher unattached to a boarding school? He didn't seem one of those loud and combative *kyai*s from the Nahdlatul Ulama, with loyal disciples and followers. *Why had I not attended to his recruitment into the school more carefully?* Sudarminto thought. *Now this simpleton is teaching my children.*

Yes, Kadipura was changing. The world Sudarminto knew had begun to slip away. But Kadipura was made up of silences. Not the silences of things lacking, but rather the silences behind things. Sudarminto understood these silences more than anybody else. He was part of this world. He had helped make it.

Flawed architecture and lack of money might have contributed to the gaps in the walls and to the windows that didn't close, but what the walls and the windows concealed ran deeper than blood.

Although people discussed troubles as calmly as they could, or avoided discussing them altogether, he soon learned that his absence from the mosque during Friday prayers had been a hot topic for some time. Some had been blunt: *Be careful, there will come a time when the distance you deliberately kept from God will cause you to fall and perish. There will come a time when these Commie bastards will come to your house in the night and cut your throat and the throats of your wife and children. Then you will regret not having been closer to the Plumbon men of faith.*

It was the silence that accompanied these words, in the straight-faced greetings of his neighbors, in the seemingly respectful nods of his students' parents, which to him was the greatest silence of all. It was deep and wide as the Serayu River. It was heavy as the gravestone of his grandfather.

❧

For Sudarminto, things had been different back when the girls were born, Amba in 1944, the twins two years later. In those days, most people had thought like him. They certainly didn't lose sleep over this shapeless, faceless God of the preachers and zealots. How could they, when life kept changing with such speed and force? The Second World War, the fall of the Dutch East Indies, the arrival and then the defeat of the Japanese, the renewed battle for independence, the Dutch aggression, the battle against pre-occupation, rebellions by the scores.

Sudarminto had lived through all this with a certain calm, a certain confidence, made possible by his quiet submission to old wisdoms passed down through generations. For centuries the Javanese had lived with a poetic prophecy that hinted at the coming of foreign rule. The *ulemmas* might scream their lungs out about Allah striking down these foreign enemies, but even before they came, the Javanese had always known they were coming. *The Wedhatama* said so: "The Javanese would be ruled by whites for three centuries and by yellow dwarfs for the life span of a maize plant prior to the return of the Just King." God might be all things to all people, but as far as the Javanese were concerned they were united by one faith: that the foreigners would eventually be banished from their land.

And banished they were, as surely as the ages that came and went, ushering change, ushering new beginnings.

But neither God nor any subversive old Javanese poem nor prophecies of the most profound sagacity had prepared Sudarminto for being the father of three daughters. Even though he taught for a living, what he taught his own daughters was different from what he taught other people's children. No theory. No science. No platitudes. Just folktales, and tales from the *wayang*, drawn from the great Indian epics, which flowed through their lives and the lives of the people around them.

It was also obvious that his choice of the name for his eldest daughter was willfully corrupting, given what happened to Amba in the great epic.

Won't people think us cruel, giving the name of a fallen woman to our firstborn? his wife had asked, all those years ago. *What sort of father pushes his own daughter toward a troubled fate?*

But it was as if Sudarminto needed to exercise his right to see how far the name would take his first child. When fate determined that his next offspring should be twin daughters, and thus ripe for their inevitable naming, he could only reflect that there was no way he could have anticipated such a twist of fate when he named his firstborn.

Surely a man was entitled to trust in his own wisdom? Besides, he'd always liked the quiet strength of the name Amba. He also had a weakness for marginalized characters, those elbowed out of the great narratives, sidelined by the puppet masters.

You do know that Amba's triumph comes later, he always told his daughters when recounting the story from *The Mahabharata*. The twins, Ambika and Ambalika, might give birth to kings, but it is only Amba who can end a war.

And darling, he told Amba privately, *you know that no woman should accept the conventions of her name, much less be trapped by it.* It was Amba's fate to rise above the old judgments, to give her name its own meaning.

Blessedly, all of his daughters seemed to know what he expected of them and proceeded to teach themselves how to breathe meaning into their names. They understood instinctively that telling is always retelling, casting the old anew.

Yet Sudarminto was also slightly afraid of them, his girls. Especially of his eldest daughter.

He found her utterly mesmerizing.

※

Since their *Centhini* exchange, Amba was aware that her father had begun to watch her more closely.

He began taking her to a lake south of town for long walks. The lake had no name, but local beliefs held it was where everything began. They would sit at the edge of a pier, on a piece of woven mat they brought from home. They would munch on a few pieces of cassava cakes soggy with palm sugar and drink water from canteens.

Sudarminto would watch his eldest daughter throw bits of cassava into the lake, and marvel at how similar they were, really.

Often he felt he was about to cross a line. Most of all, however, he felt a blazing pride. There, by the lake, he began to share with her thoughts and feelings never told at home.

Whereas Amba would think, *So this is how it feels to travel for so long and arrive in a place where you are known.*

※

"*Pak*, in the *Centhini,* Ki Amongrogo and his wife are said to meet with their family after their death. How is that possible? How do the dead communicate with the living?"

There they were again, Amba and her father, by the lake, eating snake fruits and mangosteens.

"Hmm." The word he found himself increasingly saying. "Do you believe in spirits?"

Amba didn't answer right away.

"Well, do you?"

She didn't say it, but of course she did. Every day at least one of her friends at school would talk of one sighting or another. A dead grandmother, materializing at dinner and telling stories of her life. A special corner of a house that was "our dead brother's corner," where the mood of the dead brother set the tone of the day. A friendly spirit who could keep a boy out of harm's way or reveal the fiend that murdered a family not so long ago.

Amba lowered her gaze, and something swelled in Sudarminto. He began speaking in the way she knew and loved so well.

"Amba, know that in the world I know, the dead do not sleep. They exist in the same sphere as human beings. Remember that while reincarnation may be a pillar of Hinduism and Buddhism, it is not known in Islam. Yet we in Java live with both. We are Javanese because we are both."

❧

Meanwhile, beyond the two of them, outside the vicissitudes of their family, the times were changing. Something larger was taking hold.

It had begun in 1955, the year of the first general elections for the new Republic of Indonesia. There was something acidic and shrewd in the air. At work, among his fellow teachers, politics had become more and more unbearable for Sudarminto. He often came home subdued and tired, for there was no space for moderates like him.

There were so many party emblems to choose from that people had difficulty remembering which was which, what each signified, what was good, and what was bad. But still they chose, as though it were the highest truth. Families and neighbors started to avoid, rebuke, or repel each other, just because they didn't share the same political beliefs or choose the same party.

People started to lock their doors.

Through it all, Amba watched how her father, who had prided himself on running a pretty simple ship, couldn't quite convince his wife to vote for the Nationalist Party. He'd warned her of the dangers of fragmentation, saying it was one thing to dream up a nation and quite another to live in it. Independence has its costs.

Her mother, meanwhile, was no wallflower even if she liked to pretend she was. Amba knew that she secretly understood her husband's passions, for they were not unlike her own. Ever since she tied herself to her husband, she'd waited patiently for her value as an independent thinker to be recognized. She had not slipped on these slopes, not even once. But now, somehow, she felt she had earned the right to choose her own politics. And choose she did.

One day, a few weeks after the general elections, Amba's father found his wife coming home a few hours late, the vegetables almost wilted in her shopping basket. "What happened?" he asked. "Where were you all this time?"

Even Amba could see that Nuniek looked different. Her face was glowing. She didn't even apologize for being late.

"You remember our old neighbor in Kertosono?" she asked, before he had a chance to admonish her. "The one whose aunt just died of lung disease?"

"Hartoyo, you mean?"

"Yes, that's it. Well, I just saw him speak at the town hall. He was really impressive. Talked a lot about women and their struggle. At the end of his speech, everyone applauded."

Sudarminto looked a little rattled, saying, "He's always been a smooth talker. And of course he was talking about women because the place was surrounded by *Gerwani*." Gerwani was the shortened name for the Indonesian Women's Movement, and it was closely linked to the party of this neighbor who had so impressed his wife, the Indonesian

Communist Party, a new party that had surprisingly come in fourth in the general elections, having gained a lot of traction in a short period.

"Still. He seemed to know what people wanted," Nuniek said.

"As our dear president Bung Karno said, what our country really needs is unity," Sudarminto countered.

"Bung Karno is a revolutionary, so of course he would say that. But where is the revolutionary fervor in the Nationalist Party? To unite is well and good, but tell me, where is the revolution?"

"How easily impressed you are by the power of cheap rhetoric. That Hartoyo isn't even the best of them. Did you really listen to his speech?"

Amba watched her mother retreat. Nuniek knew only too well when to stop, when to heed her husband's change of voice. She knew that you had to feel your way through a marriage, not unlike politics. Just when you thought your relationship with your husband was firmly in place, the tables began, ever so slightly and unfathomably, to turn. But as she went to the kitchen and laid down her sad and shriveled vegetables, it was plain that she was annoyed at her husband.

"Precious little good has the principle of unity done to the Nationalist Party," she whispered to Amba conspiratorially. "Didn't it, just the other day, split into two parties? One had for its symbol a chicken-feather pen, the other a shovel. Now how idiotic is that?"

Some weeks ago Amba's father had had the walls of the house decorated with the image of a bull's head inside a triangle. Then the same scenario played out so many times Amba lost count: her father insisting to her mother, "We have to choose correctly. The bull's head means the Nationalist Party and that means Sukarno."

Nuniek responded, "How about the hammer and sickle? How about the Communist Party?"

At which point Sudarminto's pedantry would border on caricature; his eyes would roll, his brows arching in mock astonishment. "My dear, just look at these two things—the hammer and the sickle. The hammer, granted, is the tool of the laborers. Fine. Now look at this sickle. What's wrong with this picture? We're talking about the working class, aren't we? We're voting for them, yes? Because they are the true revolutionaries we've been dying to have, yes? So why are we looking at a sickle? Is it not a fact that with a sickle the peasants can only cut grass, or a small branch? Shouldn't we be looking instead at the shovel, a tool that is capable of so much more? So, even the symbolism of the Communist Party is suspect. Now ask yourself, should we be voting for a party that cannot even get its emblem right?"

At which point Amba's mother swiftly, silently, almost automatically, dove into the zone of no argument, because beyond it there was only her pride in front of her children left to salvage. She would stay like that, quiet and smiling, while her husband patiently, bigheartedly, closed the discussion, as men of wisdom often did with their wives.

Amba was aware of her mother's growing frustration. Over the years, as her husband's subtle patronizing started to grate on her nerves, the feeling had started to manifest in tiny, barely perceptible acts: an insipid *sambal*, oversalted tempeh, inexplicable stains on freshly washed clothes. Amba might have been held to her twin passions—her fierce adoration of her father and her determination to be her own person and not follow the footsteps of her mother.

But in this case she felt sorry for her.

"*Bu*," she said to her mother one day, "Bapak—well, he's a little out of whack. Back in those days, all those years ago, he might have been right. In the West, so I've learned, they use the sickle the way we use *ani-ani*, the hand-knife, to cut grain."

Later, Amba would learn that politics is not about getting it right. It's about getting it wrong rightly. Then she would remember how fond her father was of saying that all the islands of their country were like a thousand little foundlings with their mouths turned toward their mother, which he called the Giant Nipples, who had to provide endlessly.

She remembered him saying, *Ten years after our country gained independence, in the chaos that was the 1955 general election, those thousand foundlings had fused into four fat suckling sons. They were the Big Four. They were the chosen ones. The Giant Nipples then spoke to the first son, the Indonesian Nationalist Party, known as PNI, and to the second son, Masyumi, or the Council of Indonesian Muslim Associations, and to the third son, the Islamic Party Nahdlatul Ulama, known as NU. The Giant Nipples told these parties, "Go over to the right-hand side of the table." To the fourth son, the Indonesian Communist Party, commonly referred to as PKI, she said, "You, stay where you are on the left-hand side of the table." Then the father, President Sukarno, said proudly, "We are all one family sitting at one big dinner table."*

Yet. The truth was, the table never seemed big enough for those four suckling sons. Besides, it was not in them, those different, greedy children, to get along. Most certainly not with that kind of mother: too various, too sprawling, too soft and porous in her constitution.

Amba remembered thinking how "family" sounded increasingly like the wrong metaphor for the Indonesian political party system he was trying to describe.

Meanwhile. When the fourth suckling, the Indonesian Communist Party, rose spectacularly, claiming a membership of three million in less than a year, his three siblings cried foul: "How can our brother be more important than we are? It's impossible."

Amba understood that anything was possible, in the tuck and tumble of those hungry, grasping mouths all sucking on the Giant Nipples, the mother who was, after all, simply an idea.

5

Salwa

Time ticked by, and the '50s became the '60s.

Amba's twin sisters were, in their different ways, growing into their predestined beauty, but Amba, too, had changed. The qualities that made her less lovely in adolescence seemed to have blossomed into a more singular kind of loveliness: those eyes, those arched brows, that soft, slightly rounded nose, a mouth that could stretch, almost at will, from a superb pout to a savanna-wide grin. She wasn't tall, never would be, but she had stature without height, and her presence changed the temperature of a room. As the Javanese were accustomed to an opposite repertoire of gestures from a woman—the downcast gaze, the lowered voice, the polite smile—people were generally unsure how to behave near her.

As ever she was not a rose, but she knew because of that she was happy.

☙❧

What Amba didn't know was this.

A month before, Amba's parents had met Salwani Munir and instantly fell in love with him. He was perfect son-in-law material. Twenty-two, pleasant-looking in a predictable way, with a thin mustache over well-defined lips and an air that appealed to them.

Salwa's parents represented two poles of Islam. His father owned a small furniture shop and was the head of the local chapter of Muhammadiyah. His mother was the daughter of a kyai (a religious leader) and was herself a leader of the local chapter of NU, the Nahdlatul Ulama.

Husband and wife bickered about religion and about politics all the time, privately and publicly. Soon home became hell, and then the town became hell for Salwa. Much of his childhood had been spent either watching this bickering, or watching people try to rend his parents into a divorce. If someone told his father that that imam who presided over the daily prayers in the local mosque turned out to be from the other persuasion, he would order Salwa and his brothers to return home and do their prayers there. At home, they would be greeted by the wrath of their mother. *How can the prayer be valid if the imam doesn't even say* ushalli? she would demand, whereupon her husband would retaliate by not speaking to her for days.

Even though Salwa's father did not appear to give physical vent to his anger, and this was something Salwa was at least grateful for, his message was clear: men and women may differ, but men still rule. And because he was eldest among the boys, Salwa would find himself nodding away, as it was not his role to rock the family boat. At times, he would feel vague nips of restlessness, the nudgings of a conscience, but he did not know for what.

As time progressed, Salwa found himself ceasing to care. What he wanted to know was this: Why was God so bent on fuzzying so many important matters, such as what was right and what was wrong? Or were right and wrong important matters to begin with? Or was the important thing to know how to be right or wrong smartly?

"Has Bapak ever hit you?" he asked his mother one day.

"Of course."

"Why have I never witnessed it?"

"Because I made sure you and your brothers never saw."

There were so many burning questions. He wondered who put those questions in his head, but in the snarls and fumes of hateful speeches and poisonous sermons he often could hardly hear himself think. Let alone ask his parents, both too blighted and used to hiding behind their masks. Or those lewd-eyed kyais whose voices, when they were not giving religious sermons, always seemed to deepen a few octaves when moistened with that favorite standby of randy old goats: Old Man *kolesom* liquor.

Salwa became even more discouraged from asking too many questions when he realized he was starting to think too much about "the pink woman."

This woman with the pink *kebaya* and the pink cheeks, who had reportedly slept with all the men in the neighboring village and who was at least ten years older than he was, had stopped beside him at the Parung crossroads on the way out of town. She had swung around and whispered, "Pinch my butt, I dare you." Now, the damnedest thing was that he was not just thinking about her, but secretly *yearning* to see her again, especially after she ordered him, there and then, in their first meeting, to feel her butt, the curve and curb of it, whispering, "Here, feel my *pantat*, and let me make you a man." It was a strange yearning, because at the same time he was fearful of her, of the things she told him, of that butt, of ever having to touch it. It was her face he was attracted to, its fire, its power, its valor.

All this took place out of his friends' sight. During a Tayub parade, a regular event in his village, he would leave home before he got into an insult match with his father's minions, who often milled around uselessly, and join his friends. He would watch them jostle each other, crying out triumphantly whenever one succeeded in pinching the butt of a sexy dancer, stuck out for their benefit. It gave him no pleasure to watch the woman break into a sweet, cloying smile, as though rewarding this disrespect to her. Or to listen to those boys, the butt pinchers, his friends, justifying their behavior, saying it was perfectly all right, in fact it was the thing to do during the Tegahbumi rituals, in which the Goddess of Rice was called to descend upon earth and bestow a good harvest. Along with all those words of prayer they had to muster in Arabic.

Lighten up! Someone would poke him. *The pinches are part of our culture.* And this, uttered so casually that nobody took offense, not even the more outwardly pious among them. It was like hearing someone say, *Yes, here we are proclaiming there is no God but Allah, but deep down we all know other gods rule this land with invisible hands.*

So Salwa would stay quiet. What was the point in trying to change things? In getting himself a new conscience? And yet.

One day, a week shy of his sixteenth birthday, he packed his bags and left home, deciding he had to get himself an education.

The first thing he did when he arrived in Yogyakarta was to knock on Johari's door. Johari was the brother of his best friend, Saiful. He was twenty-seven and by then already running a successful garage, with a steady income and a motorcycle, which helped shore up his reputation with the neighborhood girls and their mothers. He also had a reputation for generosity, and he never reclaimed anything he'd loaned to people. He was like that. He gave and didn't think twice about it.

Johari gave Salwa a small room at the back of his house. "You don't have to pay," he said. "You are my brother's friend."

For the first time in his life, Salwa set himself a goal. He vowed he would repay everybody who had been kind to him: Johari, Saiful, even his parents, who had not made his departure difficult. He would repay them by studying hard, living his life responsibly, and working, working, working.

He wanted to be a teacher.

᭠

As far as Amba's parents were concerned 1962 was a good year. It was the Year of Change. The Year of Good Fortune.

Out of the blue, Sudarminto was promoted to education inspector, a very prestigious appointment under the old colonial education system.

For the first time in his life, he desired something beyond his known world.

"I want to go to Yogyakarta," he told his wife, his voice anxious. "I've never seen inside an education faculty."

Nuniek looked at her husband. She couldn't quite pin down why, but lately he'd appeared so flat, so unremarkable.

"We can go together," he said, not looking at her. "We can visit Gadjah Mada University. The Faculty of Teacher Training and Pedagogy there is supposed to be impressive." He said those words slowly, one by one, with deliberate care, as though they had been part of his secret world.

"I've no doubt," Nuniek said carefully. "Now if we only had the money."

But how could she refuse a chance to go to Yogyakarta, even though they could barely afford it? Nuniek had only been twice to that city of cities. What she would give to go to Kotagede, to pray in Imogiri, at the grave of the great king, the author of encyclopedic tomes, to count the steps leading to the grave of the sultan Agung.

But there was no money.

❧

Not all hopes were fantasies, however. At least not for Sudarminto and Nuniek. Not in 1962.

Five days after they separately let go of their dreams, a letter came. It was from the Faculty of Teacher Training and Pedagogy of the Gadjah Mada University. The words on the page wiggled like worms in Sudarminto's wobbly vision: Could you come to our campus at 11:00 a.m. on 17 September, to attend a meeting for teachers . . . We need teachers as experienced and as esteemed as yourself . . . We plan to have 120 graduates next year and also some post-graduates and need to review our curriculum . . . We would welcome your feedback . . . We can't give you much by way of an honorarium . . . but we would be more than happy to bear the cost of your bus fare to Yogyakarta, and provide accommodation at the university . . . Please advise if your wife wishes to travel with you . . .

❧

A week later, Sudarminto and his wife found themselves on a bus to Yogyakarta. They deliberately traveled one day before the meeting and tried for most of the day to feel something of what the word *honeymoon* might mean, something they'd never had in eighteen years of marriage.

On the second day, they found themselves standing in a court-yard, next to a patchy flowerbed on which stood a board that said "The Faculty of Teacher Training and Pedagogy, Gadjah Mada University."

It was a clear morning, and they had arrived at 9:30 a.m., an hour and a half too early.

They stood wordlessly watching the people around them, students, teachers, visitors like themselves, walking along the corridors, sitting on benches, poring over sheaves of paper, everyone with their mouths open, everyone speaking their minds, everyone with things to share, everyone having a life, a real life, a big life not like theirs. There was electricity in the air, an alien charge. As the chatter accelerated it seemed everyone existed to remind them that they were not part of this elevated atmosphere.

Unsure of what else to do, they wandered around, trying to look less conspicuous. They saw doors suggesting dark storage rooms, toilets reeking of piss and cheap disinfectant, classrooms smelling of rotting peanuts and paper glue, their walls damp and yellowing under randomly hung mementos of past significance, the desks, made of cheap, dispirited plywood, taking up nearly the entire width of each room. In the library, bits of paper and discarded snack wrappers were strewn across desks and benches, and the colored, frosted windows were covered with cobwebs, the desks a nightmarish scene where roaches and unidentifiable animals were chasing each other.

Nuniek thought to herself, *Why should we be feeling this way, so insignificant? The small-town school my husband runs is clearly so much cleaner and more orderly. And why does my husband look so unattractive? Why does he suddenly look so decrepit, so small, so unfit, so unlike the respected figure he is in Kadipura?*

Nuniek tried to pin her attention on something else. But where was she to look? Up, down, sideways, farther afield? There was her husband, trying valiantly to marshal as much confident body language as he could. Her inexplicable disdain, so alien to her, returned with force: *Could he just stop fidgeting with his glasses again?* She wanted badly to snatch those glasses from his hand. She wanted to go home.

"Weren't we supposed to have made an appointment?" she whispered instead. "The meeting is at 11:00 a.m., right?"

"Yes, but I'm sure there is no need to be so formal," Sudarminto said, uncertainly, looking down again at that stupid crumpled piece of paper he'd had in his pocket for days. On it he'd printed "2nd Floor. Room B-3."

"Perhaps you should inquire at the administration office."

"All right," he said with a sigh, at long last. "Why don't you stay here? Or there, sit under that lovely tree. Let me make some inquiries."

Despite herself, Nuniek did what she was told. From a long wooden bench under the giant tree she watched her husband lurk outside the building for a few sickening seconds before finally entering. She tried not to think of him, of how Yogyakarta made both of them feel small. She saw a food stall nearby and ordered a syrupy ice drink. Along with those delicious licks of ice came a cooling breeze.

Suddenly Nuniek no longer felt so bad. The buildings began to acquire character, the faces around her ceased to look unfamiliar. A student who ordered the same drink from the same vendor, a confident-looking girl with an open gaze, reminded her of Amba. Amba . . . such a difficult child. Difficult yet loved. Lovable. Her eyes suddenly watered.

Then she was aware of someone walking toward her. A younger man, dressed smartly in black pants and a white shirt, not unlike her own husband in size, but somehow taller, elegant. He was heading for the same bench on which she sat. Look, he even nodded at her.

She began to rise to give him most of the room on the bench beside her.

"Oh please, do sit down. I didn't mean to startle you," he said, bending solicitously, as though afraid she would be hurt. "Is there something I can help you with? Are you waiting for someone?"

Is it so obvious that I am not from here? Nuniek wondered.

When the young man asked if he could sit beside her she said, "Of course, of course."

Up close he appeared even nicer, calm, quietly confident, with clear good looks. Yet there was something else about him, a loneliness perhaps, or a quiet strength, that piqued her interest.

"You're not from here, I suppose," the young man said, kindly.

"No, no. We come from Kadipura, a small town not far from Klaten."

"Oh yes, I know that town." His smile was smooth and uncontrived.

"My husband was a school principal there. Now he is an education inspector. He's been invited to a meeting of teachers here at the . . . the Faculty of Teacher Training and Pedagogy, to discuss the new curriculum. Anyway, such a long name. Often I don't remember it." She heard herself speaking in an overly maternal way, as though eager to be liked. "My husband . . . he has just gone inside the building to find out where the meeting will be held."

"Perhaps I can be of help. I am an assistant lecturer here," the man said. "My name is Salwani Munir. But please call me Salwa."

Salwa. Salwa? Something about the shade and shape of the man's lips that was so attractive, and something about his smile that brought warmth into his eyes. A smile that for a perverse instant reminded Nuniek of how it was to be both like a schoolgirl and a young woman thinking about marriage. And there was something else. Something important. What was it?

She was only half-aware of the young man telling her he might know where the meeting would be held, as he was heading there, too. "Why don't we find your husband? They might even let you sit in with us. It's far too hot here."

They finally caught up with Sudarminto in the corridor in front of the administration office. Salwa shook the older man's hand, introduced himself, and instantly Nuniek saw the change in her husband. He stood taller, his voice was steadier, more assured, the voice that distinguished him from those half-trained teaching louts back home. No longer was he the half-deflated balloon that she had stood next to outside.

But it was too early for conclusions. After their tour, the three of them arrived at the meeting room. It was three-quarters full. When

Nuniek felt her husband about to crawl back into his hole she pushed him into the room. As if complicit in the gesture, Salwa walked in next to him, tall and erect, and the moment was marked. A future son-in-law is your second future, a new lease on life.

Nuniek sat herself, relieved, on the bench beside the open door to the room. She would wait. Damn it, she would wait forever if that was what it took.

Soon the concerns of the room flooded into her ears. Classes abandoned by the children of farm laborers, teachers who didn't get their promotions, schools deprived of books, village youth more interested in marching in handed-out "uniforms" as though heading into battle than attending classes, failed harvests, staple foods that disappeared from the market, the known world changing. "And yet, *and yet*," she heard from the meeting room, a constant refrain. "We are the children of the Revolution, we have to stay faithful to the Revolution, we have to stay faithful to Sukarno, to the holy trinity of Nationalism-Religion-Communism. That is the single pivot on which our history turned. We cannot cave in to the enemies of the Revolution, we ought not to let ourselves forget the wounds of imperialism. Revolution must follow revolution without interruption."

It was nearly noon. Nuniek, bored by it all, picked herself up and went back to the bench under the giant benevolent tree. She ordered another syrupy iced drink.

Twenty minutes later, she ambled over to the canteen to have lunch. For the first time she felt unapologetic for eating ahead of her husband. She ordered two portions of everything for herself.

❧

Later, even Amba was startled by her own calmness when she first heard about Salwani Munir.

Amba's parents were anything but tactless. They knew how to keep secrets better than most. They knew how to plant and water a blessing, away from prying eyes, until it blossomed into a flower of hope. They knew their eldest daughter better than anyone, and they knew how to ride her ups and downs.

So they would wait for the right time to tell Amba about Salwani. Hell, they would wait for a year, until after Amba's final exams. By that time Amba would have just turned eighteen, and the twins sixteen. Good age, good timing.

Despite his own interest in Salwani as a son-in-law, Sudarminto secretly had problems with this view of Amba's future. Nobody knew as well as he did that Amba wanted to go to university. Even if he never spoke about it with his wife, he was the last to stand in the way of his eldest daughter's wish. He also knew, only too well, that young men like Salwani did not grow on trees. He sensed that Salwani would not settle for a small-town wife when, with prospects as bright as his, he would surely have access to women more worldly and interesting.

For Amba's own part, there were no two ways about it. She must absolutely go to university.

But there is such a thing as the heart of a mother.

One afternoon Sudarminto brought home goat meat that someone had given him as a present. He was so excited by this he took it to the kitchen himself and asked Amba to prepare a curry. (Although, he reasoned later, there was also respect in this gesture, as he knew his wife couldn't stand the smell of goat meat.) Soon the scents of garlic, shallots, ginger, candlenut, bay leaves, chilis, galangal, turmeric, lemongrass, lime leaves, cloves, cinnamon, palm sugar, and coconut cream wafted in the kitchen, filling the air with his hopes, his secrets, his conspiracies.

This seemed to be Nuniek's reading of the situation, at any rate. Which made her leave the kitchen abruptly, out of a sudden need for drama, and lock herself in her bedroom for what seemed like hours. And which forced her vexed husband to finally let himself in through the window (once the goat was gently simmering on the stove).

She wailed, "My brain is about to burst. I can't keep it in any longer. You're trying to destroy me. You're trying to take everything away from me, including my kitchen. You're teaching your daughters how not to be grateful for life's blessings. Are you really prepared to risk your eldest daughter losing her happiness?"

Sudarminto knew retaliation had no future, so he put his hand on his wife's burning forehead and let it remain there until he felt her cooling down. Then he gently took her outside and called Amba to the living room. When Amba came, he sat her down, and he and Nuniek told their daughter about Salwani.

"Meeting him has made me so happy," Nuniek said. "I haven't been this happy for years. *We* haven't been this happy for years."

It was at that moment that the strange, surprising calmness descended. Instead of erupting, Amba found herself smiling broadly, almost genuinely. She said, "That's nice, I'm really glad." Then she took herself back to her books.

The smoothness of the event shocked all concerned. For the next few days Amba's parents left her alone. Nuniek, who'd started feeling the nips of guilt, kept a lock on her mouth. She even felt the need to compensate for her impetuosity by exempting her eldest daughter from kitchen work.

This did not please the twins. Among the three of them, Amba was by far the most gifted cook, and they hated being compared to her all the time. How could it be that Amba would get all the things she wanted: a university education, a husband whom, they were told, was not just smart and educated and good-looking but also, in all likelihood, rich, or about to be rich, *and* all the love and glory?

The twins, of course, had no way of knowing Nuniek's suddenly heightened love didn't just come from meeting Salwani, the son she never had, but also because Amba had stood up for her, recognized her intelligence, on that dreary peasant-shovel-hammer-and-sickle issue some time back, the petty argument that her husband had so wanted to win.

Amba was secretly touched by the congested array of feelings around her. Especially the way her mother was suddenly so bent on pleasing her. And hearing more stories of her grandmother, whom she loved.

This one, for instance: *Your grandmother was not just a cook, but the head cook of the royal court of Surakarta before she married the school principal who was your grandfather. She never complained about life, however shitty it turned out to be. There was her husband taking a second wife, for instance, without seeking her permission. Such things could destroy a person.*

But she was such a fighter. She refused to mope and lose her dignity. And she did this by returning to what she knew best. By getting better at it. She told me many times, "We cooks have the highest intelligence, and we have opinions about everything. Why? Because the qualities we have come to know as 'taste' and 'a deft hand in the kitchen' are essentially courage, and that is the prerequisite to alchemy: a set of nerves so steely and seasoned, which always know how much garlic, how many chilis, how much salt and pepper to put into each dish, at any second, in any situation, in any city, for every mouth, for every type of hunger."

Your grandmother was also a scientist. She would say, "Cooking is not simply a skill. A cook also needs basic knowledge of physics." And a philosopher: Cooking is not unlike marriage. Learning to wait, to not put your hand into muddied waters."

Of course, Amba remembered many of the tricks their grandmother taught her and only her, for she was the favorite granddaughter. Like the trick of keeping her ginger, galangal, and turmeric in a flower pot and watering it every day just like any plant. Or getting rid of the sap on bananas by adding palm oil to the water used to boil them. Or picking the right coconut for every occasion: half-mature for traditional gravy-based dishes like *lodeh* or *opor*, young for light fish or vegetable dishes like *botok* or *urap*, and only the very young, whose skin and flesh are too soft for grating, for making drinks or cake fillings.

And there was this, another thing Amba's grandmother taught her: every woman must have her own secrets. And it was these secrets, worn lightly but faithfully, that Amba hoped would free her from the obligation to marry.

When Amba's parents sat her down and told her about Salwani Munir she suppressed an impulse to laugh.

At first she didn't quite know what to make of this name cropping up in her life. Of course she knew her mythology, which exact part in the book she and her sisters came from, knew it intimately. How could she not, with the name she'd been given? The part—no, the big joke—about Princess Amba, who, betrothed to King Salwa, was abducted, along with her twin sisters, by the great, powerful warrior Bhisma, with whom she—ha ha ha—fell in love. Princess Amba, who was not only chucked out like a diseased cow by her fiancé for having brought dishonor upon him, but also then refused by her abductor, because he loved something else more than he loved her? Something he called duty—really!—which in his case involved remaining—mother of all bullshit—chaste.

Sure, Amba adored *The Mahabharata*, some stories more than others. But there were many parts she just couldn't stand. So a woman's life was cheap back then, cheaper than an animal's—everyone knew that. But look at Princess Amba—wasn't her story a bit too rich? Wasn't she also presented as the first female monster? Depicted as living the rest of her life carrying revenge in her head, in her heart, and in her gut? Revenge as a terrible sickness, a cancer?

Her father had his own agenda, sure. It wasn't just concern for his daughters. Like any man, he too had his own selfishness. But surely it was possible to see her namesake in a different light. An Amba who was willful and strong. Who was her own woman. Who saw that what those two men, King Salwa and Bhisma, put her through was nothing more than a preparation for her mission in life: kicking good men into their manhood and burying the useless ones under a hail of her superlethal arrows.

Of course Nuniek lost no time in stressing to her daughter the positives of the connection by pointing out that the young man's name was *not*, technically, Salwa. *His real name, darling, is Salwani.* Despite her rude self, her instant, horrible laughing at this naïve offering, Amba was touched. Especially when her mother felt it necessary to add that the story in *The Mahabharata* was, after all, hypothetical, half myth; for hadn't the gods decided to suspend all disbelief for the sake of a good story?

Besides, Nuniek went on, *do you see a Bhisma anywhere? No, you don't, do you. And why is that, you think? Why? Because there is no Bhisma. How could real life give you a Bhisma as well? That's just not on the charts. But. With this young man, this Salwani, you can have the best, the ideal life. Isn't that what every girl wants? To be loved by—no, to be the beloved of—a king among men?*

But she had to be smarter than that. She shouldn't avoid her parents' grand plan of introducing her to this Salwani person. So. Outwardly she would say okay. With bemusement. With a certain casualness. But inwardly, like her mother all those years ago, she would plan her escape. The whole of escape, not just the dream of it.

Besides, now she had a reason to misbehave. When the time came, she would have a reason to escape, for her fate had been written in the stars. Bhisma or no Bhisma, there was no way in hell she would end up with Salwa. Hell, she did not need to be with anyone.

Whoever this man was, however exempt he was likely to be from the laws of prophecy, he would have to prove himself worthy of her. And he couldn't possibly deserve her.

He who doesn't know her, doesn't deserve her.

On the third day of Amba's exams, Sudarminto fell ill. He stayed home from work, slept all day, and woke up in the afternoon with his head spinning. He reached for the water on his side table, wet his aching throat, and lay again with his eyes open.

When he felt a movement next to him he opened his eyes to see his wife. His lovely wife. His heart lifted amid the haze of everything else. He reached for her. But there was trouble on her face, the kind that had lately descended upon her like the plague, affecting the mood of the house. This time, with his fever keeping him bedbound, he couldn't escape. Vaguely, he heard, or thought he heard, the words *spinster, family shame, hardheaded as a goat.*

"She can't do this to us."

"Please, Nuniek," he said sluggishly. "Be reasonable. She'll come around."

"I'm not talking about the marriage! I'm talking about her wanting to go to university! We both know that behind her sweet nods she is planning something. We do, right? So what should we do? Surely she can't always get what she wants?"

Sudarminto sighed. "Amba is a bright girl. Don't you think it's a rather good idea?"

"This is not just about that," Nuniek said, exasperated. "I just—well, I just don't have a good feeling about this. I can see it in her eyes. You know, more than anyone, she has this unruliness about her. Especially when she wants something or believes in something. It's as if there's no afterthought, no middle ground. She has this . . . this *thing*, this pride about being able to think gray, as if no one else can. She told me, the gall of her, 'Life is not black or white, Bu, there is the murky area in between,' as if I don't get that."

This part was important, Sudarminto knew. It was important to pause, to take a little breather. To acknowledge, with the right kind of silence, that she, his wife, after all, did understand, had in fact understood everything too well.

"That's *exactly* what this is all about, Pak. She always thinks I'm stupid, too stupid to understand anything, especially how the world has changed, the *pace* with which it has changed. 'These days,' she keeps saying. '*These days* we do it this way.' As though I am living in different days, in a different era, too stupid to *get* her, too stupid to see that she isn't crazy, just different. But am I? Am I stupid? Am I too stupid to believe that one day, one of *these days*, she won't do something really, really stupid, something really, really crazy?"

Sudarminto sighed again, shook his head.

"In the end she will always do things in the extreme. Wanting to go to university, not wanting to marry. She is a giant family scandal waiting to happen. *That* is what I'm afraid of. I'm afraid of *her*."

Sudarminto dragged himself up now into a sitting position. "Really, my love," he said, "could you please not jumble the issues? Let's stick to the university thing first. Now, I think there's value in that, don't you?

Besides, the world is not getting any easier. The world is, in fact, gray and obscure. She will need all the education she can have. Education includes being able to make hard decisions when there are too few rights and wrongs."

"But you and I both know she won't get to hone *that* from a university education," Nuniek said. "University will not teach her *sense*. Only a steady-natured man, a proper anchor, will give her that. Help her to create a little distance from herself. To keep evil at bay."

"To speak of evil is to invite it into your life. We shall speak of this no more," Sudarminto said, sterner now, precisely in the manner of just the sort of steady-natured man, the proper anchor, his wife might be talking about.

To her chagrin, Nuniek understood the signs, her husband's neck craning in distress, with impatience, the finality of it. She knew enough not to push too hard.

Still. "But this boy will not be around for long," she tried one last time, her voice trembling. "They still haven't even met. Maybe we should just let them meet and see. What do you think?"

Silence, then: "You're funny," Sudarminto said. "So certain that they'll be all over each other. What if they don't even like each other?"

But Nuniek pretended not to hear. "And in the meantime, let's just keep calling him Salwani, as you suggested. That way we're not actively inviting fate. Besides, you're the one who keeps telling her not to be shackled to her name." She got up. "I'll fetch you some *wedang*. I'm sorry I haven't tended to you. The combination of ginger and heat—you know. It works every time."

Before leaving the room, she carelessly paused, like an afterthought, in front of the mirror above the bureau, to tidy up her hair. Sudarminto could see her face in the mirror. He could see the back of her head: her hair coiled in a bun, her long neck, her back, her slim waist, the rounded outline of her butt under the tight folds of her *kain*. Her face swam back into view. That pretty wifely face, unlined after three daughters. That butt, stunning and taut, with its poetic tilt just where it joined with her high, proud hips. Absurdly, he felt something stir between his legs.

"Come here," Sudarminto said, his heart racing.

The history of copulation is the history of glimpses, wave upon wave of them. Marriage is about knowing how to store them in memory and unlocking them at times such as these.

They still haven't even met. Maybe we should just let them meet and see. What do you think?

Despite Amba's private misgivings, the first meeting was scheduled for the first Sunday after her exams. It was the only day to receive guests of such significance, for school took up the rest of the week. Sudarminto, who kept in regular touch with Salwa by mail, had learned that he would be passing by Kadipura en route to Surabaya, East Java, where he was going to attend a teacher-training course for a week.

And so. The time had come, Amba thought. She would be sweet and cooperative. She would not push when it was not yet time. She would not talk too much, if at all. There certainly would be no sulking, no tantrum, no ranting about women's rights. In her new avocado blouse, worn over an *overgooier*-style T-shaped dress, she would look nice. She would look fetchingly adult, what with her small but perky breasts pushing against the material just enough to be suggestive and a hint of makeup on those cat's eyes of hers. And it worked. It had to. When she came through the door she saw how her father's heart skipped a beat, and she guessed the thoughts swirling in his head. *How*

88

lucky I am, he must be thinking, *to be the man, the only man so far, in my daughter's life.*

But something happened that morning. Something sent her plan awry. For the first time in her life she was pleasantly wrong.

❧

Salwa was not what she expected. His physique matched her mother's generous description. Clear skin, honest eyes, an air of gentle reserve: check. Humble, mature, wholesome: check. Strength built upon quiet confidence, not show-off knowledge: check, check. And there was something else: a kind of altruism. It was all over his eyes. He looked like a man happiest when he was making others happy. Now isn't that interesting?

As befitted his physical form, Salwa was pleasant in a laconic way. He brought with him a gift not too ostentatious but also not too plain—a pound cake from a famous bakery run by a Chinese family in Yogyakarta, nestled in a special lacquered case. He seemed grateful to be there. His quiet eagerness seemed almost to embarrass Amba's parents, who saw that a young man with such impeccable manners, with such a promising career in a big city, was actually pleased to pay them a visit in this humble town, in this humble house.

There he sat, on their best chair overlooking the garden, wearing dark brown trousers and a white shirt tapered at the waist, with short sleeves. His muscles taut, his daily-cycling-under-the-sun color blessedly copper instead of char. His gaze warm despite his tense face.

All through Salwa's visit Amba paid heed to his body language. She was aware how out of the corner of his eye he watched her rise from her chair, her slowness deliberate, to kneel before him with an easy grace, to observe the right sequence. Pour more tea first into his cup, then into her father's, then into her mother's. She watched, not without some fascination, the twins' enthrallment. How they couldn't keep their eyes off this man, the first suitor to come into their lives, the first to dare sit in that chair, the best chair overlooking the garden, and allow himself to be mooned and mulled over like a work of art. And for the privilege of what? Private time with their eldest sister? Incredible.

More incredible still was that although they knew they must have been the most beautiful sixteen-year-olds he'd ever come across, he was unmoved by them. Amba saw this and knew she had him: she was different from other girls, different from him, and she understood that men like Salwa secretly craved what they couldn't be on their own.

Sudarminto seemed mired in his own thoughts, too. He was about to say to Salwa that he should consider teaching here, in Kadipura. But suddenly he trailed off to a mumble. He decided it would be too forward, and besides, to smart and determined young men like Salwa, the city was a dream come true. Not wanting to seem out of touch with modern sensibilities, Sudarminto tried another tack.

"Our eldest daughter," he said, nodding in Amba's direction and avoiding his wife's eyes, "wants to go to university. She's just finished her exams."

Amba gave the requisite smile. How enjoyable, this whole theater. Had her father been more observant, less eager to impress, he would have seen the veiled mockery.

"You've told me before how diligent and studious your eldest daughter is." Salwa smiled. Then, looking directly at Amba: "Which university will you be applying to, Amba? And in what field?"

"I haven't really decided," she said politely. The way he spoke, using the words "studious" and "diligent," the way he referred to her as "your eldest daughter" and the way he held back on eating the cassava, wasn't that just a little too formal? *So old.*

"I do enjoy reading and writing," she offered. "I am in the language stream now—maybe I should do English literature. At Gadjah Mada University. If I'm lucky."

"I believe we do have a very good faculty of English literature." He smiled, the poor cassava growing soggy in his palm. "Let's hope I am still there when you get in."

That thought, the dreamy respectability of it, seemed to startle Amba's mother out of her rising fear over all this university talk. Imagine that, her daughter and her son-in-law, at the same university, two educated people married to each other, working together.

Meanwhile, Amba was thinking, *Why is he not asking me what books I enjoy? What sort of writing I do?*

She said, not entirely insincerely, "Then I shall feel very safe there."

The afternoon continued in the same manner. Empty pleasantries moved things along, as did stories of childhood that were so safe, so generic as to hint of the same values and expectations. And summoned the same old polite, meaningless laughter.

Later, once they knew each other better, Salwa told Amba he had never met someone who asked what his days at the university meant to him. "Your family knows the real value of education, what it does to our soul," he said. "It is the true mark of humility and sophistication."

Then he admitted that the trip he claimed he was making to Surabaya, the reason he gave for making the visit to Kadipura—well, he had lied. He wasn't going to any teacher training. He wasn't even going to Surabaya. He was, in fact, heading to a village in Blitar, in East Java, to meet a friend from his old village, also a teacher, a member of the left-leaning teachers' association with the crazy name, PGRI Non-Vaksentral.

His friend had just married. His wife, an active member of Gerwani, was pregnant, and he wanted to move her and his unborn child to Yogyakarta. The village where they lived had become unsafe.

Every day there was news of land conflicts between the Communist Party–affiliated Farmers' Front, known as BTI, and people from the Islamic boarding schools. Salwa added, "My friend told me that every party meeting is watched over by soldiers with mouths like crocodiles, leaning on their rifles. Soldiers hardly older than you, Amba." He went on to talk of a relative who had been beaten by the Nationalist youths as they marched him down the main street and later stabbed to death, his guts spilling out onto the cement.

He also told her: "There is something in you that makes me feel safe. It's not just because you seem a keeper of secrets, someone who is therefore loyal, because half of the time I don't even know what goes on in your busy little head; all those thoughts and musings eddying from your mouth. So, no. I don't know what you're like, really. One thing I know, though: there is something about you, a woman-child, with your incredible eyes and your temperamental mouth, the mouth that has said such reassuring things to me, that makes me feel safe. For here is the truth: until I met you and your family, my life had been about sending money home, for three years, with no word of thanks, to say nothing of the lack of gratitude from my father, and only the occasional acknowledgment from my mother. But as I am the eldest son it is my duty to bear these things quietly. They are not bad people; they are very good people, in fact, but their blighted souls have made them forget how to be good parents. You reminded me of values deeper than theirs, and your values are my values. From the first day we met, the moment you used the word *safe*, I knew that you would feel safe around me and that finally I would be of use to someone. This makes me very happy. This makes me feel safe with you."

⁂

Salwa. Salwani Munir. Every time she heard that name, or thought of it, Amba's brain seemed to blank out. If at the outset she had enjoyed the wicked will-the-myth-prevail-or-will-it-not guessing game, by the time it seemed settled that she and Salwa were going to be married when the time was right—perhaps at the start of Amba's second year of university if she made it that far—she began to feel the stirrings of panic. How could she get out of this or fashion for herself a middle position in this expectation? Neither a yes nor a no? *Not* choosing being also an option?

Meanwhile, just when she started to feel comfortable with Salwa and had said yes to his suggestion that they write to each other, she felt an increasingly urgent need to escape. It was true he was good-looking; there was something remarkable about that smooth, unlined forehead, as if he had crawled one night out of his crib and fallen into a giant cauldron of anti-aging potion. It was true she admired his facility with people, his precise responses to every situation. Most of all she liked watching his poise, how he seemed always to know what to say at the right time. Even how he almost convinced her that the mental mattered more than the physical.

"The mind tells the body what to think, dearest, not the other way around," he would say, adding mind-boggling examples like, "How do you think people can fast for more than twelve hours?" or "How do you think monks don't mind not having sex?"

So how to explain this little creature burrowed inside her ear. The one that kept whispering, *You can't be tied down. You can't be tied down.*

Yet girls, even strong and willful ones, will be girls. In time, Amba learned to look forward to Salwa's letters. She enjoyed his stories about life on campus, about the independence he'd gained so early through sheer will to convert every new dawn into his own currency. She enjoyed the patient and unselfish commitment he'd shown her, one that allowed her room to grow. "We shall wait, if that's what you wish.

We shall wait until you've finished your studies. It is not love that demands," he wrote to her when they had already known each other for six months, and she again expressed her discomfort with the idea of marrying too early. Most of all, she enjoyed the fact that he knew how to write.

Of course, she did not know any other love apart from what she had read in the old books. Salwa's seemed very noble. And very reassuring. The old books spoke of love that flared and burned and scorched, love that drew furrows in the earth and moved the heavens. They spoke of life being better than death, even if in life there was suffering, for in death there was no love. The old books never spoke of love that was patient or undemanding; they spoke of love fueled solely by bodily desires, of the need to be ravished now, now, now. But how could she know how it felt to be kissed on the mouth, let alone ravished now, now, now? How was she to know which was the better love? Perhaps the point of waiting was that once she and Salwa married, that was how it would be, that other love, now, now, now, every hour, every day, until they were eventually replete?

But why did he wait so completely? Why not at least let her have a taste of things to come? Isn't desire something that does not wait for consensus?

Yet they had not so much as pecked, reverently, on the cheek, like chaste hens, after a night at the cinema. When he spoke of love it was as though he'd transcended it, as though he'd arrived at a higher place.

Not that this desire she had been thinking about so much had caught up with her fully either. She still couldn't fathom this "fire in the loins" that books such as *The Book of Centhini* suggested could cause regular folks to leap like horses and make out with anything that moved. But this was okay. Something about not knowing also steadied and pleased her, for she couldn't imagine herself naked in front of Salwa.

❧

By the time another six months had passed the year was 1963, and Amba was nineteen and a student in the English Literature Department at Gadjah Mada University. She had won. Her twin sisters had decided they would both love her and hate her, and her parents added five minutes of extra prayers for her every night. They spoke at the dining table as though she was still there with them, occupying her chair facing the window.

For her own part Amba never felt more alive. She fell in love with Yogyakarta, campus life, and literature, as she knew she would. She fell in love with hermeneutics, ambiguity, and literary theories. She fell in love all over again with her family: with her father, who understood her; with her mother, who had relented at the last minute; even with her silly but sweet sisters, who, face it, would never know the world as she was experiencing it, but whose wide-eyed faith still humbled her.

❧

How is it that some people are happy and others are not? How can you make your life meaningful when you know you are unhappy? Or does meaning come with unhappiness? Is it unhappiness or is it just a feeling of emptiness? When does a feeling of emptiness become suffering? What does it mean to be able to create great works because you are suffering? Amba hoped her study of literature would produce answers to these questions.

But that implied a process, whereas life was, well, life was now. And it was not yet the powerful, plashing paradox she was waiting to thrive on.

The trouble was, she realized, she was not unhappy. Living with her elderly aunt and uncle, an idea that had scared Amba at first, turned out to be liberating. The house they lived in, on Menukan 28, was modest but spacious, in a surprisingly neat urban neighborhood called Brontosuman, not far from the main street. There were hardly any rules, other than she should not smoke and not come home too late. They hardly ever asked questions. Not about her studies, not about her comings and goings, not about her politics, not even about Salwa. Maybe it was because Salwa inspired such faith in older people.

So Amba and Salwa went out together every two weeks, mostly on a weekend. On Saturdays this usually involved a movie in Soboharsono followed by roadside noodles, their favorite *mie thok-thok*. Sometimes they would eat fried noodles and fish cakes at a restaurant owned by a Chinese lady called Mrs. Liem, near the Tugu station. They would sit at the table farthest away from the cashier and bask in the subversiveness of it all. On Sundays Salwa would take her to the Beringharjo market to eat blanched vegetables in peanut sauce and snack on traditional cakes.

Standard outings for standard couples, one might say.

Sometimes they would pay a visit to Toko Djoen, a bakery owned by an old Chinese couple, and buy bread and cookies for Amba's uncle and aunt. Nyah Djoen, the wife, loved talking to Salwa. Even though she looked almost a hundred years old, she opened up to him in the way Amba's mother did, with a flushed, late-blooming carnality that fascinated Amba, as it was a state still unknown to her. The old woman would share her list of aches and pains as though going over the bus timetable. When Salwa tried to suggest a remedy, she would shake her head furiously, and say, "Ah, what do you people, the young and beautiful, know of pain? I know what ails me. I know it's not curable. But do you see me stop working? Do you see me complaining?"

The same old woman told them that she came to the big city with her husband and two children in 1959. "We were victims of that stupid government decree. The one that forced the Chinese petty traders out of the rural areas. We liked the countryside much more than we like it here," she said, her quick old eyes darting briefly to the family photos on the wall. "People there also liked our cakes better than people here, where everyone is spoiled by all the choices. This is what ruins their palates, for God's sake. But my husband doesn't like me talking like this. He always tells me even with a crystal ball and a magic wand we still can't make the world bend to our will. These days only rifles and batons rule the world. Our fate could have been worse. We could have been forced onto trucks like cattle or shot like pigs, like our brothers and sisters in Cimahi."

So this was why Mr. Djoen and his wife became Communists, Amba thought. She knew the Communist Party had been famously opposed to the government's relocating of the Chinese into big cities, and she knew those drowning will grab at any lifeboat. She wanted to say something sympathetic, but Salwa was already leaving the subject.

She had noticed how often he was uneasy with conversation about politics. If he talked about it at all he saw it as some kind of a task, not a birthright. To Salwa politics was a system of information, like folklore, like botany, something he had to know a little bit about in order to get by. But he surprised her when he placed his hand on the old lady's arm as though by that single gesture he could take all her pain away. He surprised her again later that day when, while taking her home, he said, astoundingly, "So they're Chinese. But does it mean they're wrong?"

That night she found herself tossing and turning in her bed, unable to sleep. She realized it wasn't what Salwa said that had jarred her, or the fact that he had said it with a furrowed brow. Rather, it was his curious lack of anger.

Whereas with her, there was little else to do but press ahead with her life, and she did so precisely because of this odd bit of contentment within her, one that allowed her to still be surprised by joy. Joy in the smallest things. Things that included meeting Salwa every two weeks, sometimes more often, and witnessing the way he touched the hearts of strangers without even trying.

In matters of the heart, however, not a lot actually happened between him and her. Soon she even resigned herself to missing him, sometimes. Eventually she realized that she had gotten what she'd always wished for: that wicked paradox of wanting to see the beloved yet not minding if he wasn't there, of being irritated by his flaws yet trying at the same to justify them as some kind of underrated virtue.

She was, in short, living the lover's dilemmas.

In mid-1964, Salwa was made head of teacher training at Airlangga University in Surabaya. The contract was for a full year. "You're a natural leader, my friend," his colleague from Airlangga told him in a letter. "With everything being such a mess, we all need a rock these days."

"Define *rock*," Salwa wrote back.

"Someone who isn't an obnoxious jerk," his friend replied in his next letter. "Someone who isn't loud, who doesn't shout. Not even, well, 'Down with Malaysia.'"

With Salwa's appointment came the inevitable question: "Surely," he said with eyes downcast, so hopelessly shy was he, "we should think of getting married."

Amba held her breath and waited for the rest.

"It's not like I can come for regular visits," he continued, trying to sound manly and nonchalant. "It's just impossible to be going back and forth between Surabaya and Yogyakarta. There's no money, and the streets are not safe. You must have heard. The road linking Central Java and East Java is dotted with electricity poles wrapped in 'Land for Farmers' posters. And then there all those land flare-ups. Besides, you can't possibly visit me if we are not married. Not that I would allow you to travel by yourself."

Careful. It's not like this is rocket science. "I understand," Amba said, for it was always the safest thing to say. *I understand.* In fact, it is what you say when you don't understand, don't want to understand. "But clearly, you need one thing, and I need another. This is not the same as wanting. You need your stint in Surabaya to further your career. I need to finish my degree to justify the sacrifices my parents have made."

Salwa looked crushed. "I know you're not ready. But I don't want to lose you."

"Distance can be a savior," she said with quiet force.

There was a momentary pause.

"You are a funny little thing," he said, suddenly reaching to pinch her nose. "Just how do you *know* these things?"

She smiled, thinking, *How can I even begin to tell you, Salwa, that to you there is no difference between close proximity and long distance? Because I know now that you think with your brain, not with your body.*

But he looked so sad that even his breath seemed to emit a whiff of desolation as he sat slumped over a bowl of soup that was rapidly cooling. This was not good. So she steeled herself and reassured him that this was about timing, not about her feelings for him.

But he was still not appeased.

"Really," she said, "it's not bad if you think about it." And really, it wasn't. A year would go by quickly, and perhaps everything would change for the better. He would be done with his program in Surabaya, he would be that much more qualified to get on in this world, and she would benefit from it. It was called, she convinced herself, "being prepared," and marriage required preparedness of all kinds.

"Certainly it doesn't make sense, Salwa," she said, more insistent now, "to marry only to separate, and God knows for how long." Besides, she reminded him, who would want to get married now with all the ugliness in the world: Seven Village Devils graffiti bleeding on walls, nights filled with the eerie beating of wooden drums, nameless corpses popping up everywhere. *You said it yourself.*

Thankfully, Salwa was at heart a rational person. So he finally nodded and said, "Yes, I suppose you're right. It doesn't make sense."

Whereupon Amba immediately sent a letter home. Soon after, just as she had dreaded, a call came through from Kadipura. "Please come home," her father said. "Your mother has refused to eat for two days."

∾

"You can't go home alone," Salwa said, his voice uncharacteristically stern. "I heard on the news this morning that an incident just broke out in Prambanan."

Amba knew the village of Prambanan was where a famous ninth-century Hindu temple proudly stood; it was somewhere near the regency of Klaten, the nearest big city to Kadipura, where another spate of violence had recently erupted.

"But Prambanan is far away from Kadipura," she said.

"That may be, but we're not talking about twenty, thirty people injured. We're talking hundreds. Your parents will have me beheaded if I allow you to travel alone."

It was true that at first Amba had been reluctant to make the journey home. She had many assignments to complete, and she wanted to be near the campus. And if she did go home, she didn't want Salwa with her. His presence would only weaken her position. Her mother would melt at the very sight of him. Yet the way Salwa described the uprising in Prambanan gave Amba the chills. In the same way as wars often begin, the latest conflict in that village had started as a minor dispute over land occupation in a small village called Saren, and it ended up with who else but the BTI—the Farmers' Front—in alliance with Pemuda Rakyat, the hot-headed People's Youth arm of the Communist Party, pitting themselves against a group of stubborn tenant farmers. It was the usual case of each party thinking they were in the right. The farmers, having formally won rental rights when the land was auctioned off for the second time, thought they were entitled to work the land with government protection. The Farmers' Front and Pemuda Rakyat had said, "Not so. This land is not yours. Get out."

Another teacher friend of Salwa's, who had been sent to work in that province, wrote to describe what he had witnessed in Saren, and Salwa read parts of that letter to Amba: "The Farmers' Front leader is this dark-skinned guy, really frightening. When he shouted, his voice sliced the air like a jagged knife, and his gums and the inside of his lips were blood red against the devil's brew of his skin. In no time, the crowd thickened. The farmers demanding their rights were barricaded by the police, the village security guards, and the youth arm of the Nationalists. But they were outnumbered by the Communist Party henchmen. By the time the dispute was taken to the town hall in Saren the numbers had swelled to the hundreds. The farmers and the local village officials were hemmed in and fearing for their lives. Then someone went to a house with a telephone and secretly called for the help of the Brimob, the Police Car Brigade. But by the time the Brimob came all the way from Klaten, divine intervention had come in the guise of an official from the district office. His diplomatic skills blew everyone away. He managed to disperse the crowd before the Brimob even got there."

"Hmm," Amba said, "I don't even know if my town has become a Communist town."

"Kadipura isn't a Communist town. At least, not yet," Salwa said, again trying to sound manly and nonchalant. But ending up sounding weak and watery and so very the opposite of what he needed to be.

When they arrived at her old home in Kadipura, everything was just as Amba had imagined it. The first sight that greeted her was a lovely length of pale nectar brocade and slippers of a matching color, displayed grandly on the wide couch in the living room. Her mother must have exhausted her savings for this, the second-most important event of her life: her eldest daughter's wedding.

"Ibu ordered the brocade and the slippers from this woman in Solo, who sells only the most exquisite stuff," Ambika said, always eager to supply details. "She has been staring at them for weeks. I asked her why she hasn't made her kebaya yet. She will only do so when we have a firm wedding date, she told me."

"You know I'm not old-fashioned," Sudarminto said to the hapless couple, wasting neither time nor words, "and you know I know that the both of you have thought things through. But what's stopping you from getting married now, before Salwa goes to Surabaya? A small, simple ceremony will do. Besides, this is not the time for ostentation. Our town has become redder by the day."

"Salwa, my son. How can I put this delicately?" Nuniek's voice slid between them. Her eyes were glassy. "People are talking. Surely you know what that means for us, day by day. The questions I face from my neighbors, from the people in the market. What's the use of postponing unless there is a problem?"

There it was, the moment Amba had been bracing herself for. Just like that, her fiancé, his every limb normally strung so tight to his backbone, suddenly gave way, like a pine tree letting all its cones fall. Completely stripped down, nothing left of him. But then something else happened.

"Oh, Ibu. You do know, you *must* know, that since I left the home I grew up in I have had no family. Now you are my family. They say you don't choose your family. But you have chosen me, and I have chosen you. Far be it from me to do anything to displease, much less to hurt, you. You gave birth to the future mother of my future children. You are more of a mother to me than any mother can ever hope to be. How can I risk losing that? A problem, you say?

"Dearest lady. My problem is I'd not known happiness until I met you under that tree all those many months ago. And that happiness won't go away just because your daughter and I will be apart for a year. The day I marry your daughter will be the happiest day of my life. But for a marriage to be successful, as you must have experienced yourself, it requires two contented people. And I know that Amba will be happiest if she can complete her studies without being tied to anything else."

I've underestimated him, Amba thought, her mind in a spin. *He's making my case, not his own. I suppose I've always known this about him, his capacity to let the person he loves love other things. This is how he loves. He has taught me to love unselfishly, too, in my own way: to accept that I may be torn by desires that threaten my conscience, and by a conscience that threatens my desires.*

"This is her first year at university, Bu," Salwa continued, hurrying on, as if fearing he would lose momentum. "Surely you of all people don't have to be told how smart she is. Yes, she will do well, and continue to do well, and graduate with distinction. Of that I am sure. But the first year can be tricky. It can shake one's very foundations. It can be overwhelming and merciless. It doesn't spare you. There are new friends, new enemies, new ideas, new politics, new activities. Then there is the city itself, so colorful, so loud, so fast. Amba needs time to absorb all these things, the new boundaries to break, passions that need to be indulged. It's best to leave her to do what she must. Believe me, dearest lady, two years will go by so quickly."

Just as Nuniek seemed almost convinced, Salwa suddenly added, as though aware of what he had just started, "I know you're worried. But I just want you to know that for our part, well, we know our boundaries."

The dam finally burst inside Nuniek. Tearfully she said, "You silly boy. You think I don't know that? That's the problem with Amba. She thinks and talks too much. But deep down, she is as shy as a putri malu."

※

So that problem was solved, for the moment. They left Kadipura triumphant, Amba returning to Yogyakarta, Salwa going onward to Surabaya. Yet this time Amba was unnerved, despite their unexpected victory on the parental front. All this business about boundaries, the one Salwa had innocently created, had set it off, no doubt.

Shyness, unfortunately, was a messier plight altogether. Women appeared shy about sex because they were expected to, and anyway most had to wait for a man who was interested in them to come along. But for a man to show no interest in sex? Amba suspected that with Salwa it wasn't just a moral show. With him there seemed to be a fundamental lack of desire around the opposite sex. He seemed very much at ease with women. Sometimes he even appeared to prefer their company to men's, but not in a sexual way.

God, but it was so maddening. His constant, chaste planting of kisses on her forehead; these chummy pats on her arm; his gentle, almost maternal squeezing of her hand in public, mostly in public; the way he cooed to her, as if toward a cute, lovable pet. Why didn't he pick up on the signs she gave him? The friskiness that came with her swollen premenstrual breasts; the exaggerated sway of her hips; the extra lubrication in her voice. What was wrong with his ear that it did not understand what a woman might mean when she said *Maas* with a drawl, or when she added an ambiguous *A-aah* to each granting and refusal?

But Salwa had plenty of virility for planning and objectives, if there was indeed such a thing. His letters from Surabaya were full of it.

"Let us not fret," she read in one. "After a year's separation, our longing for each other will take ever deeper root, like the oldest tree, like a keeper of memories and hopes. It is from so solid and respectable a foundation we will marry, build our family, do all the customary things married people do. And from that foundation you will be able to say, with pride, 'I am the wife of Salwani Munir . . .'"

Such triumph! The sureness of every *will* in that letter. The implacable faith in the pride that must inevitably suffuse all her actions: *you will be able to say, with pride, "I am the wife of Salwani Munir . . ."*

Amba didn't know whether to laugh or cry. Her first impulse was to destroy the letter. How could this educated man support her wish to gain independence for herself, and yet in the same breath tell her how fortunate she would be to call herself his wife? Nonetheless, she put the letter in the box with all the others he had sent.

When she was alone again, in the tranquilizing light of her Spartan room in Yogyakarta, for the first time in many months she couldn't sleep. A part of her, she realized, was becoming soft, like a marital bed, too willing to settle. The night was no longer Tartarean. Love was unsexed. Blue was simply blue. Is this what is meant by growing up? Losing the fire? Becoming wise? Or is this what is simply called being a woman?

There was a simple enough reason, of course. She wasn't sufficiently roused to change things because she was not discontented. She didn't have what people called "problems." She didn't agonize about anything, not even how studying literature would be "of service." It was true that she was not unhappy. In fact she might be happy. She had everything she had wanted from life, except for Salwa to suddenly turn into the God of Sex. Her days on campus were a rich and heady mix of beauty and revelation, of the innocent and the not-so-innocent, of the fast and the faster, of clear-eyed idealism and easily inflamed feelings, of harmless flirting and unexpected friendships, of spontaneous poetry readings and invitations to go hiking in the mountains. She had no right to want more.

❦

Six months after Salwa left, he already seemed part of some distant past, like history, like a creature of night, like a face in an old photograph. His letters would arrive without fail, every first and third Monday or Tuesday of the month, always with the same measured tone and level of engagement: no longings, no missing, no urgency—only formal endearments. Amba's longing to find something in the details, in the possible hidden meanings in his choice of words, soon wore off. She had discovered a new love. It was another language—the English language.

❦

When Amba, opening up uncharacteristically in a letter, reported to Salwa that she was in awe of Tagore's poems, he wrote back, "You're too much of a romantic."

"I don't think so," she replied. "This is me returning to old loves."

Salwa's next communication came slowly, as if he had taken time to do a bit of research: "You must like that part about the children."

For a few days Amba refrained from replying. She liked the poem she thought he was referring to but was not about to be drawn into something *he'd* singled out, not knowing the first thing about literature. She realized she had become a bit of a snob.

"I like the thirty-fifth poem in *Gitanjali*," she wrote at long last. "The one on freedom. Freedom from fear and frozen habits."

Why make it harder than it already is, she thought, in a return to that annoying nonfeeling: the half self-defeat. *Not everybody understands poetry. Even* understand *is not the right term. Not everybody reads the same*

106

meaning into a poem. How can they if a poem often doesn't know its own meaning?

But no sooner had she thought this than she felt that horrible sinking feeling again. *What's the point in stressing this impossibility to my long-distance fiancé?* she thought. *What's the point in saying that's exactly the problem, that children are free because they are pure, because they are earnest, because they don't understand the first thing about guilt and deception? That they enjoy things not for their obvious reasons; they enjoy things just because they do. That in this they are like poetry. Like the poem that is hard to get. You might have been right about me liking that particular poem, but I like it precisely because I don't want to have children.*

It was 1965. Amba had kept up with politics enough to know that President Sukarno's affections for the Communist Party had become more blatant. Like a consummate adulterer getting too old for the game and deciding to go out-and-out public with his not-so-secret girlfriend. As a result, scholarship programs like the Ford Foundation were under threat. They were no longer able to send the best PhD students from universities like hers, Gadjah Mada, to study in the US. Sukarno's growing ambivalence toward the West was unmistakable. He was too in thrall to Maoist ideas and the fervor of his new ideological bedfellows to see that things were spiraling out of control.

Then it came, the foreign minister's announcement: "No Indonesian will go to America on our watch."

Things started happening, and happening fast. The US withdrawing its assistance from Indonesia. The Information Service libraries and the Peace Corps finding the raids and harassment so untenable that they packed up and left the country.

Yogyakarta had always seemed distant from Jakarta, but now there was a sense, even in the local newspapers, of a fundamental disconnect between decisions at the top and the needs on the ground. Politics revolved solely around the presidential palace, and every day there were more reports of raids, persecutions, diatribes, and alerts. All heavy on judgment but scant on facts.

Feigning ignorance was becoming impossible. History had knocked on the door. Soon it wasn't content being a guest in the living room; it also wanted to snuggle in bed with you. Even Amba felt its force. She began waking at odd hours, like a criminal held to her sins. Fear began to dog her, and even the words on the pages she studied, the calm and bounteous curves of the English texts, could not shut out the noises of the night. She started to dread nighttime, because nighttime meant sleep. The simple, earthly delights of poetry, the joy of morning birds, the first half minute of raindrops—everything that did not demand to be seen or admired, much less subscribed to—lost its power of simple earthliness. Even her stabs at writing her own poems, which had become more urgent to her in her solitude, ran out of gas.

Bear with me dear poem, / for I have nothing yet to say.

Then came the final straw. For several months Amba had willingly, almost slavishly, given her Tuesday and Thursday evenings to the wonderful English conversation classes that were held in one of the classrooms in her building. They were part of a comprehensive English language program funded by some foreign organization, the last of its kind to miraculously survive. Amba's favorite new friends came from this class. They were either English language majors, or studying for the English teaching certificate.

Despite her occasional dark moods, something about her fellow students touched her. They were happy, sunny, generous people. Their lack of irony was bracing. They were unafraid of making mistakes or appearing like fools. They shared their books cheerfully and listened to each other with genuine interest. They were fiendishly unaffected by the dark clouds of politics.

But one Thursday evening she found herself standing in that darkish corridor outside the room she had become accustomed to entering, only to find the door locked. The room usually alight with warmth, good humor, and the English language. The room in which she was hoping to catch Tara for ten minutes, before the flock descended, before the estrogen fest began, to go over some lines of poetry they had traded the week before. Instead, there was a sign on the door, which said that the conversation classes had been discontinued. Where had all her friends gone? She stood there, for a very long time, her head and chest heavy.

Tara was pure joy. She was their tutor, one of the last American teachers who had stayed on after everyone else had skipped town. She was the best reason for going to these classes. She was young, only in her twenties, and she had a bright, easy smile. When she laughed, hearts opened up around her. She had a different kind of sunniness from Amba's classmates. It was one fueled by hope, or faith, or something else.

Tara was also generous lending her books. "Here. Read them. They are Communist poets," she'd say as she handed Amba the poetry of Pablo Neruda and Paul Eluard. She also loaned Amba books of Federico Garcia Lorca's and Else Lasker-Schüler's poetry, which Amba immediately took to.

But most precious was her introduction to the selected works of Sylvia Plath, which Amba received in the form of a small notebook, in Tara's handwriting, copied out from her own books. No one ever had given Amba a more thoughtful gift. Most of the poems dated from the early '60s to the months just before Plath's suicide at the age of thirty, in

February 1963. There was something about the manic energy that drove the lines, the violent emotions and the brutal but searingly precise imagery, that shook Amba to her soul. Here was a poet who offered herself up to be flayed and sacrificed for being a woman, but in so doing, also sought to avenge womanhood.

In exchange, Amba introduced Tara to the work of her favorite Indonesian poets, including Chairil Anwar, Amir Hamzah, Asrul Sani, and others whose poems she translated as best she could. Tara was especially taken by Amba's work on a poem by Subagio Sastrowardojo, about the first man who was sent to outer space. The poem describes a man who is literally "hurled out of his home," and who demands, in protest, "a line of poetry / rather than promise-choked formulae / that got me thrown out so far / from the earth I happen to love."

"How noble and sad to be an individual," Tara had told her. "And America is at fault. We have abandoned poetry in favor of scientific progress. We think we can conquer the world with knowledge and machines."

"We Indonesians are no better," Amba offered. "We tend to think everything can be resolved with prayers and sorcery."

But on that dark evening when Amba had stood alone in that dark corridor, she knew Tara was gone. And her American friend had not even sought her out for the return of her books. When she finally ventured outside the building, she ran into another student from the class, sitting under a tree.

"Try not to be too sad" was the fellow student's attempt to comfort her. "Everybody has their limits, even if Tara's tolerance for things seemed more expansive than most. But these foreigners, they are funny. Sometimes their love for our country far exceeds their love for their own. I wouldn't be surprised if one day she came back."

Amba sensed there was something in Tara that was like her. Tara might be confident and knowledgeable but, like her, she wasn't yet speaking from a point of achievement that would mean something to her parents, to whom letting her go was a sacrifice.

For a few days Amba found herself inconsolable. The world hadn't ended, the sky was the same pasty gray-blue, and if anything the noise had become louder. Yet she felt the heft of her bereavement in every little thing. It was as if a great atrocity had been committed by unknown powers, yet she seemed the only one in the class to feel its devastating impact. She felt like that worst thing—a victim. Nothing around her seemed to be improving. The feeling of loss was everywhere, in the house, the dusty streets, and the clammy classrooms. Salwa's letters kept coming but she felt less and less inclined to write back. He was in Surabaya, she was in Yogyakarta. It was 1965, and it was everyone for him- or herself.

Sadness demanded a big heart. And hers wasn't that big.

So she returned to poetry. Soon she was finding it, too, everywhere—at the university library, in the flea market, at the homes of friends. Soon she was reading again with the fervor of a new convert, a monkish dedication, knowing she needed this unsullied time, even if only for a few hours every day.

Soon poetry's magic began to envelop her. She loved how the lines she recited wrapped themselves around her tongue. Often they shook her very core, moved her to tears, and in such moments grief and joy were one and the same. She began to translate, madly, furiously, with more focus—lines, poems, short stories—in a way that sometimes took her away from the rest of the world. She was also moved by the grace with which this internal life and her formal life coexisted, how they steered clear of each other without envy or judgment.

As with any worthy relationship, she struggled in this love affair. Increasingly she realized there is no such thing as word-for-word equivalents with another language. When she translated a line, never mind an entire work, she became aware that the original ceased to be, as she had led it to a place where it could not survive in its pure form.

A famous translator once said prosody embodies the vastness of the human voice. And so Amba found herself, bit by bit, opening up to fellow students and teachers, women and men. Often they were activists, most of them passionate, most of them human—hard for them not to overlap.

Soon, as with Kadipura, the memory of Tara and of those English conversation classes began to fade. Her room at her uncle's house developed a new history: a chest of drawers full of new objects, a desk brimming now with books, dog-eared to the hilt, a vase crammed with pens, pencils, spoons, straws, sticks of every kind. When her aunt brought her some flowers, she said, without so much as a pause, "These are hard times. Flowers are a bourgeois comfort. Or a poet's conceit."

The sounds in her room, too, grew more meaningful: the creaking of her desk, her own insomniac groans as words filled her head with other worlds. Her aunt reported other sounds, too, sounds she heard in the wee hours of the morning as she fetched herself a glass of water: "I swear, it sounds to me like you're dreaming in English." An allegation she took care not to refute.

And later, "Others pray before the dawn of a new day, yet you read poetry."

Reading poetry is a sort of prayer, Amba thought.

❧

Not only had she stopped answering Salwa's letters, she had almost forgotten what he looked like. When her friends asked her about her fiancé, she blushed no more. Before long, she stopped writing to her parents, too, for they reminded her of Salwa, and even if she knew that sin was one thing and guilt quite another, often she didn't feel guilty at all. If anything, she felt like something was soaring inside her, bearing her aloft, as though her life was about to change.

⁂

In retrospect, it was a perfectly ordinary day. The difference was that Amba went to campus uncommonly early that morning, to check some references in the library before handing in a major assignment.

Two unexpected things happened.

First, she saw a notice in the hallway: "Private Classes. Native Speaker of English. An FF Program Veteran." There was a classroom number and a time written at the bottom, in smaller print.

Amba stared at this notice for a long time. How exciting. Finally, another native English speaker. And how extraordinary. Because she hadn't seen a foreigner on campus since Tara left.

She resolved to register immediately for a private class with this unknown teacher, but that determination was eclipsed by the second unexpected occurrence: a newspaper ad she'd noticed in the university broadsheet, which had half piqued her interest; here it was again, tacked beside the other notice. Being together on the same corkboard made both seem somewhat consequential. It said: "Looking for an English translator for a small project in a local hospital. Must be willing to stay for at least two weeks. Fees, accommodation, and all expenses, including transportation, borne by employer. Please write to Dr. Suhadi Projo, Jalan Kemenyan 15, Kediri, East Java."

Kediri. An area where, according to the radio and the newspapers, violence was on the increase. Where not only the hospital was likely to be primitive, but where the roads were likely to be dangerous, and the youth militia from both sides of the ideological divide probably prowled like jungle cats in the night. *Kediri.* The very word seemed full of malignancy. Yet Amba registered the moment as having a certain rightness and largesse to it. A big, booming feeling filled her chest, like a portent. She would go. She would not be afraid. She could save people. This would be her ultimate test of courage and will.

By nightfall her sense of the day's glory had overtaken Amba wholly. It was time to move on with her life. Yogyakarta was too small for her. This was a chance to put her new translating skills to the test. Sending off her application for the East Java position made her feel modern and adult. And she somehow knew she would get the job.

Part of her determination came from knowing that her English language fluency would not mature without some kind of immersion. The other part came from knowing that taking such work, despite it being only short term, would help repay her parents, even if only in pride, for the generosity of all this separation, for the way she had shut down their world in order to open up hers.

The final element in her decision was Salwa. Amba did not want to be the one who waited.

6

Kediri

After I'm gone, come visit me every Thursday /
read me a letter into my dreams.

There were certain lines from *The Book of Centhini* that surfaced on
the horizon of her mind's eye, like stripes of light that glinted along
the ocean, and this often happened when she was trying to empty her
mind or remember other lines in a different language. Then she saw,
like a ghostly scrawl on the window of the train, more lines: *Should you
eat sambal today and get yourself bitten by a snake, just remember that
it's Thursday* . . . But why Thursday? How was it different from other
days? She rested her head on the window frame. The rest of the lines
flooded in: *On certain days you have to avoid heading east because it will
bring you ill fortune. You can still head east, but you might do so after going
westward first.*

She smiled. Nice piece of logic, as trains didn't exist in those days.
Then it hit her. Of course it had to be Thursday. Thursday was her
birthday.

It was late afternoon, and a good twenty minutes had passed since Amba left the railway station, walking under an asphalt sky. She found the hospital hidden behind a vast thicket of rubber trees. It was a long building with a shingle roof. A crowded open-air canteen took up most of its front yard. Walking past the curious eyes at the canteen she kept her gaze straight ahead. *Don't tempt fate.* She reached the lobby and was about to enter when she heard the roar of engines behind her. She turned to see three motorcycles slow to a halt in front of the building. The riders wore the green berets of the Indonesian Army. Her blood ran cold. The sight of soldiers never had scared her before, so why was she scared now? She hastened inside.

As instructed, Amba went on to register her name at the administration office. Before long, the young woman behind the desk showed her to the glass-cube room inside the office where she would spend the next fourteen days translating reams of medical documents for a doctor.

"A foreign doctor?" Amba asked, with a flicker of hope.

"No, Indonesian," the young woman replied. "But he has been seconded here by a foreign relief service because the previous doctor, an American, fled the country."

Amba nodded, knowing this scenario well.

"This new doctor," the young woman said with a sudden blush, "is a graduate from a German university. He is, how shall I say it, very un-Indonesian. His mannerisms, even his face, seem half European."

Before Amba could ask anything else, the young woman added with a whisper, "He's the kind who stays, if you know what I mean."

The kind who stays. Amba turned those words over in her mind as she deposited her bags in the corner of the room. *Am I,* she wondered, *the kind who stays? Have I not run away from everything that is constant in my life? My parents, my sisters, their worried letters, the emissaries they've sent—mostly the grown-up children of my parents' friends who happen to live in Yogyakarta, people I've never seen before who ask invasive questions about how I am, what I'm doing.*

And Salwa. Of course Salwa, so far away in Surabaya. The man she was meant to marry, the man Amba hadn't thought of for weeks. She tried not to think of the last letter she wrote him, about her decision to come to Kediri. "To be useful, however dangerous, however crazy," she'd written in explanation, asking him because of that, could he just try to understand and be supportive, and could he also not tell her parents? So now, here she was, in a place teeming with those ominous soldiers on their motorbikes, a place where everything seemed to be simmering. Was she willfully plunging into strife? Was she deliberately courting danger?

It stunned her, quietly, to feel this vital and unspooled, like a character out of a wayang story appearing on a blank screen, entering an epic poem whose story was not yet decided by the puppet master. Even her hair caught the electric moment. It blazed. She was ready for anything, whatever cards life dealt her. *She was ready for more.*

She would meet real flesh and blood. Her love would cover the sick and wounded like a silken sheet. She would offer herself to anyone who needed her help, especially the doctor, that man whose face and whose mannerisms were half European, who had given up that other world to be of service here. She would put aside her unplucked past to tend to others' blighted present. Even though she was here to be a translator, not a nurse, she would help tend to the needy. She would rub them with balm and flower essences. She would grow a garden in their souls.

❧

After pointing to a chair for Amba to sit on, the young woman left. Amba pulled her headscarf, something she did not always wear, closer around her face. An old man, perhaps a male nurse, entered the room. He seemed surprised to see anyone there.

He asked, "You're not from here?"

Amba shook her head. Why are people so nosy? "I'm waiting for Dr. Suhadi Projo," she said flatly. "He knows I'm here."

"Why have you come here?" the man said. "A young attractive woman like you, to this dangerous town?"

"Well," Amba said, trying to keep her composure. "I'm here now."

"You shouldn't be traveling alone," the man repeated. "You must understand how precious life is."

When the man left, Amba began to feel the pinch of impatience, pins and needles in her bottom, an ache in her foot she hadn't noticed before. Through the window she saw it was suddenly darker outside, as if a warrior had shot down the sun. *Is the head of this damn hospital never going to come?* She stared again at the peeling sign on the wooden door: "Sono Walujo Hospital."

Suddenly she was sick of all the warnings, the advice people gave when they wanted to keep order in their world. Her aunt and uncle had fallen for her lie as if they were children, but still it hadn't stopped their warnings: *Make sure you always travel in a group. Be sure to always say you are married.* It had never occurred to them that their niece could be doing something other than staying with friends in some accommodation in the city center, poring, as she'd told them, over some joint project, something bigger than herself, than all of them, something rare and brave and adult. All adults liked to warn you about life's dangers. They did so not because they knew about the world, but quite possibly because they were cowards.

Joy never lasted more than a few seconds. A few minutes if you were lucky. After that, time and space started to swell and shrivel. Amba couldn't see what time it was, where the hands on the clock were pointing. She couldn't make out the dark lettering on a corroded brass panel. Other objects fell into focus and disappeared. All that registered was this room, soaked in carbolic soap, where the weak electric light set sine waves dancing on the floor. Footsteps passed the office door, now vaporous, now heavy, now diminishing again.

The hospital was nothing like what she had imagined: it was small but not pinched for space, and while it looked frayed here and there it seemed surprisingly orderly. The head of the hospital, when he finally appeared—the man who'd advertised for a translator, then written back almost immediately to say Amba was hired—wasn't exactly as she had imagined him either. Dr. Suhadi was slightly stout, wore thick glasses, and had a nervous tic. When she got up to greet him, he said, "Oh no. No, please, don't get up." He did not look her in the eye.

At that very moment, a bunch of soldiers walked past the office, with their cold, hardened profiles and hair shaved close to the scalp. They turned their heads, looking her up and down, down and up, through the office window. She was almost grateful for the doctor's reticence.

"I am Amba," she said.

"Yes, yes, of course." But there was a faint dismay on his face.

"I am the translator."

"Your name—is it not something else?"

Oh, God, she thought with a jolt, *have I come to the wrong place?*

"No, my name is Amba. Amba Kinanti. My father—his name is Sudarminto."

"Sorry, my fault, then." But the panic—yes, it was a kind of panic—hadn't left his eyes. "When I was looking at your application, I only saw the name Kinanti. A name I've always liked. My wife, she is a Kinanti."

Before she had time to think about the doctor's strange reaction, he swiftly ushered her into his office, another door along from the glass cube. The room was all bare walls and uncluttered tables, unlike the offices she was used to, which generally seemed to house occupants who were bent on leaving no surface untouched. On the wall there was a framed photograph of President Sukarno, taken when he was still young and lean and impossibly handsome.

Dr. Suhadi pressed on with the details of Amba's job. She was to be at his office every day, promptly at seven in the morning to start the day's work. She would be translating English documents into Indonesian. With what? Why, with a typewriter, of course.

"So what exactly are these documents?" she asked.

"Mainly research papers from British medical journals. Tropical diseases, anesthesia—he's interested in those kinds of things. He's quite funny that way. He is himself a surgeon but he deliberately wants to keep updated on other aspects of medicine. I'm talking about the doctor you will be assisting. He believes his English is not up to scratch."

Amba heard the hesitation in Dr. Suhadi's voice.

"He says so, anyway," the doctor said. "I have no way of knowing. My own English is poor. Maybe he's a perfectionist. You know how these graduates from overseas universities can be, so exacting, so hard on themselves. Their second language may be nearly perfect, but they say it isn't good enough for scientific work."

"I heard he studied in the West, in Europe," Amba said. *But the doctor says he isn't able to read English well enough*, she thought, feeling both disdain and a surge of anxiety. *How is that even possible? Surely his English will be far better than mine?*

"That is true," the doctor said, meeting her eyes for the first time. "He studied in Germany. But, you see, not everything foreign is English."

Silence fell between them as Amba let those words sink in. *Now how stupid can I get,* she thought, watching her new employer fuss about his desk with studied concentration. For a while there was only the sound of paper rustling and toneless humming, like a pulse in doubt. She was used to this—a gesture often adopted when words fail. She looked up.

A cicada was trapped in the room. It bumped up against the ceiling, clawed onto the wall behind Dr. Suhadi's head, weightless.

After five minutes of shuffling, he looked up.

"Forgive me for asking this, Miss Amba. But you're not married, I take it."

Amba shook her head.

"You know it really isn't secure out here in this district," he said, apologetically. "I feel responsible, bringing you here. This hospital is pretty safe, but I can't guarantee anything, and you just never know in this, er, political climate. You must look after yourself. Don't wander around alone, for a start, especially at night. And lock your door at all times."

"Okay," she replied. *More of these endless warnings.*

"You seem very young."

"I'm not *that* young."

"Believe me, you *are* young."

"So why did you pick me? You must have seen my age on my application?"

"Yes, but I didn't realize . . ." The doctor trailed off, looking down. "Actually, you're the only person who replied to my ad. The only one brave enough to come to Kediri." Then, to save himself more embarrassment, he stood up, saying in a kinder voice, "Let me take you to your room. It's across the way, in a separate wing. It's a nice room."

He took Amba's bags for her in an almost fatherly gesture and she followed him wordlessly out of the office, through the corridor, and across the courtyard to another wing.

The room was small, the bed was small, but then *she* was small. She told herself quickly that everything was to her liking, no problem whatsoever, the bed, the tiny wardrobe with its lone hanger, the mirror with a sink below, the low table pressed to the far side of the bed, even the color of the wall, a rather indeterminate blue, a duck's-egg blue, a shade she hadn't expected despite having absolutely anticipated the leaks on the ceiling and the depressing 25-watt lighting.

She vaguely heard the doctor asking her whether she wanted to refresh. "The women's bathroom is at the end of the corridor. There are five or six showers there," he said. "There are always tea and snacks in the common room, starting at four o'clock. In fact you're just about right on time."

She nodded politely, though something about this remark, uttered in the manner of a gentle but authoritative uncle, reminded her of Salwa.

"You won't often find Dr. Rashad around this time, though. He usually takes his tea when the others have left."

Rashad. Not a Javanese then.

"We're glad you're here," the doctor said, not looking at her. "It's a good thing."

Before she could reply, he turned around and opened the door. "And please," he said, still not looking at her. "Please just lock your door."

After he left, the last thing Amba felt like doing was take a shower. But she could hear the trickling of water already. The sound of wet, anonymous bodies. Girls, giggling. Something about this brought her back to Kadipura, to the way she and her sisters were taught to respect clockwork, and to treat 4:00 p.m. like the cleansing hour.

It wasn't until the sunlight receded that she decided to leave the room. She looked herself over once in the mirror, ran the tap, and dabbed her face with water, once, twice, that should do it. She wondered once more about the doctor for whose benefit she was there. It shamed her to think of her earlier *faux pas*, when she mistakenly let slip the impression she thought all things foreign were inherently English based. How could she have allowed herself to sound so dumb? And how elegantly the head of the hospital got out of that conversation. It was an elegance that was as familiar to her as her mother tongue.

❧

The sound of crickets and frogs filled the air: it was time for evening prayers. The gray-blue sky looked cast in iron. As Amba walked along the corridor she thought of peering into the common room in case her doctor was there and she could introduce herself. But she decided against it and instead walked into one of the wards, and then the next, telling herself she must get a sense of the patients and their diseases.

Most of the wards were full. The patients seemed settled and resigned to their ailments. There were none of the horror scenes she expected. The nurses were not the middle-aged women wearing the white triangles on their heads she'd seen in comic books; instead, they were petite, upbeat, mostly young, working in groups, cackling, chuckling, their shoulders touching, like slow-moving vignettes of optimism and camaraderie.

When she nearly collided with a nurse as she entered one ward, Amba stopped, not knowing how to introduce herself. Fellow worker or short-term guest? Of course they must see her only as a stray, a face they'd never seen before.

"Don't go in there," the nurse said.

Amba noticed her sweet, friendly face, her scent of soap and afternoon tea.

"Oh," Amba said, dumbfounded. "Why not?" A response she immediately regretted for its stupidity.

"It's a special ward for patients with serious injuries," the nurse said with a smile, though it was clear she was insisting upon the necessary demarcation. "Haven't you heard? They've come from as far as Jombang. More land trouble there. So much blood and chaos."

Amba walked outside, into the dark and a light drizzle that steadied her. *Into the night I descended alight*—that was how she would later remember this moment. A rain so fine it was more like a gossamer veil. What cruel, sweet pain.

✹

From where she was standing, in the hospital's courtyard, the only objects she could make out were the things chosen by the dying light: idle horse carts, bamboo bushes deep in sleep, an abandoned pile of buckets. She walked on, into a garden that suddenly opened up to a wide space, ending in a tight barricade of trees. She heard the slapping of wings as birds tried to sneak into pockets of warmth amid the leaves. She could hear the gentle snap of twigs and their descent to the ground.

There was nobody around. Then she saw a flash of light, a strange sheen blooming from the thicket of trees. It refracted through the land-scape, infusing it with sadness. Strangely it was blue.

Later, Amba would learn that Bhisma had never taken colors for granted. He would ask her endlessly about how she perceived different hues, listening intently to her descriptions, whether a poetic burst about a sunset or a reflection on a fruit as banal as an eggplant. When she finally understood the reason for this it would be too late: he would be long gone.

For now, she walked toward that light.

✹

He appeared from nowhere, as they all must. Or, perhaps, he simply came from behind a tree.

He was unusually tall. Easily more than six feet, a height that seemed to cause him to stoop a little, understandable in this part of the world, and made Amba feel tiny. For a moment—it's love talking, after all—the air seemed to deplete at his appearance, rendering him a resplendent blue and everything around him barely perceptible.

She knew instantly who he was. Her doctor. She lost no time in deciding he was the most striking man she'd ever seen. The details of this first impression would come later: in their afternoon walks together, in the wee hours beyond work, leaning close under the half-light of the common room.

"Dr. Rashad?"

"Yes. Are you the translator? Miss Kinanti?" His voice, slightly lighter than baritone, sounded amused.

"Yes. Yes."

Dr. Suhadi must have told him that was her name. But what, pray, is in a name?

She said, "I start tomorrow." She could barely breathe.

The drizzle changed its mind and deepened. They found shelter under an enormous banyan tree. Sitting side by side on one of its snaking buttress roots they looked out at the rain, backlit by the hospital. Amba smelled the faint scent of leather, or was it wood, on him. The scent of paper, perhaps? Old books, fading letters? For a while they simply sat there, absorbing the night, the patter of the rain.

Finally he began to ask questions—the standard niceties of conversation like where she was from, what had made her leave, why she was prepared to come here in such dangerous times to stare at English medical manuscripts. She told him a little about her life in Yogyakarta and how she loved it. He didn't ask how old she was. He didn't ask, as she wished he would, if she had ever been kissed. Instead he told her in return that he'd spent long years in Europe and had just returned for a couple of months. He didn't tell her why he doubted his English, why he looked like a Eurasian prince.

She couldn't stop looking at him. It should have been quite dark here under the tree, with the rain beyond, yet she could clearly see the translucent green of his eyes, how the irises were flecked with gold. Perhaps it was the glow of lights from the hospital buildings, or perhaps he contained his own light—whatever the reason for the unearthly illu-mination, his eyes showed that he knew the world, had seen many things.

She also couldn't help but notice his perfectly-shaped ears, his long neck, his lips of shale, his wavy hair just the right amount of unruly. Then she realized that her own hair was down, and she knew for deco-rum she should put it up. But she was many miles away from her mother, and even though she could hear in the back of her mind a little voice saying surely there was a law somewhere against opening up like this crazy giddy flower, to a man you just met, she was also many miles away from her Qur'an mentor.

They must have talked for two hours. The sort of hours they say breeze through when it's the right kind of talk, the right kind of feeling.

"I didn't expect this, meeting someone like you here," he said.

Someone like her? She asked what he possibly meant by that.

He didn't answer. He simply gazed at her, and in that moment she realized something she and Salwa had never had, and never would have. In suspense, she waited for him to go on.

But he seemed to change his mind.

"It's late," he said. "I've forgotten the time, and look, the rain has stopped. I have my evening rounds. Yes, there is all this research I'm doing. But I'm still a doctor in this hospital."

It took Amba a moment to realize that he was leaving to attend to some burning need, a burning need that wasn't her. She knew that the light would follow him, and she would be in darkness once more. Fear caught her in the stomach. She got up just as he leaned to offer his hand, and she rose to his chest. The surprise of proximity sucked the air from her lungs.

Dr. Rashad strode back toward the hospital. Amba scurried to keep up, thinking how returning to this place together, this place of light and healing, suddenly felt like returning home. Then instantly, guiltily, she thought of Salwa. She couldn't see herself returning to any place with him in it.

As they drew closer to the hospital's glaring light she again stole glances at the man beside her, looking for flaws, for any sign of ugliness. But she found only heightened splendor. *Who is this man, this beautiful stranger? Does he have the sort of parents I have, does he have siblings as beautiful as he, do we have similar notions about family and duty?* Something he'd said earlier, beneath the banyan tree, resounded in her ear: *I know something about responsibility. Just don't ask me about politics.*

7

Precipice

It was nearly 7:00 p.m. when they reentered the hospital. They encountered no one Amba recognized, and she assumed the nurses had changed their shift. There were many people milling around, patients, patients' family members, nurses, hospital staff, men in uniform.

Dr. Rashad stood above them like a beacon, not just because of his height but also because there was an innate sense to the man that he was a doctor, a healer, someone with an important job to do. She fell a few steps behind, thinking, uncomfortably, that she was just a small-town girl, and she hadn't even started her job here yet. Vaguely she realized that in this place, this difference would always stand between them.

Feeling maudlin, she followed him all the way to the pharmacy. What now? There was nothing she could offer to help him with; her job description had been unambiguous from the get-go. She was employed to translate English language documents for a doctor who probably spoke English ten times better than she did, and that was all there was to it. Yet here she was, the hardheaded sister of Ambika and Ambalika, breaking free at last to live her own life. And here she was, already utterly undone.

The minute that thought hit her, Dr. Rashad turned, all purpose and barely-contained frustration. "Excuse me," he called out, "Can I have a nurse here? Where is the stethoscope? It's missing. Bring me one please, room 6, now." He swept past her as if she were a poster on the wall and disappeared.

She later learned the rooms where they each stayed were not far apart; only three others separated them. But during these first minutes that followed her loss of him she could think of nothing else but to duck for cover.

Once back in her room she was flooded with shame. The shame of being so blatant in her adoration; he must have seen it under the tree and felt repelled. That would explain his sudden decision to leave. Worse than that was the shame of feeling that he'd rather be elsewhere than with her.

The next morning, at dawn, she decided she would pull herself together and have her breakfast in the dining room ahead of everyone else.

It was 5:45 a.m. when she started to make her way along the corridors she had followed Dr. Rashad along the previous night. Listening to the echo of her own footsteps the shame hit her again. Of course she was ashamed of herself. What had she been thinking, to rush the most important meal of the day just so that she could avoid a man who was clearly out of her league? A man who knew she was out of his league and had sent her a clear sign that he was not interested?

And yet, where else could she go? It was not yet six, and her first day at work hadn't even started.

෨෨

Hospital: warehouse of the used and the superfluous, the half-here and the half-there.

Unconsciously, in some internal bid to think before deciding on a course of action, she wandered into the east wing, where the wards were replaced by other rooms, other closed doors. One door was labelled "Mortuary." She imagined fresh-swaddled corpses behind that door, lying on slabs, waiting for more soil to be dug outside. How would she get through this first day?

Ten minutes later she was sitting alone at one end of a large communal table in the dining room. Before her was a platter of pallid papayas and anemic bananas shaped into come-and-get-me petals. At least someone in the kitchen had a sense of humor, she thought.

The minutes that followed were nerve-racking. Each time she heard footsteps approaching, her chest clenched. She wanted to edge into the shadows so that he—if he came, if he ate breakfast at all, if he was a human and not a ghost—wouldn't see her the moment he entered the room. For he would enter the room, at some point, right? Or—and here Amba's heart gave a little jump—was it possible that he might spend his nights in another woman's room? One of the nurses perhaps?

She felt nauseous. She had to make an effort. She had to eat, for one thing, to not be nauseous. So she did, and tasted neither heat, nor cold, nor sweet, nor salt. She could have been swallowing air.

When a group of nurses arrived, fresh faced and carefree, for some reason they all chose to sit as far away from her as possible. She watched them, overhearing the way they joked about the trivial and the grave as though they were of the same importance: recipes, hairstyles, baby names, rape injuries, mothers who died of poisoning. She wanted to join them, but how could she leave her safe place? Who knew when that damn doctor might walk in?

She noticed one of the nurses, the one who had spoken to her earlier, was really quite pretty. She wondered if he had looked into that girl's eyes the way he'd looked into hers.

Finally she made herself sit up a little straighter, telling herself that fear was debasing, jealousy even worse. All her life she'd schooled herself not to be afraid of anything, and, like her father, her mother, and her grandmother, she believed that there was always enough space within in which to keep secrets. Secrets make you strong. They wrap you like the softest of fabrics, so sheer you could hardly see them, yet they cover you with their warmth. Holding on to a secret, she reminded herself, means you are not dependent on anyone; you do not fear so easily.

She picked herself up and walked to the door, not minding that the nurses didn't acknowledge her. If she exited with a thirst in her heart it was not because they hadn't spoken.

Dr. Suhadi told her he always arrived punctually at the office at 6:45. On her first morning at the hospital, Amba sat waiting for him on the bench outside the office. She had beaten him by a quarter of an hour, sitting there watching other morning people do their morning things.

When Dr. Suhadi arrived they nodded their polite good mornings, he unlocked the door, and then they went on avoiding looking at each other. A half hour later she was comfortably ensconced in her glass-cube room with her typewriter and was well into translating Dr. Rashad's documents, when Dr. Suhadi left the room, saying he must attend to his morning rounds.

As it turned out, the manuscripts gave Amba little joy; one, on tropical diseases, contained, on just a single page, thirteen words she didn't understand. Whatever had made Dr. Suhadi think he could entrust such an impossible task to a young hick, barely twenty years of age, with no work experience and no formal training in the English language? Surely she had made everything clear enough when she applied? Whatever made *her* think she was up for the job?

Through the room's small open window she could see the gray swath of sky. Soon a light drizzle dampened everything in the courtyard, filling the air with pollen. Amba felt her eyes begin to smart. Then they, too, broke out in their own drizzle.

Hours passed. Not only did she have to hold back her tears, she also had to constantly check the meaning of new words, as though collecting pebbles for a mosaic. But this was a world she could love, she decided, because it was, after all, the world of the doctor who had bewitched her. The doctor who now seemed to have fallen off the face of the earth.

❧

She lost track of time. Her narrowed vision shrunk each letter to an ever-more-foreign blur. She could no longer hear sounds; instead she felt them: The ceiling groaning with the weight of termites. The walls cracking and turning to rubble. The slow movement of a wheelchair in the corridor; the sound of a gurney passing, bearing, no doubt, another body shrouded in white cloth, soon to be memory's cloak.

Then, a sudden twist on the doorknob. The feeling of air and light being sucked out of the room.

Amba looked up with a frown, expecting an errant man, and saw instead a god.

❧

He just stood there at the door, a manifestation of absolute whiteness. Whiter even than the pages she was paid to soil with her inadequate English. Gleaming, in fact. If you looked at him closely, of course, he wasn't white at all; he wasn't even off-white. More like the translucent flesh of snake fruit. And she, what color was she? All she knew was that she was definitely not herself. In fact, if she was honest, in those few seconds she stared at the apparition the same way her sister Ambika responded to men. Or worse.

But unlike the men who looked at Ambika, the doctor she had been dreading and dreaming of seeing all day wasn't just not looking at her; he seemed determined to look the other way.

She tried desperately to understand this dark thread of sightlessness, the flash of fear in his eyes, but her thoughts couldn't go beyond the vision she saw the previous night, when he had emerged from the trees. He had seemed fine when they sat talking under the banyan tree. She hadn't mentioned her fiancé or talked about her sown but entirely unharvested life. So why was he acting like this now?

Assistance came unexpectedly with the return of Dr. Suhadi, who sailed into the room and took the matter out of their hands. Amba, nervously returning to her work, tried to steady her gaze on the word *herbaceous*, then a little farther along in the paragraph, the word *hollowed*, just before the blessedly straightforward *stomach*.

"Come, come, doctor, today's your lucky day," Dr. Suhadi said, ushering the hapless Dr. Rashad into the room. "This is Miss Kinanti. Pretty name, isn't it? I assume you haven't met. She's our translator. We hired her all the way from Yogyakarta."

Her sudden shyness was unbearable. She listened, her eyes downcast, as Dr. Suhadi prattled on about which documents he had already passed on to be translated, inquiring whether Dr. Rashad was happy with his choice. When Amba finally dared look up she saw something else happening. Dr. Rashad was finally, actually, looking at her.

"I'm sorry, but you said 'Kinanti' just now. Such a pretty name. Quite rare for a first name."

"My name?" she said. Hadn't she told him last night? But now she wasn't sure—she might not have told him her name. No, in fact she hadn't. Was he simply trying to hide the fact they had already met—as indeed, she was? Baffled, she didn't answer.

"Yes, but is Kinanti your first name?"

Dr. Suhadi tried to step in. Clearing his throat, he said uncertainly, "Oh, her first name?"

"Amba," she said. "It's Amba."

For a while no one spoke.

"That's not a name you often encounter," she heard the younger doctor say at long last. There was a faint trace of a forced smile, but she'd heard the way his tone changed. Was that a quiver in his voice?

Something caught in her throat. "Yes," she said. "No, I mean no, you're right. Not a very common name . . ."

Meanwhile, Dr. Suhadi was rattling off some of the names from *The Mahabharata* commonly found in Java: Krishna, Yudhistira, Abimanyu. "But yes, yes, Amba is certainly quite rare, for why would any parents name their children after . . . ?" Here he stopped to catch his breath. "After an avatar of the goddess Durga?"

Amba, about to say something in protest, saw the head of the hospital blushing deeply as he scurried to his desk and reached for a stack of paper, then looked up at Amba and the equally bewildered Dr. Rashad.

"By the way, about that toxicology report," he said to the young doctor, "now I'm pretty sure it isn't quite accurate." Clearly still unsettled, he muttered some standard information at Amba, by way of introducing the hospital's protocols—equipment she needed to keep away from, how to mitigate a power failure. Then, apologizing for having to rush off, he bolted.

In the silence that followed Dr. Suhadi's departure, Amba sensed a shift of ground. Dr. Rashad, who had been standing immobile near the door, unexpectedly walked toward her, all impressive height and gold-flecked eyes, and held out his hand. His grip was strong and clean and colorless.

He said, "When you hear what I'm about to tell you, Amba, I know what you will think." Again there was that waver in his voice as he spoke her name. "But let's try to live with this as sensibly as we can. I mean, it's just life, right?"

She held his hand, uncomprehending.

"My name is Bhisma. Bhisma Rashad."

And of course, he too, he of all people, tried that again, that same old tired trick he was clearly struggling with. Smile. Smile as much as you can. It's the only way forward. *Folks just can't get by without smiling in this country,* she thought inanely. Then, mumbling an excuse, she abruptly got up from her desk and left the room. Left the smiling Dr. Bhisma Rashad to drown in his own unsmiling bog.

She sat on the bench outside the office trying to catch her breath, to reassemble herself. She could hear the white noise in the near distance, but the corridor had strangely emptied of life. After a while the air resolved into normalcy again, and soon she noticed that the blurred beauties who were passing the office—the nurses—all slowed down, poking their heads in to ask Dr. Rashad—no, *Bhisma*—questions that sounded to her either trivial or plain silly. It was clear they all wanted a piece of him.

That's it, she thought, picking herself up, *pull yourself together.*

Amba returned, taller now, to her desk and her typewriter. She had not much choice, really. She had to either love him or kill him.

From the corner of her eye she saw him flipping through the pages of a document she'd completed. He mumbled at some of the more obscure words she had come up with, words like *withered* and *respiration,* and occasionally broke into a nervous laugh. An irritating nervous laugh.

When Bhisma finally left, she was almost relieved.

The sudden stillness was a welcome respite. Looking up at the clock, Amba was surprised that it was already midday. The last thing she felt like was lunch, and the prospect of sitting in the dining room over a plate of food she'd rather feed to the cat, with nurses who didn't want to talk to her, was not inviting. But her curiosity won out. She knew lunchtime could reveal what was obscured at the breakfast table. Someone—anyone—was bound to utter his name. But would she be able to prevent her blush?

Her mind returned to scenes from the night before: how she followed his slender form back to the hospital; how, as they came closer to that source of artificial light, she noticed things that had not been so apparent in the light he seemed to carry within himself; how he had worn a blue shirt, the tail end of it flapping against his taut rear; how he had looked back, to make sure she was keeping up.

No, she would skip lunch. He might be there, and if he was, how could she control herself? The quickening pulse? The sudden stuttering? Her heart hung open as though it had just been skinned halfway? And it wasn't just that. If the names *Amba* and *Bhisma* were uttered together, and entered public discourse, it would tempt fate. For, indeed, one could not die without the other.

Mercifully, she didn't even have to break for lunch to experience all that she dreaded.

A gaggle of nurses suddenly descended upon the room. Her head was spinning. The brain was not meant to register so many human types.

Nor voices.

"So handsome and aristocratic."

"It's weird that he should end up here."

"He's a German university graduate. He even looks German, so why did he agree to being sent to this hellhole? Shouldn't he be somewhere grander?"

"Have you noticed he disappears a lot? One or two days you don't see him, then suddenly he appears the next morning."

"Well, he brings in those new patients, from the violent clashes. He really cares. I've seen him attend to them."

"I heard he's red."

"He looks PNI."

"There's supposed to be a look for that?"

"I love his name. Rashad. So charismatic, so strong."

"What kind of name is that? Arabic? Malay? What?"

"He's so handsome."

"It still doesn't add up. The only reason he's in this horrible place is because he must care about politics. Otherwise, he would be in some major hospital in a big city."

I know something about responsibility. Just don't ask me about politics.

"Maybe he lied about graduating in Germany. Maybe he never even went there."

But she couldn't stand this.

"Sorry. Excuse me." Amba heard her own voice fill the room. She felt her cheeks reddening. "I don't think any of it was a lie. Well, for one, he calls himself Dr. Rashad, not Dr. Bhisma. In this I'm sure he's very European. From what he told me it isn't compulsory for an overseas graduate to end up in a bigger hospital. In fact, he said that the university he attended in East Germany, in a Communist city, encouraged its students to come to places like this. It fits with what is required of him here I guess, if it's true that he's a leftist. It's a form of *turba—turun ke bawah*—after all. Getting down to work. Perhaps for him, it's like doing social work."

One of the nurses seemed pleased with this sudden rush of insight. "Yes, yes, that's exactly what he told me, too," she said, chirpily.

Amba felt her heart snap in two. *So it's true. Men are all the same.*

"Are they interesting, the documents you translate for him?" the same nurse asked, oblivious to Amba's jealousy. Amba felt the collective narrowing in the other women's gazes.

"Oh yes. Some are about new revelations on tropical diseases, findings only published in British journals. And an awful lot on anesthesia. He's interested in those things. He thinks knowing about them makes him a better surgeon. Anyway, it is all mightily difficult, and my English is not quite up to par, but I think it's really lovely to find a doctor who"—Amba was about to say *cares* but decided not to—"takes time for such things. Especially," she added, before the skepticism around her turned into something more, "because many doctors in Indonesia couldn't care less about research. But we do live in hard times."

An instant—shorter than a blink.

"Oh, I think it's splendid," the friendly nurse said.

Amba didn't leave the office until 8:00 p.m. Whenever the young doctor came back to check on a report, or to talk to the head of the hospital, or perhaps to assuage his guilt by pretending to look in on her, she ignored him. It was possible that her strength made him slightly fearful of her.

The next morning Salwa's letter arrived. Why wasn't she surprised? In fact, although Amba had virtually stopped writing to Salwa, his letters kept on arriving. And this letter, even though she wished it were, was far from ineloquent. In fact, it was anything but.

Beloved Amba,

I don't quite know where to start: I have to admit it's not commonplace that a man knows his fiancée has gone into hiding and conspires to keep it a secret from her parents and friends. But love is trust so I try not to fret.

However, this deception doesn't mean I don't miss you. I miss you all the more because, after our long separation, I find it even harder to imagine you in your new environment. I trust your first few days at the hospital have proven beneficial, not just for the hospital but also for you. I must say I was a little surprised, and not entirely pleased, when you told me of your plans, and I worried about the pains you must take to travel that far, alone, in a crowded train, with your heavy bags, and under such dangerous circumstances. I've lost count of how many times I've wanted to leave work and join you. But I understand your need to be of service to others, and it makes me respect and love you more. I also understand your need to be independent. I did have a plan to leave here, to come to see you, but at the last minute I decided against it. I decided not to alarm you in any case. There would have been complications. I wouldn't have been able to stay the night at the hospital, and for you to ask to stay elsewhere would raise questions. Now if we were married . . . But again, I understand why we must wait. I just hope you're well. You must always tell me the truth about your well-being.

Woe is still the flavor of my days at Airlangga University. The teacher-training program that I run is not going well. Students don't come to classes, and

*sometimes we have no choice but to cancel if attendance
is too low. It's not that I didn't anticipate this happening
with the political situation being so volatile. The Faculty
of Education is cash strapped, and travel funds are the
first thing to go. Besides, the roads are not safe, and we
never can be sure when a friend may turn into an enemy.
There is no use, I find, in keeping a log on the people who
might harbor ill feelings toward us. Even our neighbors
can turn against us, or turn us in, whenever they feel it
is expedient.*

 *Last week I had the opportunity to leave Surabaya,
so I decided to stop by Kadipura for three hours. Meeting
your parents and your sisters would be a balm, I thought.
It was then that I realized that I love your family in a
strange way.*

 *Your mother seems most pleased with my homebound
ways and the fact that I always try to look her up whenever I can. She is so kind and attentive—and as beautiful as ever. She treats me even better than a son. By
that I mean there's none of the fussing and reminding,
no shared past to pluck anger from in times of strife. She
told me she understands there is something in me that's
like an ancient book that has long lain remaindered at
half price. Perhaps it's true I am a work picked up and
leafed through frequently but that nobody wants to own.*

 *Your father is different—no less loving but really just
different. I guess the right term is philosophical. He has
told me not to be afraid of anonymity. It's often easier, he
said, to accept someone without a family. Come to think
of it, he's right. He's an impressive person, your father,
although I find there is something in him I can't reach,
something that begs me to look the other way.*

As for the twins, their fame is such that most people see their beauty before they really look at them. I wonder how that is, living with such a cross. They, too, seem scared by the weight of their reputation and have learned to understand it by proxy. But one thing is sure: your family, soon to be mine, surely misses you. They cast almost no shadow in your absence.

You must tell me more about the hospital, about your work there. Tell me about the people you've met. The kind of dreams they have. The sort of freedom they envisage for themselves.

Talking of freedom, during my last visit to your home Ambika suddenly pulled me into a corner and told me she wanted to talk to me. She said it was proper because I was practically her brother. She assured me she had only the most boundless love for you, and that you always come third in her private prayers, after your deceased grandparents and your parents. She prays, above all, for your health and prosperity, and that the joy of marriage and childbearing are yours ahead of everybody else's. She told me that this means I am now in her prayers, too, for I am an integral part of your happiness. Then she whispered to me—and this was the main reason for her concern—that while she hoped for so much, there was something she was a little worried about.

After I managed to coax out of her the unrest she feels about a certain fire in you, she told me you have a feeling of imprisonment you can't control, and that everybody in the family knows about it but has resolved to live with it, hoping it will never break out in any way that might harm you.

Now of course we all know that it's a dangerous thing to feel imprisoned, because that implies you have a need to break free.

I do hope that when you are my wife you will have no cause to feel this way, much less the need to satisfy it. With God's blessing, you will be safe, safest in my hands.

I don't usually speak God's name, even though I was raised by a devout family. But it is to Him that I presently commit your care and protection; may you return home safe, and sound, and soon.

Ever your loving Salwa

Earlier that morning, before she saw the letter, Amba was at it again, at the far end of the same communal table, bent like an old woman over an empty table, craving something else, needing to leave. It was not yet dawn when she entered the dining room. She had to be done before the crowd descended, and of course she got what she deserved. There was no coffee, no one in the kitchen, no alarm ringing, no one being buzzed, no antiseptic smell, just the silence of the room and the dogs and cats looking at her for an explanation. When a kitchen hand finally came with coffee and a few slices of toast, she ate longingly, desperately, like a beggar.

She wondered if Bhisma had beaten her to breakfast. She thought of asking the kitchen hand, a pale, pock-marked girl of about fourteen, whether she'd seen him, whether he'd eaten his breakfast here, and if not, where he usually took it. Perhaps, like a dog with a bone, he'd saved his breakfast to be buried later, in a secret place? As if looking for reassurance that she wasn't slowly going mad, she almost called the girl and asked if, by any chance, she had found him simply glorious. A light went on in her head, and she stopped herself. What could possibly be sadder than this? How much lower could she go?

The face of her fiancé suddenly flashed in her mind, like a star, an instant of hope, as if offering a temporary absolution. Salwa, who had a prophet's face, the face of love unsullied by desire. But Amba had not thought of him for so long. Why should she start now? With nothing to sustain her but her pathetic thoughts, she left a shallow pool of black muck at the bottom of her coffee cup and walked, with heavy steps, in the direction of her room.

She paused as she passed what she knew to be Bhisma's room, but the world was so quiet, the water and the trees so still, and even the birds refused to signal to her what they knew. Reluctantly she went into her room and slumped on her bed, her back against the wall. There was still more than half an hour before she expected to start work. She had decided to make beating Dr. Suhadi to the office a temporary personal goal. At least she could give herself that.

Then it all came back as she drifted to sleep: the woody smell of him, that strange blue light, those eyes.

A little after 6:30 a.m., she woke with a startle, five minutes behind schedule. She quickly washed her face, grabbed her copy of *On the Eve* to hide away with during her lunch break, and ran to the office. This was not as she had planned, arriving out of breath.

When she got there, the door was unlocked: Dr. Suhadi had beaten her to it. Amba lost no time in starting the day's work, a few pages of a journal article. The first lines stared at her mockingly: *In China, the prolonged and targeted use of salt containing diethylcarbamazine resulted in the elimination of lymphatic filariasis as a public health problem.*

Just as she had pulled herself together, there was a sudden rush of activity outside in the corridor. She heard gathering footsteps, voices upon voices, the screech of wheels scraping the floor. The air shuddered. She stood up, wanting to see what the fuss was about. Wanting to see if Bhisma would tend to the commotion.

She stepped out of the office to see a mad whirl of people and gurneys racing past, ribbons of blood trailing. She had never seen so much red, this otherworldly red that was neither candy nor paint, but life leaking away. There was debris everywhere: gauze, plastic bits, masks, empty bottles of disinfectants. She felt a surge of adrenaline. Keeping her body flattened to the wall, she sidled along the corridor, looking for Bhisma, hoping to see his height hovering above the chaos. But there was no sign of him, and she dared not bring herself into any of the wards, or the operating rooms, where she knew the real work was done. Eventually her sense of self-preservation asserted itself. She went back to the office, feeling useless. She thought of Bhisma saving lives and almost wept for the sick, furious love she felt flaming inside her.

It was then that the letter from Salwa was delivered to her desk.

At 12:45, after the longest six hours of her life, Amba heard bottoms thumping down on the bench outside the office window. The nurses and administrative staff were on their postlunch break. A cloud of cigarette smoke added to the aroma of black mud. The door from the corridor opened. She looked up to see Bhisma's face. Lovely and lethal. A wounded animal.

The next few minutes were a blur. Amba got up, and, as if trying to escape fate, she scurried past him, out of the office, down the corridor, and into open air and the safe unknown. It wasn't until she reached a bench in the courtyard that she realized he had followed her and sat himself next to her.

Her heart was racing. She couldn't lift her eyes. She saw his clean, pink nails, bitten to the quick, the specks of blood on his white jacket. Inglorious details that made him even more glorious in her eyes.

Finally her breathing steadied. She asked, "What happened?"

"Another clash between the youth militia groups," Bhisma said, heaving a sigh. "It's the usual suspects around here—the People's Youth, supporting the Communists, and those Banser guys, representing NU. Twelve were wounded, seven and five respectively. Two are dead."

Bhisma's voice was low, heavy. He went on, as if it might help lift his mood if he talked. "Of course, I knew when I came here this place was a furnace waiting to explode. I just didn't expect it to be this bad."

He paused.

"I knew because my friend from the local branch of LEKRA had warned me, when he asked if I could help out at the Union of Sugar Workers."

"Oh. Is that where you go, why you often disappear?"

He looked at her strangely, as if unsure of what her question meant.

"Perhaps you did not hear that several weeks ago the village head of Garum, only around five miles away from here, was hacked to death?" He was suddenly at it again, in part, perhaps, to deflect her question. "He was PNI. So then all the other Nationalist supporters, those from NU, too, rose in fury against 'those Commie bastards.' You should have heard them. The things they shouted. 'We'll hack you to pieces, shove your innards down the throats of your bitch mothers.' Those kinds of things. And so there they were, hunting anyone they thought was a Communist, or a sympathizer. They threw stones through the windows of houses and set them on fire, they dragged the people out and beat them to a pulp."

Bhisma paused and then said, "You know, Amba, I thought the worst of it had passed. But who was I kidding?"

She felt her pulse quicken. He said her name! He said it without wariness, without hesitation, as though he had accepted it. The sick humor of their situation.

But he was still absorbed in what was happening outside their world.

"I should have known," Bhisma continued, "with violence and intolerance on this scale, nothing is ever laid to rest. This morning, for instance, I found that two of the patients on my operating table were boys from Garum, both barely out of their teens and not even Communists. Later, when there was more time, I got one of them to talk. It might be possible that they were targeted because of what happened in Kanigoro several months ago."

Is he always this intense? she wondered, still not trusting herself to speak.

"Mind you, this is just my theory," he said. "But this morning's clash might have been partly ignited by NU people and their Banser allies. I suspect they wanted vengeance for what happened in Kanigoro last January. It was payback time."

How hard it was to talk about people's brutality and how easily violence began. Even if a violent act was committed under the guise of changing things for the better, once begun, people often didn't know how to stop it. It went on and on and on until no one could even remember the first wrong that needed to be righted. She wanted to say something about this, but he had spoken again.

"You're right, I do disappear." A hint of a smile. "Sometimes. And when I return I bring new patients from the union."

Just as well he clarified this, because she was not good with platitudes, or, worse, with filling an uneasy silence. Slowly she forced herself to speak. "You said you thought this morning's violence was partly ignited by NU. Did something else happen?"

"Yes, now there is a new source of violence. At least that's what the guys in the emergency ward told me."

They both rose from the bench with a sense of urgency, as if sharing the same thought: *perhaps we would learn something useful back in the office now.* But there was a new *we* in the air, and that alone was something.

❧

Sure enough, Dr. Suhadi had returned, all doom and gloom. With news to make their hair bristle.

"Apparently something big happened in Jakarta this morning," he said. "The 7:00 a.m. news. Did you hear it? There was this army guy, a lieutenant colonel—I think Untung was his name—who went on the radio. He said a group calling itself the September 30th Movement had kidnapped and killed six Indonesian Army generals. Apparently this included its highest commander—Yani? Nasution? Anyway. The group claimed that it was preempting a coup, and it looks like they've taken over all media and communication outlets. Whatever that means. The same group has also whisked President Sukarno to safety, or so they said."

The air in the office seemed sapped of vital substance. Outside, people were milling around. No one seemed to know how to react, or what to expect. The sense of tension was physical, the feeling that something momentous had taken place, something uncontrollable, with the power to determine who would live and who would die like a dog in some ditch.

Suddenly there was this terminology, too, names she didn't understand—*General Council, Revolutionary Council*—which nobody had ever heard until they were spoken on the radio. She didn't know what they meant, what they replaced. *Why do we need even more words,* she wondered, looking around at the anxious faces of the nurses, the medics, the janitors, the kitchen staff who had gathered at the office, recognizing the significance of the hour, but hadn't the foggiest what was going on.

When Bhisma bent down and whispered, "Would you like to go back outside? Get some fresh air?" she offered no resistance.

She followed him wordlessly, not really noticing which way they were going until she saw the banyan tree they had sheltered under only the night before last. They ducked under the curtains of aerial roots and entered dense shade. They found the buttress root in no time, the one they'd perched themselves on previously. They sat and stretched their legs, breathing, grabbing for something solid to hold on to.

A mild wind rustled. Bhisma found his voice again, but this time it was not as sturdy as before. He said something about how hard it was to know if the situation called for sadness or for fear. Or what was meant by a revolutionary situation. He looked at her, stripping her with those eyes. "Don't you think," he said unsteadily, "that the world is on the brink of change?"

"The brink of change?" she repeated, her head reeling.

A rush of silken air, like the scent after a downpour. Bhisma gently took her hand, cupping it palm up before bringing it softly to his lips. A whiff of musk, some kind of flower, iron. *I'm not dreaming,* she told herself. *I'm not . . .*

Then there was warmth on her lips, a sweet wetness—so sad, so long, so blue, and into her mind swam the words of Turgenev's Elena, before she vanished into the ether, something about being brought to the edge of the precipice and falling over.

Only an old black dog that had followed Amba and Bhisma to their refuge under the banyan tree knew where the couple had been. He saw everything, and later he carried his knowledge calmly back to the hospital, where the nurses and doctors in the common room attacked the snacks heaped on plates while avoiding every mention of politics, and the cooks and cleaners itched to be released early from duty because the streets weren't safe and they hadn't received their paychecks in two months. The old dog settled, dozing behind a door, his nose pressed to where years of footsteps had grazed the floor.

They had said good-bye guiltily, walking separately back to the hospital. When Amba saw Bhisma an hour later she greeted him calmly, her face a well-behaved mask.

But once back in the office, all she could think of was that kiss. Her *first* kiss! So long and yet so brief. Why did he have to stop? Why not kiss her forever?

At around 4:00 p.m. the friendly nurse, the one she liked—the one she was jealous of—unexpectedly brought Amba a tray of food. Steamed rice, sautéed long beans, and deep-fried tempeh, with sambal on the side.

"I didn't see you in the lunchroom today," the nurse said. "You know, it's not good to skip lunch."

Amba knew food didn't last long in that place, and it was not as if she had earned this royal treatment, not having tried with the nurses and the hospital staff, not having been more open to scrutiny as all newcomers were expected to be.

To make amends for her earlier sin of childishness, she made a big production of eating. It was the only way a stranger's kindness could be acknowledged and a beloved one's absence endured.

Time dragged. It was a quarter to nine in the evening, late by any standard. Dr. Suhadi was still in his office. There had been no talk of overtime, but today had been no normal day. When Bhisma finally walked in he announced that he'd sutured some fifteen wounds inflicted by jagged knives and machetes: ugly, unspeakable things.

Unexpectedly, he went over to Amba's desk. He stooped over it, picked up some of her translations, leafed through them. Occasionally he read them aloud in a chirpy, put-on tone. Amba knew he was trying to act casual. Feign familiarity. And wondered if he was aware that her hands trembled like his own.

Dr. Suhadi finally threw down his pen and said wearily, "Look at all this useless paper on my desk. How can I deal with it? There are so many more important things to worry about. Twenty-six more patients in this hospital today, more than half of them in critical condition. We're short of almost everything we need—sterile gauze pads, bandages, irrigation syringes, not to mention basics like cleaning equipment. We're even running out of food! Another week and there will be no more painkillers, no more antiseptics."

He'd said too much. His voice caught in his throat and he began to cough as if his own lungs were about to give out.

The rest, silence. At 9:00 p.m., the recorded voice of a two-star general by the name of Suharto boomed from the radio. He said something to the effect of having taken charge of the Army, that he would crush the "counterrevolutionary" forces of the September 30th Movement, whatever that meant. His voice was calm, authoritative, with only a slight quiver hinting at suppressed anger. The broadcast was swiftly followed by news of the kidnapping and murder of the generals, an official statement from the armed forces denouncing the coup, and a standard assurance that everything would be done to "restore peace and order and safeguard the president."

For a few minutes Amba, Bhisma, and Dr. Suhadi just stood there, mute. Quite a motley crew—what were the odds.

In Jakarta many things could change in less than twenty-four hours, so Amba was told, but here it was as if some ghostly wind had rushed in and just as quickly rushed out again, leaving things seemingly as they were. Dr. Suhadi said how strange it was that General Nasution, apparently the assassins' main target and their only escapee, had joined Suharto in the studio yet had neither spoken nor assumed control of the Army himself. "Nasution is way more senior than Suharto," Dr. Suhadi said. "He holds the highest military rank in the country. So why not seize control himself? Why stoop to this unknown?"

Dr. Suhadi seemed to want to stay with the subject and talk some more. Amba had not intuited this aspect of his. But it was late and not the most eloquent of hours. Her mind was a jumble of emotions. She shot a pleading gaze at Bhisma: *Please don't start talking—get me out of here. Look at me, look at what you've done to me. You kissed me this afternoon, you kissed me long and hard and deep.*

As they walked the empty corridor Bhisma stroked her arm softly. "Sorry. Sorry for being such a pain."

She didn't react.

"Please," he said again. "Don't be afraid of me."

He ran his fingers along the small of her back and told her it was absurd, of course it was absurd, but he felt as if all that fate bullshit might actually explain this absurd feeling.

"What feeling?" she asked.

"The feeling of you having risen from the deepest part of me. You have to believe me," he pleaded. "I can't explain this, but that is truly how I feel."

That night, Amba allowed Bhisma to enter her room. He gathered her in his arms like something delicate and precious, laid her down on her bed, covered her with kisses. Then he looked at her. He looked at her hard and tenderly. The pear of her, the soft and yielding mounds, the tuft of hair down below. He took his time. He took his time with his hands and his mouth and this hard, dripping, pulsating alien organ—the one she'd heard so much of but hadn't seen before then.

They stayed there, on her bed, until an hour before dawn.

Obviously there were questions. Too many questions.

"Don't think," he said. "Just close your eyes."

But when the deed was done, and she was no longer the Amba she knew, she thought of babies, of children running on sand, of a gentle and kind sun bearing down on them.

Later, Bhisma told her all he had ever wanted was to be an anesthesiologist. It was his mother who insisted he become a surgeon, saying it was the most noble of all the specialties.

"I have never been one for money and fame," he said as he ran his fingers through her long, thick hair. "Being a heart surgeon, or an internist with a private practice and a big house, the fancy car, the beautiful wife from a respectable family, your children enrolled in the best of schools, invited to all the genteel parties—that's not how I pictured my life. That isn't the way to live. Besides, with all those money worries you're likely to die of a heart attack before you reach fifty.

"An anesthesiologist is different. An anesthesiologist is an island, a republic. He is slave to no hospital, to no system. He has the simple yet very important responsibility of putting his patients to sleep so they can be operated on safely, painlessly, and come out of it alive. But somebody needs to stitch up the wounds, and now that is what I do."

He must have sensed the awe in her silence, because he immediately became self-conscious and said, "Not that it is something to boast of." He chuckled. "In stitching, it's true, I create lines to hold together lives. That takes some skill. But it's not like I'm an artist. It's not like I can draw the lines of a landscape."

A considered pause, and then: "It's not like I can draw your face on my skin, which I really wish I could do right now."

"How odd you are," Amba said. "You speak as though you're a poet."

"Funny you should say that," he said, looking at her tenderly. "I'm no poet. But I love poetry."

He told Amba he was a boy from Menteng, the privileged heart of elite Jakarta, and it had been two years since he, aged thirty-one, had returned to Indonesia from Leipzig. Still unattached, he was a definite catch. After months of renting a small pavilion in Pasar Minggu, South Jakarta, his parents, who lived in the big house that had been bequeathed to Bhisma by a dead aunt, decided it should be turned over to him at last. To be precise, it was his mother, Miriam Rashad, who made this decision.

Miriam had a way about her. Bhisma described how his mother, all salt-and-pepper hair and high cheekbones, had walked out of the notary's office saying triumphantly, "Son, now you own the place. Your first house. Now you will look bona fide. You have something to show for all those years away slaving for an education. Because it won't do for a man of your age and professional standing to be seen not to own anything."

Miriam had produced four children but only one son. As a woman with only sisters she often told her siblings it was this boy, who took more than thirty hours of contractions to bring into the world, this sweet-faced boy who opened her up and made her a woman. It was her son who taught her about motherly love, even if he'd disappeared to Europe for years, only to return with funny ideas about property, parliamentary democracy, and patriotism.

He was unused to Indonesian bureaucracy. Family matters, too, unsettled him, and socially his body language betrayed him for what he had become, not only the person who had just returned from Europe with a German turn of mind, a first-class degree, and a rare set of skills, but an idealist, the man who would single-handedly change the world.

His father's people were from Bukittinggi, a city on the west coast of Sumatra. He came from a line of Minangkabau, a people used to honing their expectations against the peaks of volcanoes and mountains and the high roofs of their houses. Bhisma's mother, Miriam, meanwhile, came from Central Java. She was a noblewoman by blood rather than a member of the Dutch-era priyayi bureaucratic elite, so Bhisma's lineage was all about pedigree. But contrary to the doctrine of docile Javanese femininity, Miriam took on the matrilineal tradition of the Minangs with fervor, becoming the undisputed ruler of the family. His father might have given Bhisma his surname, but it was his mother, a Javanese behaving like a Minang woman, who decided the important things in his life. Bhisma admitted he liked to think that he had successfully manipulated traits from both families in his tendency to go for strong women, who would help him make important decisions in life, while still being himself: self-sufficient, self-contained, self-aware.

When he was growing up he was often ashamed because he had such a formidable and domineering mother. While he adored her he also recognized how her resourcefulness and competence often had a way of disabling him. This feeling followed him to his first year in Holland, when he was sent, at seventeen, to Leiden to finish his secondary schooling. To compensate for the burden of his parents' relative wealth, he had often lied to his peers.

Later, at university, his favorite stories, the ones he told his Indonesian as well as his Dutch friends over and over again, were about not having any money for almost half of his first year of studies in Holland, about having to eat horse meat for days on end, and about being thrown out of a French truck, in the days of the Indochina War, because the driver mistook him for a Vietnamese.

Money transfer was indeed slow in those days, and he did have to go through the occasional days of scrimping whenever his allowance came late. Yet he knew he was secure, because one of his sisters had told him that his education was funded entirely by money held in a trust his father had set up sometime in the early '30s and that sum had been thrust into his guardian's hands for safekeeping, to be doled out every month with Swiss-clock precision. Sometimes he'd wondered if the delays were his parents' bourgeois method of teaching him the hard way.

He admitted he had also exaggerated the story about grinding through extra lessons, slaving to catch up with his Dutch, German, French, and English and European history and geography, which he knew little about. Despite private tutorials eating up his free time, in truth he actually received dispensation from numerous exams, including Dutch, which he'd learned as a child.

There was an odd look of pride when he said this, how he had told tall tales. As if he needed to furnish himself with proof of the delinquent in him, a bad-boy streak. Part of it a rich boy's entitlement, of course, to being cut some kind of slack, to a certain impunity.

She wouldn't say it, of course.

"But I had to believe that I was suffering. You know how that was?"

Do I know how that was? "Well," Amba said, nuzzling against him despite his strange, slightly off-putting speech. "My life has been so much simpler. So no, I don't understand your rich-kid-with-a-conscience dilemma. But I understand how some people can be lucky. I sense I am among the lucky ones, for regardless of any real effort on my part I ended up mostly where I wanted to be—in college, in Yogyakarta, and now here, with you."

Something tugged at her after she said that last bit. Still, she couldn't believe that here in this hospital, in this very room, the warrior Bhisma came to life from ancient stories, breathing the very same air. Was she dreaming this? Did the gods send him here to test her? Was he having her on? *Come on. Show something of what you have learned, your own wisdom.*

"But as for you, you're not merely lucky, you're blessed," she heard herself say. "And your biggest blessing is that you have found a purpose in life. You are like Turgenev's Insarov, who so enthralled Elena: you have chosen your path, your aim."

It sounded hollow even to her ears. She wasn't sure that was what she wanted to convey, but it just went on and on, the story of their contrast: Bhisma had indeed lived the life of someone she never dreamed of meeting.

As a member of the Indonesian elite, Bhisma was able to study at a Dutch university. That wasn't even an anomaly, it was a given.

When his parents waved good-bye as his ship left the port, their tears were more of pride and self-justification than loss. They had paved the way for him to return and make himself useful to his native land. So he internalized those platitudes forged by the conceit of noblesse oblige: *I shall return to help prevent diseases, preserve health, and cure the ill. I shall dedicate my life to service to my country.* Yet all along he felt there was something in his motivation that was banal and bogus.

He knew he had acquired the looks and mannerisms appropriate to his endeavor, but he wasn't sure he wanted to return to his home as the finished sculpture people had already perceived before he left. Europe would play a part in molding him, but not the Europe of his parents' desire.

Yet it was always clear to him that he had to go back to Indonesia. He was his mother's life. Her death would have been on his head had he not returned. He knew that as the only son his specialness infused each sin he committed and each good deed he performed.

So he came home ashamed. He knew his blessings—education, opportunity, knowledge of the world—were not shared by many of his friends, or by most people in his country. This shame was what Europe had also given him—the shame of being a privileged man as he walked the sodden streets of Leipzig and Berlin. On those streets he often longed for "*Wolken und Vögel und Menschentränen,*" the "clouds, birds, and human tears" that he felt would provide a home for his heart.

"To me they were like words of prayer," he continued. "Especially whenever I threw flowers into the Landwehr Canal, where Rosa Luxemburg's body was tossed in 1919, after she was shot by the right-wing militia. Those were her words, and they were the words that kept me going as I steeled myself to go back home."

Then, just like that, an aside: "Brecht—do you know him? Well, he had a similar effect on me: he had this innate sense that joy and goodness are what human beings are made for and deserve. But he was a womanizer to boot, and he made many enemies because of the way he treated his women. For all his progressive ideas he did once say that relations between the genders was a contract, one in which the men could demand a tremendous amount, while women had to give a tremendous amount."

"I would have hated him," Amba said. And meant it. Remembered the loyal men in her life. Her own father. Salwa.

"I knew you would." Bhisma laughed. The worldly man, blasé, perceptive, thinking nothing of it. "Yes, he was something else all right. Not the nicest guy by any stretch. But I love most of his work. Maybe something about my admiration is biased, too. Maybe it has something to do with the harsh way the Left often treated him, a harshness I suspect was class-based and which I can relate to. Like mine, Brecht's family belonged to the bourgeoisie. But even if, in many people's minds, his understanding of Marxism and his critique of capitalism, indeed the entire moral force that drove his art, could only be superficial I didn't care. He and Rosa. My God."

∞

When he had left for Europe a decade before, he, too, had been enthralled by Sukarno's charisma. He was not exempt. And he still maintained that admiration to this day, even if he was dismayed at how dependent the Indonesians had become on their leader.

Bhisma's hero worship had begun to dim in 1957, after Sukarno proclaimed the concept of Guided Democracy. Among some of its disturbing results was the president's increasingly hostile stance toward the West. How different was Sukarno's rhetoric from the social patriotism that washed over Germany on the eve of the First World War? Where true Socialists had made few—or no—gains, there was no ground for patriotism. He had believed that fervently.

He also found Sukarno's growing cult of self-love more than a little disgusting: "the Great Leader of the Revolution," "President for Life," countless titles with the word "Noble." He decided to ask a friend what would happen if Sukarno were suddenly to die. This friend, a Dresden graduate who had been active in the Association of Indonesian Scholars, gave him a skewed look and replied, "The revolution will carry on, my friend. And you shouldn't even be asking such questions."

Since then Bhisma chose to stay silent on these matters. Once, in the presence of old friends and a handful of cousins whose main preoccupation in life seemed to be the latest Sukarno gossip, he protested, "Why is morality always about sex? Why can't you campaign to have those corruptors hanged?" The others just looked at him and laughed. Someone even suggested he should get a nice, sophisticated girl from Menteng to keep him honest.

∂∾

The night hours were passing, soft and slow and susurrant. It was around 3:00 a.m. Amba felt as if time had shifted, and she now inhabited another world.

"What was Leipzig like?" she asked.

Having never been abroad—having never even traveled to Jakarta—she couldn't begin to imagine a place with such a name. She pronounced the *z* like a trill and was not even sure why Germany was divided into two.

"Things certainly tasted different in Leipzig," Bhisma said. But he was distracted. Fixated, on the small of Amba's back.

And now, something about her question seemed to arouse him. He told her to lie facedown and started to kiss her neck and shoulders. For a while there was only the sensation of her body succumbing, his weight on her, the sound and feel of his lips and tongue.

Then he told her that he was not proud of his secret taste for contentment, but seven years in Leipzig, for all its darkness, taught him to single out beautiful things. He had loved the Gewandhaus Orchestra as though he'd belonged to it, and he had a collection of cherished spots on and around the Pleisseburg. He told her how every city was different, how Leipzig was quite different from Leiden, where he'd lived for three years, and from other cities he had traveled to in Western Europe.

Leipzig was a sad, dour secret, a walled-in garden, a place lost in time. He could still feel the sting and pulse of that city, its hidden shortcuts through buildings and unmarked lanes between the blocks, the many ways of ducking the Stasi on his way to meet his friends. His closest friends were a radio playwright whose work never got aired, a lonely Jewish anthropologist, and a cross-eyed sculptor.

In a detached tone, he told her about Monica, a radio journalist at the Rundfunk der DDR, who after her nightly talk show would read him the love poems of Brecht and Paul Celan, the sort of poets East Germans read, especially after the latter's wish, in the '50s, to distance himself from the West German literary and political establishment, but whom she had loved. Monica, who had run away to the West—no surprise there!—and was never seen again.

"You must miss it," Amba said, not quite sure herself what she had meant by "it" but wondering all the same how it must feel, returning home from a place so strange and different, and so far away.

⁂

Like all secret lovers, they had decided on the ground rules.

In the mornings she would arrive at the office first, around 6:20 a.m. Bhisma, who was sometimes required to accompany Dr. Suhadi on his early morning rounds, would appear at the office around 7:00 a.m. They would be courteous to each other, even cordial. He would peer into her glass-cube room and say something friendly but bland, like, "Good morning, hope you had a nice rest. How is it going? If there is anything you want to discuss with me please do not hesitate!" He might sit with her to discuss said things, but never for more than five minutes. They also agreed not to eat in the dining room together.

Nobody had told her that when two attractive people tried to obscure the real nature of their relationship they would only highlight it. Nobody had told her about nature. What the situation had meant to her was one characterized only by the tonal emotions, those she could recognize, even name: restraint, denial, discretion. But it was not easy, suppressing her desire to touch him, to feel his warmth whenever he was near. Needing some sort of affirmation that they were in on it together.

But she realized these rules were not too difficult for Bhisma. She soon came to discern an innate aloofness in him. It was as if he'd decided that he could only take small doses of people at a time, unless those people were lying on a hospital bed. As if he had learned a certain survival skill, because people actually expired on him, died, no more breath left, went away, never to be seen again. As if he had to learn how to live on without real attachments, without the pain of missing, the gravity of loss.

She couldn't fathom his relationship with the head of the hospital either. Or maybe it was because Dr. Suhadi was not a terribly interesting person to start with. How about the nurses? They, too, also seemed to be slightly afraid of Bhisma, or else in awe. They watched his every move as if waiting for the weather to change. Were they uninteresting, too? Was she *that* interesting, come to think of it?

Still, he often disappeared without explanation. She remembered vaguely his medical work with the Union of Sugar Workers, but because he often didn't tell her where he'd gone, she started to become jealous of that mysterious elsewhere. Maybe it was just the not knowing. About how, for instance, having spent a decade in Europe he remained irrevocably Indonesian, but at the same time maddeningly foreign. And why his eyes often bore into hers as though to find something he'd lost.

She wanted to discuss the import of their names, but Bhisma was too blissful to care.

"What should we do about it?" she asked.

"What is there to do about it?"

"You don't understand."

She agonized for the umpteenth time over whether she should tell him about Salwa. He believed, obliviously, that the two of them could rewrite *The Mahabharata*. But it didn't occur to him that a Salwa existed between them—a Salwa who had lost the thing most precious to him because she had given it to Bhisma.

But Bhisma would know. After all, reality had a sick way of mirroring myth; surely years of being abroad didn't wash away this instinct? And even though the only red she and her lover felt was the red of their desire, in this world where there were so many uglier reds in people's hearts, surely this would be the reason the two men would eventually meet.

Salwa would find out, they would meet and fight, then both would be done with her, and she would be twice broken, forever.

But again and again she put off telling him, because the fear of losing him had also turned her into a coward.

※

One day, in the office, Amba could tell something was bothering Bhisma. Later, during their break, he told her he had received a phone call from Yogyakarta.

"Someone needs surgery back there. It's quite urgent. I am bound to this code, so I can't name him. It will be a complex procedure, and only I can do it. It was my good friend Untarto who rang. He's with CGMI, the student arm of the Communist Party. He said the man who needs surgery is a security risk. So we need to keep him away from hospitals."

Amba felt her stomach churn. She understood that his skills were needed, that he would run the risk, for his beliefs, of performing this clandestine operation in Yogyakarta. But where were the declarations and reassurances he had lavished on her before? Telling her how he didn't want to be apart from her for even a minute? *Why is it,* she thought, *that men have a way of compartmentalizing their needs?*

In her bed that night she clung to him, as if in so doing she could make history change its course.

It was the third day of October. All morning, rumors and clashing reports filled the hospital. A stream of new victims arrived, to be transferred from vehicles to gurneys and quickly wheeled inside. Fear and confusion reigned. The television in the common room had been fixed, but the scenes of soldiers with their rifles and combat gear looked grainy, as if the images of skin, sky, and weapons were as flat and drained as death. The news reporter announced that the September 30th Movement rebel troops had been eliminated from all strategic spots in Jakarta, and the chairman of the Communist Party, D. N. Aidit, had fled to Yogyakarta.

"Thank God! Down with the Commies!" Dr. Suhadi said, relief in his voice. "As for Aidit, he's a dead man."

Amba realized that whenever someone made an anti-Communist remark, Bhisma kept quiet, his expression tense.

By late afternoon, Dr. Suhadi's tone had changed. In his office he told Amba and Bhisma and the other doctors he had called in, "Apparently there's been an out-and-out Communist Party coup. I just received a phone call from my brother-in-law in Yogyakarta. He told me yesterday, sometime before dawn, an army unit led by someone called Major Mulyono took over the National Radio headquarters in Yogyakarta. The guy now controls the Army. He even had the gall to announce he is now the leader of the Revolutionary Council."

He continued gloomily, "No other way to look at it, but this is a big deal. My brother-in-law said he saw with his own eyes the might of the Communist Party. He found it gut-turning. CGMI, the People's Youth, the workers' union, and all the other affiliate groups, all gathered on the city square, shouting their allegiance to the Revolutionary Council. No other party was present."

"But what does it all mean?" Amba asked. "Can this Major what-ever-his- name-is really command the Army? What's happened to Aidit? Or that other guy Suharto? And where does Yogyakarta's royalty stand in all this?"

"My brother-in-law told me this Major Mulyono has said nothing about deposing either Sultan Hamengkubuwono or Sri Paku Alam. The two kings are, after all, the leaders of the civil government of Yogyakarta. Clearly the Army is divided and being torn apart. This Mulyono guy is quite crazy, though. Apparently he also kidnapped two of his superiors, and of course many in the armed forces would perceive that as a sub-versive act. The rebel troops might be in control for now, but they are edgy and on the defensive, especially after their recent antics in Jakarta got them in trouble. The whole situation could get out of hand at any time. In any case, my brother-in-law was worried enough to send my sister and their two children to stay with family in Bantul.

"Honestly, Miss Kinanti, I think you should go home. I'm not sure whether it's safe for you to be away from your family for much longer."

And yet, he still had time to change her name, not being able to bear the storm to come.

Night could not arrive soon enough. Sometime after 10:00 p.m., Bhisma sneaked his lover into his room, no easy task with staff wander-ing around the building much of the time. Then came another task, no less difficult—keeping sounds soft: the rasp of pillow sheets, the surge of skin against skin, the bed's clicking and clinking, their breathing, their moans, their cries—red-hot trickles of sweat building to rivers of want—cries that couldn't be denied.

Amba knew that when they were together like this Bhisma thought nothing of news, politics, betrayal. His only thought was her, the intrigue of her body, ways to make all parts of her flare, the parts that hurt, the parts that cried out to be found, the parts that preened, and the parts that longed to be rebuked. She felt like a bruise within her own skin, first purple, then lime green, then yellow, which he tended to so gently. He was a balm to her every wound. He filled her. He took her whole, like the sun, in his mouth.

Later, as they lay on the wet salt of the sheets, he asked her to think back on the moment they met. "Do you remember the tree, the dog, the rain? Can you see them? Would we have felt differently about them had we known they were the prelude to this?"

She said nothing. Just closed her eyes. *All the better to see.*

He went on. "If we had not known their names, if we had called them by different names—mountain, bird, wind—would it have made any difference? Would we have felt differently toward each other? How can our names matter? How can they make you other than you, and me other than me?"

His scent of rough wood and the smell of her sex in the afterwarmth of their coupling lifted her like a glittering veil. An aroma sent from the gods purely in their favor. How grateful she would be if the same source could remove Salwa from her story so she could live her name more easily.

As ever, she was surprised that she felt no guilt, either for thinking such thoughts, or for choosing to keep her lips sealed about that other name, the name of her loyal fiancé.

The next night, Bhisma took Amba to a low, secluded rise, well away from the hospital and looking away from the lights of the town. As they lay counting the stars together, Amba pointed to one bright star.

"There," she said. "The one that seems at times to be red. Can you see it?"

Bhisma mused that if it was red it could be a planet, perhaps Mars. Then he seemed to hesitate. "Sometimes I see only shades of gray, and I have to guess the color by its light. I can't tell if the berets worn by the soldiers who come to the hospital are red or green."

It was midevening, the air still holding the trace of twilight. Amba tried to imagine how this unseeing affected his perceptions, his world. But it wasn't uttered, the medical name of this condition. Neither did he say it, that it was a disability.

And so, accustomed to seeing her lover only in the most favorable, even godlike, light she responded to the revelation the way she did to his stories, his many shades of tenderness, his every touch. She absorbed it as simply another intriguing attribute, a beautiful imperfection. Little did she realize that one day she would come to wonder whether he saw the color of his death through his dying eyes.

8

Your Face Holds the Sadness of a City

On October 6, 1965, the night before Amba planned to return to Yogyakarta, she suddenly developed a case of acute shyness. The thought of being with Bhisma both excited and scared her. *It isn't entirely an unlovely thing,* she thought, *recognizing this kind of vulnerability in oneself.*

Early that morning there had been a fresh burst of activity in the hospital. Green Berets jostling with armed civilians. Dr. Suhadi was away attending to family matters. The hospital felt like a sinking ship. Half of the staff disappeared by 3:00 p.m., and the building buzzed with news of Banser troops attacking the Communist Party headquarters in Banjaran. There were casualties. Communist Party members ran for their lives, their headquarters burned down.

In the afternoon Amba went to the warung on the front lawn to buy a bar of soap. A throng huddled near an old radio, as though being as close as possible to the instrument of news gave them comfort in knowing what was going on. She stayed, listened.

It was all about rage. Rife, rampant, full of rancor. General Nasution's five-year-old daughter had died. On that wretched morning of October 1, she had taken the bullets meant for her father. Now, after five days of fighting for her life, her tiny body had succumbed. Folks couldn't bear it. They wanted someone to pay.

The word *Gestapu*, an acronym for the renegade movement—clearly meant to sound like Gestapo—and its variant, *Gestok*, were on everybody's tongue, in everybody's livid breaths. But nothing ignited hatred more than the acronym for the Indonesian Communist Party, PKI. Everyone moved with disgruntlement, with poison in their hearts. Time and emotions were spinning out of order. Thoughts of killing friends and neighbors were made public. "I'm going to kill that bastard, that fucking Communist pig," the warung-keeper hissed as he handed Amba her soap. "And his entire fucking Communist family."

Now she was alone in the office, on a night like this, and Bhisma was nowhere to be seen. Had he forgotten this was her last night at the hospital? Their last night together?

She heard a gathering noise. A storm, she realized belatedly, bearing down upon the city. Perfect. It was like an interstellar production of Socialist propaganda. As if the heavens had decided to get in on the act and make people superfluous.

Soon the earth seemed to be retaliating, refusing to be subdued in this theater of rage: she could hear it in the mad swaying of trees, in the deep groan of the building, in the creaking and cracking of everything around her. It felt as if the entire planet had decided to buttress her indignation, give her a little push, because up to this point she had been shamelessly, scandalously quiet. Because for all her conceit, of not being the proper Javanese girl of her mother's heart, histrionics were not in her genes.

The clock on the wall said ten to nine. A hunk of iron pressed on her chest. She was propped up behind a desk she would never see again, in a town she had barely seen outside the hospital walls, her legs heavier than lead.

The night was getting on, and she still had no clue where her lover was. Was he still tending to patients, at this hour? Was he smoking in some private place he kept from her so that he might wallow in his memories of Leipzig and the more sophisticated world that was once his? Had he gone out, to Banjaran perhaps, to help victims of the recent clash, forgetting that this was their last night together? Was he nearby, in another woman's room, a woman whose beautiful belly glistened with the mixed sweat of their passions?

When did she become this jealous person?

It stunned her, this thought. So new, so unexpected. That she loved Bhisma with a jealous heart. That she loved and resented him for being indispensable to other human lives, and because she wasn't the only person he thought about day and night. She felt aches in her bones, in her belly, in her head, and they stayed in her like pesky, impossible ghosts. When she was not aching she was numb. If she stood she felt no sensation in her feet, in her hands; she was like a portable hole moving from place to place.

This is not good. I have to get out of this. I can't keep moping and mooning.

Resisting the urge to leave the office seemed like the place to start. To not go into the corridor and stick her nose into hospital schedules, on the off chance that she might find out where he was. To not look for him, much less beg him for an audience. Even though she was not a proper Javanese girl, never would be, she'd rather be caught dead than be found lusting after a man.

Which also meant that she had no choice but to go back to Yogyakarta tomorrow, as planned. Bhisma would be there, too, performing the emergency surgery he'd been so elusive, so mysterious, about. She couldn't bear the thought of not seeing him. But Salwa soon would be in Yogyakarta, too. What were the chances that if she and Bhisma were together they might all bump into each other?

Done. Done with work, with duty, with translating, with waiting. She viewed the scene for only an instant. Ivory book, pencil holder, blue notebook, all packed up and the finished documents piled in a neat stack on the table. At least she'd done a good job with those. She thought of leaving a note, of crafting it for maximum effect: "Dear Dr. Rashad, here is the last of the translations. It has been a pleasure to work for you." More: "Sincerely, Amba Kinanti." But she didn't. Pride: what a nasty thing. Nasty and corrosive, often sounding no different from vanity.

Pride. Did she have any left?

And yet. Had he ever talked of the future with her? Had he ever said he wanted her to be part of his future?

Amba looked out the window and fittingly there was only darkness. It was time to call it a night—especially on this night of all nights. The decision couldn't wait, and she was the only one who could make it.

They bumped into each other in the courtyard, close to ten. Bhisma looked disheveled, feral, his eyes glowing in the dark.

"I've been working nonstop for fifteen hours," he said. "I've come home to you."

Amba woke to the sight of her lover's head on her hips. For a moment a rush of feeling, a primal tenderness, washed over her. She reached gently and cradled his head in her arms. *To think that there is such a*

thing as love. It took her a while to hear the sounds of the night: voices, the echoes of bootsteps. Soldiers.

"Oh God," she said. "It's one in the morning."

Bhisma finally stirred.

"There are soldiers everywhere," she said.

"What are you doing," he said drowsily. "Come here."

"What are they searching for? What if they find us?"

"Don't worry," he said, sitting up. "We're safe here."

"What do you mean? How are we safe? They can storm in on us anytime."

"Maybe, if you were in *my* room. But we are in *your* room, and you are a woman. So we are safe. They won't storm into a woman's room."

"I can't believe you. Just listen to them! They're *soldiers!*" He was too calm. That was no good. "Soldiers kill. No one is safe."

"Shush. Why should they kill anybody? Why would they kill you? Nobody could kill someone so beautiful."

"How can you know what they're looking for? If they find you here, I'm done. I'm worthless. I'll be the slut."

"That word could never apply to you. If they do come, this is your room, and *I* am the intruder. *I* am in the wrong. If anyone is to be killed it will be me."

"They'll kill both of us. Me for being the slut, and you for sleeping with the slut."

"No one will kill anyone, and stop talking like that."

The shouting outside was diminishing. But her nerves were shot.

"Have you noticed the janitor? Have you seen the look on his face, the way he watches me, his eyes following me everywhere? I swear he's a spy. I don't know for which camp but I'm sure he's a spy. I've seen the way he looks at you. He probably sees you as the enemy. You've seen how it is. There's no one to trust."

"Nobody will kill someone so beautiful," Bhisma repeated, gathering her into his arms, pulling her against his chest. His calm was quite of another world.

The night outside began to soften and settle, and soon, like all troubled lovers, like all troubled lovers with not much recourse, she, too, settled, for what was available, what brought ready solace: sucking, skin, saliva. Once again she let him wipe her clean of fear—with his hands, his tongue, his throbbing manhood.

❧

Later, because the moon was out and the night had quieted down, she relaxed. Back in love, pure joy. Tangled together, rich with each other's scents.

She imagined them married. *Is this what married people do?* But the moment she thought of the married people she knew other than her parents—her aunt and uncle, her teachers, parents of her friends—she was convinced they all must be bogus lovers, bogus people. Were they even human, these people who went about their lives saying they were in love yet looking the way they did: washed out, dead eyed, dead?

Amba looked at her lover again, his long-lashed eyes closed, his breath still a little labored. What should she say? What is the etiquette at this moment? When all night with his fingers, his mouth, his cock, he had filled her, making her whole.

Do other people in other beleaguered cities, in other bedraggled rooms, on other bedazzled nights like this, experience this woozy happiness, she wondered. She felt by turns shy and assertive, tentative and exultant. But why think of other people? She and Bhisma were here, now. They were the only ones.

"Tell me more about you," she whispered.

❧

He wanted to talk of first times.

"They're always the hardest."

Not mine, Amba thought. *It has been utterly magical.*

He wanted to talk of a different kind of first times.

The first time he returned to Indonesia from Europe, for instance. "I felt choked by a strange petulance, almost anger, and it seemed to fan out inside me. The feeling consumed me, often for days, and later, when it deflated, I felt so used, used up. Like a car or something, like last season's model, an expert devoid of grit."

The worst of it were those early days of living in his parents' house. The house in the old-money area of Menteng, amid longtime and new servants, neighbors stalking him on the street because he was so uncommonly brilliant, relatives who came and went. They all commented on why he had to study for so long. Was he failing, was he not smart enough, did the university make him retake exams? Why was he still single at his godforsaken age of thirty-one? And why, before his mother—*his mother!*—had given him the house, had he owned nothing of his own?

He told her about the tree house he had long outgrown and the little shed in the backyard where his sisters would lock him in at night when he'd done wrong or told a lie, where he had a name for every rat in there that kept him company. He conjured other memories in a slow, dreamy voice: the lonely rattle that followed the sound of the *tokek* lizard like an axiom, how his mother used to keep his wayward coins in a woven pouch in an attempt to teach him frugality.

"I don't easily forget," he said. "And certainly not those things. Those coins, for instance, tinkling as they hit the ground. They were the bearers of my childhood. I feel these things in my bones. Coming home was like renewing an old love, but it was beauty and pain in equal measure. Each new meeting, each reacquaintance, seemed like a bereavement."

And suddenly, this: "That same feeling assailed me all over again when I first met you. Until you came into my life I felt I was enveloped in a strange listlessness, a sense of barely engaging with the world on my own watch. There was no hurry, no urgency. But you, you've changed everything. You bring with you an altogether different bereavement, and it makes me want to both stay and flee even more."

"You want to flee from me? Why?"

"I'm not sure. I'm going to sound really cheesy in a minute. But it's like"—he paused for a moment—"your face holds the sadness of a city."

She tried to feel his words, the sound and the sight of them, like a poem. Nobody had ever spoken of her in metaphor.

But he didn't stay with his thought. Later, she realized it was part of his charm. The thing that kept her waiting, burning. "So there I was, in my midthirties, not bad-looking, if I was to believe what I was told. And accomplished—I had university degrees to prove it. And lonely as hell. I felt like I had walked the world and still couldn't pinpoint what it was that gave me pleasure, or disappointment for that matter. I've seen so many cities, had many women, none of whom stuck around for long, and now my eternal wandering has led me to you."

He came back. He came back. He hadn't forgotten. "You, child-woman, with your hungry, curious, giving body, your amazing eyes. Your . . . surprising thoughts. You're quite unlike anyone I've ever met. You've shown me something I've never seen. A different path. And stranger still, all I can do, it seems, is follow where you might lead."

She just sat there, too overwhelmed to respond.

"You're not convinced?"

"You're sweet, but how could I be?" she said, finally, lightly fingering his arm. "You've known women much smarter and more worldly than me, no doubt."

"How about I tell you this," Bhisma said. "And if this doesn't convince you, then I'm doing a poor job in loving you. On the eve of returning, I wrote to my sister Paramita about how part of my nostalgia for home involved the hope that I might find an Indonesian woman I might truly love. Until that point I had never been with one. You're right, the women I was with in Europe were all gutsy, bright, and independent, and not the types to stoop to fate. They opened my eyes to the world and enriched me as a human being. Through their pain, their memories, often through their language. But in the end I always felt there was something inside me they failed to reach or speak to, something rooted in my childhood, perhaps, to the multiplicities that built me before I arrived on those foreign shores. But I also knew that being with an Indonesian woman wouldn't automatically set me right, or that an Indonesian woman would necessarily better understand my entirety. Despite this, I told Mita I had a powerful feeling that my true fate awaited me back home."

Amba's heart sped. She wished she were a real poet, one who could respond in verse, with something smart, and sensitive, and singular. Something quiet but dazzling. But it was too late, he was drawing closer, and now he was bending his head and taking her nipple in his mouth. Turning the divine into the carnal again, knowing where the switch was.

In the minutes that followed, she realized it was this private Bhisma that she loved, not the Bhisma whom she was jealous of. This private Bhisma who desired her, who only a few hours ago had pressed himself back against the candlenut-colored wall of the corridor beside the courtyard to catch Amba by the arm as she rounded the corner heading to her room. Snaring her, so that in the evening light she glowed like a firefly.

Lying beneath him now she knew as surely as the moon was her friend that she would leave nothing in him unturned, and he was falling in love with her over and over again.

❧

All night Bhisma talked. She marveled silently at how willingly she listened to his stories while offering none of her own. Was it because her life paled in comparison to his? Was it because none of her stories was worth telling, because they weren't about faraway places and the wills of rich dead aunts and imperious mothers? But still she kept quiet, unable to face the consequences of offering up her truths, immense yet somehow inconsequential, while resenting nothing of this other life. This socialite life with its norms and codes he was merely reexamining now, or so it seemed.

"The early '40s," he said, "stick in my mind like a leech. Those were hard times. My parents, along with the rest of the population of the Dutch East Indies, heard again and again that the Dutch had rejected autonomy, had rejected giving our archipelago independence. My father, Asrul Rashad, may have had a family pedigree and a reputation as a respectable book publisher, but like everyone else we had to live a life of thrift and vigil. Our house in Menteng even had a small bomb shelter, buffered by piles of gravel, just in case. We were waiting for another war. We were waiting for the Japanese to invade and take away everything we knew."

One conversation between his parents stayed with him. It was midafternoon, and Bhisma, sneaking out of his obligatory nap, was slinking noiselessly toward the window, beyond which his friend and neighbor, Tony Muis, waited with a bagful of new marbles. Those *kelereng*, as those pretty, glassy things were called. They were both five years old, and barely out of short pants. It was then that he heard his father's voice from the living room.

"That's it?"

"Well, yes, what's left to barter at any rate," he heard his mother answer. "Tomorrow we will run out of eggs. Our rice supply is also depleting—a week, if we're lucky. Unless I get to barter these."

Intrigued by the sound of paper rustling, Bhisma had peeped around the door. He saw his beautiful, regal mother wrapping fabric in newspaper, those lovely kains.

Her voice rang out again. "Maybe we should just sell everything we own. Our bed, if we must. We can always sleep on the floor, on a woven mat. But our children, they *have* to go to school—our youngest in particular."

There was a silence, before Bhisma heard his father's voice. "Yes, our youngest. We must do everything we can. I won't settle for anything less."

Bhisma felt his throat constrict. He knew what *barter* and *sell* meant, and although he was too young to completely understand, he could tell from his parents' faces, from the tone of their voices, that the safe life he knew was changing. He was hit by a sadness so deep that he didn't feel like playing anymore, shiny new marbles be damned. He turned and tiptoed back to his bed, where two of his sisters, Maya and Paramita, were sleeping.

He lay on the edge of the bed, listening to the light snores of his eldest sister, Rosida, who was ensconced in her own bed, on the other side of the room. Listening to sisterhood, security, strength. He lay there for a long time, trembling, until he broke into tears and had to cover his face with his pillow. He was crying for his parents, for himself, and for his shared bed because, God forbid, what if they should want to sell that, too?

Twelve, thirteen years passed. Their world had survived the three-and-a-half-year war with the Japanese, only to get sucked back into the unfinished business with the Dutch. But when the Dutch handed over power in 1949 to the Republic of Indonesia, 340 years of Dutch colonial rule in the archipelago ended. Suddenly, things got better for Bhisma's family. The house remained the same, but the furniture changed. There was real teak, not the cheap wood of years past. The family's publishing house, which Bhisma's father started after he quit his newspaper job, had a new lease on life. By the mid-1950s Bhisma's parents had a new office car to take them everywhere, while he himself became the undisputable ruler of a nifty new bike, a Fongers, no less, which he loved more than anything. Life didn't only get better; life was *good*.

Then one day another overheard conversation between his parents halted Bhisma, now seventeen years old, in his tracks.

"Have you heard from the good man from Ambon?" His mother's voice, from the living room. "Is he coming soon to pick him up?"

Bhisma knew "him" could only refer to the two men in his family—himself and his father—and the question was addressed to his father.

"The good man from Ambon," impeccably mannered and soft-spoken, with astonishingly perfect Dutch, or so it seemed to his mother (who repeated this observation many times afterward), came to their house the following week. Bhisma's parents introduced him as Tomas Lisapaly. They all had tea in the living room, conversing only in Dutch.

Lisapaly had lived for many years in Holland before retiring there with his Dutch wife and his two Indo children. He had been an *Inspecteur van Onderwijs*, an education inspector under the Dutch East Indies. He had met Bhisma's father during a recent visit to Java to look for his brother's grave. The brother, a medical doctor who fought on the side of KNIL, the Dutch colonial army, had been detained by the Japanese and died in one of their prisoner-of-war camps.

At the start of Lisapaly's search, nobody knew where his brother was buried. Then he met a man who suggested that a certain Mr. Asrul Rashad, a coffee plantation supervisor turned Jakarta-based journalist, might be in the know. Together Lisapaly and Bhisma's father went on the trail and found the grave, less than half a mile away from the police academy in Sukabumi, West Java. Indebtedness had brought Lisapaly to this house now.

A month later Bhisma found himself waving madly from the deck of the *Willem Ruys*, an eight-hundred-passenger schooner heading for Rotterdam, with Lisapaly standing next to him. The man to whom, from that moment on, he would report his progress at school, to whom he would turn if he was being mistreated, the man who would be the head of his new family in Leiden.

"Think of *Meneer* Lisapaly as your foster father," his own father had told him.

Bhisma had felt his stomach contract. How could a boy have two fathers?

As the world he knew receded, he thought he could smell the lingering sweetness of his mother's favorite house freshener, the intoxicating burst of gardenias brought inside on certain nights, mixed with the aroma of his father's cigar. But now those scents, too, seemed to be fading away.

He tried to digest what it would mean, being adrift on foreign waters for twenty-one days to get an education, then to return after who knew how many years to a home dependent on the promise of young people such as himself. Shouldn't he be crying, too? Wasn't saying farewell supposed to be one of life's greatest crises? He'd read this—in Papa's office—in Voltaire's *Candide*. But the tears did not come.

Later, much later, when the ship had left Port Said and entered the Red Sea, he finally wept. He wept for his parents, his sisters, for his classmates, and for Tony, his best friend. His best friend, who came from a poorer family, and to whom he had left his Fongers bicycle—but with whom, for reasons that seemed so unfair to him, he could not share his future and his good fortune.

Amba, enveloped in her lover's arms and stories, tried to wave away the thought that if she had been part of Bhisma's childhood she, too, might have been left behind. Might not have been important enough. But Bhisma had just given her another kiss—the longest, deepest kiss of all—and she was ready for anything.

He talked the way he made love: unhurriedly, intensely, often with his eyes wide open.

She remembered one of her university friends saying that when you lose your virginity there are two types of lovers: cocky and inexperienced, or generous and unselfish. The first one, she had said, would more often than not hover above you like a scared fly, while trying to keep his soft and scared appendage in clear sight of his aim. If he succeeded in pushing his thing into you he would suddenly bear down on you with his full weight to make sure his appendage remained inside, not slide out like jelly. While he did this you'd notice his eyes closed in pained concentration. *You'll feel heaviness on your chest and pain in your vagina, not to mention the general feeling of turning into mash. You'll feel a little cheated, too, as you realize the moment you've been waiting for all your life is potentially an initiation into lifelong torture.*

The second type, this friend had said, would be all eyes, hands, and tongue, stroking and licking and penetrating you in a thousand exciting ways. He would divert you from pleasuring him for the right to pleasure you, as if he didn't have any other need but to see you come and come and come. It's like a generous way of teaching you about pleasure, about the many ways it can make you feel, because you didn't know anything about it, because of all the things your parents taught you they didn't teach you this, and you did not live before he opened you up. Also, he is grateful to you, for opening him up.

It was clear which category her lover fit into. But had he been like this with each of the other women he'd slept with? Had he always been this deft and tender and madly in love? And had all the other women responded in kind?

Bhisma reached for her again. "You're so gorgeous." He sighed. And, then as though having to qualify the platitude of that last line: "I feel I can really for the first time in my life *talk* to a woman. Really talk."

But that's it. The very thing she had wanted to hear, just when doubt began to creep in, when her brain started thinking brainless things, when fear took over. He knew how to do this so well, the right tone, the right angle, the right timing, the right language, and that was part of the problem. Amba tried to forget how unmoved she had always been whenever her fiancé said the same mush.

"Do you know anything about the Maluku Islands?"

"Not really," Amba said, shaking her head. "Not much beyond what the history textbooks taught me. Weren't they once called the Spice Islands? I know they are a long way away, to the east. When I was little, I often mistook them for Irian Jaya."

"I knew nothing about them either, until I went to Holland," Bhisma said. "It was mainly Tomas Lisapaly, who taught me things. Especially in the first weeks before school started. How in the nineteenth century, clove cultivation had slipped out of Holland's grip, and the Maluku monopoly was no more. How the island of Ambon paid dearly for this change, how for every *eugenol* and batch of Chinese five-spice powder produced, a Catholic church and a *mestizo* local had taken a fall. The result, he told me, was that thousands of Ambonese, whose ravaged island had been practically demoted to a colonial footnote, were absorbed into the folds of the Dutch colonial administration. So, you see, I did learn something.

"Anyway, by 1830, ten percent of Ambon's population had moved, dispersed, to other parts of the colony. They were loyal, almost to a fault. They were molded for lifelong service. By the time the Japanese invaded, Ambonese comprised half of the local troops of the Royal Dutch East Indies Army. They were Christians and spoke and dressed like the Dutch, Lisapaly included. It was always a given that people like him, a colonial civil servant, were to be sent back to Holland upon his retirement. So when the Republic of South Maluku was declared, in 1950, and promptly crushed by the Nationalists, he and other civil servants went to join the twelve thousand or so Ambonese soldiers who were shipped to safety to Holland."

The point of this whole preamble, Amba realized, was that her lover had truly loved his Ambonese foster father. Despite his Dutch-leaning political views and his quiet, laconic ways, Tomas Lisapaly had treated Bhisma as a son. His wife, *Mevrouw* Lisapaly, too, was always kind and attentive to him, with a laughter that matched her girth.

He paid her the same loving tribute. "She cooked a mean *stamp-pot*," he said. "I came to look forward to it, especially on those cold, stabbing winter nights that could really drag you down. I loved hanging around in the kitchen, watching her pound veal cutlets with a heavy steel mallet, the coupling of bacon and sausage in a cloud of her mashed potatoes, the thick steam that rose from her boiled cabbage, clinging to the pots and pans like body odor.

"In those days I was looked down upon, in the street, by neighbors, by friends of the family. But not by my foster parents. They were wonderful. They might even have loved me."

Yet often, after dispensing polite good nights to his adopted family, Bhisma found himself alone in his staid and puritanical room, with the timbre of certain words pressing upon his ears. Words like *opvoeding* and *geschiktheid*: "upbringing" and "suitability." Words uttered frequently at the dinner table, especially when the Lisapalys had members from "the Ambonese gang" join them for dinner. Words that disturbed him because he'd heard them used just as frequently by his parents, especially by his mother, whenever Lisapaly came for tea.

A letter from Paramita, his favorite sister and the most avid reader in his family, attempted to explain: "*The whole* geschiktheid thing goes back to 1884, when legal access to European equivalent status in the Indies required one to be suited to European society. This was defined as a belief in Christianity, fluency in spoken and written Dutch, and internalization of European morals and ideas."

"What does it really mean, internalization of European morals and ideas?" Bhisma wrote back. "What does it mean beyond being able to display familiarity with European norms?"

Then one crisp morning, after not having heard back from Mita, Bhisma found himself taken to the Christelijk Lyceum, about a fifteen-minute drive from the Lisapaly home on Lasserstraat, without a single indication, much less pearl of wisdom, from either his real or his foster family. He didn't miss the fact that he was taken to a lyceum, not a Hogere Burger School, and that this was, for all intents and purposes, a great honor—that is, for those used to measuring worth through the gaze of the colonizer. He knew his enrollment at the lyceum implied that he would follow the same trajectory as privileged Dutch people: graduate from a Dutch high school, matriculate at a Dutch university, and become ever more Dutch.

He and Lisapaly spent no more than five minutes in the principal's office. In those long minutes, during what seemed like a very warm and personal exchange, in which not a single paper was produced, as though everything had been settled long before Bhisma had even set foot in the Netherlands, nothing seemed real. All of it could be a dream. Someone asking him, "Are you cold?" and him shaking his head, bravely, unyieldingly, even though he *was* cold, Holland was so cold. The principal, a tall, brisk, bushy-browed pole of a man, smiling, rising from his chair, saying a few words in Dutch, to which Bhisma mumbled a pained reply, and leading him out of the room. Walking down a long, cold corridor, before entering a big, cold room, the sunlight utterly useless, a big, cold room with a class in progress, and some two dozen Dutch faces looking up at him and staring.

All too much, of course. He hadn't the language, the wherewithal, to know what to do, despite his so-so Dutch, his own passable height. He was much moved by everything—the principal, for one, with his fingers tap-tapping him on the shoulder, coming to the rescue. After all, it was his job. Announcing: "I have here a new student. He's just arrived from Indonesia. His name is Bhisma. He came to Holland alone, without his parents, without other members of his family. That is a brave act. I hope you will all make friends with him."

I hope you will all make friends with him.

There was a rush of feeling, and he was determined to do his best. There was much past injustice, yes, and there was no erasing history. But it was up to him to turn it into his own strength, his own currency. It was, to put it mildly, the price of privilege.

The first day went by without any problem. So did the second and third days, although he felt inadequate in almost every subject: French, Latin, natural sciences, and geography. They all seemed to be about Europe. Only in math was he a superman. So much was he the reigning king of numbers, those Dutch faces in his classroom would sour whenever he took to the blackboard. He remained the champion of math until the day he graduated.

But the words from his sister's last letter stayed in his mind: the idea that any Dutchman could arbitrarily pronounce a non-European fit or unfit for European society. Did the reverse apply? Would this give him, when he returned home, the license to expel those Europeans who had remained too long in the Indies, including their children? Did their self-exile from Holland make them traitors to their race—did it make them unsuitable? What even was the basis of such a discrimination? What defined "suitability" to any society? Who decided which individuals would be deemed suitable and which would not? Something about this upset him greatly.

One evening, in the struggling light of a late-winter thaw, he watched the European faces of his host family as they sat around the table: the tight curls of Julius's *caboche*, the plump, buttery Saskia, and the caramel glow of Jeroen and Rieke, both picking reluctantly at their string beans. A golden European family gathered at a European table, their supper prefaced by the grace of a European-looking God who transformed water into wine and bread into flesh, put knowledge in a bite of fruit and immortality in a cup. A European-molded family with shared morals, culture, and perceptions, feelings that united them, yet said nothing about who they really were.

How was it possible to become so remote from your roots, Bhisma wondered. Would this happen to him, too? What *were* his roots?

This question came back to him after he left the Lisapalys to live by himself in a small but cozy flat on Vesterstraat. "What is the point of an overseas education if you don't even learn to live alone?" Mita had written imperiously. When he took a long time to reply—he was busy getting an education, after all—Mita sent another letter: "Mama told me to tell you that we have enough money to support you. So go start your independent life. Be an adult. Impress the world."

Whom was he kidding, putting up a show of independence to his friends, entirely on his parents' money. Life was short, and there was so much to learn, so much routine to fall into. But also so much fun to be had, if he was honest with himself. More things happen than one can carry, that much he knew. But he also knew his profound need to suffer was a false pretext to begin with; he needed only to justify his good fortune, which he could pretend was hard enough yet did not wipe out the fact that he was blessed. So he'd better be good at it.

Soon he found himself biking every Saturday night to Roebels, near Pieterskerk, to meet up and drink with Jeroen Lisapaly and his friends. In one of the pubs they frequented, he met Liz Manuhutu, and fell for her.

Liz, a regular in Jeroen's "Maluku" clique, was Ambonese. She had shoulder-length hair, with a black curtain of bangs hanging above her stunning topaz eyes. She had high cheekbones, an almost Latin face. She was a year older than Bhisma, but she singled him out.

"When you're done undressing me with your eyes, we may, perhaps, talk?" she'd said with a laugh.

"I'm sorry," Bhisma said, blushing. "It's just—I've never seen eyes as singular as yours."

"That's all right. You have rather nice eyes yourself."

He discovered, despite their increasing closeness, that Liz did not talk much about herself. One day he found her in the pub, alone and crying. He had hugged her and asked what was wrong. She had been fired from her job in an antique shop not far from De Burcht, an old fort. Just that afternoon, the owner of the shop had found a chip on a treasured nineteenth-century porcelain plate. He had blamed Liz.

"Surely you'll get another job," Bhisma said.

"I don't care about the stupid job," she said. "I'm upset he said *zwarte kut* to me. He called me zwarte kut. Can you believe it? In front of everybody else in the shop."

Jeroen arrived. Bhisma asked him to look after his bike. He walked Liz back to his flat on Vesterstraat. When they had shut the door behind them, Liz asked where the bathroom was. After a few minutes she emerged, wearing neither blouse nor bra. He let her walk past him, her breasts firm and lovely, like the cat she was. He watched her inspect his dusty bookshelf, running her long, approving fingers up the spines of the more succulent books on offer. Still not meeting his eyes she stood by his desk, leafing through his scattered notes. He found himself throbbing with desire. Suddenly they were clinging to each other, kissing a kiss that went on forever. Bhisma was not yet twenty, and despite all the admiring glances he'd drawn from women throughout his time on this foreign shore, he had never made an advance, didn't know how to, nor expected this. The kissing never stopped until they were both naked, limb on limb. They stayed like that until daylight sent flashes of silver through the shutters.

Amba, naked herself, and molded to the warmth and scent of Bhisma's skin, wondered why he told her all this, why he *felt* he had to tell her in such intimate detail. Again she felt the stirrings of jealousy, that idiotic, inglorious thing, but more than that, she was aroused.

What Bhisma remembered was that at one point in the late morning Liz had looked agitated. She dressed and left the flat to make a call from the phone booth, but not before asking him whether she could stay one more night. When she finally left the flat, a week had passed. She didn't tell him where she was going, and he expected she would soon be back. Later, as he stripped the bed of its sex-stained sheets, he found a small notebook filled with addresses and phone numbers.

He thought she would come back. When she didn't return that day he was worried. Reluctant to publicly disclose their relationship without Liz's consent, he wasn't sure whether to ask colleagues about her. After a few days he remembered the notebook. On instinct, he called a number on the first page, somewhere faraway in Westerbork, in Drente. He was told he was speaking to Gerard Manuhutu, Liz's cousin, and they agreed to meet.

Gerard was twenty-three, untethered and confident, over six feet of raw bone and sinew. His face was flatter than Liz's, but with the same chiseled features. From their first meeting Bhisma sensed something dynamic flowing between them, a new energy kicking in.

In his sprightly Dutch, Gerard explained that in the year since she'd moved to Leiden, this was the first time Liz had returned to her parents' house. "Her parents don't exactly live in Westerbork. They live some six miles away, in an ex-KNIL camp." He told Bhisma that he had been living in Holland for five years before Liz and her parents came with the rest of the Dutch colonial army troops who had been demobilized to settle in their allotted spaces in the Drente province.

Bhisma still remembered his heart seizing at the slight quiver in Gerard's voice as he related the story of their arrival in Holland from the Maluku Islands. Already dispirited by their lukewarm reception, they felt disgraced as they were told they would be housed in a place that had served as a Nazi concentration camp, a place where scores of Jews were tortured and starved before being transported to the gas chambers in Poland. Anne Frank had been incarcerated in one of the units there, not far from where the Manuhutu family was made to live. "This part of Drente, and its inhabitants, came back into Dutch hands after the Germans conceded the area, eleven years after they took it," Gerard said. "Some eight acres of land surrounded by dark forests and noiseless fields, with the nearest village, absurdly, some fifteen miles away. Yes, it is a place of wreckage and complete isolation—an isolation that none-theless cut a wide swath with its silence. This is how the Dutch showed their gratitude to the people of Maluku, who for centuries fought the enemies of the Dutch and even died to defend the Dutch crown. *'Door de Eeuwen Trouw.'* My uncle's dream of a Republic of South Moluccas was essentially the dream of a people rejected by both sides."

Something about Gerard galvanized Bhisma. Soon they were spending almost all their spare time together. He still met his friend Jeroen from time to time, but he increasingly found Jeroen had very little to say that was new, and there was a complacency to him and his life of stamppot and pea soup and legends to thrill the children—so many nephews and nieces, so many kids!—that Bhisma found groan-ingly dull.

Now he understood there were real dangers in the world, ideas that changed people and cultures. But they were tucked into corners. They hid in the dark. Only those who were really seeking and listening and asking questions would find them, and Gerard, primal, virile, strong, was among them.

Months passed, and Bhisma heard nothing from Liz. After their week together she seemed to have gone cold on him. But then one day she appeared at the door to his flat, announcing that she was moving to Amsterdam.

"I am dying to breathe Amsterdam air," she said dramatically. "But do not despair, we might sleep together again one day."

"Fine by me," Bhisma said, slightly surprised to find that he wasn't too sad. Why should he be when Gerard was still there?

More months passed and Gerard hadn't only become his best friend, he was also his window to a new world. He knew about things, matters even bigger than the desolation of the Westerbork camp, worse than discrimination against people of color. They saw movies together, salivated over books they couldn't buy. They biked keenly and leanly along the Nieuwe Rijn and, during the midterm break, took their bikes with them on giddy train rides to Brussels and Paris. Gerard believed, with furious clarity, in a future of Communism and what it could give to mankind.

"My brothers in the camp detest white people. They also detest Indonesians. But I don't," he said.

"And why is that?"

"Because Rosa saved my soul."

Bhisma knew nothing of Rosa Luxemburg, so the following night he borrowed two biographies from the library and started to read. He learned how this brave German Jewish woman, a dedicated leader of the Socialist movement, was executed without trial, without audience, without any word or gesture that would dignify the moment of her passing. Instead, her body was thrown into a canal as her soul struggled to hang on to her skeleton. Reading her words, Bhisma found he was surprised by her calm, by its strange vigor and mobility. For all her protestations against injustice and oppression, for all the tender eloquence of her laments, there was an absence of hatred in her anger.

Bhisma felt himself change, as if new roots were growing inside him. Gradually, his visits to the home of the Lisapalys at Lasserstraat 23 became less and less frequent. He still felt close to them—they were his first love, after all—but there was now another layer between him and their reality; an intoxicating otherworldliness had crept into his starry-eyed but nonetheless unremarkable life. The feeling increased when he started working as a receptionist at a surgeon's private practice in Morsweg.

As he arrived at this point in his story, Bhisma propped himself on one elbow, gazing down at Amba. "Of course I had to earn my own money," he said with a grin. "I already had difficulties explaining to Gerard how I could afford my flat."

There it is again. The apology for being privileged, Amba thought. Yet she abandoned herself to the moment, as he bent down to kiss her stomach, then instead of moving lower so that he could see and smell and savor her, he let his tongue travel upward, over her breast, her clavicle, her neck, and finally her ear.

"I must kiss you in this special place," he said, his voice turning hoarse. "Because these days you are not only my lover but also my listener."

⋙

There was a faint sound of footsteps outside. *It must be past three in the morning,* Amba thought as she drowned, their loins linked, in Bhisma's kisses. Outside, branches close to the window stirred in a breeze, knocking against the glass and the walls. Suddenly she thought of Salwa, which immediately made her think of her parents, their shock of knowing, and, yes, they would know, and she started to sob.

"My parents will kill me," she said, all choked up. "And you. They will kill you. Or perhaps I'll have to kill myself."

Bhisma was staring at her strangely, as though it was too much information, too much of the wrong information. There was no reason for feeling so tortured; weren't they—she and him—a good thing? She knew he was no fool. He was trained to be quick on the uptake, alert all the time, even after days of minimal sleep. She suspected he could see through her. Perhaps this was the moment.

And so out it came, all of it: how torn she felt because of her naïve commitment to Salwa, his blind devotion, the way he was with words (*not like yours, but still*), with people (*with certain people, but still*), her father's admiration (*not one to belittle, and still*), the way he made her mother's eyes light up in his presence, his admirable reserve, his touchingly lucid letters, and the fact that he, too, was no fool. Coming to a faltering finish, she said, "So there it is. There is a Salwa. Yes, and a Salwa who is kind, noble, wonderful, in fact. Wonderful . . ." She couldn't go on.

Her heart beating too fast. The silence damning.

"Be with me, then."

She couldn't believe it. "But I'm as good as married. There is no other way for me. You have to . . ."

She stopped. She couldn't say it. And not because she believed in marriage, or was afraid to be alone and grow old without a companion, or because she wanted a way out from Salwa. Not even because she wanted to prove the myth wrong by having Bhisma choose to be with her out of his own volition. Unlike Ambika, she had no expectation that men would fall at her feet to their own ruination. She had fallen in love with him, pure and simple.

And yet.

She started again, "You have to . . ." But her shame was too strong. Again she couldn't say the word.

But he was already kissing her again, kissing her face all over as though it would disappear if he didn't mark it—*I was here and she is mine*—and her body collapsed once more to his touch as though she was a putri malu, the shy plant, the shy princess. Once more she succumbed, all language spent.

There was a moment when he stopped. Bruised with want and hope, she tried one more time: "I can't go back to Salwa. But you and I, we have to . . . you know. We have to . . ."

Panic rose within her as nothing came out of his mouth. And she didn't ask for it.

⁕

After Bhisma had gone from her bed, Amba waited out the final throes of night, her belly sticky with his seed. She knew that in an hour or so she had to start packing, but it didn't seem pertinent; she had hardly brought anything from Yogyakarta and purchased nothing in Kediri. She wanted to spend her last hour in their room, in their blue room, drinking in the details of their time together, the exactness of his scent before and after he came, the feeling of being made whole. She wanted to drown in the lines she had so loved in one of T. S. Eliot's poems, "to be conscious is not to be in time" yet "only through time time is conquered."

She went through everything he'd told her about his life. She was drunk on the idea of him, and everything about him that she wasn't. But what was he going to do now, now that he knew everything? Now that he knew that there was a decision to be made, that she was not a free woman. They hadn't even discussed how they would say their public good-bye, or whether they would meet again after Kediri. And there was no thought given, now that she was no longer a pure flower for her future husband to pry open, to what her future entailed once Salwa knew.

It was not an easy image to store: how Bhisma had looked, in that split second before he walked out her door ahead of the dawn—as if someone had thrown icy water at him, leaving him struggling to argue against its substance. He'd looked as though the weight of Salwa's presence in her life had just hit him full force, and that knowledge was too much to comprehend—as if he could only deliberately misunderstand it for the moment, shelve it, in her absence, like an artifact, only to dig it out later, when he felt he was ready. Suddenly, she saw the image of Ambika: crouching in a corner of their house, gazing longingly at Salwa with her mind and breath full of fire.

Then something even more vivid and urgent than worry washed over her: a certain fatalism about what had to happen. With that came the sadness of realizing she had changed, and part of that change was this sudden, urgent, obsessive complicity in her own destruction.

9
Bumi Tarung

October 7, 1965: the appointed day Amba and Bhisma parted, less than eight hours after they last had been together. It was a clean moment of reckoning, free of tears and protestations. The sun was cruel. There was no ceremony. A hospital is a place of perpetual exit.

An hour after he left her room, Amba had again gone for an early breakfast, her nervous tic, her staple defense, unsure where to peg her despair. It wasn't accomplished without effort. As on her first day, and the next day, she slid into a corner of the dining room like a pathetic, scared mouse and forced herself to eat a piece of toast to calm down. Bhisma was nowhere to be seen. She hadn't even asked the question she'd always wanted to ask him: *Do you ever eat breakfast?*

Dr. Suhadi was particularly nice on this, her last, day. With no intention of milking her to the last drop he decided there was no need to keep her working right to the last hours of her contract. The expression on his face when he escorted her to the front of the hospital, she realized, was of relief. Did he know what had been going on under his nose? But Dr. Suhadi said nothing about Bhisma. Instead he said pleasantly, "Thank you so much for your hard work. You did very well." And because her eyes were misting over, he quickly said, "Anybody else, even a certified translator, would have taken double the time. Have a safe trip home. Please be careful."

He had offered the hospital car to take her to the station. It was unmerited, an act of kindness. He must have known.

She also noticed he didn't suggest she return one day and visit the hospital again. When she had said good-bye the real test was to walk straight, with a clear sense of direction, to the place where the car was supposed to be waiting. No fumbling, no hesitation. She turned around once, to wave to Dr. Suhadi because suddenly she felt the need to see his face for the last time, which reminded her of Bhisma, to whom a certain measure of largesse was not alien. But Dr. Suhadi had gone. Amba walked on, her chest heavy, her bags keeping her on gravity's path.

Then, just like that, she caught sight of her lover's tall silhouette out of the corner of her eye. *Surely,* she thought, *this is where I pretend not to see him, make him pay for his callous silence.* When he approached she avoided his eyes, keeping her own steadfastly on the ground.

"Amba," and now he said her name, no more *sayang* and *mein Liebling* of their private nights. "Baby. I have to see you again," he said quietly, a little desperately, as he leaned closer. "Can we meet in two days' time? The operation in Yogyakarta must be done soon. It may be hard to persuade the hospital to let me go, but I promise I'll somehow work it out."

She didn't answer.

"Say something, please."

A group of chattering people fell quiet as they passed. It seemed to Amba that everyone was watching.

Her mind was in turmoil. She could stop him right there, fix him on the wrong side of the fault by saying *good-bye, say no more, I don't want your words* (and sounding like she meant it). Or she could keep him at arm's length but not to the point of burning her bridges, in case he did not end up abandoning her—and that would require coldheartedness and considerable acting skills. Or she could break down and throw herself at him.

Bad options, all of them. So she lied, instead. She said that she had received, that morning, a letter from Surabaya, telling her that Salwa wanted to see her that weekend, and that if she didn't appear, her parents would send out a search and rescue mission.

"Can't you buy some time?"

Why do you want more time? Amba thought with irritation. *Time to make a commitment to me? You could have done that last night. No, you simply want time for more sex, more off-loading of your life story.* "I don't think so. It's too complicated."

But then that same mistake again. She looked up. They locked eyes. And he had her. Had her completely.

That seemed to be the way of things with them.

Four days later, they met in a secluded area outside the Sonobudoyo Museum in Yogyakarta.

But before their rendezvous, Amba had had to do a few things. When she arrived in Yogyakarta, she immediately went to a public phone booth outside the station and called Rien Oey, a fellow student at the university. They talked, and Rien said she had a free room at her place, which she described as more spacious than most cheap student lodging and conveniently out of the way. Amba was welcome to stay for a couple of nights. Funny how things just sort of fell into place.

Once they got to know each other better, Rien mentioned the threats her family had received from unknown people who would spring out of nowhere, mostly in the dead of the night, demanding that they leave town if they still valued their lives.

"Is it because you're Chinese?" Amba asked.

Rien shrugged in the manner of someone who was used to intolerance and replied drily, "They think we're Communists because we are Chinese, and because we're Chinese we can't possibly be Muslims."

When Amba appeared at Rien's doorstep, straight from the station, she was only vaguely aware of Rien's expression—one of shy admiration. Then she began to notice, every time she entered the room, her host's eyes light up. Unsure of how to behave, Amba kept stories of Kediri to herself, and showed she was more interested in listening.

"You were only gone for two weeks, but already the city has changed drastically," Rien said. "People are scared and unsure and waiting for something big to happen. Recently I went to visit my friends from the Nationalist Party–affiliated Christian student organization in their boarding house, but they didn't give a fuck about me. They were all too busy with self-defense exercises. Some were even learning how to use weapons. When I suggested that was extreme, they just kind of pounced on me, like a pack of wolves. 'Where the hell have you been, you dumbass?' they said. 'Those People's Youth guys were already armed by pro-Communist forces. Yogyakarta is turning redder by the minute. Even our campus is overrun by those CGMI morons. Haven't you noticed?'"

And there she was, all those nights, sleeping with a friend of CGMI. Amba cleared her throat, then said, "But surely there is the Army . . ."

Rien looked at her, seemingly surprised at her guest's poor grasp of the situation. "Well," she said, haltingly. "I'm not sure myself. Since the so-called attempted coup was crushed in Jakarta, the battalion that was allegedly tasked with murdering General Katamso and throwing its weight behind the Revolutionary Council has disappeared from the scene. But then we heard their commander was preparing a new move, some kind of desperado guerrilla warfare. Now both the Muslim and Catholic organizations are gearing up for that." Leaning closer toward Amba from across the table: "You know, you can't be too careful. You just can't. Everyone is a spy these days."

All the while, on the wall behind Rien, hung a portrait of an unknown man, his painted eyes like real eyes, spying and monitoring.

You can't be too careful, Amba repeated to herself. *Certainly not of a man who makes love to you like there's no tomorrow, but won't talk of tomorrow with you.*

❧

When she met Bhisma at the museum and told him about her conversation with Rien, Bhisma laughed. And laughed again, after stealing a thousand kisses under the shady trees.

"You ever thought she might be a little in love with you? And that you should bolt before it's too late?" he said, his handsomeness undiminished, his perfect hair perfectly ruffled.

Amba, annoyed by his easy dismissal of her fears, thought, *Is it just me or is it true that you are a little misogynistic? Not like Salwa, certainly not like Salwa, with his irritating fascination with women as wives, but you, you don't really respect women. Not really.*

He was still oblivious, laughing. "And me, should you bolt from me?"

Amba tried to disengage from his arms, but no chance of that; it was all about him, his desire. Newly intoxicated, she heard him mumble the opening lines of the Neruda poem Tara had introduced her to, the ones she occasionally read to him in Kediri: "I love you as certain dark things are to be loved, in secret, between the shadow and the soul." The lines seemed so familiar to him. Was it possible that in his secret, shadowy way, he had encountered the poem long before they met, courtesy of his European friends? *Is it possible*, she thought suspiciously, *that he has whispered them before, in the same velvety voice, to Liz, or to the many other women he has mentioned but not named?*

Despite these petty thoughts, she too had her longing, and it, too, must be sated, must be sated *now*, but where could they go? Taking her lover to Rien's place seemed distasteful, Rien who adored her and had been so good and selfless, who had asked no questions. Then there was the not-so-trivial matter of her respectability, the image she must maintain in public at all times.

Later in the afternoon, after they were done snacking and sipping iced tea in a nearby eatery, holding hands under the table like teenagers in heat, Bhisma told her he'd take her to Gampingan, where the Bumi Tarung artist colony was. *It is the safest place in all of Yogyakarta,* he said, *because there we can be together as man and woman, and nobody will bat an eyelash.*

On the way there in a slow-moving *becak*, Bhisma turned once more into the Bhisma of Kediri, the lover with stories. The place they were going to, he said, was a haven of left-leaning artists, mainly graduates of the National Fine Arts Academy. The guy who founded it was a painter and sculptor from Medan. His name was Amrus Natalsya. When he was still a freshman in the academy, President Sukarno purchased one of his sculptures, and he became a sensation overnight. It gave him clout, and that was how Bumi Tarung came into being.

"This guy is one of a kind," Bhisma said as the becak trundled through the slate-gray and faint pink dust of low dusk, the wind teasing and fondling their hair. "He isn't interested in beauty or harmony. He creates art that is politically charged. He actually *believes* that art has to serve the Revolution. But he's not like most artists of the Left who only paint muscly laborers, or farmers with giant sickles and soldiers with rifles. His work is actually good; it is what one would call alive."

"Like Neruda?" Amba offered.

"More or less. Or, like Sudjojono," Bhisma said, looking momentarily moved. So much that he leaned over and planted a quick kiss on Amba's lips while keeping his eyes on the back of the becak driver. "You've heard of him, yes? He is, well, he towers above everyone. The artists from the Bumi Tarung colony are made of the same stuff, the same spirit, more or less. And they are certainly no mere imitators."

And he went on and on, a little like a university professor lecturing an undergraduate student about the merits and flaws of the school of Revolutionary Realism. About idealistic boys who grew up to become idealistic men who went on to change the world.

The becak ride itself was lovely, and Amba felt a knot forming in her stomach at the thought that such simple things should not be taken for granted. Yet there were no women, of course, in this constellation of fine people he spoke so passionately about. Does Bhisma care about women and their fate? Do all women have to be fierce warriors and die like men, as Rosa Luxemburg did, to earn his respect? Does he care about the mountains, behind which every day the sun rises and sets, about life on the side of the road, about the color of twilight in certain clear afternoons, so beautiful it is almost unendurable?

But she *saw* him, of that she was sure. Saw the fine salt-dirt lines on his neck and his forehead. Saw the wetness of his shirt where his armpits ran with sweat. His intellect might be a weapon, his worldliness his shield. Might it be that the world was a frightening place for him, for it held far too many shapes and flavors and colors for him to handle? Whereas she, unarmed, wide open, pregnable, with everything to lose, she held this man whole, the man whose taste resided in her throat, whose words replayed in her ears like childhood songs.

Their becak pulled up in front of a red brick building on the corner of a small street, at an angle with the Fine Arts Academy. Curiously, it was shaped like a fort. The driver jumped down to check the address. Amba felt the silence settle upon them, but before she could decide how to break it, Bhisma's mouth searched for hers and, again, they snatched a hurried kiss. The becak driver returned and shouted, "This is the place."

The lovers dismounted. As Bhisma paid the driver it seemed that he sensed Amba's hesitation. He said softly, "Okay, this might not look like the safest place in Yogyakarta. I might have lied. But it is our best option right now if we want to stay together."

He led her to a modest-sized patio, where a few men, who all looked the artist type, were gathered in a searing, smoke-filled conversation. Although this wasn't altogether unfamiliar territory, Amba felt strongly that she and Bhisma were outsiders, always would be, and that Bhisma's slight nervousness, his stoop and his put-on friendliness, combined with her guilt and uncertainty, must be a dead giveaway.

A man with long, frizzy silver hair rose and greeted them with open arms. "Well," he said. He seemed genuinely surprised and happy to see Bhisma.

"Well. Look who's here. A guest from East Germany! What have we done to occasion this?"

The two shook hands.

To Amba the silver-haired man looked near-extinct, yet she sensed he still smoldered. An aging lothario.

"Please, sit down," he said, appearing a little unsure about Amba but smiling broadly.

When seats had been found for them he filled them in on what the group had been discussing: the political situation. "Amrus's artwork was burned by an anti-Communist mob in the lobby of a Jakarta hotel recently," Silver Hair said. "Everybody is scared shitless. Many of our artists have not returned. Gone into hiding, most likely. The big man himself recently called from Lampung and told everybody to stay away for a while and to lie low."

"So why are you still here?" Bhisma asked.

Silver Hair laughed and shrugged. "Danger, brother, is part of our struggle."

Then, as though remembering something important, something he'd missed, Bhisma turned to Amba and said, "Isa and I have been friends for a while. We met for the first time in Vienna, in '59. The World Youth Festival was held there, and he was one of the artists invited by the Austrian government."

Amba nodded, unsure how to respond. She wondered why Bhisma hadn't introduced her to everyone. Yet there was nothing new about this ritual; in this part of the world women often simply didn't get introduced, they didn't have to be acknowledged; it was enough that they were present. So why was she fretting?

There was a brief question mark on Isa's wrinkled face, she was sure, but Amba looked away, fixing her gaze on the two pieces of *wingko* cakes offered them on a banana leaf, so familiar, so sad and so dejected. How could she not be reminded of home and of the beloved faces of her parents. And Salwa, Salwa again, whose face she could barely remember but who she knew would never be embarrassed about introducing her to anyone.

Her thoughts were interrupted once more by the ongoing conversation among the men. Isa asked Bhisma how things had been at the hospital, why he was thinner, whether it was because of turba. The other men broke into laughter. It was quite clear, Bhisma lent himself to some light taunting: the Menteng-massaged rich boy who'd gone to Europe on his parents' money first, before he won himself a scholarship, with a face like some goddamn prince.

Turba, shorthand for *turun ke bawah*, "going groundward," was almost too easy a jab, for it reflected the perception among the Left that bourgeois boys like Bhisma felt more acutely the need to spend real time among the underprivileged, in order to display their commitment to the people.

"Turba is a way of life," someone mumbled in their midst. "That's why we are all emaciated."

Which was followed by a roar of laughter.

No one addressed Amba as the conversation dragged on, with Isa doing most of the talking. They talked about Nationalist Party members who feared for their lives. They talked about the righteousness of the heroic brawls that ensued after a leftist wayang performance. They shared their stories of the dead.

How much longer? She wanted to stretch her legs and get away from all the smoke. She longed to get out of her clothes and lie down. She hated feeling so exposed.

Something about her anxiety seemed to catch Isa's attention, as though he had just remembered that she was there and that she was the reason for Bhisma's presence, this bourgeois boy who was too handsome for his own good.

"I'm sorry, but you must be tired," he said to her. "Would you like to rest?"

She was relieved by this unexpected kindness. She shot a quick glance at Bhisma, watching him struggle with those guilty green-gold eyes. *Do your goddamn part: you owe me at least this.*

"Folks"—Bhisma's voice finally filled the space—"I'm so sorry, I nearly forgot. This is Amba. She is studying literature at Gadjah Mada University."

She realized Bhisma didn't explain her relationship to him. Not his girlfriend. Not even his friend. She felt a shooting pain in her chest as she realized there was nothing she could do. He couldn't say either of those things. She was his lover, yes, because she was sleeping with him, yet she was someone else's girlfriend, someone with whom she hadn't slept, but to whom she was engaged to be married. She was not Bhisma's friend—precisely because she *was* sleeping with him. And as to *lover*, the closest word to the truth, that word could not exist, not in this world of theirs, at any rate. You were either someone's girlfriend, and that implied you were not married yet to each other (but were most likely going to be), or someone's wife. Friends did not sleep with each other; they did not do the love thing.

She also realized that while he nodded in her direction he made no attempt to touch her or sit closer to her.

Whether time, at that pinprick moment, had expanded or contracted she couldn't be sure, but finally one of the men addressed her, asking about the faculty of English Literature she studied under. Was it true that not all the lecturers who were sympathetic to the Cultural Manifesto were given the axe? "Firing lecturers on the basis of their beliefs is a scandal," the man said. "What a gross violation of our ideals of a Communist future free of human greed and moral degeneration!"

Of course. They were not interested in what she thought, because she was a woman. But shouldn't Bhisma care? Shouldn't Bhisma come to her defense because he loves her?

It was at that instant she realized how little she knew about the man sitting next to her, the man into whose hands she had, by coming here, now entrusted her life. What was he thinking, as he sat there, brooding, withdrawn, a little more than attenuated? Had he simply decided just like that, that it wasn't the time to speak up for a woman, even if that woman shared many of his opinions, to say nothing of his secrets? Was he being tactful or cowardly? Was he conservative or radical? How did it come about, exactly, his open-armed welcome into this Commie lair?

Blessedly, Isa interrupted. "The room at the back is empty, if you want to take a rest, Comrade," he said, nodding at the doctor. Amba's handsome whatever. "Why don't you take your . . . er, friend to see some of our paintings?"

Lying together that night in a room with a packed-earth floor, and on a cot made of wooden crates, with a mattress so narrow it could barely fit the two of them, Bhisma was visibly perturbed. He lay on his back, a zigzag of white sheet over him, as though practicing the final calm before being lowered into the ground.

Sensing her equally foul mood he kissed her shoulder. "Do you love me?" he asked.

She didn't say yes or no, just nodded. She pictured the earlier scene, Bhisma in that crowd, the air of veiled condescension thickening around his stint at the hospital, the fact that he had been brought to their midst by someone whom he liked and who liked him back, the fact that try as he might, he knew he was more familiar with the cadences of an East German pub than the shifting realities of a place like this, with its deceptive codes and expectations and local language of struggle. He never would fit in here completely, by dint of the way he looked. Even stripped of history, of context, there was no getting past that face, that body language.

Amba thought back to the hour they'd spent earlier, looking at the paintings. She didn't know a great deal about art, but it was hard not to have an opinion. She knew which works she enjoyed and which she didn't, though not necessarily why. Because the paintings were mostly illustrative, they made themselves rather too conveniently available to appraisal. Bhisma seemed to appreciate certain canvases that attempted to tell a story rather than to merely describe, and those that revealed the unexpected. In one, a worker, clumsily rendered, seemed to want something for himself. If you followed the worker's eyes you knew he wanted something else, something beyond the painting's narrative, compelling you to finish his thought. In another, a train symbolizing man's bright future raced through a landscape and on toward the sky with its sun, its moon, and stars; it didn't seem to want to stop, and yet she had the impression it would rather go someplace else.

Beside her, Bhisma was drifting off to sleep. *Trying to read this man,* she thought, *is like trying to interpret those paintings, half lovely dream half nightmare, so out of place, so out of time.* Bhisma, who had soaked up the philosophy of Lenin, ducked the Stasi, and lived behind the Berlin Wall; doctor, lover of poetry, worshipper of Rosa Luxemburg and Bertolt Brecht; a man who had lived with hope, apathy, fear, despondency but also luxury beyond her wildest dreams.

Later, perhaps, she would learn to trust her own reading of the world, just as he would, perhaps, learn to stop reading the world too much. But for now it was his gaze that had helped her reach—for the right words, for the right feeling, like reaching for the stars. Her enchantment, the bright star in her sky.

℞

What did it matter if he was a Communist at heart or not? He made love to her with such unadorned hunger he was her guide to her own mounting need.

"Do you believe in what they believe in?" she asked.

"You heard that guy with the long hair?" he said, sleepily, his face buried in her chest.

"Which one? Almost all of them have long hair."

Bhisma smiled, perked up. "The skinny one with the goatee. The one who talked as though they were all saints on some giant purification mission."

Every time something bothered him like this, Amba realized she was perversely happy, happy to be included, to be integral enough to join the storm brewing inside him.

"The thing about people who speak for Communism," he continued, "is that very often they don't know their Marx and their Marxism. While it's true that that gray old man often referred to history itself as an actor, people often mistake him for a historical determinist. In fact no other thinker stressed human agency more than he did. In the end, Marxism, as with all the other isms, is upheld as an encouragement for people to seek this, well, purity. Those who believe they have found it become absolutists forcing it onto others, punishing those who do not comply. Then the ism they swear by becomes more like a fundamentalist sect than a secularist program for social change."

Amba ran her fingers through his hair, couldn't stop looking at him. "You know, where I come from, religion—for you are talking about religion, yes?—wasn't like that," she said quietly. "At least not before the loud turbaned folks started to overrun the place. I grew up with the gentlest, most selfless people. I grew up with the kind of Muslims my parents are. People so spiritual they glow with kindness and good deeds. But suddenly the community changed. Every day now once-simple people are at each other's throats, saying, *I am right and you are wrong, I am pure and you should burn.* The farmers are the same. They talk about Islam, *their* take on Islam at least, as though it was the only truth, and yet they're just as bigoted and sadistic."

Bhisma smiled. She reached to kiss it, this smile on those lips she loved. He pulled her close.

"My family has always been secular," he said. "They never demand freedom from sin."

"Is this a sin?" she cooed. *Don't turn your head away. Let me look at you. I love you so much.*

He looked at her long and hard. "You are a lovely, pure thing," he whispered. "But you see, I know something about living in fear. In Leipzig, the Stasi were ruthless. You lived by their fascist rule, couldn't move a muscle without looking over your shoulder, expecting a death-blow at any moment. Folks were forced to live behind closed doors. No wonder many of them went nuts."

Only half listening, she pressed her hand on his chest. "Is this loving a sin, too?"

He smiled, but didn't answer.

"Tell me something I don't yet know," she said, feeling emboldened.

He played the game. "I love you more each day," he murmured, "and I don't know how we will be together, or how soon. I know I have told you before that to me your face holds the sadness of a city, a sadness I'm not sure I can endure, but now I know it is becoming more and more difficult for me to leave."

With one deep look she rose to mount him, in that habitual pin-prick of time. The moment felt so close, so fitting, as if she had trained for this place, this motion, all her life. When they were done again, after that familiar pulse had passed, and they lapsed into that vague melancholic ache, they held each other the whole night.

As Amba drifted between sleep and wakefulness, she remembered how, when they had met that afternoon, at the museum, their first reunion, his eyes had gone all soggy. It was the first time she realized he, too, must be in love with her. It was the first time she had felt wedded to another human being. She knew that a part of Bhisma, however buried and quiet and uncertain, felt the same way. As if their bodies, the fount of their lovemaking and the jelling of him and her, knew the ultimate truth.

Should she distrust that feeling? Should she fear it? What if she was driven to such a feeling because, deep down, she needed to invest the carnal with the divine to give their relationship sanction? Is it true the body knows more than the mind? That it is more resistant to being tricked than the mind is? She didn't know how to make sense of this feeling, much less discuss it with Bhisma.

But how can you objectify, individually, something you could only attain when two people become one? How do you discuss such a thing without urging it to a premature end?

In the morning, when she awoke, the sun was up and Bhisma was not in the room. Amba saw that he had tidied up, his bag and jacket and her few clothes and toiletries set neatly on the corner table.

The compound was dead quiet, as though it had folded over, with only the occasional punctuation of someone coughing. *A smoker's cough no doubt,* she thought, as she quickly put on a fresh shirt and yesterday's skirt, brushed her teeth and her hair without the aid of a mirror—this being such a man's world. As she left the bathroom she caught a glimpse of three men in the front room. Bhisma and Isa were deep in conversation with another person whose face she couldn't see, and seemed to be speaking in whispers.

She glanced back at their room to check if she was missing anything, a note perhaps, but found only a cold cup of coffee and a plateful of *nasi gudeg* on another table. If it was for her, maybe Bhisma had had his breakfast ahead of her. If it was for him, then she was an off-the-books guest.

Fifteen minutes later she found herself walking out the gate to the courtyard, deliberately avoiding Bhisma, Isa, and the mystery guest. She walked all the way to the main street, which was deathly quiet as well. Across the street, in the courtyard of the Fine Arts Academy, she saw two banyan trees. It was too much; she almost laughed. And yet her rawness won over. She felt mawkish.

The trees' canopies were so dense they seemed to wait with bated breath for something yet unnamed, a malady, a curse, or an act of beneficence, while the branches reached as if for something to hold other than each other. Her head spun. What was preoccupying Bhisma? Did it have to do with the patient he had come to operate on? Who was the mystery guest she'd just seen him talking to?

I know something about responsibility. Just don't ask me about politics.

As ever, when those words of his came back to her, sounding so grand in their finality, she had no idea what they actually meant. What politics did he mean? Had he not abandoned his responsibility at the hospital to be here, in this city, to help someone in need? Was this something he was doing for the sake of politics?

It would not be until later, after Bhisma vanished from her life, that Amba would arrive at a conclusion that never before entered her mind— that at certain critical junctures, politics and duty are one and the same. But on that quiet morning, standing on a corner in Yogyakarta, with the harsh heat of the sun only beginning to cut through the moist morning air, and the scent of her lover rising from her own warmth, Amba wanted only to believe in one truth, the highest truth—the truth of their lovemaking. It seemed that sex had started to become neither something to be set apart from "love," nor a mere ancillary to it, but, rather, its supreme articulation.

She tried to still her mind, standing before the silent twin banyan trees, willing them to love her at that moment, to love and forgive and feel sorry for her in that warm and random way of strangers. But this only brought on a new rage.

Why am I back here in Yogyakarta, she thought furiously, *stealing forbidden moments with a forbidden man? Here, in my fiancé's town, his town before it became my town, his town before there was an Amba, before there was an Amba and Salwa, before there was an Amba and Bhisma. The town he had to leave in order to build a future in another town, a future for his intended—for me.*

Why am I doing this? Why did I not return straight to the house of my aunt and uncle to stop them from worrying? Why do I not care what my family in Kadipura must be thinking, having not heard from me at all in these dangerous times? Times when our world has turned, all of a sudden, into a dark, demonic place, a place of mournful horror and futile fury, where bad news has no place to go but inside, into our hearts, riveted there like a reminder that we do not exist in this world to be happy.

Have I ceased to care about the people and the things I used to love? Here I am, so captive to this new, treacherous feeling that I prefer to be with a man who sets me agog with his exciting stories, rather than a man with whom I may only be able to trade boring cleverness each day but who will keep me safe? What kind of a person have I become?

She thought of her forbidden lover's impassioned, almost reckless decision to come here to Yogyakarta for duty, to save the life of someone he didn't even know. *Is it possible,* she wondered, *that his recklessness has rubbed off on me? Is it possible that I have edged myself closer to danger because I believe that the closer I get to the source of my biggest fear, to that great moment of reckoning, the more likely I might be able to avert it? Could I possibly forestall the battle that could make me twice a widow? For is it not true that the only way to deflect the inevitable is to will it to happen?*

But all these thoughts and questions were too much. She returned to their room, making sure she wasn't seen by Bhisma and his companions.

She needed to do the right thing. She had to bring herself closer to Salwa. She pulled one of his old letters from her bag. She hadn't realized it was there until she took out her toothbrush and toothpaste the previous night. She started to read, willing the letter to speak to her:

Beloved Amba,

You know what we both want to be right now, what we should be: we should be together, married, you with your degree in your pocket, and me with my program done and a new job awaiting. Common sense, pure and simple. Aah, this thing they call faith, or what you will. Where would we be without it? But please don't think I'm losing it, for it is the only thing I have to keep me going these days. I know there is no decree against my showing up at your doorstep one day, announced or otherwise, but I also know you are deep in your studies, so critical to our New Life, the one we are heading toward. And the last thing I want is to disrupt your studies.

Besides, too many disturbing things surround us these days, especially in Yogyakarta, I've heard. How I wish I could go back and keep you safe. But we all have to learn to live with this feeling, I suppose. Things are also getting ever more disturbing in Surabaya. You know I'm not one to complain, but there is so little at work these days that makes me look forward to waking up in the morning. Often when I get home, I feel teary with tiredness. Ever since the start of the Manikebuist purges of the past year, things have gone from bad to worse. Three trainers I'm relatively close to have not received their paychecks for over a year, and just last week they were told to pack up their bags and leave. Not only am I still reeling from the unfairness of it all, but I also have to find new people to replace them, the right new people, who will have not only the proper skills to be good teachers, but also the right teacherly values. (Your father's example always comes to mind.)

As with everything in life, it is always easier to destroy than to build, especially characters and values. And one of the most important values to learn in life is that we should respect one another not on the basis of power, or politics, but because of one's merits, good deeds, and devotion to a cause. Politics should not rule over everything else. It should not replace the time-tested foundation of our lives. I really do believe in this.

My God, did I just write all that? I must sound so pedantic to you. I'm sorry, my love, but here you have *it—your future husband, the head of a teacher-training program, talking like one, writing like one.*

On to happier things, then. I don't know what you think of this idea, but since I have been duly triggered back to Kadipura, to your family, I have a good mind to introduce my father to your father. Lately things haven't been so good for my father. He lost his job and position at the Muhammadiyah three months ago, following his arrest by the police on fabricated charges. Anyway, not to bore you with the details, it is enough to say he was detained and interrogated for three days. He has high blood pressure, and on the third day he buckled and fainted. My mother stepped in, bringing some of her NU kyai friends to his aid. They managed to persuade the police to release him, and my father has since been looked after at home.

Surprisingly, something positive has come out of that frightening episode, even if it lasted for no more than two days. My mother and my father united, if not in love then in solidarity, despite their politics, despite the choices that chained them. But when I looked into my father's eyes I knew he was, deep down, crushed and weeping for his life. He needs weeks, maybe months, of recuperation, and this can only be brought about by a change of scene. This is how my idea of taking him to Kadipura to meet your father came about.

See how I'm missing you so much, that your birth-place has become to me my magnetic north, the one place to which the needle of my compass would swing without demur.

Forever,
Salwa

Salwa's words rarely moved her, but now she found herself helplessly in tears. His words had the believer's poetry to them, a strange spiritualism, something that dared defy separation, impossibility, even asymmetry. Yet the facts remained: he wanted what she had more than she did. It was he who wanted Kadipura more. It was he who wanted and understood her family and their history: her father with his secret books; her mother, who prized stability; her easily awestruck sisters. He saw Amba's home as a miniature temple that wasn't entirely clean-cut but nonetheless safe because it never tried to be different. It was Salwa who understood that love was will. It was he who was good, whereas she was nothing but fickle, disloyal, and irresponsible.

Ever since she'd embarked on this sea of desire, ever since she had entered those strange new chambers, her room and Bhisma's at the hospital and now this room with no mirror at Bumi Tarung, she had plunged into a new world, a world built in a mere fourteen days but far more captivating than the poems of Eliot and Neruda, than the novels of Steinbeck and Turgenev, because it spanned Jakarta, Leiden, Berlin, and Leipzig, and its name was Bhisma. Yet she couldn't picture him in Kadipura. She couldn't see him with her father and mother, being part of their safe but small lives.

Her mind was made up. She must end this wildness, her adolescent indulgence of adventure and escape. She was no child wanting to run away from home.

When Bhisma returned to their room, she burst into tears.

Bhisma was worried, that much was clear. He kept apologizing, explaining that he and Isa had been speaking to Untarto, the friend who had requested help with the secretive surgery, who had arrived early in the morning frazzled with fear. But he seemed devastated by her tears, which made it so hard, because Amba knew that for once she had to keep her mind clear and stick to her resolution. And she did. She told him she had to go back to her uncle and aunt's place, send news to her parents.

"Yes!" she said. "I have parents, in case you've forgotten. I'm not some stray cat you picked up from the street."

"What's happened to you? Something must have happened."

In a voice that she realized was edged with hysteria she told him again she was leaving. She couldn't help herself. "Besides, you keep telling me things are getting out of control and dangerous. You should be agreeing with me on this!"

"Yes, things are getting out of control," Bhisma said, his voice once again turning grave and otherworldly. "Untarto has just told me things are getting rapidly worse. Even he wasn't aware of how porous the pro-Revolution forces really are here in Central Java. Nothing is known of the fate of Major Mulyono and his Battalion L—it seems like they have been forced out of the city, to Boyolali perhaps, where they might or might not gather guerrilla forces.

"Aidit is still around, but he has nothing to hang on to. The Revolutionary Council is practically toothless; it has lasted barely a week. Untarto thinks the Communist Party is woefully ill positioned. They should be leading the National Front, but instead they have become isolated. At the mass action event he organized with CGMI last August, they managed to get thousands of people from all the Nationalism-Religion-Communism parties to fill the streets of Yogyakarta, but only two weeks ago, when the Party tried to organize a similar initiative, they couldn't get one-tenth of the number. Untarto said the Red Berets, those CIA hacks, infiltrated the city disguised as becak drivers, scaring supporters off. We can curse them any way we like, but it won't change a thing. The Army is no match for the Special Forces."

She sat on the edge of the makeshift bed, tears coursing down her cheeks, her thoughts a confusing whirl. Did this moment call for her—again—to put Bhisma's needs, his objectives, first? Why did he keep talking goddamn politics when he forbade people from asking him about politics? Here he was, throwing information at her like the evening news when all she wanted to do was stand her ground, trying to say to him, *Bhisma, listen, this is my hour.*

Bhisma's attention finally found her again, the faraway look leaving his eyes. He cupped her face as he said, "Oh my dear, dear girl, shush now. Let me hold you."

She pulled back from his touch. "No, please, I have to go. How can I explain just disappearing like this? My family will try to find me. Perhaps my aunt and uncle are searching already. If things are as bad as you say, I could be putting them in danger."

Then, like music: "Are you going back to Salwa?"

She had not expected this. Or the desolation in his voice. It was as if the tables had been turned, and now Bhisma was the wounded one.

A long silence passed. When she didn't answer, it was not out of spite.

᠅

Half an hour later they took a becak to the house of Amba's uncle and aunt. Her handbag felt heavy on her lap.

"I know this is probably the best way," Bhisma said, squeezing her hand, sounding genuinely shattered, "but we'll meet again. If we do have to part, surely it is only temporarily. For now stay safe with your uncle and aunt. There is a house on Terban Street I can stay in. Untarto told me it's not wise for me to stay at Bumi Tarung. The house belongs to a sympathetic doctor who is out of town, and it isn't far from Panti Rapih Hospital, where I will perform the surgery. Who knows, you might be able to join me there."

Amba stared at the road ahead. Soon the becak ride would end, and she probably would never see this man again. But he was back on the subject of his passion, things grave and political, explaining how hush-hush his mission was, how the identity of the patient was still unknown to him, how it was likely that the Party had involved Untarto due to his Catholic family ties. "Panti Rapih Hospital is under the bishop's protection," Bhisma said, "and how could a bishop say no to helping a Catholic in need?"

She thought desperately, *Bhisma, please spare me the details. Do I need to have the full political picture of everything that involves you? Shouldn't you be focusing on the fact that life—along with the complexities of our real lives—is driving us apart?*

"Just as you couldn't say no to Untarto because you love him?" she said, aware of the edge in her voice.

She didn't know where it came from, this pettiness. But Bhisma seemed to have missed it. Instead he was gazing at her with the same remote intensity she always saw whenever he was about to convey something of importance, that chillingly self-absorbed look. In that moment she knew she could not change her mind about leaving.

Amba decided resentfully that she hated this Untarto. Why was everybody in Bhisma's life always so larger-than-life, so impressive? His own mother, Gerard, Liz, all those artists whom he met in Berlin, Amrus, Isa, and now Untarto, whose face she failed to catch this morning? Why did she, in contrast, always feel so small and of so little consequence? How could Bhisma devote so much time to his talk of Untarto when he had only minutes left with her?

She remembered seeing her reflection in a shop window that morning, when she had walked out of Bumi Tarung. Noticing how thin she'd become, those dark circles under her eyes, those funny bruises their lovemaking had left on her arms and shins.

So, now. This was what she had decided, and she'd better stick to it. The becak had reached Plengkung Gading, where the beautiful dream had to end. She disengaged her hand from Bhisma's. She was not going to speak. No regrets, no tears, absolutely no tears. She would step out of the becak and leave. But then she heard Bhisma's voice, and the words she so wanted to hear.

"For God's sake. It can't end like this between us."

Ten minutes later, from the street in front of her aunt and uncle's house on Menukan Street, she watched him leave.

"I'm going back to Bumi Tarung to speak to Isa one more time," he had said before climbing back into the becak. "Then I will go to Terban Street and await further instructions."

What comes next? Amba thought as she entered the house. She was told by the maid that her aunt and uncle had gone to a funeral. For a perverse moment she regretted not asking Bhisma in, after the maid had retreated into the kitchen. *If* she'd retreated, *if* she weren't judgmental like everybody else, *if* she could be bribed, *if* she weren't a spy. Anything would have been worth an hour or two of more kisses, more touch, more skin against skin—anything to prolong the dream.

But Bhisma had said it, hadn't he? *We must meet again.* How could he say that and not mean it? In haste, before dismounting the becak, she had told him the only way to contact her was to phone Rien and leave a message; she would go to Rien's twice a day to check. She told him Rien's phone number, and Bhisma had jotted it down on a piece of crumpled paper and put it inside his wallet.

Back in her familiar room, Amba locked the door behind her. She sat on the bed, looking around at her desk, her bookshelf. Sights that used to give her joy, which now seemed lifeless. This room that she used to escape to in order to live had become part of the house's barren, sad quietness. There was no one here who needed anything of her, no one wanting her. Is this what abandonment really meant?

Somewhere inside her a lassitude began rising. She was too beat and sad to fight it. She collapsed onto her bed and lay there, inert. *I have to move,* she thought in a momentary panic. *I have to move to keep myself whole.*

In the minutes, in the hours, that followed she felt that the bed was her only comfort. She imagined that if the bed could speak, it would say, *Think of me as how all your beds will be from now on, as you spend your life in love's barren aftermath. Think of the man you think you will return to lying next to you in your marriage bed, and the next bed you share, and the bed after that—barren beds for the rest of your lives.*

So learn to love me, for myself, in this moment, for I am the one place where you can dream of the man you love, and I won't tell. I am your only heaven between now and your final bed.

Amba managed to pull herself from her inertia when she heard her aunt and uncle return. They were overjoyed to see her, relieved that she was safe, and trustingly accepted her story of staying with a friend.

In the evening, after dinner, she retreated into her room. She wanted to return to the balm of Turgenev, resume her interrupted reading of *On the Eve.* But she knew that would only bring her back to her days in Kediri. Instead, she picked up Pramoedya Ananta Toer's translation of *Of Mice and Men* and began to read. But the words seemed to shift on the page so she soon gave up. She reached for the English poems she had copied out from the library, poems that had filled and fed her soul for the past two semesters, finding and reading over and over certain lines that she needed in order to believe: Neruda, for one, and yes, Wallace Stevens. Always Wallace Stevens. Especially the ones that spoke about twin souls beyond the reach of night.

Then a darker impulse made her reach for Larkin, a poet rejected by her friends as unhappy, even mean. But there were poems of his that, from the very beginning, she couldn't help but love. Despite their being gloomy and anti-love, anti-life. How chillingly apt his words seemed to her now. These, in particular: "This is the first thing / I have understood; / Time is the echo of an axe / Within a wood."

She couldn't bring herself to read another poem, "Home is so Sad," in its entirety, for despite her fear and sorrow of losing Bhisma, she did miss home. She missed her talks with her father by the lake and scooping her mother's famous warm black porridge onto banana leaves and serving them to guests. She even missed her childhood with Ambika and their precious finds, the shells they made up into necklaces, the trinkets silent wells hid, and both of them being in love with the formless promise of everything.

There was, true, some comfort in what ". . . stays as it was left, / Shaped to the comfort of the last to go / As if to win them back," but she was too bereft to stew in difficult truths. She had to push Sylvia Plath away, too, even if her hopeless admiration for the poet, partially a condition of youth, no doubt, never ceased to satisfy her, if too easily and too soon. Right now, what she needed were lines that soothed like a parent.

Midnight struck. Amba turned off the light, hoping dreams would be gentler than this despairing wakefulness. She began to drift into sleep. Plath again, trying to force her lines through: the poem about windows and echoes, a song for the morning.

Startled back to consciousness, she thought fearfully, fitfully, *How speedy it could be, that slide from living to only half living, and from virtual bride to symbolic widow.*

10

Vanished

The next day, Rien had two messages for Amba: *I will call you this after-noon at three.* When that call didn't materialize, another, two hours later: *Sorry. So many interruptions at work. Will call you at seven.*

For the second time that day, Amba walked the twenty minutes from her aunt and uncle's to Rien's. She was moody, a little scared, not knowing what to expect. It was terrible, missing someone like this, as if existing without sight or taste.

When Amba returned to Rien's in the evening, she sat dumbly in the living room. As usual, Rien said very little. She went to the kitchen, came out with a bowl of vermicelli soup, put it on the table in front of Amba, and disappeared into her room.

Bhisma's voice on the phone wasn't all that clear, his tone clipped and matter-of-fact. Clearly, he was not alone. "I'm done with my work here. It was exhausting. I have to return to Kediri the day after tomor-row. Can we meet in the morning?"

The usual doubts crept in: Was it all about the mission for him, with romance on the side being simply one of the perks of revolution? And should she not be making her own calls right now, to her family, to Salwa?

When they met again the next day, returning to the place of their first tryst in front of the Sonobudoyo Museum, Bhisma was accompanied by a young man wearing thick-rimmed spectacles. The man was introduced as Yahya, a CGMI member from the engineering faculty of Res Publica University. Amba, stiffening for a moment at the name of the university, soon relaxed, realizing the young man, an engineer, in all likelihood wasn't an acquaintance of Salwa's, who, like her, went to Gadjah Mada University before taking up his post in Surabaya.

"Yahya is my eyes and ears in Yogyakarta," Bhisma said. "He knows the city inside and out."

True to this description, Yahya took them to a small eatery on Trikora Street, one that nobody seemed interested in. He stopped at the door, saying, "I have to make some phone calls. I will be back here for you in half an hour."

Amba and Bhisma settled down at a corner table. She almost couldn't bear to look at his face. He reached underneath the table to put his hand on hers and said, "You are so beautiful. I miss you too much." When Amba didn't respond, he leaned close, saying gently, "Can't I miss you? Can't you look at me?"

She met his eyes, and seeing how the restaurant's faint lighting deepened their gold-green and bronzed his skin, she forgot all her resolutions and forgave him everything. When Bhisma asked if she had seen Salwa, she shook her head. When he asked whether she had tried to contact him, again she shook her head, intensely aware of his fingers interlacing with hers.

When she found her voice she asked how the operation had gone. He had told her nothing on the phone except that it was done.

"Yes," he said, heaving a sigh, which Amba recognized as something he often did when he was about to explain something difficult. "The surgery was successful, under the circumstances, but the patient won't live long. I tried to let Untarto know, but he couldn't be reached. No one knows where he is. Thankfully the doctors on my team had a contact to report to about the patient's condition."

"So who did you operate on? Someone famous? A Party bigwig?" She only asked for the sake of expediency. She didn't even want to know.

And it must have been obvious from her tone, because Bhisma didn't respond, and she wondered if he was angry, thinking her flippant and spoiled. Yet it might be that there was a problem, a huge one. Something women were not privy to; not her kind anyway.

Then there it was, the statement she'd been longing to hear, pried from his tongue, no doubt, by the shock of separation: "I've been thinking. Let's go away, you and I, after I'm done with the surgery. Somewhere safe. Jakarta perhaps, or Bandung." But then, almost as soon as he said it, the eagerness in his voice evaporated as he continued flatly, "But you are determined to go back to Salwa."

Something rose in her. "Come *on*. I can throw this back at you. Aren't you determined to go back to Kediri? Aren't you tied to your contract? Why do you always make it sound as though you're the noble one, making all the sacrifices, and I'm somehow incidental—just something on your way?"

"Sorry," he said. "Sorry."

There must have been tears in her eyes or something stupid like that because he then softened. "Look. Sorry. I didn't mean to. It's just that everything seems so . . . polluted right now.

"When I'm working, meeting with my comrades with barely enough time to eat, drink, even bathe, without you there with me it is as if all I touch bites and infects me. Even the water seems contaminated. But someone has to do the stitching."

She tried to focus on the fact that the day before he had performed a major operation that presumably took many hours, sapping his energy, knowing as he stitched his patient back together that the life beneath his hands still might not hold on for long.

"You're with me now," she said, deciding to wait before bringing Kediri up again, trying to rise above it all. "Can't you, for once—"

"I won't be away for long. A week, at the most." Again, that sudden inattention to what she had just said. "I'll try to find a doctor to replace me. It won't be easy, but it isn't impossible. Then I'll come back to Yogyakarta for you. I'll go with you to Salwa and ask him to give you up."

The shock of his last line had barely registered when the waiter arrived to take their order. After which she barely heard what Bhisma requested—some fried rice, was it, or fried noodles—thinking how it didn't matter. They would share whatever they had, for that's what couples do.

Later Amba would recall how right then, in that depressing eatery, the present willed itself into her mind through a Gumarang Orchestra song playing on the radio: something about a sad twilight, a twilight in which everybody died. Then someone changed the station to National Radio, where the last strain of a choir was heard, an old, feisty independence song . . . *The patriots of the proclamation, I am your protector* . . . Remembering that apparently irrelevant detail, she would realize that there are moments in life when the future is hastily articulated and thus sealed, because it is the present that rules, and the present always changes, often so fast it can hardly be experienced.

The fried rice they shared was swimming in oil, probably the reason no one else came into that restaurant. But she couldn't care less. She was walking on air. In her giddiness she began to babble, unleashing a torrent of thoughts, anything that would not ruin what he had just said, the proof that mattered to her as much as his love: that their future was not going to be the future spelled out in *The Mahabharata*, that their lives would not mirror the myth. Meanwhile Bhisma's hand was stroking her knee underneath the table—emboldened, perhaps, by the moment.

It was at that point that Yahya entered the restaurant. "I'm sorry I'm early, but you have to go," he said to Bhisma with panic in his voice. "I have a message for you from Untarto. If you're still going back to Kediri, to the hospital, you better leave this afternoon, before three. I will have a car ready. Best not to take the train, he said."

Clearly it was more an order than a request. She felt the sudden wrongness in the air, like the unclean taste of refried oil in her mouth. It was astounding, how Bhisma leapt up, as if to a military instruction, but even more shocking was the way he suddenly pulled her to him and kissed her on the mouth, in front of Yahya. Then he extracted a wad of cash from his wallet and left it on the table to pay for the food.

There was no time to take her aside to follow up his earth-shattering statement of minutes earlier, no suggestion of how or when they would meet again. Instead he and the younger man spoke quietly, urgently, after which Bhisma told her that he had to make haste, and Yahya would take her wherever she needed to go.

"You know where to call me if you need to," he said to her before he hailed a becak.

She waited for more, for the reaffirmation of his love, but the becak sped away as if here, in this city, nothing waited for anyone or anything anymore.

Of course there was no way for her to know that in only a few more days, beside that same road, across from that very restaurant, another separation awaited her. One that would leave a gaping wound that neither Bhisma nor time would be able to close or dress, and an infection she would live with for the rest of her life.

The following hours beat upon her like a hammer. Everything—the weather, the food, the news—turned nasty. Forty hours after Bhisma left to return to the hospital in Kediri, Yahya suddenly appeared at the doorstep of her aunt and uncle's house, telling her aunt he was Amba's classmate at the university.

The news he whispered to her, the news he wanted her to convey to Bhisma over the phone, was this: Untarto had been kidnapped. A group of unidentified people had taken him from the house of a local union official. Yahya told her to tell Bhisma that while he believed the union official was the main target, Untarto was taken away in the back of a truck after, according to witnesses, putting up a fight and being beaten to within an inch of his life.

When Amba asked why Yahya hadn't called Bhisma at the hospital, Yahya said, a little evasively, "It could arouse suspicion."

Questions crowded her mind: Why, for instance, had Untarto had a say in Bhisma's itinerary? Why, indeed, did Bhisma have to bolt to Kediri that very afternoon just because Untarto said so? How exactly were Yahya, Untarto, and Bhisma connected? How exactly could a phone call between Yahya and Bhisma arouse suspicion? But she knew better than to press for answers. And she was worried for Bhisma, how this news might affect him.

"Take me on your bike," she said. "I will call Kediri from my friend's house."

Yahya rode like a madman, rising on a pedal, then sinking back with erect intensity. Sitting on the rack behind him, Amba couldn't understand why the news jarred her so. She hadn't liked what she'd seen of Untarto, but wasn't he one of Bhisma's closest friends? Someone who meant a lot to him, and whose death would cause him to grieve and perhaps even compel him to come back to Yogyakarta, and eventually to her? Then in the heat and the whir of the ride she remembered how clandestine the surgery had been. In fact everything to do with this damn Untarto had been hush-hush. No, things couldn't be good. She had to know more before taking any action. Realizing she couldn't risk Rien being part of whatever was happening, she said to Yahya, "No, it's no good going to my friend's. Take me to the telecommunications office."

Fifteen minutes later, Bhisma's voice was in her ear. She was aware of his effort to keep his cool. What was it that she heard in his voice? Sorrow? Fear? Anger?

"I'll be back in Yogyakarta tonight," he said. "I just have to sort out things with Dr. Suhadi."

From his voice Amba wondered if he had expected it. His friend, his much admired friend, possibly dead. So horribly, so soon.

For once she let it go, his seeming indifference to her own voice, its naked, shameful longing.

❧

Meanwhile, Yahya was talking to someone in another phone booth. When he came out he was shaking. One of his comrades confirmed that Untarto was indeed dead. His body was found in an abandoned building near Fort Vredeburg, his skull cracked open.

❧

The next day, as Yahya escorted Amba to the house where Bhisma was staying on Terban Street, they saw soldiers on both sides of the street, moving in packs, standing in impatient rows as a blur of armed youth groups unrolled posters and set up placards.

"Everybody's here. Everybody, bar none," Yahya whispered, listing all the different groups' political acronyms, the stupid legacy of the times, *do we even care.* But at that moment it did matter, it mattered whether GMNI was there and PMKRI was not, whether there were more Banser or more HMI.

Amba thought it strange how all the while Yahya kept holding up his hand in front of his face, as if trying to blot out the sun, even though he wore wraparound dark glasses. Only then did she realize he didn't want to be seen, because he was a mark, he was a target, how could he not be. Then the details hit her: those throbbing neck veins, the heat in his eyes.

So he, too, was scared, and that somehow made her own fear permissible.

As they entered the living room of the quiet house near Panti Rapih, Bhisma was pacing the room like a caged animal. It was as if he was in a zone of anger that eclipsed everything except for what was too big to contain within himself.

It took some getting used to his presence, his nearness, the morning light bleaching everything white, his face in this strange house, another world in the same history lesson. It was like being plunged into an icy stream on the hottest day of the year.

He spun when he heard her voice. Strode straight to her, scooped her up, kissed her like mad. All the right gestures, the right urgency. The Bhisma she liked and missed. But she immediately sensed the discord, the duality of him giving vent to everything but her, everything she wanted him to rein in. Hearing Yahya sob behind them, the valiant, unperturbable, go-to guy Yahya, she knew the mood would change, and he would despise himself for it. Then quietness reigned.

Someone had to say something, and the someone who spoke was the public Bhisma, the Bhisma who had to play a role for others, detached, unsentimental, the good doctor. There was no Amba and no love to be conceded in this persona. That Bhisma was for behind closed doors, for rooms with no mirror to offer reflection.

And now that morphing had occurred, almost as fast as she intuited it: he told them in a flat, slightly defeated tone how he returned to Yogyakarta in a car loaned by the ever-generous Dr. Suhadi Projo. Bhisma's voice warmed, briefly, as he thanked God for Dr. Suhadi's driver and how they had bested all the civilian and military roadblocks along the way, thanks to the magical words "Sono Walujo Hospital" adorning the old Dodge, along with the stethoscope Bhisma wore around his neck. More thrilling drama, such as only politics could produce.

She disliked herself so much at that moment, but she disliked Bhisma even more. When he walked toward a door that led to the kitchen, she didn't offer to help. He hadn't asked if they wanted a drink, but he returned with coffee anyway, three cupfuls of it. She ignored the uneasy call of convention—wasn't he European, after all, and Europeans were used to equality between the sexes—and accepted the black muck that was handed to her.

But the problem was Yahya. He was the liability. He was too voluble, his words spilling as if he couldn't keep them in.

"I knew something was wrong with Untarto. He was really down these past few days. That's the problem, you see. He always believed that being a leader meant never showing you were scared. Never showing you've lost hope. 'A *commandante* has no right to his true feelings,' he kept saying. But, like me, he didn't—couldn't—always trust what the Party people said. Those CDB guys in Yogyakarta always looked down on us, preferring to put their faith on those People's Youth shitheads. Look at them now! Assholes.

"Untarto told me that Chairman Aidit, safely tucked away in his hiding place, had told his confidantes that he refused to work with CDB because they're so fucking hopeless, because they always focus on other Party organs and have no clear strategy whatsoever. And yet, he was such a hypocrite, because to others in the Party he said, 'Let's not get petty. Let's work with the CDB if they are willing to work with us. Unity is the only way. We just have to wait out this period of conflict. When our enemies are strong, we retreat, but when they are weak again, that's when we attack.' I mean, Aidit's starting to sound like Sukarno! That's what you get for sleeping with each other for too long. It all makes sense now."

"But they look very strong right now," Amba said.

"Yes, but that's because they're in attack mode," Yahya said doggedly, looking more and more attractive with every indignation, with every word of protest. He was wiry, he was surprisingly muscular, he was a force field unto himself.

"Brother, what do you think? We must work together. It's the only way," he said, looking at Bhisma, who was just as oblivious to her heat, her swellings. "I just hope they know what they're doing, our comrades in the union who believe we're finally consolidating. A week ago Untarto . . . A week ago he said there were plans for us to rearm."

"How did he propose we do that?" Bhisma asked.

"Apparently last week some of the union guys managed to break into the Air Force armory. They got out with quite a load of handsome souvenirs."

Bhisma was about to respond, but this new Yahya, this Yahya unleashed, was too much even for Bhisma. He stood up. His urgency wouldn't wait.

"I have to go," he said. "Please don't call the last number you used to contact me. I'll be on the move. Here, use this," Yahya said, hastily writing a phone number on a piece of paper before shoving it into Bhisma's hand. Then he left.

Silence, finally. This time Amba didn't wait, neither for the familiar return of demureness, nor for his cue—their kiss was long and fiery and rough.

And when that was over, when the breathing had calmed: "What was it that you told me once?" she asked. "Something to do with you and boundaries?"

"What's that?" he said, his face momentarily confused. "I'm not sure of anything I've said anymore. I guess I was talking about Europe. There I felt that those boundaries, if not my own, which are irresolute at best, then of the ideal Communist, were firm: in the case of defeat, the revolutionaries had to admit that they have lost, then go die in the sanctuary of the Party machinery. You don't break ranks, go AWOL. But here it is different. Here the butchers get to decide our fate."

"So why is Yahya so hopeful still?"

"Who knows," he said, sounding exhausted. "My friend Untarto is dead, and he was our guiding light. Maybe his death is some kind of warning. Maybe I'm wrong, maybe Yahya is wrong, maybe we're all wrong, there is no hope."

"Maybe the real question is," she said, "what if you're not wrong? Rien told me the other day that no one knows what's happening. Who's strong, who's not. The whole city is just waiting. Nothing makes sense. The enemies of CGMI and the Party are also preparing themselves for an inevitable clash, and Rien's PKMRI friends, all scared shitless of the People's Youth, are apparently in training day in, day out. They're arming themselves, too. God knows how they've managed."

He didn't even believe in God; at least, he never spoke of God. *But does it matter?* Amba thought. Grief and faith often look the same. And then, because he didn't reply, she said, "Bhisma, what will happen to us if civil war does break out?"

He still did not trust himself to speak. His face was inscrutable, a patchwork from another world. "It's bleak, I know," he said quietly. "But you *are* going back to Salwa, are you not? So shouldn't you be worrying about what will happen to you and him?"

But lovers are lovers. They didn't make it beyond that room as they pulled each other down to the floor, called by that urgency of skin against skin. She never had a problem with this part. The problem was always afterward, postfact. That high-pitched anxiety, for instance, rousing like an ogre after a nap.

First she chided Bhisma for his earlier statement about Salwa, saying how absurd it was for him to think that she would be returning to him, after everything that was said and done. Then she had to mention again how he was taking forever to decide on a plan, on their loss of momentum.

"Unless, of course, you only desire me because I'm like no one you've ever been with before? Is it true you only came back to Yogyakarta because of Untarto? Had it nothing at all to do with me? Did you love him so much that you didn't mind sacrificing your duty in Kediri for him, but not for me? Is it because I don't deserve such selfless love because I'm still here? Because I haven't died?"

When Bhisma failed to defend himself she added bitterly, "What do you gain by coming back here to Yogyakarta? It's too late. He's already dead. There is no way to prove to him how devoted you are."

Where did it come from, this cruelty? She was doing herself a disservice, of that she was aware, but somewhere within her there was a loose screw she had no idea how to fix. She looked at him, not sure what she was pleading for. Rebuke or lenience. Rage or compassion. For he was certainly capable of rage, she knew that, too, and it was her luck that that capacity was buried under years of hard training in patience.

Instead of lashing back at her, he sighed. "It's true, Untarto is no more," he said, his voice suddenly so old and denuded. "But he would have wanted us to persevere for our ideal, which is bigger than him. And that is exactly what I'm trying to do: not admit defeat. You may have no faith in me, and rightly so. You probably think me delusional because, at the end of the day, you also think that I'm a bourgeois boy constrained by the limits and boundaries of advantage. You probably think someone like me incapable of a life dedicated only to the Revolution. But to refuse to succumb is something else. It takes a different faith."

But his timing, as usual, was off. Amba felt herself withdraw, annoyed anew at his unbecoming bout of self-pity. Self-pity that surely *was* a bourgeois trait. She wanted to say, *You have faith. Congratulations. But are you not putting words into my mouth? Are you not, in fact, saying what you think about yourself? Are you not saying these things precisely because you're* not *dedicated to the Revolution?*

Not surprisingly, he went on. "I know any doctor may find himself in a position where his choice could mean life or death. Each moment branches, each moment changes. I'm not the sort who fights in the street or shoots from behind a barricade. I operate differently. Yes, perhaps I'm the sort who gets defeated in the end. But if I don't do anything, in the end my life would mean nothing. I would be a doctor who knows how to heal but chooses not to, and there's nothing worse than that.

"Perhaps you see me as someone who left his country for too long, who has come home thinking he can see everything so clearly—a country of blood and tears, a country that cannot make promises—and thinking he can fix it. But that's not what happened. I came home to a changed world, and I quickly realized with every passing day that this country has been overrun by butchers."

This self-justification, was it to mask his sorrow? She just sat there, listening.

"You wanted to know the identity of my mystery patient. Well, it was Untarto's father. Not his biological father, but his spiritual one. A man who has been a leading light in the Communist ideology and who invested in Untarto all his hopes for the future. Now Untarto is dead at the hands of the butchers, and the ideology he has promoted for so long may share the same fate. That is how our world has changed. That is why my power to heal feels useless sometimes. I can't make a difference. I can't make it meaningful."

Amba felt nauseous; it might have been the coffee. She took deep breaths. After her earlier outburst, how little she felt now.

"Look," he said, softening. "I know this is hard for you, and you're right: I don't have a plan yet. While CGMI is still so divided, and those close to Untarto are still sitting targets, I may have to remain here. If you feel your own safety is compromised, if you can't wait any longer, go. Go if you must."

Amba just sat there. How silent the ruins were. And how surprising that her tearlessness seemed to unleash something in Bhisma. And it finally came, the closest to rage she'd witnessed in her lover.

"You may not see it now," he said. "But deep down you know that your Salwa will save you. That man whom you've told me is so noble and kind, who will give you a new home, a family, *respectability*—whatever that means. That blind, deluded Salwa, who can't even see that all this, your postponing of your marriage for a year, your daring flight to Kediri to make yourself useful—yes, even you being with me—is all about running away from him. But if you think he's worth it, that he's the safer bet, go back to him. Don't let me stop you."

Back in her room at her aunt and uncle's house later that afternoon, Amba dug out her tattered copy of *The Mahabharata* and read the part where Bhisma refused Amba. She stared them down, those two pages, stared at them long and hard, so hard as to crush them. *I would read no more poetry until I've killed our story, mine and his. Killed it with the bare fists of my will.*

At around 7:00 p.m., there was a knock on her door.

"A Dr. Rashad is here to see you." It was Amba's aunt, her voice tentative and strange.

Amba rushed out, partly to forestall any guesses her aunt or uncle might make, partly to stop Bhisma from encroaching further on the part of her life that was not his. It happened too fast, passing too close to the hideous statue of the Garuda lamp beside which her uncle sat reading in the living room, veering away and slicing her knee on the sharp corner of a glass table, the blood welling, her cry of distress. Bhisma, descending like a being from another realm, with that smell of wood and that blue brilliance. Bhisma, kneeling beside her, as her aunt and uncle rushed to get towels, whispering the lie he'd told to get to this point—as a doctor based in Kediri he had met Amba and wanted the address of a mutual friend. Bhisma, speaking like a lovesick boy, as he grabbed one of her aunt's precious embroideries from the table to stanch her wound: "I went crazy, seeing you leave. I shouldn't have said what I said. I'm such a louse. Forgive me."

That he found her by asking Yahya was obvious. That he couldn't stay, once he'd cleaned, disinfected, and bound the cut on Amba's leg using the water, lotion, and bandages that Amba's aunt, ever a practical woman, had hurriedly gathered, was also obvious. Like everyone in her family, her aunt and uncle were besotted with Salwa, and soon they would start asking questions. Bhisma might have been desperate, he might have been European, but this—this *propriety*—he got it, he recognized its clarion call, even he had to observe it if he truly cared about her. So he told the worried elderly couple, "It's just a teeny-weeny cut, Pak, Bu. Nothing to worry about," and helped Amba to her feet. "And I will see Dr. Rashad out," Amba said, quickly.

Safely out of earshot, and clearly suppressing his urge to touch her, Bhisma muttered, rather inanely, "Tomorrow afternoon? Can we meet at the same restaurant on Trikora Street? 5:00 p.m.? From there we will go together to a memorial for Untarto. My CGMI friends are organizing it, in the small auditorium behind the Baperki Building at Res Publica University. I have to be there. Just that one commitment, mein Liebling. Please bear with me. Starting tomorrow we'll have a lifetime for me to make all this up to you."

∞

An early-morning temper was starting to become a pattern. It was no different the next morning, when Amba was searching for a particular red blouse, one she'd had specially made for a musical event on campus. There was a sense of things happening too fast, but at least life was moving and was no longer the agonizing stasis she had lived on some nights past. The search for the red blouse was stupid, she knew. But it might please Bhisma's CGMI friends that she had made such a choice, the color symbolizing their ideals, to show her acknowledgment of the sacrifice of their fallen comrade. She wasn't sure why she wanted to please them. If nothing else, she thought, she would at least please Bhisma.

She found the blouse, and it was pleasing enough to the eye, judging from the smiles around the breakfast table. Amba's aunt said the color suited her, then enigmatically commented on how handsome her doctor visitor was and asked where he could be from with that name, Rashad, a Sumatran name, surely? Salwa had better be careful, her uncle offered, as if complicity was something you could simply will in order for it to take shape. How little they knew.

Too fast, too, was the way she barely skimmed the letters that arrived for her that day as though in stern reprimand, her heart racing, her eyes seeing but refusing to read. Ambika wrote, "Bapak and Ibu are worried. Please send us news. Hope you are safe," while Salwa, uncharacteristically brief, almost telegram-like, simply wrote: "Beloved, I hope you are well. I will come to Yogyakarta next week."

Too fast, this dismissal of things once loved, and this denial of how desire destroys.

❧

Politics once more reigned.

As Amba entered the restaurant, her heart sank at the sight of Bhisma and Isa deep in conversation with several other men. Could she and Bhisma never be alone in public? She nodded at her lover and smiled weakly as Isa stood up to shake her hand. But her red shirt appeared to work its magic. She wasn't sure what passions she stoked, but whatever they were the men seemed wildly approving.

"Welcome, Miss Red," she heard one say, rather unimaginatively, as she sat awkwardly next to Bhisma. When she felt his arm slide around her waist she began to relax, thinking, *Good, this won't be one of those nightmare conversations between several men and one woman where the woman feels like an outcast.* But Bhisma was distracted. He was nodding at Isa, urging him to continue what he'd been saying before Amba came.

"So you see, those generals in Jakarta are very smart," Isa said and sighed. "How can Chairman Aidit match them? He keeps saying he's got the People's Army behind him. But who is he kidding? What army? What people? Soon the Special Forces will completely overrun Yogyakarta. They have already penetrated Semarang and met no resistance there. What I don't understand is how we got into this mess in the first place."

Bhisma looked at Amba. Unexpectedly he bent and kissed her on the cheek. "What do you think, mein Liebling? Are you as pessimistic?"

Joyful at being so clearly acknowledged by him in front of his comrades and included in their discussion, she simply shook her head. All she could think was that soon none of this would matter. Soon there would be all these *mein Liebling*s uttered in public always.

After they paid for their drinks the group headed gloomily out to the street to walk the short distance to the Baperki Building. A huge crowd was gathering, clearly and loudly anti-Communist, milling in front of the post office, protected by their soldier comrades. There was some serious chanting going on. As they tried to make their way through, Amba heard Isa say to Bhisma, "Can you believe that shit? They're saying they'll take over the university."

They reached the courtyard in front of the building where Untarto's memorial was to be held. Two rows of men dressed in black stood guard, a menacing presence, like shadows taking their places in a history book that was yet to be written. The crowd was swelling. Bhisma, holding Amba's hand, pulled her in his wake toward the group of mourners who had gathered in front of a tall, craggy, brooding door that opened to another courtyard. Yahya emerged from the throng to greet them, looking a little ridiculous in an oversized army jacket. Despite herself, Amba was relieved to see him.

In no time they were ushered with the other mourners into a small auditorium, already packed with CGMI and Perhimi members. Isa disappeared into the crowd, and for a few minutes all eyes were on Amba and Bhisma. They were introduced around as Dr. Rashad, a good friend of the dearly departed, and "*Mbak* Amba"—nothing more, nothing less, the *Mbak* indicating clearly that she was not married, and the absence of a more formal introduction indicating she was, well, not much of anything. It was during this moment of self-pity, with Bhisma ever more distracted by the many comrades who greeted him, that Amba sought refuge with Yahya. As she was chatting with him, she saw a woman walk confidently up to Bhisma, a woman who she quickly realized was outrageously beautiful.

"Dr. Rashad?" Amba heard her say as she extended her hand. "I'm Rinjani, a close friend of Untarto's. He was very fond of you and often spoke to me about you."

A woman to distrust, for sure, whose aura was cold, as though her veins were made of metal. But her beauty was indeed extraordinary, and Amba quickly felt diminished by its impact. That smile! Those perfect white teeth!

Amba tried to ignore the exchange between the woman and Bhisma, for fear that something in Bhisma's reaction would justify her insecurity. But how could she not see how splendid they looked together? Even their heights complemented one another, the woman being only a little taller than Amba but very lean and elegant. It was too much, those big eyes, those long legs, those firm and rounded breasts and that perfect skin, the way she wore her sleeveless maroon shirt, casually and seductively, the straight-backed, confident way she stood, the way she met Bhisma's gaze squarely and spoke with quiet authority. She looked like a woman who deserved a man like Bhisma. She looked like his match. Amba hated her. And seeing Bhisma's warm response as he shook the offered hand, she hated him.

How was it possible that they had never met? Or was this woman the reason Bhisma was so attached to Untarto? The reason he was prepared to drop everything, including his responsibilities in Kediri, to come to this memorial service?

"He was your great friend, too. I'm so, so sorry," Amba heard the woman say, her sickeningly slender hand still in Bhisma's grip, a slight quiver adding even more charm to her firm yet alluring voice. "But he lives on, *bung*. He lives on."

Mercifully, not a minute later, the crowd was asked to be seated, although there were only a few rows of seats and at least four hundred people in the room. Bhisma made a production of seeming reluctant to take one, but he nodded at Amba to sit, which she did, and then she heard him suggest to Beauty Queen in a more elaborate way that she also take a seat. Amba saw Rinjani smile and shake her head. Not wanting to run the risk of the two of them standing close through the memorial service, she called to Bhisma, begging him, rather pathetically, to sit next to her. Was it a flash of annoyance she saw on his face before he finally sat beside her? Amba blushed. How childish she must appear.

The air in the auditorium was still and oppressive. It stank like hot lead. Glancing around, Amba realized she wasn't the only one to think of wearing red; there were flashes of it throughout the room. Looking down at the dust-covered floor she could make out the faint lines of what used to be a badminton court. Along the walls were stacks of bricks, drums, iron beams. It all made the place feel makeshift, and bare lighting gave everything a slightly sugary look. On a door near the back of the room a wooden board said: "Universitas Res Publica."

Around 7:30 p.m. someone switched off the lights and lit candles. A man made an announcement, but the acoustics were hopeless, with too much echo, and there seemed to be no microphone. Amba couldn't focus on anything except Bhisma's presence next to her, loose fitting but real, like a favorite borrowed jacket. The room was noisy, strain upon strain of voices thickening, flooding over each other. A choir broke into song to their right. Amba didn't recognize the tune, but the lyrics were clear: *The blood of the people flows . . . everywhere people are poor and suffering . . .* Before she knew it the people who were sitting also rose to sing. Some, including Bhisma and Isa, hammered the air with their left fists. As she stood with them mouthing the words all she could think was, *Who do people in the room think I am? The girlfriend of this magnificent man next to me? A CGMI member? Does Rinjani think I'm Bhisma's girlfriend? Wouldn't she be curious to know? Is she jealous? Does she wish she were me?*

The choir stopped, and a woman recited a poem, by the garbled sound of it, her voice barely rising above the din. All Amba could make out was: ". . . let us endure this separation, for I am forging the days, clearing forests, and walking in night's wake, all in the name of our children, children to be raised, children browned by the sun . . ." Despite her distaste for large crowds, everyone acting like a single entity, Amba found herself moved.

Her gaze traveled up the wall to Untarto's portrait: the beloved's face captured, immortalized, looking benignly at all of them. It seemed a fitting tribute, in this smoky, sweltering, anything-but-serene room. On the verge of clapping when the woman finished reading, she caught herself in time, remembering these people were mourning, hugging and folding themselves into their silence.

"Why is there no microphone?" she heard Bhisma whisper to the young man next to him.

"Ever since we recaptured this building, we've had only one generator," the young man replied, "and its wattage is low."

"What do you mean? This building was recaptured?"

The young man looked at Bhisma incredulously, as if to say, *What planet, pray, do you come from?* But he explained, "Around two weeks ago parts of the campus, including this place, were attacked and occupied by forces of the extreme right. Somehow the Regiment Commando just allowed that to happen. But being complete dunces the occupiers slackened their vigilance, so we, with the help of members of the People's Youth and Perhimi, managed to reoccupy the building."

A man stood on the raised platform underneath Untarto's portrait and began a speech. It was more of a call to action than a eulogy. Suddenly Bhisma's name rang in the air. Amba watched her lover walk toward the portrait, feeling as if she was seeing him anew, like that first instant when she saw him emerge from behind the tree. The room was quiet, as if the mourners were struck by his height, his bearing. His beauty.

His speech was short, and his voice, like the others, was barely audible. She heard the name *Che Guevara* spoken, followed by a quote, something about oppression and injustice. Amba couldn't help it but there she was, relentlessly impressed. It must have been glorious, to say nothing of unexpected, to be the center of so much respectful attention, and yet Bhisma took it all in his stride. As if he was born to such princely surprises.

After three more people spoke, Rinjani, of all people, was invited to say some words. The room seemed to still as it had when Bhisma took to the podium. She was a blazing goddess—who cared what words came from her mouth? *How unfair,* Amba thought, staring at this woman, *not only to have been created that way but to be the one every man adored.* And then came that pathetic thought: *Why was I never the beautiful one, like this woman, like my sisters? If I were so beautiful surely I could change my fate?* The rising whispers among the men were no help: "Is she CGMI?" "Heard she's from Jakarta," "Party member?" "She's too beautiful to be a Communist," "God*damn.*" Gross, braying laughter. Yet this was what it sounded like, a man's world. All these men not listening to Rinjani's words about her friend Untarto because they were too busy ravishing her with their lustful gaze.

After nearly three hours the memorial was blessedly over. Amba itched to leave, but there was still the wake—the social hour. She decided to walk around a bit, to give Bhisma some space after chaining him to the chair. Ten minutes later she was relieved to see him and Isa motion her to leave the auditorium. She began to follow them, but suddenly Rinjani was in her way, saying to Bhisma, "That quote from Che, it was perfect. Thank you."

Bhisma stood smiling and seeming unsure of what to say. Or did he just want to linger in her presence?

Suddenly she heard Yahya's voice behind her, like a guardian angel. "You should leave now. There are People's Youth members outside, and they've been instructed to defend the university against the right-wing forces. It won't be pretty."

Meanwhile, Amba was looking in desperation from Bhisma to Rinjani and back to Bhisma again. They were chatting now.

"Yes," she said, "but Bhisma . . . He doesn't seem ready to leave yet."

Taking stock of the situation, Yahya ducked his head and whispered, "The three of you, Bhisma and Isa, too, must go now."

"Are you sure it is so bad?" she asked Yahya. "The students, aren't they just HMI, the Student Alliance? Surely they won't attack?"

"We'll be lucky if HMI is the only force we're facing," said Yahya, unconsciously fingering the blade of the dagger hanging from his waist, as if testing it for strength. "I was just told that there is an entire troop from Regiment Commando 72 out there. A Special Forces platoon as well. If that's the case, we're toast. That's why our side has been trying to amass as many people as we can since this morning, so we appear stronger than we actually are." Yahya's eyes fixed on Rinjani as if, like all the other men, he couldn't help himself. "Who is she?"

Amba, trying to look disinterested, said, "A friend of Untarto's, is she not?"

"El Commandante never mentioned her," Yahya said with a snort. A generous gesture of solidarity, entirely unmerited.

Emotion is embarrassing, but she could already feel the sting at the corners of her eyes. "I'll make sure we leave now," she told Yahya unsteadily.

She waved at Bhisma, catching his eye. Smiling, he waved back, seeming to understand what she wanted. Her determination faltered when she saw Rinjani place her hand on Bhisma's arm, as if to detain him again, but to Amba's immense relief Bhisma continued toward her. There he was, her lover, not anyone else's, weaving through the crowd to be at her side. He was hers, and she loved him. How could she have doubted him?

Suddenly, deafening noise blared from the direction of the courtyard, and the sound of the national anthem blasted into the room. The crowd left at the memorial service froze. The overhead fluorescent lamps stuttered into life for a few seconds, then died. The room looked bruised, a sickly green.

The sound of an explosion—or was it a bomb falling?—shattered the air. The room shook. Amba heard screams; people started to run. Bhisma reached for her and pulled her against him. "Wait," he hissed. "Wait for the second bomb. That's the rule." He wrapped his arms around her as the rattle of gunfire bounced off the concrete walls, and dozens of uniformed men charged into the building, brandishing their rifles.

Amba's ears whistled as she saw the mourners respond, seizing chairs, boxes, bricks—anything they could find to throw. Blood spattered, people screamed, a crush of people tried to make for the rear exit. Somewhere in the commotion, she saw Yahya, not running but crouching with his knife, his face turned savage. Others too, familiar faces, armed, feral, poised for the inevitable face-off. Then somebody shouted, "Grenade!" and Bhisma pulled her down, her shoulder smashing against the floor.

Amid the strafing she saw something that looked like Yahya's army jacket fly through the air. Was Yahya hit? Where was Bhisma? Was he the man she vaguely saw staggering toward where she'd last seen Yahya?

She struggled to her feet. In the thick cloud of grime it was impossible to breathe, impossible to think, impossible to remove from her mind the image of Yahya's flying, misshapen jacket. Her face was coarse with soot, tears, and blood. She cried out for Bhisma, but her voice strained. Thinking she heard him calling, she ran through the dust, stumbling over debris and soft, yielding bundles, just one of a swarm of terrified people wanting only to stay alive.

A young man wearing a bandanna grabbed her wrist. She followed him out a door, buffeted by scores of people, scared, scarred, stumbling, afraid of losing sight of him as he led them along a winding path through the blundering confusion. Then, inexplicably, the young man stopped, telling them all to disperse. Amba saw an alleyway that looked safe enough. Unthinkingly, she dashed its length, ending up in a courtyard behind an unfamiliar building. To the left and to the right of her, people were panting, wailing, getting aggressive with one another.

"We're trapped!" someone shouted. "The place is overrun! By tomorrow we'll all be dead!"

Not one face was familiar except for the face of the bright moon that hung above them, its brutal light exposing them all.

Amba felt nauseous from the stench of blood and gunpowder.

Suddenly, a moment of clarity. Of realizing that Bhisma was not with her.

BOOK 3

Amba and Adalhard

Yogyakarta, 1965

11

The Third Man

When a woman wavers between two men—the one she didn't get and the one who didn't get her—she usually encounters a third. This is how the third man came into Amba Kinanti's life and how his story should be told.

For Amba it started with dreams both foul and fair.

In the days following Bhisma's disappearance, her heart sick with sorrow, Amba started having vivid dreams. Maudlin, abusive nightmares with baby-burning witches and gods with deformed cocks. Nostalgic images of Kadipura, of her parents and her sisters and her corner on the porch where they took their tea in the afternoons, the lakeside where her father and she often sat, her father opening *The Mahabharata*.

Once, Bhisma and Salwa appeared together in her dream, as the book dictated. But instead of taking up arms and hacking at each other, they were sitting down under a vast banyan tree, the way warriors always do, talking about great revolutions and ideas that would transform the world. Meanwhile, she was peering at them from behind another tree, eavesdropping. She could hear every word. The Amba of this dream looked sad, disheveled, and old, and her purpose was vindictive: to aim her arrow at Salwa's heart. She would wait for the right time and kill Salwa first and then herself, and then the gods could have a field day blaming one another for the loss of a very important thread in their celestial narrative. She, Amba, would be the noble princess who exited the world so that Bhisma, the ultimate warrior-healer, the man who saved lives, would prevail. Because he must. She was going to take Salwa with her to end his suffering in the world, his and Bhisma's, from everything that she had done.

Suddenly, in the dream, she saw Bhisma lean toward Salwa, the man who was supposed to be his rival, his fiercest foe, and say, "She doesn't know it yet, but I must leave her. I must leave so she will have a future."

The horror of that dream had woken her. The horror of how in the dream Amba, on hearing those words, had changed her aim in a sick split instant, and the desolate sound of Bhisma's groan before his body hit the earth.

Some nightmares were grimmer. In one she saw her father dashing through the dust in a smoky battlefield, amid the ringing sound of gunfire and the swish of arrows, soldiers screaming and falling around him. He had in his trembling hands an open page from *The Mahabharata*, something he seemed to want to get rid of but couldn't. Soon a naked woman who looked like Rinjani, a perfection of limbs and breasts, appeared. She began to devour soldiers, both dead and alive.

In another, Bhisma and Salwa appeared in her room, their faces dewy and transformed by lust. They offered to take turns fucking her. "Why not?" they said when she protested. "Won't it be fun?"

☙

After the chaos at Untarto's funeral and Amba's sick moment of realization that Bhisma was not with her in the courtyard, she swallowed her fear and frantically began looking for him.

The streets had almost emptied. No one wanted to be part of more trouble. Yet she went around anyway, asking each person she saw if they knew, or had seen, Dr. Rashad, describing his appearance. Each time she was met with a shaken head, a blank stare.

There came a point—it might have been half an hour later, she couldn't say—when she gave up and started to run in the direction of Rien's house. Halfway there she found a becak that stopped for her. Something in the driver's frightened eyes suggested he was glad for her company, and the two of them talked about everything and nothing to keep fear at bay. When she got to Rien's, she asked her whether she could borrow a spare shirt. As she described the events of the past hours, Rien's face paled. "I had no idea you were so involved with CGMI," she said quietly.

Hugging Rien good-bye, Amba didn't have the heart to say she could never return because she didn't want to bring danger to her friend's doorstep. Instead she kissed her on the cheek, thanked her for everything, and quickly left. Somewhere between Rien's house and her aunt and uncle's she threw her red top into a random bush beside the road. At the house, she couldn't look her aunt in the eye when she said, "Sorry, all night I was at Rien's working on an assignment, and the phone wasn't working." Then she locked herself in the room and cried herself to sleep.

The next morning Amba took a becak to Bumi Tarung. The artist's compound was deathly quiet. She was met by one of the painters, who had not said a word when she had arrived with Bhisma. He remembered her and introduced himself as Tarigan.

He told her Isa and some other CGMI members had been arrested in the night, and the others had gone into hiding. He had elected to stay behind to man the fort. He was sympathetic enough, but he had no news of Bhisma's whereabouts. Amba felt her last hope seeping away. She asked to go to the bathroom, and there she spilled the entire contents of her stomach into the sink.

As she left, she vowed to the hapless artist that she would not stop looking for Bhisma. As in ancient books, there are words one utters that will become sacred.

Salwa was the last person in Amba's mind. When his message arrived in the mail saying he couldn't make it to Yogyakarta, a familiar relief washed over her. "Beloved, I can't come. Several people in my office have been arrested, and I have to shoulder their workload. Please bear with me."

For days after Bhisma's disappearance, Yogyakarta seemed like a city unspooled. The people rejoiced at the overthrow of the Communists, doors were flung wide, and joyous ululations filled the streets. The Special Forces rolled into the city with their tanks, and jeeps, and trucks, and their happy songs, and the requisite *veni-vidi-vici* swagger. Thousands gathered to listen to the Red Beret commander, Colonel Sarwo Edhie Wibowo, who addressed the crowds in full combat gear. The Red Berets had rounded up hundreds of the enemy in one night, and there was no doubt in the people's minds that those murderous

Communist rebels with their inane September 30th Movement and those sniveling People's Youth scoundrels and their kind were annihilated once and for all.

Astounding how similar the face of freedom can be to the face of fascism.

᠀᠈

But not everybody was caught up in the hum of history. Some, like Amba, felt they had to leave behind their history altogether.

There was, for one, the agonizing pretense of good humor she had to assume for her aunt and uncle. Day in, day out. After about a week, she decided she couldn't stand it anymore. She had to leave Yogyakarta and make a new beginning elsewhere. Salwa had written that he was coming in late October. To escape him, and to escape her family, one of whom could appear at any time, she couldn't stay with her aunt and uncle much longer. Besides, she felt vulnerable there. So many things could go wrong. Someone at Untarto's memorial might have pegged her for CGMI and ratted to the authorities. Bhisma might have been arrested and tortured for the names of comrades and supporters. Even now the authorities could be looking for her.

She could hurt Salwa and her family in so many ways.

Someone at Bumi Tarung, for instance, might have confirmed that she was at the compound not a week ago, there with CGMI affiliate Dr. Bhisma Rashad. Could this lead investigators to her family in Kadipura? Would they hurt them? What if they went after Salwa in Surabaya, or found him on his way back to Yogyakarta, and took him in for questioning? Should she risk traveling to Kediri on the off chance that Bhisma might have returned there? Could she risk a visit to his parents' house in Menteng, in case he was there?

Crippled by anxiety, she held out for a few more days, hoping Bhisma would find her and make good on his promise to take her away, to start their future together. The minute she left the house, it would be harder for Bhisma to find her. But on the seventh day of hellish indecision, the goddess of fortune seemed finally to shine her light upon her. Her aunt and uncle announced that they had to go to Solo on a pressing family matter.

"We might be gone a week. Will you be all right living here with only the maid?"

"Of course, of course," she had said. "I'll have Rien keep me company if I get too scared. Or I can stay at her house occasionally."

But she knew she must leave, and not only the shelter of her relatives' house. She must, somehow, leave Yogyakarta as well. Disappear into the anonymity of Jakarta, find work, start again. She knew jobs didn't magically surface when you needed them, and Jakarta would be even more competitive than Yogyakarta. It would be less friendly, less welcoming, less easy to bend and boss around. She had not finished her degree—in reality she had no credentials whatsoever—yet there was no other way, she had to wear the courage of her own conviction and survive on her own.

Not that she had nothing. She had saved a little of the monthly allowance her parents sent her, and there was the translation fee she received from the hospital in Kediri. Enough to manage for several weeks, and those weeks, she told herself, can be as short or as long as you make them.

Within two hours of her aunt and uncle leaving the house, she, too, was gone. She didn't leave a note. She found herself a small room in a boarding house in another area of town. The owner's wife, with one look, must have recognized the desolation in her eyes. She told Amba that she ran a business, a small but popular canteen, and she needed help with the cooking. If Amba could cook, she could have the room in exchange.

Amba, who could work magic in the kitchen, quickly became an asset. She knew her savings would not last long, so it certainly helped not having to pay rent.

Chopping onions and grinding spices left plenty of time for thinking, and her thoughts were soon overtaken by the problem of what she should do about her studies. How could she throw away what she had achieved so far? She had to complete a degree. Without qualifications how could she hope to get a reasonable job? She had no idea if it was possible to transfer from one university to another, but she was determined to get some kind of accreditation, proof of the classes she had successfully completed. Then, she thought, she could transfer to a university in Jakarta. She had to find someone on campus to help make this happen.

Suddenly even the word *Jakarta* frightened her. It was a city she knew little about, a place she wasn't even sure was all that safe. But when Bhisma had said he'd take her there the name absorbed traces of Bhisma's hope for their future, and that had been enough.

Now it was the city of impossible dreams.

Another week passed with no word of Bhisma. But something else happened: a sign. The presence of something new within her, a new soul. That presence grew and filled her consciousness, as if conceived in the blossom of her purest dream. She remembered their last night together and how, as he emptied his seed into her, she had felt thick with contentment, enormous with joy. *This must be what it means to bear a child,* she thought.

Bearing the fruit of love, and understanding that to love is to accept, and to accept is to protect, the child quickly became her priority. How quickly she learned to love her new body.

※

Amba knew she was running out of time to take control of her life. Without Bhisma to help shape her future she had to shape it herself. She spent every spare hour in the university library, plotting her escape to Jakarta or enlisting help in looking for ways to transfer her credits.

One day, she found a woman in the English Department office who advised her on the procedures of transferring to another university. The woman also gave her the names and addresses of a few professional translation offices in Jakarta she might want to apply to. For the first time she felt she was on to something.

And so it was that, as she went about the campus, she saw again the notice she had seen on the hallway notice board, all those weeks ago, when she had decided to apply for the job at Kediri Hospital. The notice was in the same place, unobtrusive, a bit meek, but now slightly curled along the bottom edge: "Private Classes. Native Speaker of English. An FF Program Veteran. Every Weekday from 10:00 A.M. to 3:00 P.M. Apply Room 11."

As before, something about the notice distracted her. Again she stared at it for a long time, wondering who this native English-speaking teacher could be, and how, in this day and age of Sukarno rejecting the assistance—even the presence—of foreigners, this person had dared advertise his background without fearing arrest. Had things changed since the events of October 1? Another Tara? She felt a surge of hope.

She found room 11 and pushed open the door.

※

Adalhard Eilers possessed many admirable qualities rarely found in the average human being, the most endearing being the gift of contentment.

But when he fell in love with Amba he felt as though he'd never before known joy. He fell in love with her the moment she entered his classroom, even before he had greeted her and introduced himself. Even before she had said, feeling none of the timidity she'd shown the other two men in her life, that she didn't want to attend his classes; she just wanted to engage him for English conversation.

"Come again?"

"Just conversation," she repeated.

"You just want to talk? For a whole hour?"

"Yes." Then she added, because courtesy dictated that she should, "Sir." Then, faltering a little, "If you don't mind?"

He was about to say something just as polite—*And please don't call me sir*—but she got in first.

"I mean, I think my English is adequate, but I need more practice."

Adalhard hadn't heard English spoken so perfectly since he'd left Jakarta. To be precise, he hadn't heard English spoken so perfectly since the brief time he'd spent training panicky would-be local economists worried they'd miss going to the States because of the ban on sending students overseas. Of course he didn't tell her that. She was shy—he could see that beneath all her vim and snap—and he suspected she was troubled, even if she had donned colors meant to obscure it. But he was not one for psychoanalysis.

"You can start right now if it suits you."

At first she seemed startled by his lack of resistance. She looked as though she'd prepared to fight for what she wanted, her mind and body tensed to make her case.

Like a little gecko, he thought, *its tail still determined to fight long after it has been severed from the rest of it.*

"Yes. It does," she said, almost absentmindedly, looking at the wooden chairs arranged in front of the foreigner.

"Please," he said in Javanese. *Mangga.*

He even got the accent right, Amba thought as she obliged.

There was a pause as they settled down to new roles, to a new beginning.

"You might start by telling me what your name is," he said.

"Before I tell you my name," she said, looking embarrassed, "we must settle on your fee. I have very little money. I don't know your rate, but I'm sure I can't afford it. Besides I am only here for two weeks at the most. I have to leave. I am moving to Jakarta, you see, and before going I must improve my English."

He smiled and said, "Payment is not necessary. I am still employed here, and I'm actually glad to have a student. As I'm sure you know, your government frowns upon us non-Indonesian academics. My expatriate friends have all left. I could have left with them, seeing that my research project has ended."

Her eyes lit up for a moment. "Why didn't you leave?"

Adalhard later told Amba he didn't immediately answer because he was quietly vexed by his own explanation. He pretended not to hear her question. "Pardon?"

As she politely repeated the question he noticed her eyes. They could be the eyes of a widow.

"The rector asked me to stay on. He said it would be good if I could help students who wanted to improve their English. I like it here, but I was at a loose end, and I want to be useful, so I agreed. I'm very grateful to him. Besides, things can change . . . and the truth is I have nowhere else to go."

"Really? No family, no home?"

He'd spent many years now in Java and was used to this kind of nosiness. But she seemed to ask with feeling, with genuine empathy.

"No, no family," he said. "Unthinkable, isn't it, to an Indonesian. But my father recently died. My mother I hardly knew." And before she asked, he added, firmly, "And no, I have no wife or children. I'm quite sure I am unsuited to both."

He watched her blush. He could see the quick mental adjustment she made, keeping her thoughts to herself. To buffer her confusion he said blandly, "And you?"

He told her later he had recognized the look, that *guarded* look, yet something in him refused to dwell on it.

She offered, carefully, "As I said, I am going to Jakarta."

So she's running away from someone, Adalhard thought.

"Oh," he said. "Perhaps, then, we will focus on Jakarta for our conversation in this lesson. Tell me, what will you do there?"

"Teach English? I don't know. Perhaps work as a translator. I've done that already." Then to Adalhard's delight she smiled shyly and added, "I love reading. I love poetry. Shall I read a poem to you?"

Producing a notebook from her bag, she did.

"Eliot," he said, enchanted. "'Burnt Norton,' the first poem of *Four Quartets*. Where ever did you find him?"

"In a book donated to the campus library. I copied it into my notebook so I can carry him with me everywhere," she said, clearly pleased with herself.

He leaned back and heard his own sigh, released as though from its own yearning.

"So you enjoy poetry. That's wonderful."

"I read poems to myself every day."

"Only in English? How about Indonesian poetry?"

"Yes, some. But less and less now. Nowadays Indonesian poets are so predictable. Their lines sound like slogans. Most are about the struggle: *Workers of the world unite!* I know there are exceptions, but I feel a poem can't be made to say things alien to it. It can't be a . . . How should I say it? It can't be a tool."

Adalhard was an economist. He knew his Benn and Rilke, his Celan and Trakl, and he liked most of his fellow Americans, at least those who had a modicum of irony. He was about to agree, to say he, too, had long hardened himself against the instrumentalization of art, but he remembered how, just before he came to Indonesia, he'd stumbled upon a rather lovely translation by Michael Hamburger of a poem by Benn that had tugged at his heartstrings. Quietly, suddenly, he realized that everything had changed. This woman had single-handedly disarmed him, and suddenly he yearned to read that poem again.

He kept these thoughts to himself because he knew, at that moment, that he wanted nothing else in the world but to care for her.

"You already know my name. But you still haven't told me yours."

"It's Amba," she smiled. "From the wayang. I'm the woman twice scorned."

And, as if to prove the power of coincidence, the strains of a song playing from some radio was turned up by an invisible hand in a room nearby, gliding them into the aptness of the moment.

"*Pangkur palaran,*" Amba said.

"Yes, beautiful, isn't it?" Adalhard smiled, thinking there were moments in a man's life that could happily be the last he experienced before he departed from this world.

"So where are they now, those two men who scorned you?"

He couldn't believe he said that.

She couldn't believe he said that.

Adalhard Eilers had arrived at the Faculty of Economics of the University of Indonesia in Jakarta at the end of 1963 on a research grant. The faculty later sent him to the University of Gadjah Mada in Yogyakarta, where he would be based while undertaking fieldwork to investigate marketing systems in agriculture. He was not loud like some Americans tended to be, and his Indonesian was fluent enough. "You'll get by easily," his friends in Jakarta told him.

They were right. Everyone at his recently adopted campus, from his research assistants to the dean and the university rector, took to him instantly. He was even given his own small office. People responded easily to his misshapen but kindly face and his strangely effective Indonesian. When he found accommodation in the village of Purbalingga and asked if they'd let him stay even though everyone else of his kind had bolted, his host, a simple peasant with a wife and five children, said, "Sure. Pay the usual rent, and when you have time teach us some nice, useful English words."

He established a class in the village and before long he drew women and children like a magnet. Something in him reminded them of a time when everything was not so dark and difficult—he was like a benign father, the odd teacher, the kind who came only once in a lifetime, the kind who actually listened. They came to him unbidden, and he was quick to show appreciation.

As a boy, Adalhard had grown up in Bavaria, in the valleys of Leutasch, the region that produced meatballs the size of tennis balls but also whipped up the most exquisite trout in almond sauce. His mother he only knew through pictures his father had set lovingly into frames. His father, who worked for Daimler-Chrysler, moved his son with him to Munich, and then to Cologne, and then to New York, where he became country director. For most of his youth Adalhard felt like the boy who stood outside and peered into the living rooms of others, trying to remember what life was like inside and wondering why so much of the light and the warmth was shot through with loss.

Hardened thus he sailed through his studies and found his years at Princeton a breeze. When he received word of his father's death, he went back to New York to bury him. Then he returned to the research center at Princeton and asked to see the list of overseas places that recruited foreigners. He scanned through the list, which wasn't long, mostly places in Southeast Asia. But the names mostly meant nothing to him. He inquired about postings to the Philippines, but the advertised positions had already been filled. He considered Indonesia. On a whim he'd once taken electives in the country's religious history and mystical traditions. There was something about the language, the music of it, that he'd liked.

One day several months earlier, walking with a friend in Berkeley, he'd stopped at the faint strains of a soundscape so rich and strange and haunting. He later learned it was *gamelan*.

He returned to the list. He saw there was one research position in Indonesia, on Java. The next day he knocked on the door of the office of the director of the research center, sat down, and presented his case. His academic record was impeccable, added to which he was a known polyglot. The director had to admit to himself that Adalhard possessed a detached, nothing-to-lose quality that suggested he would be adequate for the task. He sent the young man away to think about his decision one more time. Adalhard was at the director's office door first thing the next morning to sign the forms. Then he packed his bags. A week later he dropped his house keys into his friend's mailbox and left for the airport. He had three thousand dollars in his backpack, money he'd found in a drawer of his father's desk. He hadn't planned anything other than getting to Java, much less thought about how long he would stay. Most certainly he hadn't planned on falling in love.

They met every day. Amba needed a wall with a city inside it that she could draw and color to her own liking, and this not-unattractive stranger with the mousy hair and kindly eyes became her companion. He placed no demands on her whatsoever and spoke beautifully the language in which she wished to be understood. But there lay beneath that language one much older, and one which he couldn't learn until she let him.

Will you listen to my story? Of course you'll listen.

When she asked Adalhard whether he was prepared to listen to the story of her previous relationship, he did not know what to say. He felt there was something slightly insensitive in Amba's invitation to peer into her life, to be told secrets she had shared with two other men he had never met. But she was so bewitching, and every time she so much as looked at him he felt his heart crumble. He found he wanted to know everything about this woman, every single thing that made her laugh, cry, and want. With her, everything seemed so simple, like the falling leaves that formed a bed on the paths they walked upon. He nodded along, feeling serene in his own wordlessness.

And so he listened.

He, she'd said. *He*, always referring to the one man, even though there were two. And every time she said that word it carried the weight of earth, wind, and fire. It had the depth of the deepest waters. Adalhard instinctively knew he could never replace that one *he*, the man who had fathered the baby in her womb. Adalhard knew that his role in Amba's life was to provide stability, to be the ballast. He would be the one who would fall into step beside or slightly behind her, hearing the droplets of her sigh before they fell to the ground. He would be the *he* who knew the cyan of her sorrows, the viridian of her jubilations, the *he* who understood that everything about her tended toward green. He would be the *he* who grabbed her before she slipped, who steadied her, who straightened her back when she was slumped and tired. Adalhard knew that while Bhisma would always be the *he* who owned Amba's dreams, he, Adalhard Eilers, would be the *he* who never vanished.

೨೭

One day Adalhard and Amba left the campus together, he clutching his bag and she hugging her notebooks close to her chest. Stiff breezes drove away the clouds, and for an hour it seemed that the two of them shone in the uncommonly golden afternoon. Adalhard longed to touch her arm, but he knew she was still too full of the other *he*.

They settled down in a small eatery, sharing a serving of *pecel*, blanched vegetables with spicy peanut sauce. Shoulder to shoulder they pored over the newspaper Adalhard had bought, trying to make sense of the news of the day. More than 250 people were reportedly massacred in the district of Boyolali, dozens of organizations had been disbanded, and people had been detained everywhere: hundreds of students, artists, women activists, lecturers. Then Amba read that the Army had stormed into Bumi Tarung that very morning, and many artists had been arrested.

Now, she thought, *it's just you and me, Adalhard. I can't go back to my parents. I can't go back to Salwa. I have to find a home for the child growing inside me. I must find a new life for us.*

A busker stood on the doorstep of the eatery, playing his sitar and singing a song that bore the intimations of a different kind of fate. Years later, looking back on this moment, neither of them remembered how the word *Rinjani* entered their conversation, but they both agreed perhaps it was in the song. But seeing the sudden change in Amba, her face turning ashen, he asked her what was wrong, and she admitted that she was jealous of a woman who bore that name. Why? *Because she was too beautiful, so beautiful it hurt.*

"Too beautiful?" he said and chuckled. "What does that even mean?"

You're too beautiful, he thought.

Jealousy, Amba knew, clouds judgment and poisons all common sense, but as she thought about how to answer Adalhard's question, the facts remained: Bhisma had vanished, Rinjani had vanished, and there was no evidence of them not having vanished together. Then suddenly a memory hit her like an uppercut to the jaw: an image that she could see so clearly now, despite having no memory of it all these dark days and weeks. Had she blanked it out of her mind?

Now, vividly, she remembered how in that dust and commotion in the auditorium, as she had clambered awkwardly to her feet, she saw her lover's towering figure looking around frantically. Was he searching for her in the terrified throng or trying to decide in which direction to run? She had called to him, that much she remembered, but the place was in an uproar, and her voice seemed to stick in her throat. He was too far away. Then Bhisma had turned, bolting in the wake of a running figure in a red shirt. The running figure of a young woman, a young woman who was unmistakably Rinjani.

Now Amba knew she couldn't linger, seeking that lost life she'd had. The sages might claim that true love requires humility, but she finally had to concede that nothing good could come out of a relationship in which one person loved the other person more. She knew this truth because it worked both ways: Salwa had loved her more that she had been able to love him, while Bhisma's love had never seemed enough, and she'd always felt she was the one who loved too much. With that dawning perception came the realization that she needed a new story. She needed to be free of both men. She needed a man who would understand that she must be the center of her own story, she and the new life growing inside her—for nothing else mattered.

❦

They were out on a hill not so far from Yogyakarta, staring out at a valley bounded on one side by a once-gleaming river. Sitting in the sunlight beside Amba, Adalhard did not understand why she suddenly announced, so emphatically, that she didn't want to find Bhisma anymore.

"You shouldn't give up. I can help," he said.

But how could she explain to him her insecurity about her own lover? How could she admit to the parts she had so often had to patch in her mind, like a sickness, like a failing, every time she tried to justify her love for Bhisma? Up to this point she had shared with Adalhard almost everything about her life, but now she couldn't disclose her last revelation: how Rinjani's eyes, lips, breasts, hips, and the way her lover had followed her, kept getting in the way of her memory of Bhisma. How she could no longer tell what was reality and what was imagined, because jealousy sullied her memory of the man she loved.

Amba met his gaze. What was it that was so soothing and so reassuring about this foreigner? He had accepted her, understood her, allowed her to efface him, even use him as a garbage bin for all the anguish she needed to discard, yet he had never lost sight of her pain. She momentarily felt ashamed for being so self-centered, but then, somehow, she felt vindicated. He valued her story. He absorbed it, made her feel snug. It was as if, by opening her entire world to him, he made her shame and guilt seem trifling. Her gratitude to him was immense.

"I no longer want to search for Bhisma," she finally said. "It's over. He hasn't found me, and I doubt he is even looking. I want to get away, leave for Jakarta as soon as possible. I don't feel safe here. I wonder if I've ever felt safe."

Adalhard saw himself reaching out for her hand and holding it in his. His face was earnest and if it had surprised him, this nerve, he didn't let it show. An intimation of what was to come suddenly took hold of her, but she didn't take her hand away.

"I know this might sound absurd," he said, his voice gentle and assured. "Perhaps it will be the kind of spur-of-the-moment decision that means spending the rest of one's lifetime dealing with the consequences. But you have a baby growing inside you, and you have to take care of yourself and this baby. If you don't like what I'm about to say, if you feel you can't accept the idea, please tell me now because I will pack my bags and go straight back to New Jersey, even if it means leaving my heart behind. But if you feel that you can accept me, accept the idea of being with me, then this is what I propose."

Amba remained very still.

Adalhard took a deep breath, then whispered his plan.

12

Good-bye

November 1965

Mas Salwa,

   After my long silence you must already have guessed what I need to say to you.

   I cannot marry you.

   I write this letter not to justify myself, because nothing I can say will ever redeem my disloyalty to you. I wish upon my soul I could be more of the daughter my father and mother—they themselves paragons of loyalty— wished to raise, but sadly I am not. But I know you are one such warrior—a man so honorable your cosmos has no place for the likes of me. I and my word have no value in the world of rectitude you've built for yourself, and rightly so.

   As I said, I shall not embarrass you further by tendering so crass a thing as a justification. But seeing this is very possibly my last letter to you, I want, if I may, to recall a moment between us that has very much stayed on my mind.

Do you remember that day we went to the rice fields near Pujasari, a week before I left for Yogyakarta? The day was bright and breezy, and we were treading gaily along the edge of a levee when suddenly you stopped in your tracks. "Look down," you said. "This embankment beneath us was once the path to hell." I followed your gaze, seeing nothing but the gravelly footpath below and the weeds trying to reclaim life through the cracks. You spoke of the scores of people who had once been massacred there. Sounding so stricken, so emotionally invested, you nearly broke my heart as you pointed out to me the fracture line on the footpath. Do you remember when you said, "That's the line where all hope ended. Roads have a way of ending where people have died. It is strange how nature sometimes obliges us"? When I looked beyond the rice field I saw no horizon.

Before I left to make a new life in Jakarta I returned to that spot. I was alone. I wanted to remember. I wanted to say good-bye to you, to thank you for having loved me, for accepting the thousand tiny hurts I inflicted upon you and continuing to love me when such love was no longer possible.

I also wanted to see if my memory held true. But there was still no horizon. Still no sign of what—other than the ties to everything that lay outside us—should have bound us, soul to soul.

Mas Salwa, this may not be your truth, but it is mine and I am only as good as my own memories.

So with this I take my leave. Again, forgive me. Know that this comes with love, however you choose to see it.

Amba

ॐ

Jakarta, November 5, 1966

Beloved Bapak,

As you can see above, I am writing from Jakarta, where I always dreamed I would one day come, though not quite under these circumstances. I am still not used to this city. It is a strange place: the gray gets into your eyes, the tall buildings and statues make you giddy.

I have written and rewritten this letter many times. It is the letter I should have sent you a year ago, before I gave you reason to wonder if I had fallen off the face of the earth. I know there were many separations and farewells in the stories you told me. I remember when we talked about how it is possible for a loved one to never leave us, for by looking in the eyes of someone else we love we will also find our loved one there. You and I both know it is possible for a daughter to leave her father, to travel to cities so far on the map, and yet not a day will pass that she doesn't hear his voice, even in sleep, like a cry for help, for restoration.

I have learned almost everything I know from you. I know, from you, there is still much I must learn. But you taught me about feeling safe, and about belonging without the stain of absolute possession. That is why, at this moment, the business of writing this letter is so hard: I do not know if I still have the right to call myself your daughter. I do not know if you have discarded me from your heart, erased my name from your mind, given me up to fate.

I do not know if asking for your forgiveness is still possible.

But now it is time for me to explain. I made a decision about my future without seeking your consent. I know you taught me to be an independent thinker, and I know in the past you sacrificed much in order to accept my decisions—no matter how wise or stupid—even if deep down you might not have understood my reasoning. I knew you were bereft when I left home to go to the university in Yogyakarta, even though you gave me your blessing. I even knew you were a little unsettled about my decision to study English literature: even though you saw the value of that language, at the same time you secretly worried that I would forget my roots. You feared I would change into someone you wouldn't recognize, someone who wasn't your child: a person who chose to arrange her thoughts and world in another language, a language that was not yours.

I know how you worried, perhaps more than anything else, because Salwa and I decided to live apart for a full year. Yet I didn't make this decision only to serve my own happiness. Please believe that your happiness, and Ibu's, means a lot to me. But I have never forgotten something you once told me by that lake, back in the childhood that was so dear to me. You said there was no black and white in this world, no ultimate right or wrong.

At the time I wasn't yet acquainted with the wonders of the English language. I didn't then know the words for the myriad shades of black—jet, ink, ebony, coal, raven—much less the names of carbon-containing pigments—bone, lampblack, drop black. I did not know yet that in this alien language that has eased into my own, black is not always evil; it is not always scary or calamitous. I did not know then that in the poems of lovers and losers alike, black can even bring peace. And that the reason the world is so fraught with violence is because Black and White are cast as enemies, as absolutes: Us and Them. Do you remember saying once, lightly, perhaps in jest, that black might even be the color of light?

I did not know then what you really meant, but it was with this in mind that I made my decision to follow color and light. That meant I had to disappoint Salwa. I did not arrive at that decision with the intention of hurting him. I made it because I respected him. He was so upright, dutiful, loving. How could I subject him to a future with someone so undeserving of him? With me? I always knew I would fail him because I could not love tidily. I did not know how to love something so noble, pure, and kind. For me love could not be duty. I only knew how to love body and soul. That meant loving a thousand colors, loving what makes you feel alive. It also meant loving imperfection.

Such a love is not the fate of everyone, but it was mine, albeit only briefly.

It was a love that opened my eyes to all that was wonderful, a world that resisted easy definitions. And from that love came a new path for me, my own path, and a fate that is entirely my own, for it produced a tiny being—a granddaughter for you and Ibu. She was born four months ago, in July, a child born out of a love whose shape and charge I learned from those pages I've read ever since I was a young girl—those pages you first read to me from The Mahabharata. A love that fuses the sensual and the spiritual, each fortifying the other. My daughter is the child I could never have had with Salwa. Forgive me for saying this, for I have no right, but I know, Bapak, that in the deepest trough of your heart you've always known that Salwa wasn't my fate. You've always known the love between him and me was not such a love.

This does not mean I have not suffered for my choices. It wasn't easy to decide which would be the greater punishment: to go home and spend my days seeing your wounded eyes, Ibu's face sullied by shame, my beautiful shining sisters abandoned by their suitors because of the scandal I brought to the family, or to cut myself off, to disappear with the man I chose instead of the one you chose, to never return to my childhood home, to never again listen to Ibu's singing or be able to ask for your blessings during Eid Fitri.

Now I must live with the consequences.

It is funny how, when I reached this stage of self-surrender, I was reminded of a scene in the 136th song of The Book of Centhini: the scene where Lady Tambangraras was setting off to find her husband. You will know that before leaving, she composed a short letter for her parents. It said, "Dearest Mother and Father,

I've left my home to journey, and to journey is to enter Deep Contemplation."

This thought gave me courage and it gives me courage now. The courage to hope you might understand why I did what I have done. I had to journey so that I might keep the places and people I love close to me, and so that I might be safe in the hearts of those I loved. And, Bapak, despite what has passed between us, it is you who pointed me to the manner in which Centhini vanished on the wedding night of Amongraga and Tambangraras, telling me it was your belief that it was in tribute to that vanishing that the Javanese bestowed her name to The Book of Centhini. It is you who taught me that vanishing can be the sign of resurrection, as black can be the color of light. You taught me to not pass judgment too easily. You taught me to not color my world only black and white.

Right now your granddaughter is asleep in the next room; I can hear her tiny breathing. She is very beautiful, strong yet fragile, not quite of this world. I named her Siri—Srikandi. What else can it be? I am learning the one true thing in this world is the love of a parent. The happiness of seeing your child happy.

Oh, Bapak. You have known all along, haven't you, that heaven is far from just? Or perhaps it is just in its injustice? You told me we can mock, scold, deceive, denounce, lament, plead with, kowtow to, befriend, and even make love to the gods, yet we must never expect too much of their goodwill. You gave me and my sisters our names, and surely that invited fate to do with us what it will? The rest we have to make for ourselves.

I feel so close to you at this hour. It is as if you were here, in this room, large and looming and real, asking me to come home.

Your loving daughter,
Amba

BOOK 4
Samuel and Amba
February—March 2006

13

A Rough Landing

The city of Ambon and later Buru Island, sometime in late February 2006

When Samuel Lawerissa entered his assigned cabin on the state ship
Lambelu he found a woman and a man sitting on two bottom bunks,
facing each other. They were past middle age, and they weren't talking
to one another. There was a faint stench of vomit. The woman clutched
on her lap a small suitcase that looked frayed and bruised. Samuel didn't
dare look at her face. He didn't want to get involved.

But her face was one he recognized. She had stood out when he
saw her earlier, in the throng of bodies fighting their way onto the
ship. Samuel had watched as she patiently moved through the ocean of
people—people who were visibly sick and tired of this trek from the city
of Ambon to the island of Buru, which many of them had to submit
to weekly, their loads of vegetables, goats, and bicycles groaning along
with them. It was impossible not to have noticed her dignity in that
turmoil, and along with her interesting face there seemed an unease
and a single-mindedness: it was too much to expect more than a single
sighting, let alone finding her in his assigned cabin.

He had no expectations when he boarded the ship. His ticket belonged to a friend who had taken ill at the last minute, and he was surprised to discover the ticket read "First Class." It was his first time in possession of such a thing.

Despite his flustered entrance and the clamor of the door as Samuel opened and closed it, the woman's posture remained ramrod straight, her pose unflinching. The man opposite her, meanwhile, reclined on his bunk and propped up one knee in easy repose, as if to say, *I'm in this with you, but don't expect too much from me. I'm just going to do what I like.* What gave them away as a troubled couple was the look the woman shot the man in response to his offhandedness, and how she stiffened, clamping her small case more tightly with her still-shapely arms.

Samuel put his bag on the third bottom bunk and sat down. Nothing was said, but the air was full of implication. He guessed the man was not her husband. There was something that suggested the couple might have met only recently. There wasn't between them the laid-back synthesis of two people who had known each other for some time. But he also detected a certain air of dependence about the woman, the way she glanced across at the other man as if secretly waiting for his cue, as if her decisions were hinged to his. As Samuel sat on his bunk he saw her shoot the man a look, as though to say, *Oh no, here goes our privacy.* Or even, *Oh no, what now?*

The silence stretched, threatening to become awkward. Samuel decided to end it.

"Good morning," he said to the cabin, avoiding her eyes.

"Good morning."

Samuel was aware of the man looking him over. His eyes were steel: *Don't mess with me. I've met guys like you.*

"Sorry," Samuel said, acknowledging his inadvertent intrusion, and having been raised that way.

Finally, Samuel felt the ship in motion, cast off.

"What now?" he heard the woman murmur to the man.

"We sail and we wait," the man said. "Are you hungry?"

"No, no." She shook her head. "Food is the last thing on my mind. If I eat I'll be sick again."

Samuel observed the way the older man regarded his companion. He seemed smitten but trying hard to conceal it, and who wouldn't be? She seemed in her late fifties, perhaps even in her early sixties. Yet her glorious cheekbones and sulky, pillowy lips seemed uncracked by time, and there was something alluring about her air of resigned patience. In contrast the man's calm seemed superficial. There was something of violence about him. Samuel noted the way he clenched his jaw, his quick, impatient movements. Samuel was intrigued: they seemed very different. What was she to him? And why did he seem familiar?

"I shouldn't have brought this," the woman said.

Suddenly her eyes were on Samuel, including him in the conversation. *Luminous,* he thought.

She nodded at her suitcase. Samuel smiled but said nothing.

"I should have brought something softer. Canvas, maybe," she said apologetically, childlike almost.

The older man rustled on his bunk, obviously uncomfortable with her openness. "The case is fine," he said. "Say, why don't you go up on deck for some fresh air?"

Samuel saw her shoot him an anguished look.

"I'll stay here, watch our bags," said the man, oblivious to his lack of gallantry.

She shuddered, reminded perhaps of having traversed the ship earlier to get to the cabin through that sea of indifferent people, their smelly bodies and oily faces pressing from all directions. The man laughed and turned to Samuel. "Hey you, Mas, where are you from?" His teeth were too even and white.

"Ambon, Pak. And you?"

"The lady is from Jakarta," the man said with a self-satisfied laugh. "I'm from everywhere."

Jakarta. Jakarta could mean almost anything, as folks tended to end up in that city one way or another. Samuel decided, observing her sharp, narrow nose, wide forehead, and sensuous mouth, that the woman probably was Javanese. His impression was reinforced by her gracious smile at the rather undeserved jab.

"Will you be staying in Namlea, Bu?" Samuel asked her politely.

She seemed disturbed by the imposed intimacy of the space. There was nothing but the width of a bunk and the light bulb between them. A *Yes* or *No* would have sufficed, but she did not answer him.

"We might," the man said, coming to her rescue. "Namlea is the safest place to be."

"It's not your first time on the island, then?"

The man smiled dismissively. "Not for me."

The man's answers, Samuel noticed, were slippery. He pressed on. "Are you going there on business?"

"I'm here for melaleuca oil. Among other things."

"Perhaps, if you have time, you could take Ibu," Samuel said, nodding respectfully at the woman, "to Jikumerasa. Do you know it? It's a lovely, little-known beach."

"What's worth looking at there?" the man asked, his eyes knowing more than he let on.

"Anemones. And the color blue like you've never seen."

The woman seemed intrigued. For the first time she seemed willing to join the conversation.

"Yes, it's a beautiful place," Samuel added. "The sea the bluest blue."

"Oh," she said, looking genuinely enchanted.

"Anywhere to stay there?" the man asked sharply.

"Not yet. In a few years, maybe. For now there's only a smattering of fishermen's houses," Samuel said.

"Hmm," the man responded, looking doubtful.

"The village is poor," Samuel added. "No electricity and a lot of sun."

"Hmm."

Samuel couldn't read his face. Caught up in the cat and mouse of the exchange, he blurted, "I can take you there if you like."

"You live there?" said the man, seeming newly interested. "You have family in Buru?"

"I did. Once. Now I visit only occasionally. I'm mostly in Ambon."

"Any idea how to get hold of a car in Buru?"

Samuel hesitated before offering, "I could probably arrange for one."

Samuel saw worry spread across the woman's face, as if this wasn't part of the script she'd agreed to.

"No. We're in a hurry," she said. "We won't have time, not even for the bluest blue."

The sun burst through the porthole, drawing the man's attention outside. "Amazing," he suddenly said, almost to himself. "To think that once upon a time, they discarded us at dusk."

He didn't turn back, and his voice had become infused with sadness and distance; the voice of an old person.

"They always discarded us at dusk," he repeated, still in his own world.

"I'm sorry?" Samuel said.

"I still wonder why that island stays mute," the man continued, "but now I realize the island doesn't have the answer, and we've stopped asking why. Even from the beginning we didn't ask why."

He stopped, as though deciding whether to go on. And did. "Because they fed us, and they fed us well. We were like beggars invited to a feast. And after all that fat and coconut cream they stuffed into us in the six days it took us to get to that island, our questions died in our bellies. That's what they intended. They wanted us overfed and subdued. Because fat meant safe, because fat meant we couldn't fight."

The woman closed her eyes as though she had anticipated this moment, had seen it coming, this quiet but stunning flare-up on his part. And accepted it, as if it was his right.

"They worked us like slaves, it's true, but fat meant obedience. Fat meant defeat."

He had been a prisoner, Samuel realized. Part of the roundup of the suspected Communists, all those years ago. Surely. That's why he's been to Buru before. He is an *eks-tapol*, as his kind is known.

The woman arched her back and looked directly and unapologetically at Samuel as though to warn him, *Watch out, he will tell his story to anyone who will listen.*

"Sorry, may I know your name?" she suddenly asked, ignoring her companion.

"Samuel," he said, not without fumbling. "And yours?"

"My name is Amba," she said. "Look at me. Do you think it so improbable that my name ended the battle of all battles?"

Samuel felt ashamed that he didn't know his Javanese mythology better. He remembered vaguely the story about a princess kidnapped by a warrior. The name sounded familiar, but not much else.

"Perhaps I should eat something, after all. Samuel, will you keep me company?"

Most passengers avoided the restaurant like the plague even though it was the cleanest spot on the whole ship.

Perhaps it was the arctic air conditioning. (They passed two women hurrying out, and he overheard one say, "Who do they think we are? Penguins?") Perhaps it was because the damn place was reserved for first- and second-class passengers, and folks generally knew their place. The people on the crowded decks might do just about anything, but no one without the proper ticket would ever enter this room and sit at these tables. Not even the thugs from Ambon, who were known to roam the state ships. No, they'd rather be at one with the stench and stink from the toilets, the wet litter of rotten food leaking from plastic bags and waste bins, and the body odor and vomit soup of a thousand people.

Once they had settled themselves, Amba asked, "So, Samuel, what is it that you really do?"

Sitting so close to her unsettled him. "The breadfruit," he said nervously, pointing at the basket of fried breadfruit on the table between them. "You must try it. It's locally grown, I'm told. Best breadfruit ever."

She smiled and chose a piece. After one bite her face lit up. "I don't normally eat deep-fried stuff," she said. "At my age, one has to be so careful. Ah, but this is too good. The soil where this fruit was grown must be excellent."

"The soil on Buru is rich," Samuel said, uselessly. "Come, Bu, why don't you have some more?"

"Amazing durian sauce," she said, dipping the breadfruit deep into the bowl before taking another bite. "I wonder who first thought of this combination?"

"Yes, if we only knew," he said, "but that's the beauty of our cuisine. No one knows who started what. All we know is that these dishes are just there, and there are so many variants of them. Most of my friends eat this for breakfast," Samuel continued, realizing he was enjoying these empty niceties; they were not something he was particularly used to.

He watched a dribble of the sambal slide down one of her long, fine fingers. Then he saw her bend her head and, with her pink, pointy tongue, lick it clean. He was strangely drawn to this woman, to her tiniest gestures.

She repeated her question about the work he did.

"I worked as a journalist for a radio station in Ambon," he said. *Tread carefully.* "Before that I was in Surabaya, freelancing. I'm afraid I've been the hopeless romantic, wanting to spend my life as a writer. You know, be wildly successful writing travel journals, novels, epic essays about life." He laughed, a little nervously. "But I had to make ends meet, so I became a copywriter, then a reporter at a daily, *Jawa Pos.* I stayed there for quite a while."

Her eyes remained fixed.

"I found Ambon more volatile than Surabaya. Opportunities came and went—so I worked odd jobs as well. Even drove a van and became a tour guide, the works."

"And your family?"

Predictable questions, Samuel thought. *But I know what she wants to find out. Am I a bastard who abandoned his wife and children for a bohemian life? Did I come from some well-heeled, respectable family only to abandon all the advantages offered to me to hit the road and find my true self?*

"Mine was a typical Ambonese Protestant family," he said, deciding to keep the story simple. "The sort that spoke and dressed like the Dutch and wanted no other master. My grandfather served in the Dutch Army during the Japanese invasion. His forebears had done the same, and his grandfather had actually relocated from Ambon in the nineteenth century to serve the Dutch East Indies throughout the colony. My father believed there were none better than the Dutch. He was a proud, formidable-looking man, all furrows and wrinkles, with a hawkish nose, but he was taunted and harassed for his affiliation with the Dutch colonialists. He took the 'black dog' insults that were hurled at him with pride. 'Never bite the hand that feeds you,' he used to tell me."

For an instant she seemed distant, as though caught by a stray memory.

"Sorry," she said, when she became aware of Samuel watching her. "I didn't mean to be presumptuous, but I wonder . . . Am I right in thinking . . ."

"Please, just ask," he said. "Don't apologize. I mean, none of us in this archipelago knows enough about our neighbors' history, right?"

She considered this. Perhaps she was making up her mind about him.

"Your father," she said slowly, as if paraphrasing with care. "He was involved, then, in the Republic of South Moluccas, serving the Dutch. And he later fought for your people's secession from Indonesia?"

"You may be thinking what most people think," Samuel said, smiling. "That my father and his kind were traitors. That during the '50s and early '60s, after the collapse of the clove monopoly, they were the worst kind of maggots, siding with the white men who had murdered and oppressed our brothers. But no. Like all people of Maluku, we are proud of this legacy. We've learned that one can't undo one's history."

"You and I," she said at long last, "we're as different as night and day. It still vexes me, after all this time. We have such different outlooks and ideals. We even look nothing like each other. How then are we supposed to see ourselves as neighbors, as brothers? And feel that we share the same national destiny?"

Samuel understood she wasn't conceding, merely not disagreeing, and it seemed that was as much as she would, or could, say.

Amba straightened her back and sat in the upright way of their first encounter in the cabin. "Perhaps your ancestors came from a faraway place," she said. "Were they Arab?"

She wasn't his first acquaintance to think that, with his bone-marrow skin, jet-black eyebrows, and golden eyes. So he told her of that part of him that was Chinese. And how that, one day not so long ago, led to him join other fifth-generation Chinese Muslim families in Ambon in a battle against their Christian neighbors.

"Yes, that conflict. How terrible. Have you killed anyone, Samuel?"

"Two men," he said, seeing that despite the gall of her question she was surprised. "In both cases it was a choice. Either I died or they did."

She seemed momentarily troubled.

"And you, Bu. What are you looking for in Buru?"

Suddenly he couldn't see the black of her eyes. It was as if the core of her had suddenly vanished into the ether.

When Samuel and Amba returned to the cabin, the man they had left behind was leaning against the wall beside the murky porthole.

"It'll be a rough landing," he said.

Something in him had changed.

Turning to look back out the window, he said to Samuel, "You, too, may know this trip well, but there our similarities end."

They had been sailing westward for six hours. All three of them picked themselves up.

"So soon?" Amba said. "I thought there was still over an hour to travel. I didn't realize we were so close to shore."

"I'm afraid we're not so close," Samuel said. "The new pier is still being built. This ship has to anchor more than a half mile from the shore, and then the passengers are ferried across in small boats—some no more than outrigger canoes. I'm afraid it's a slow and tedious process."

"Really. When will the pier be completed?"

"I have no idea," Samuel said. "But they do a surprisingly good job with construction money in this part of the world, unlike in Java. I gather you flew into Ambon? So you'll have seen the high standard of Ambon Airport. The standard is similar here. Wait till you see the new police headquarters. You'd think corruption was a relic from the past."

❧

There was a moment during their struggle to reach the outrigger when, pressed by the jostling crowd, Samuel felt he could not breathe. In front of him Amba still clutched her small case to her chest, her fine nose flattened against someone's skinny shoulder blade. When there was a slight easing in the crush, he reached out and pulled her toward him, then kept his arms around her protectively until they moved closer to the disembarkation point. For a while they seemed to oscillate between indignant bourgeois shouts at line jumpers and gestures of compassion from fellow sufferers.

It certainly was not a dignified place to be. How easily a person could fall to the floor, be trampled on, cut short. And in that steaming mélange of body odor, bad breath, and impatience, Samuel saw something else: how the charisma and presence of Amba's traveling companion quickly turn to dust. He struggled to stay beside them, but made no move to help. It was left for Samuel to push a path through the crowd, to find breathing room for Amba lest she pass out.

Ahead he could see an outrigger boat looking just about as solid as the rope ladder's dozen rungs dangling above the water. At the top of the ladder, Amba froze. She turned to Samuel, her fingers clutching his jacket. Unable to persuade her that the only way to get down to the boat was to let go, he finally scooped her up and half lifted her over the side, passing her awkwardly down to the waiting boatman.

Later, when she was able to laugh about this, she admitted to Samuel that aside from being frightened, she had felt something strange—it was hard to say—like a tingle of indecorum.

"I'm fine, I'm fine, I can manage," she presently shouted, as he lowered her to the small boat. At the same time her suitcase began to slip from her arms. Lunging to grab it before it fell into the sea, he lost his footing. When he finally righted himself the boat was pulling away. Her companion, released by Samuel from the responsibility of all manner of luggage, had also managed to scramble down and was now squeezed in beside Amba.

The fishing boats that came to collect the passengers and cargo buzzed like flies around a big hunk of carcass. The one Amba was in, painted with blue stars on the prow, tried to maneuver its way back. Samuel, Amba's case held to his chest, readied for the jump, but the little boat lurched away again from the ship's side, dragged back by the pull of the waves. Something in the theatrical hyperbole of it all appeared to annoy Amba.

"Forget it!" she shouted. "Wait for a steadier boat!"

But then, as though responding to a prayer, the boatman in another outrigger laden with passengers shouted to Samuel to throw the suitcase down: "Hey, you. Throw the damn thing here. I'll transfer it to the other boat." Casting a desperate look toward Amba, Samuel tossed the suitcase down. He saw her looking back, seemingly transfixed by the strange, crazy, cinematic beauty of that instant when he'd chosen the heroism of the leading man over a certain kind of safety. Then the star-dotted boat bore her off toward the shore, and they lost sight of each other.

※

Night fell like a great blanket over the port city of Namlea. All the town's activities focused on the thousand people belched out by the tubby, inert vessel a half mile away, who were now scrambling all over the pier. The pier itself was no more than a rickety wooden structure leading to a beach stripped of both sand and coral.

The Question of Red

How many times have I seen this view? Samuel thought. Nothing of Namlea's scenery moved him anymore.

He finally saw Amba, sitting alone on the dockside, watching people making their way up the rocks of the shore, having been deposited on the edge of the sea by those gnat-like fishing boats. She seemed befuddled. For the first time Samuel thought she looked her age.

From a distance he observed that she took her shoes off and put them on again, rolled up her pants and rolled them down again. Then apparently realizing there was no need for a headscarf—and it was true that in the port of Namlea not many women wore them—she removed hers.

After losing sight of Amba in that mad welter of waves and boats in Kayeli Bay, he had seen her again as she and her nameless companion made their wild jump to the shore before disappearing into the waiting crowd. Now, having found her again, he was having a hard time taking his eyes off her. But, for some reason, he was reluctant to approach.

Her companion finally emerged from the madness on the dock with a porter in tow, having paid his way through, no doubt. It seemed he had found her suitcase—her absurd suitcase—and at the sight of it Amba's face lit up. The porter was smiling crazily. God knows how much the man had tipped him.

Still holding back, Samuel watched Amba and her companion trade words, the man glancing every minute or so at the screen of his cell phone as if anticipating a text message or a call. Clearly they were waiting for someone. Samuel was curious, doubting now his first impression that the man and Amba had known each other for some time. What exactly was their relationship? If they were lovers, why pick this godforsaken place for a lover's escape? If they were related in some way, which seemed to defy the laws of biology, why all this edginess? And this niggling thought somewhere in the back of his mind: *Where have I seen this man before?*

A figure approached the duo, a stout local. Introductions were made, and then Amba's companion laughed—no, bellowed was more like it. They embraced. But no sooner had smiles been traded than shouts began to splinter the air. Amba's companion had his hands on his hips, his manner aggressive. The local stood his ground but soon left.

Beyond the lights of the pier Samuel could see the sky was no longer the gray green of dusk but pitch black. He checked his watch. It was after 8:00 p.m. Being out at night without support, even in Namlea, was inviting trouble. Wiping his brow Samuel self-consciously made his way down toward the stranded travelers.

As he approached, Amba looked up. "Hey! Samuel. Is that you? It *is* you. Come and join us, please."

Her relief seemed genuine.

"I see you made it ashore," he said, noting the relief was shared by her companion. A brief but sweet detail.

"Yes, we did, as did my suitcase." She smiled guiltily.

"Are you heading downtown?" the man suddenly asked Samuel.

"I am," he said, knowing what was coming next.

"That fool who just left promised to get us a van. Then he came back to say he couldn't get one. Do you think you can drive us instead?"

The man's demeanor had changed; now he seemed a little less high and mighty.

"Well, on the boat I said I could get you a car. But I don't own one."

The man said impatiently, "Can you get someone to rent us a van?"

Samuel, trying to figure out what he was up to, said, "Let me see what I can do." *This guy acted like fucking royalty back there on the boat, but now that he needs something, ingratiation fits him like too large of a coat.*

"But here's the thing," the man added. "Maybe we're not going to Namlea."

Despite himself, Samuel was taken aback. To go anywhere else on this island, at night, with a woman like Amba, was out of the question. Where else could they possibly be heading?

"Sorry, I don't follow," he said.

"I know it's late. But if you can get a vehicle, how much would you charge for a whole day? From now until 8:00 p.m. tomorrow?"

Samuel was not prepared for this, to be asked to be—what? Their driver? Their guide? Their security, for fuck's sake? *Who are these people?* But Amba was staring him down, and the man, despite his arrogance, was looking on, his manner expectant. Samuel found himself weakening.

"I think I can organize something. Just pay me the same amount you were going to pay your driver," he said, picking up Amba's suitcase. "Come then, follow me. It's not far from here."

Samuel was right in assuming that Hasan, his policeman friend at police HQ, would be eager to rent out his van. As the younger man walked toward it with the keys, he leaned close to Samuel and whispered, "No dents, no trouble, okay? Forty percent and you bring me the money when you bring back the van."

"Don't worry, brother."

"Who are these people, anyway? Are they from Jakarta? Where are they staying? Who are they visiting?"

Samuel shrugged. "Your guess is as good as mine."

"That woman. Not bad-looking, is she?"

Samuel felt an odd surge of pride at those words. "She's older," he said nonchalantly. "But well—you're right. Maybe that's why they want to travel at night, to get away from perverts like you."

They both laughed.

"You're not going to stop by the police station? Check them out, just in case? That man with her looks like trouble."

"Nah," Samuel said. *It's tempting, but no. Not yet.* "I have a feeling it'll be better if they stay below the radar for now."

"But sooner or later someone at HQ will find out about them, whoever they are."

"Just relax, okay? I'll get their story. You can't help but talk about history on an island like this. You know that as well as anyone."

But he couldn't stop wondering if he had made a huge mistake by committing himself to these strangers, especially if the man was, as he suspected, an eks-tapol.

☙

All three were quiet as Samuel, following the directions Amba's companion occasionally muttered, drove the van out of Namlea. He had no idea where they were going, what their final destination was; in fact, he was still waiting for the man to tell him his name.

Hasan's words clung like a leech to Samuel's mind. He knew that strangers to the island, especially strangers looking as if they might have money, would be a target for anyone who could sniff out potential gain. *Buru*, he thought, *is like a festering wound. There will always be bad luck here.*

Even when he was young, Samuel understood that history is not always on your side, but for the most part it knows its place. He'd learned to keep silent when people started ranting that they hated Communists, as if by doing so they would rid themselves of the filth that soiled the air they breathed. He also knew he was ignorant of many things, and soon learned the necessity of taking notes. Some six or seven years into the newspaper game, he'd gotten pretty good at picking up scents and nosing out trouble.

Take Amba's companion, he thought, bringing himself back to the present as the van headlights pierced the anonymous dark ahead. *He might be trying to pretend to be something else, but he must have been one of them, a Communist.*

He had met targets before whom he'd actually liked, and he knew that whatever this couple was up to was no ordinary case. There was no love lost between him and the cocky man, but he definitely respected her. So, driving them through the night he worked out his excuse. He was sticking close, as he'd been trained to do. Call it surveillance, call it keeping your ducks in a row—whatever, he'd keep them close. But this time he would do it his way.

Under normal circumstances, he would by now have sent word to headquarters, to Major Kusno, to say he had acquired a target and to say roughly how long he needed before backup was sent in. But he'd been doing this long enough to know that reinforcements were often sent in before a request was even made, making a bloody mess of things.

Samuel would not let Amba get caught up in all that. He'd known that as he drove off with a cursory wave to Hasan, when he'd felt the overwhelming urge to protect her.

The drive inland was slow, dark, and steep, and still Samuel didn't know where they were going. The man, sitting in the passenger seat next to him, turned to check on Amba in the back.

"Not long now," he said. "Twenty more minutes. Thirty at most."

In the rearview mirror, Samuel saw Amba's ghostly face nod and smile by the low glow of the dashboard lights. Despite her age, it didn't disturb him one bit to be caught in her web.

"Two-thirds of Buru is hill and mountain," the man told her. "Belts of them, like a girdle hugging the island, northwest to north, northwest to south, north to south. Somewhere in the middle there is a waterway that links Lake Rana to the Waeapo River—*wai* means river—and the river runs through the island from west to east, cutting the landscape in two."

"What's that outside?" she asked. "All I can see are dark silhouettes."

"Palm and rattan, mostly, and shrubs of all sorts," Samuel interjected, trying to be useful. "There have been a lot of changes in Buru, but out here in the country it looks much the same as it always has."

"Oh," she said, her voice far away. "And Namlea?"

"The Dutch made Namlea Buru's capital city in 1919, after the great floods of the Waeapo River destroyed Kayeli, the first capital. Now Kayeli is like a lost city," Samuel said, feeling he had piqued her interest.

The man said, "Are you tired, Bu?"

"No, I'm fine. I'm enjoying this."

Samuel sensed she was waiting for someone to clear the way so she could ask the hard questions. But the man, completely oblivious, resumed his unasked-for geography lesson, describing the marvel of bracelets of mountains streaking southward until, at Waraman Mountain, they turned westward, wending toward Lake Rana.

"From Lake Rana the mountains move in chains to the north, peaking in Fud Siul and Fud Fadit Mountain before curving and completing the circle at Siahone Beach."

"The mountains block access to the interior," Samuel interjected again. Just because he could. "This is the only road. The government never bothered to make another. They just slapped asphalt on the old path before the president's visit a few years back."

"The *current* president," the man added.

Glancing in the mirror at Amba's face, Samuel could see her letting this bit of information sink in: the *current* president. Then, to his surprise, she said, "Amazing how many presidents we have gone through in rapid-fire succession since Suharto slammed the door shut on those twelve thousand people sent to this island almost four decades ago. And many of them for crimes they might not have committed."

It was the first political statement he had heard from Amba. He glanced at the man sitting next to him, but his face gave nothing away. *Clearly the type of person accustomed to living in darkness,* he thought. His earlier unguarded outburst in the ship must have been out of character.

"Have you heard of the sago palm of Ambon?" Samuel asked casually. "I mean the sort they sell in markets around Java."

"Yes, yes, it's legendary," the man said.

"They mostly come from here, Buru," Samuel said, glancing in the rearview mirror. Again he saw Amba's face light up. He had guessed she'd be the type of big-city person who enjoyed conversations about earthy things. Perhaps she was from a small city herself.

"What I saw at the harbor looked like a vibrant economy."

"Well, after all, Rome wasn't built in a day," the man said. Despite the harebrained cliché there was a curious fondness in his voice. "The place we'll stay is where Unit IV of the prison camp used to be. The prisoner unit closest to the sea."

"Savanajaya," she said, almost in a whisper.

So she's familiar with this part of the island's history. Yet she claims she hasn't been here before, Samuel thought. *Where did this familiarity stem from?*

The man turned to Samuel, a little too briskly, Samuel thought.

"Hey," he said, his face betraying nothing, however, of his feelings or his knowledge. "Is it true there's a warung somewhere near where we're staying? Some people told me there was."

The story was coming together now. *This bastard's playing me,* Samuel thought. Very few knew of this eatery, and fewer still had business there. This man—these people—fear and beauty be damned, were after something, and the man definitely knew his way around.

"You must mean Warung R. M.," Samuel replied casually.

"Ah. Is that its name? Well, then, how about we stop there to eat before they close," he said. "By the way, my name is Zulfikar, Zulfikar Hamsa. I'm not sure I told you earlier."

⁂

It was close to 9:30 p.m. when Samuel pulled into Savanajaya. In 1972, this compound, known as Unit IV, was the first to be dissolved. Overnight the collection of buildings went from a prison unit to a village. Warung R. M. was a roadside hut, dimly lit by two or three bulbs, 40 watts at the most, standard in Buru and elsewhere in the archipelago. The three travelers left the van and collapsed at the rickety table outside. They ordered without expectation. The girl—*waitress* was hardly the right word—sprang into action. Soon two bowls of *soto* (chicken soup) were laid on the table, along with a plate of raw vegetables, fried tofu and tempeh, and a half dozen or so pieces of lemongrass-crusted chicken, fried to near death.

"We have some chicken liver left," the girl said. "Are you interested?"

"No," Zulfikar said, speaking for the table.

Instead he ordered sambal and not one, but two different varieties of sweet soybean sauce. *Kecap manis*: a keen cultural marker, seemingly tailored for Amba's benefit. Samuel wondered if this gesture would touch her Javanese soul. Then again, she might not know that in most eateries in Buru you could find a bottle of kecap manis. It was practically a religion. But she didn't seem impressed, much less moved. Something deep inside seemed to hold her captive.

"The family that runs this place came out here in 1979 from a small town in Central Java," Samuel said. "The husband was an eks-tapol."

Deliberately, he let the word breathe.

"I'm not sure if you knew," Samuel continued, treading carefully, "but when the prison camp was abolished, the inmates with family were given land, which they worked and sweated over, and it paid off. I mean, look at this place. It's a little rough, but they're doing well."

"The barracks?" Amba asked slowly, her voice flickering as though her heart had skipped a beat. "What about the barracks? Are there any of them left?"

Her interest in the older parts of the island unsettled Samuel. What was it these two were looking for, anyway? He really should be doing his job and filing a report—one of his key instructions from police HQ was to report on any Jakartan arriving on this island, especially any wealthy ones. If they were here to nose around for business opportunities, they'd have money, and his buddies at HQ would surely find a way to get their hands on some of it. This, strategically, was where Samuel came in. Right now he should be arranging a spot where the couple could be amicably ambushed and taken to HQ for questioning. If he let things drag on for too long the military would find them, and they would be out of his, and the police's, hands. Either way, in the normal scheme of things, they would soon be his responsibility no more.

But his instincts told him this unlikely couple had not come to conduct a business transaction. Amba knew too much about the prison camp for her trip to be either about melaleuca oil or the tourist's enchantment with being waylaid by arresting shades of blue. And Zulfikar had been here before, possibly at Savanajaya—he carried the look of someone who had smelled and tasted this earth.

"The barracks?" Samuel said, returning to Amba's question. "All gone, all twenty-two of them. Except the art center at Savanajaya."

"Actually," Zulfikar cut in, "Savanajaya has more history than any spot on Buru. If it were daylight you'd see we're surrounded by rice fields. Most of the first prisoners were sent here. They began working the land when they arrived in 1969, and year by year they transformed the place into a mini-Java. Before they knew it, the unit had all the basic infrastructure of a standard Indonesian village—roads, buildings, sanitation.

"The tapols who remained here for the duration nearly all ended up bringing over their families. The families—well, they were shipped here from Java as a reward from the government for the tapols' hard work. Anyone who understood the politics of dictatorship knew that the government wanted to give the impression it was a benevolent regime, not as inhumane as most people thought.

"So even before the prison was abolished, Savanajaya became a village, the place where all tapols with family lived and enjoyed the status of warga—citizen. That's a vintage term now, but then it was New Order lingo, to make the general populace accept them as respectable."

"What about those without family?" Amba asked.

"Redistributed between the other units."

"So having a family was an advantage?"

Samuel detected a slight edge to her voice.

"Well, yes and no. For many it was not," Zulfikar said, his voice suddenly turning grave. "For most tapols I've known, bringing their family to the island was the same as getting a life sentence. It meant you would live and die on Buru. There was no going back, ever, either for you or your family. The truth was that for most of the men, knowing their family was free, far from Buru, gave them hope. Knowing they were free was to know that part of them still lived in the normal world, breathed the air of freedom, did the earth's good work that they'd been cut off from doing." His voice cracked a little as he added, "If you really loved someone, you wanted them to be free of this place, and free of you."

Despite the softness in Zulfikar's voice, Amba stiffened, as if having to block a painful memory. Her eyes darted around the place, her face registering her distaste for the unpainted aluminum sheets forming the walls of the warung, plastered with bikini babe calendars.

"I promise you'll understand more in the morning," Zulfikar finally said. "Things are always clearer in the morning."

❧

Following the directions of their waitress they made their way to the sparse group of houses nearby. After negotiating with the caretaker of the neatest-looking of them, Zulfikar acquired three rooms: two at the back, for Amba and for himself, one facing the street, for Samuel.

"We are all out of light bulbs. You don't mind a candle?" the caretaker said to Samuel.

"No matter," he said with a shrug. "Darkness is my friend."

Zulfikar gave him a sharp glance. Then he affably suggested a game of poker. Samuel politely declined. "Sorry, it's been a long day. I need to sleep."

He didn't tell the old man that there were several reasons why he felt it would be best for him to retire early. Firstly he knew that even though it was late, someone from the military or police intelligence could stop by, sniffing around, especially if they had a direct line to the caretaker, and Samuel certainly didn't want to be seen by the military.

Secondly, he had a fair idea that Zulfikar suggested the game as a guise for pumping Samuel for information he wasn't prepared to give.

Lastly, he didn't want to watch the wick of the candle burn down. For some reason the thought reminded him of the sadness he occasionally caught in Amba's face. He'd rather lie on his bed and think of that face. He would let the thought lead him to darkness, until he was completely at the whim of angels and demons, both scotching his sleep.

❧

In the end, both men stayed up half the night checking on Amba, but Samuel was certain he was the more vigilant of the two. He knew she hadn't slept but had spent the night listening to the dark. He knew that because of the many times she had risen from her bed, from near midnight to the bone chill before dawn, checking and rechecking the lock, presumably to allay her fears. Through the night he also heard Zulfikar prowl both inside and outside the house. Yes, daybreak was long in coming. But when the sky began to pale and Samuel made his way to the common room, Zulfikar had beaten him to it. Samuel backtracked and headed for the bathroom for a quick shower. When he returned, Zulfikar was still sitting on the chair.

The older man pointed surreptitiously at the servant's quarters, and said, "That man who let us in last night, there's something in his eyes I don't trust. I bet he's told the military we're here."

Samuel wasn't sure if he should nod or shake his head. Suspicion is a natural state in situations like this.

"How is she taking all this?" Samuel asked, taking a less direct tack. "I mean, there seem to be so many secrets in the air. Is she not afraid?"

"Oh," Zulfikar said, his voice suddenly sorrowful. "She is very afraid, I can assure you. It's possible she hasn't been this afraid for a long time, nearly as long as you've been alive, brother—she's at least fifteen years older than you."

"Pak," Samuel said, unsure if he was about to offer a subterfuge or a confession, "believe me when I say I've seen a thing or two—bashings, knifings, friends turning on friends in self-defense, nights spent on hard, damp floors with no blanket. Hell, I, too, have known fear like an old friend."

Momentarily it seemed as though Zulfikar was regarding the younger man with a fresh pair of eyes. When he recovered he let out a guffaw, baring again those two rows of too-white, too-even teeth. "So when did you decide to repent?"

"I left Buru in the early nineties. I lost weight and learned to fly straight, and I've kept at it ever since."

Zulfikar leaned closer, as though the restless night they'd shared, coupled with this new honesty, had cemented something in his mind.

"I know you've guessed I was an eks-tapol," he finally said, his mouth wrapped around his cigarette. "You're a smart guy, and you're right. It's all true. I was in the third batch." He eased back again, blowing rings of smoke in the air. "Now that *that's* out of the way, this is what I need from you. Can you help me find the grave of a man? He, too, was an eks-tapol, and last I heard, he's dead."

"Which unit was he in?" Samuel asked, relieved at the sudden candor between them.

"Sixteen."

"Which unit were you in?"

"Same unit, different barrack. But this man I'm looking for—or his grave—he and I were good friends. We didn't meet on the transport ship. There were too many, over a thousand of us, like sheep. But we'd bump into each other early in the mornings when we collected our tools from the unit warehouse. Sometimes we shared corvée, you know that word, for unpaid forced labor? Tasks like being directed to carry equipment or supplies from the central logistics building in Namlea to the logistics building in our unit, or the other way around. That happened when our unit supplies dwindled. I'm talking rice, cooking oil, sugar, salt, salted fish, agricultural implements. Later we sought out each other at the concerts in the art center. We became close. He couldn't sing a note, but he knew his poetry. Western poetry mostly. Soon I found out he was a doctor, a damn good one.

"When I found out his privileged surname I expected him to be a typical Menteng kid. You know the type? Comes from money, has the right connections, doors open at the slightest mention of his family name—in other words, someone to keep at arm's length. For a long time none of the rest of us could figure out what he was doing here. Hell, we were suspicious of everybody.

"Then the story came out. He was someone who, well, cared. Hell, he was—and these days it's no longer politically correct—an *idealist*. He wanted to heal, not only individuals but also all of fucking humanity. He wanted to make a fucking difference. How's that for a life goal, eh? As for me, I'd be happy enough writing letters of complaint all day. But the real irony was that he wasn't actually a Communist Party member. He was not even officially from any of the Party affiliates. But one day in 1969, in Jakarta, he was scooped up and taken to Salemba Prison. Turned out he had friends at CGMI in Yogyakarta and among LEKRA artists, and at different points in his so-called career he'd offered his services at a Gerwani-run clinic in Tanjung Priok and helped out at a small hospital in Kediri. *And* he just happened to be a graduate from a university in East Germany. All those things combined finally got him arrested."

"So in order to end up here he must have been transferred from Salemba to Nusakambangan Prison," Samuel said. "But he wasn't even a diehard?"

"Well, let's say he was almost free from any formal affiliation, though he always surrounded himself with people from the Left. In Jakarta, typically, he had friends in HSI. Again, he wasn't a member, but he attended their meetings anyway. Another factor in what did him in. Poor bastard."

Samuel might have been way younger than Zulfikar, but he knew those acronyms and organizations like he knew his own family. Anyone who'd spent time on Buru did: HSI was the Association of Indonesian Scholars, CGMI was the leftist student organization commonly associated with the Communist Party.

Zulfikar suddenly said, "He was a bit of an unknown quantity, really. He kept to himself when he was not out saving the world. Not once did he ever speak of women, or even women friends, which made it all the more unexpected when Ibu here contacted me to ask for my help. But part of me wasn't surprised. He was the handsomest sonofabitch I've ever laid eyes on."

This touched on a thought already spinning in Samuel's mind, a sense of familiarity. He definitely recognized Zulfikar from somewhere. Could he possibly know this mystery man as well?

"Give me a name," he said.

Zulfikar Hamsa leaned toward Samuel and whispered it, as if the walls had ears: "Bhisma Rashad."

It was at that instant Samuel remembered how he knew Zulfikar. But before he could say anything Amba opened her door. She smiled at both of them with a brightness they could not ignore.

"Good morning, gentlemen."

When Amba said she wanted to get a better sense of the land, Zulfikar suggested that, before they did anything else, they drive the van up to a lookout point not far off.

Samuel was getting jumpy. His friend Hasan at police HQ had been messaging him since 9:00 a.m.: *Where the hell are you? What are they doing? Have you learned anything?* He had set his mobile to "Vibrate," and it felt like a landmine buried in his pocket. He knew that he and his companions wouldn't be able to stay off the radar forever. He could almost hear the rumor mill grinding.

The road was unpaved. Rocks and grit sprayed the underside of the van, sounding like heavy rain on a tin roof. This time Amba rode in the front seat, wedged between Samuel and Zulfikar. She would see and hear better there, she'd insisted.

Samuel was acutely conscious of her arm and hip, warm against his side. Every now and then he dared a quick look at her and marveled again at her generous, cushy mouth, her eyes so clear they could cut through icebergs.

Zulfikar narrated as they drove, pointing to barren stretches of land where a building used to be, slapping his hand against the dashboard to get Samuel to slow so he could explain this or that to Amba. She listened with unnatural attention, her laser-like gaze taking in the whole of the landscape, as if this was a university assignment, a prerequisite for graduating life. Samuel found himself listening, too, although he knew the story of Buru well enough, all the while trying to ignore the buzzing phone in his pocket.

Zulfikar asked Samuel to stop as they passed the shell of a concrete building standing in a field. He pointed at it and explained that it was a typical barrack. Mainly oblong shelters some fifty-five yards wide, with roofs, pillars, and walls made of sago, each housing about fifty people. Most of them rank and overcrowded but way better than the prisons in Java.

Samuel stepped on the gas again, continuing along the bumpy track winding up the mountain. He felt his phone vibrate again. How long would it be before the officials in Namlea caught up with them? He wanted to catch the older man's eye, to signal him somehow, but with Amba between them, and Zulfikar's attention pinned to the world sliding by the van's windows, there was too much going on.

It was a glorious morning, the sort you looked at and thought, *it is wonderful to be alive, to be a human being, bewildered by so many colors, the hustle and retreat of hours, the keeping things in and wanting to say so much.* The spread of light, like a long benediction. The grass still a little moist from the morning drizzle, but warmed now under the overlay of sunlight. The gravel on the road surface loose and contented, obliging one's every footstep.

A munificence that seemed to touch the older man, too. "There's this one thing we used to do. It's about creating our own secret spaces.

Like a kind of resistance. Take me, for instance. I can't live without writing. It's a necessity. Without it I go nuts. So I found a small clump of bamboo among some shrubs, and that was where I left the things I treasured, including the copies of my letters. You see, the guards censored everything that actually got sent off the island so we could never say what we wanted to say. So some of us wrote two versions of every letter. I rolled my copies into long tubes of bamboo and hid them among those plants. Even if they would never be read by anyone it was my way of staying true to myself."

"Anybody else do that?" Amba asked.

"Well, there were some," Zulfikar said.

"Even him?"

"You could say that."

It was the first time she had alluded to the ghost. Samuel felt her body tense against his and then shrink somehow, as if she was trying to contain and compress the emotions the name evoked.

There was silence in the van for a while until Zulfikar continued with his memories.

"Thank God there was work," he said.

Thank God, Samuel thought. Where would anybody be without it? How could anybody survive anything?

Zulfikar went on to tell the story of a political prisoner who found a simple but expedient way to make sure he and his friends did not get crushed by exhaustion. Worried about the prisoners who had to go up and down dangerous and slippery cliffs to transport water for their fields, this man remembered how the vegetable farmers in his hometown on the highland of Dieng, in Central Java, coped with similar conditions.

One day he suggested to his fellow prisoners that they apply the same method, showing them how to create pipes of bamboo through which they could transport the water directly to the fields. "A wonderful man, a wonderful writer," Zulfikar added. "Hersri is his name. A practical man of letters. So you see, they did exist in the prison camp. They were the ones who made a difference."

They had reached a fork in the road. Samuel slowed the van, waiting for Zulfikar's signal, and surreptitiously pulled his phone from his pocket. They were out of signal range. He leaned back, relieved that for a moment he didn't have to worry about Hasan's text messages.

He was only half there, as the conversation went on.

Thinking, Amba had mentioned. "Did you ever have time to think?"

It was obvious Zulfikar hadn't thought this through. "You'd think we would have so much time for that," he said, a little hesitantly. "But I really can't remember. At night you were either exhausted or fighting off the mosquitoes. I don't think you can even begin to imagine. The barracks were damp, malarial, partly open to the elements. We slept on bug-infested bunks, so close together that everybody lived with somebody else's BO and bad breath. But despite the barbed wire that surrounded our shelters, despite the beatings and humiliations and the fear that we would never get off this godforsaken island, we weren't that badly off. I mean, compared to those in other prisons."

The details of such days were gentle to the ears. Even he seemed surprised anew at how much they had. Every day they were able to smell the air and feel daylight on their faces. To go out into the forest to burn limestone, fell trees, catch fish. To hunt and raise cattle. He spoke of the arts center, his eyes hazing over: there was so much music, so much music-making. *How normal could it get: coming home from a hard day at work, playing the guitar, lounging in front the TV.* This was even better: you got to put up your own attractions, live them, laugh them, even if you didn't have to love them.

"And then there was the planting: the planting was important, too. The slavery bit was shitty, but it was part of the deal, and at the end of the day you still got to plant your own spinach and morning glory, your eggplant and your genjer, stuff you'd grown in Java, have a bit of home sprouting around you. You even got to teach native people about plants other than sago—as miraculous as sago was. The lucky ones got to spread the love even wider and bed the native women."

He suddenly sat to attention and shouted, "Here, stop. Pull over."

Samuel jerked the van to a stop on a broad rock platform leading to a precipice.

"We're here?" Amba said, her voice suddenly childlike. Samuel climbed out of his seat and turned to offer her his hand. She squeezed it like a brief gesture of thanks before jumping out of the van.

Shortly, from the outcrop where the three of them stood, the rice fields that were once woodlands gleamed in the sun like an unexpected gift. But the stunning vastness of the landscape and all that it obscured— the years of hard human toil that went into it, the mass humiliation, the blood spilled—wasn't the only thing that took Samuel's breath away. It was the look in Zulfikar's eyes.

"They miscalculated, you see," Zulfikar said, after a very long silence, his tone grim, almost cruel. "Suharto thought this island would become his Communist graveyard. But what we tapols found was a rice trove, a new soil, a new life. Plant almost anything in this Buru soil, even a political prisoner, and it will live."

But his eyes were surprisingly moist, and Amba caught this, too, so much that she had to look away from the view, fearful perhaps of stoking her own grief. On every side of the valley jagged mountains rose from the earth, like a pod of surfacing whales.

"Amazing," she muttered under her breath. "It's like, like a nod to Nietzsche."

"Who?" Zulfikar said, leaning toward her.

"Nietzsche," Amba repeated softly. "The German philosopher. That brilliant man who went, one day, to climb some mountains in the Alps. He stayed there awhile and wrote words that changed lives. Those mountains wouldn't have been too different from these, only snow-covered."

Zulfikar smiled politely, but it all went past him. He was used to knowing what he knew and sticking only to that.

As he was now. "When I got here in 1970 there were no fields. It was wilderness. The local people hunted pigs and deer and went deep into the forest to look for the sago palm, or if they lived by the sea they caught fish. The more enterprising of them planted cassava and sweet potato if they had arable land, but they were basically clueless about agriculture. But now look. Thousands of acres of paddy and pasture, farmland and irrigation channels, clove and coconut trees. To think that we created a miracle. A miracle that wasn't even ours."

Watching Zulfikar lean out over the edge, Samuel suddenly felt irritated. He wasn't sure where it was coming from. So the man still had his wits about him and was a fine storyteller. In the best of times—or the worst, Samuel couldn't decide—he was telling tall tales, creating a past fit for the ages. Or something he could tell his grandchildren about. Samuel had no issue with that, because that's what you do. You tell stories, because stories are all that's left. But who the hell did this old drone think he was talking to? It seemed that his stories weren't so much directed at him and Amba as to his friends and enemies from thirty years ago.

His anxieties resurfaced, rose up his chest. He glanced at his phone. Another message from Hasan. *Someone from wherever it is you're staying reported to HQ. An officer is arriving this morning. Don't veer too far from Savanajaya.* Samuel looked at his watch. It was already close to eleven. There wasn't much time to decide on a plan.

While Zulfikar continued to wallow in his past, Samuel walked some distance from him and Amba and made a quick phone call to a contact, a man named Julius, who he thought might know something about the eks-tapols on Buru. When he mentioned Bhisma's name the contact said, "Yes, I know Pak Bhisma. At least I know his name." Samuel told Julius he would call back with a place to meet.

The call over, Samuel switched off his phone. No use in transmitting a signal. It would only help the police officers who were tracking them down.

Samuel returned to the storyteller and his captive audience. "I just called a contact of mine, someone who may have information about your friend," he said, enjoying the satisfaction of stopping Zulfikar midsentence and having Amba's eyes fixed on him.

Zulfikar, who had clearly lost track of time, glanced at his watch. "We need to go now. I also have to meet a contact, an old friend of mine, at the school in Walgan. How close is your man? Can he meet us there as well in, say, half an hour?"

They all hurried back to the van. Samuel reactivated his phone and called Julius to confirm the meeting. During the call, he saw the beads of sweat gathering on the nape of Amba's neck. Suddenly she turned and said she needed to go behind the bushes.

As they watched her scurry away, Zulfikar said, "Your contact, how do you know him? Is he safe?" When Samuel hesitated, the older man, looking sapped, said, "Well, no matter. We'll be gone from this island in no time." Looking toward the bushes that hid Amba, he said, "We just need to make sure the rumors are true. To give her closure."

"I'm sorry, I don't follow. Rumors?"

"About Bhisma's death."

"What if they aren't? What if Bhisma *isn't* dead?"

"This guy Bhisma, well, she was once very much in love with him," Zulfikar said, lowering his voice. "They were lovers, more than forty years ago. But then they were cruelly separated and never saw each other again. You understand what I'm saying, yes? I myself am doubtful that the guy is still alive. But if there is the slightest chance that he is, she won't let go. She just won't, she's that type. And that's no good. She absolutely needs to get on with her life, be at peace with her past. I mean, that's what we all want, right? At the end of the day."

꿮

Samuel knew the village of Walgan. It was once part of the penal colony and the ideal place to be. If the police or military spies were intent on finding them, Walgan was an unlikely destination for most visitors to Buru. Going there would probably buy them some time.

Everybody was silent as Samuel drove the van back down the mountain. He still couldn't make up his mind about Zulfikar. He had suffered, yes, but what made his suffering so special? This was Indonesia, after all, where everyone had a personal story that would break your heart. How about the suffering of his own family all those years ago in the early 1950s, and their horror when they realized on their arrival in Holland that they were not allocated respectable abodes but stashed away instead in some godforsaken part of the land in an ex-Nazi concentration camp? How about his own suffering, being shipped off to Buru, never to see his parents, brothers, and sisters again? Besides, it was clear that the old codger didn't trust Samuel, not fully, anyway, and so what was there for him to give?

As he drove he was aware of Amba watching him. It was as if she had recognized a new—or was it old—emotion in him, a secret shade known to few. *But this is hardly the time to get carried away,* he thought. *There is a time for everything.* As he slowed the van in front of the school, he said to her, "We're here. Do you feel like getting out? The two contacts will meet us here soon."

Before them, framed by the windshield, was SMA Waeapo 3, a high school so postcard pretty it might have come from a kretek commercial. The building boasted a Javanese-style roof, three tiered and tin red, with a large courtyard. On the front lawn, stone seats were gathered around stone tables, three sets of them, all in the shade of a tall and motherly meranti tree.

"How wonderful!" Amba's voice rang. "Just look at this. The red of the building, the blood-red burst of the hibiscus flowers and the blue of the fence and the signs, so marvelous against the green of those tear-shaped trees." She stepped down from the van, onto the path once trodden by hundreds of eks-tapol, and turned to say breathlessly to Zulfikar, "How is it possible that they built a school this lovely on the site of a prison camp?"

It was close to midday. People milled about the school and the nearby mosque. Samuel glanced around nervously, hoping he wouldn't be recognized by an informer. It was a futile thought, however, since everyone on this island was a snitch. He watched two men working across the road, building a low stone wall beside a house shaded by banana trees. They cast sidelong glances as Amba walked by. They knew the three strangers had no business in this settlement. They wouldn't hesitate to file a report.

Samuel and Zulfikar kept silent, keeping an eye out for their contacts. But like the workmen, Samuel found it almost impossible to keep his eyes off Amba.

"Where are they?" Zulfikar said, nudging Samuel impatiently. "We haven't got much time."

"I don't know. Julius isn't answering his phone."

"Your contact has a phone?"

How do you think I called him? Samuel thought impatiently, wondering again what planet the old bore thought he was living on. Even Samuel's six-year-old nephew and the janitor at the Ambon train station had cell phones.

Zulfikar stood beneath the meranti tree, looking distressed. A cyclist wearing a black T-shirt emblazoned with the laughing face of Saddam Hussein passed by, giving them a pointed stare. Zulfikar waved him away, a patronizing gesture as musty as the waver.

Samuel noticed a short man wading through the thin crowd of passersby with a sense of purpose. "Pak Zul," the man called to Zulfikar when he was closer. His strong Melanesian features, unusually flat face, and deeply notched, protruding jaw, suggested he wasn't from Buru.

Zulfikar shook the man's hand.

"This is Jacko," he said. "Jacko, meet Pak Samuel."

"Pak," Jacko said, shaking Samuel's hand. Amba stood a few feet away, deliberately it seemed. "Bu," Jacko said to her, but he did not reach for her hand.

"So, Jacko, my man," Zulfikar said with one arm around his old buddy's shoulder. "Have you heard anything about Pak Bhisma?"

"I haven't heard anything, Pak. Not since *that day*," Jacko said. "Folks said he didn't turn up."

"This was two years ago. 2004. Jacko here is talking about a reunion of the eks-tapols who had made Buru their home, for old time's sake," Zulfikar explained. "You'd think we'd get together a lot, but no. We avoid each other like crazy whenever we can. So this was a big thing. Now we just refer to it as *that day*."

He turned back to Jacko and said bluntly, "We're here because we have reason to believe Pak Bhisma is dead. Please, help me here. Have you heard anything?"

"No, Pak. Nothing."

"You sure?"

Jacko looked at him earnestly. Yes, he was sure.

Zulfikar sighed. "Can you take us to where he lived—or lives?"

"Nobody knows where he lives."

"Someone must know."

"Nobody's seen him since that day. They say he disappeared. Just like that, like a ghost."

"Look, Jacko. Somebody wrote anonymously to Ibu here, saying he's long dead. Seems like it was somebody from Buru."

Jacko nodded, and then shrugged. "S'pose that's possible."

"Do you know who could have written to Ibu? Someone who could have written her an e-mail?"

Jacko's face was blank.

"Is there a roadside Internet warung here?"

Blank again.

"A *warnet*?" Zulfikar tried one last time.

Jacko's eyes began to wander. The guy was losing focus.

"You see, Jacko . . . My friend here, Pak Samuel, he has a friend who is coming any minute now. His name is—" Zulfikar looked at Samuel, a little desperately.

"Julius," Samuel said.

"There you go. Julius. Do you know a man named Julius, Jacko?"

Jacko thought a little, his eyes downcast, and then looked up. "Yes, yes, I might know him. When you and all the other prisoners left, I stayed, remember? I stayed and got married here. I know Julius—he's my wife's cousin. He told me he was often asked by the *tonwals* to help the prisoners carry provisions to Mako—the command headquarters. There was so much mud and dirt on the road, it always slowed down the warga."

"How come I don't remember this Julius guy?" Zulfikar said.

"Well, that's what he told me, Pak."

"Do you see him much, this Julius?"

"Yes, yes," Jacko said, a little impatiently. Then he thought the better of it, and said, "On and off."

Samuel watched the exchange with interest. It was clear Zulfikar wasn't prepared to trust a contact that Samuel produced. *So what the fuck are we doing?* Samuel thought. *Nothing more than plucking up disparate elements and forcing them together, forcing people to relive parts of a mutual history they might rather forget.*

With that unsettling notion in his head he hunkered down next to where Amba sat patiently on one of the stone benches and waited for Julius.

An hour later, all five were in the van heading to a settlement at the bottom of the valley they had seen earlier from the mountain. Jacko and Julius, their contacts-in-arms, had both been adamant that Bhisma was last known to reside there—before he wandered off to other parts of the island, away from familiar eyes. Jacko explained that the place was a special transmigration area, where the eks-tapols who chose to stay on in Buru after '79 were given priority land. From the lookout earlier that morning the distant settlement surrounded by emerald paddies had looked like an ugly, sprawling brown blotch dotted with white, less a commune for a New Life than an uneasy cluster of survival. Samuel, staring down from their vantage point, had thought, *So this is what freedom looks like.*

During the drive Zulfikar kept up his conversation with Jacko, speaking in a wobbly mixture of Ambonese, Indonesian, and sign language. Julius, a large-headed man with a square-jawed, impenetrable face, was quieter than Samuel remembered him. He, too, had served as a paid informant at the police HQ and had been among very few people in that sordid business Samuel felt he could trust. But something had changed now. Julius seemed restless and kept fidgeting. He seemed to hate being here. But as the van drew closer to the settlement the guy suddenly perked up. Pointing to a green stand-alone building with a Javanese roof, he said animatedly that the last meeting of eks-tapols had been held there and went on to describe the gathering.

Samuel was aware of Amba's eyes scouring the terrain ahead, as if for a sign or a portent, anything that might explain what had happened to her eks-tapol lover.

Then he heard her voice, so low, as if talking to herself. "Why would Bhisma end up in such a place? I still find it hard to believe. He who was so wary of walls and barbed wire. You'd think that his years in East Germany would have taught him to be careful, to look after himself, but no. He just had to know the other side of everything. Walls. Borders. Ideologies. He just couldn't let things go."

It was Julius who stepped in to fill the silence that followed. "We must find Marko. He's the *lurah*, the chief of the settlement. Let's not lose any more time."

When Zulfikar began muttering about the dangers of returning to Savanajaya, Julius offered his house for them to stay in overnight, after their meeting with Marko. It was not that far from the settlement, he said.

"Good idea," Zulfikar said grimly. "Tomorrow we will have to travel fast, and I have a feeling it would be a best to avoid the places we've already been to, like the school, like Warung R. M."

Surely that's stating the obvious, Samuel thought. *'Cause now we're on this wild goose chase.* There had to be a more efficient way to find out about this Bhisma. If it wouldn't blow his cover he could simply call Major Kusno at police HQ, come clean about the two visitors, tell him that they were only on the island to learn about the fate of a friend, then offer his share of the month's trade so that he wouldn't be further indebted to the good policeman in the future. Surely Kusno would know where any remaining eks-tapol would—could—be found on the island. But how could he risk Zulfikar or Amba learning he worked hand in hand with the police? That he was an informer, a traitor? Even if he didn't understand why it was so important for her to find out whether Bhisma was still alive, he could not risk losing Amba to the police. They would mistreat her, be nothing but stupid and boorish and wrong.

There was her voice again. "It's so peaceful here."

Samuel, reminded once again of her need—this foreign land—and of his own need to please and protect her, immediately threw the idea of calling Major Kusno to the wind.

Marko, the settlement's unofficial head, whom Julius said was from Sumatra, possibly Bangka or Palembang, had the face and bearing of an old guard: rough-hewn, suspicious, territorial. When they arrived at his house he eyed Zulfikar as though he'd come face-to-face with a worthy opponent.

"Bhisma Rashad used to live just there, at the corner house," Marco said in between incessant puffs from his cheap cigarettes. "He always kept to himself, never mingled with us. Sometimes we wouldn't see him for days, weeks. It seemed like he resented our presence. *Needed space*, he said. As if we didn't."

"Did he live with anyone?" Zulfikar asked.

"No one. I told you, he was a loner. And it's not like we cared. Most of us were too busy trying to make our own lives to bother with such fripperies as friendship." Marko went on to describe how the men who stayed on in Buru really never recovered from their harsh experience, despite making a new life on the island. "Some of these warga, you know, they just can't get out of the past. They mistrust everyone. They think they're still the same people, that the world is still the same world from forty years ago."

There was much bitterness in Marko's voice. Yet he clearly didn't want them to leave. So they ended up listening to his long list of woes, from the barbaric treatment of the eks-tapols to the shortcomings of the present government, all the while dying to be released. After what seemed like an eternity, he eventually gave Zulfikar the name of someone who lived high in the mountains above Lake Rana, a man known as a healer.

"Go and find him. He might know something." Then Marko laughed a rather unsettling laugh. "But don't tell me I didn't warn you. That healer is a prick. Big time. The kind of guy who'd boasted that he could give us special powers, powers that would make us untouchable. He said that all the time, when we were still in the prison camps.

Turned out he was a wanker. Loved only one guy, gave whatever powers he could to him. Want to know how we found out?"

How do you tell a foul-mouthed guy to respect a woman in his midst? This was a new territory, even for Samuel.

"One day Bhisma and a couple others were caught stashing timber planks out in the woods," Marko said. "That was one of the things we did to survive, hiding some of the quota of timber we had to cut where the bushes were dense, then sneaking it out later to sell, so we could buy a few things or pay for favors. We all did it. Anyway, Bhisma and these others were caught, dragged back to the barracks, and beaten up for good measure. The strange thing was, Bhisma didn't seem to feel anything. I mean, he was sitting there, with a hail of fists raining down on him, yet none of it seemed to hurt him. He showed no sign of pain at all. Afterward he didn't bruise either. So we assumed he'd been given the healer's powers. That's why I think this *hombreng* might know where he is."

After another half hour of Marko's torturous reminiscences and charming linguistic prowess, Zulfikar shot Samuel a look. They would learn nothing else from this man; it was time to go. With hurried thanks they left.

As they walked back toward the van, Amba said sulkily, "Well, that was rich. Special powers? I can't believe it. Did he truly think we're so provincial? So stupid? So . . ." She was running out of words. Still incensed by the earlier assault of such winning words as *hombreng* (homosexual) and others, no doubt. "I mean, just because his name is Bhisma? That the guy felt he *owed* him his mythical right? He's not even Javanese. He's not even anything. Maybe we should just go home."

"You're tired, I understand," Zulfikar said. "But if we go back now, you'll never get your answers. Is that what you want?"

Samuel wondered what Amba meant by "home." And it was she who had insisted on the journey. Why, then, would she give up so easily? It was getting late.

"So, Julius, where is this house of yours?" Samuel asked loudly.

Five minutes later they were at Julius's house, where the only solace anyone could offer a sad and disheartened Amba was a black T-shirt six sizes too big, a cup of lukewarm tea, and a fly that hovered drunkenly above it for a full minute before falling in.

❧

Samuel awoke to the sound of knocking. He saw Zulfikar opening the door of the house. Outside were three men. *Where's Julius?* Samuel thought. *Why didn't he open the door?* One of the men, a burly guy of about fifty, burst in without an invitation, his eyes darting around. He had the air of someone trained to watch, assess a situation, and take immediate and decisive action if required. Zulfikar seemed to be playing dumb, trying to steer the men away from Amba. Feigning terror, he gabbled that there was no money to be had.

"I never forget a face," the man said ominously, squinting at Zulfikar. "Weren't you in a unit down by the Waeapo, back in the camp days?" Shifting his gaze to Jacko, he said, "And you. I remember you. You used to hang out with the prisoners. What name did they give you at the barracks?"

By now Samuel had wiped the sleep from his eyes and sat bolt upright. Where was Julius? Panic set in.

The bully said to Jacko, "Dog, right? Something to do with dogs."

Zulfikar drew a long breath while Jacko huddled with his arms around his knees, trying to shrink from view.

Black dog, Samuel thought. The term was a downright insult at the barracks, thrown around only when the intent was serious. It was the name given to the Ambonese who assisted the Dutch back in the colonial days, and on Buru it became the name for despised tapols who became informants for the guards. Then it dawned on Samuel that it wasn't Jacko but that shit Julius who was the black dog. Julius who, with his offer of hospitality for the night, had planned to inform on them, and like sheep they had dumbly walked right into the slaughterhouse.

"And you!" the man said, shifting his gaze back to Zulfikar. "Aren't you the one who helped decide who got off the island first when the prison camp closed down? You were quite the favorite with the prison camp lords then, weren't you?" The man's hectoring stopped short when he suddenly noticed Amba, who was so obviously not local. His voice was as sharp as a blade as he asked Zulfikar, "Is that your wife?"

"Yes," Zulfikar said without hesitation.

Amba inched toward her "husband" as subtly as she could. Samuel felt a twinge in his heart as he watched her seek Zulfikar's protection.

"What are you here for?" the burly man asked Zulfikar.

"Business, sir. This Jacko here is my local partner. We do business through Firma Abdulalie, in Ambon. You know them, yes? Their main office is on Jalan Sultan Babullah, the one with that famous seafood restaurant just across the road. Best seafood there is, and ours is the best oil."

Samuel had to hand it to Zulfikar. The man's wit was unflinching, and he had to admire it. But the burly man shifted his attention, and now his eyes were on Samuel.

"You! Have I seen you before?" he demanded.

"I'm not sure, Pak, but you could have."

"Where do you hang out?"

"Namlea, Pak, mostly," Samuel said. "I have friends in the police force there."

Samuel, aware of Zulfikar's glance, wondered for the umpteenth time, *Doesn't he know? Hasn't he guessed that I'm a sometime informant?* But he couldn't second-guess Zulfikar. Maybe he'd assumed this all along and factored it in.

Who was this ugly sonofabitch? Samuel couldn't place him among the policemen he knew, although he did look vaguely familiar. Another informant? Working for the military, the Green Berets? The man had a crew cut beneath his cap, and his body was ropy with cords of muscle although they were slackening with age. More of a threat than Samuel had originally thought.

"Who do you know at police HQ?" the man demanded.

"Oh, just a few junior sergeants from the tactical unit, mainly in internal security and crowd control," Samuel said dismissively. "You know how that is. They're always being reassigned so that they'll actually have something to do."

"And you've been staying here since when?"

"Since last night."

"Why not in Namlea?"

At this point Zulfikar rose. He had produced, from thin air it seemed, a slim lacquered box, which he opened and offered to the brute and the two men behind him. As they reached eagerly for the cigarillos Zulfikar patted their leader on the shoulder. The scary guy looked again at Amba, up and down, and winked at Zulfikar, who played along.

Samuel felt sick. How could Zulfikar acquiesce to this game? But who was he kidding? After all, Zulfikar came from a generation of men who, despite their insistence on female purity, still thought of women as no better than gambling chips. And yet, his brazen display of chauvinism might be what saved them. He looked over at Amba, who had remained quiet the whole time. She looked diminished, shrunken into herself. But she would know as well as he did that there was no other way; she had to suffer this indignity if they were to get out of this situation.

Zulfikar was presently ushering the men outside, taking that stupid, sickening laughter with them. His gamble seemed to be paying off. Eight cigarillos later he came back into the treacherous house alone.

Samuel and the others waited ten minutes to make sure the men did not intend to return. Then they clambered back into the van and set off. There was no time to lose. Samuel couldn't remember what had been said about where they were headed next, but Julius had overheard all their discussions. If that thug who'd crashed in on them remained suspicious, how long would it take his superiors to deploy a team?

He mentally kicked himself. He should have known better than to involve Julius. The road he drove along shimmered with heat. Jacko was navigating in the seat beside him, while Amba, suddenly a slip of a thing, a ghost, rode in the backseat with Zulfikar. He could almost hear the hum as Zulfikar's mind calculated how much of a liability he was.

The episode at Julius's house still filled his head. But it was the memory of Zulfikar claiming Amba as his wife that stayed with him. What a sleazebag. What an asshole. He imagined the conversation when Zulfikar took those men outside, the sly nudges, the leers: *You saw her. Yes, she's something, isn't she, that woman, even if she's getting a bit on in years. What I said back there in the hut, you know that wasn't true. She really isn't my wife, but you know women. You've got to keep them happy. They need to keep their respectability intact even if they'll jump at the slightest chance to misbehave. Women. Ha! But what can we do? We have no choice but to tolerate them.*

Samuel gripped the steering wheel more tightly as the vehicle wound on toward the blue cummerbund of Fud Siul, the mountain that only yesterday Zulfikar had spoken of. It felt like it was the only thing he had control of, for now.

Jacko, sitting next to him, seemed to sense his tension. "Don't worry, Pak Samuel," he said. "It won't be too difficult to find the healer's house."

After miles of listening to nothing but the gloomy, grating sound of the van's spinning wheels, Amba seemed to revive. "How long have you known Jacko?" she whispered to Zulfikar. She was probably afraid that Jacko, too, might turn out to be a traitor.

Zulfikar seemed to like the unexpected question.

"It was on Nusakambangan," he said, "that strange, foul island, the ugliest and most vulgar of prisons. People still say the word *Nusakambangan* as if it were hell on earth. And it was." He leaned forward to touch Jacko's shoulder. "Brother. You remember, don't you? We were there for five months before we were shipped off to Buru. You were no bigger than my son was at the time. A little imp, really. But that's how it is. You take your friends as they come."

And then the story.

"How important that was, to have a sense of humor on that boat. Yes, we told jokes. Lots of them. Jokes mostly of the last supper and the they'll-soon-have-us-walk-the-plank-and-feed-us-to-the-sharks-at-the-end-of-this-all-but-we-don't-care-because-life-is-good kind. And we had songs! Lots of them! Name it, we sang them all. On our last morning we went up on deck to see heavenly sunlight lighting up everything, the bowsprit, the gunwale. Then we saw it. Buru, stretching before us like a dozing *whale* . . ."

There were more disembodied words: *landing craft . . . marching the beach . . . the first mile . . . mangroves . . . Transit Unit . . . pouring rain . . . mosquitoes . . . festering sores . . . purgatory . . . krinyu the healing plant . . . human chariots . . .*

Samuel heard the last words with a jolt. "Human chariots," he echoed.

"That's right," Zulfikar said. "That's what we called ourselves when they made us transport people, VIPs, on our backs."

"I know," Samuel heard himself saying, the abruptness of his confession startling even himself. "I remember those words. I saw it many times when I was a child of only thirteen."

Suddenly it was impossible to hold back the secrets of his childhood that, over the past two days, had seemed so important to hide. Now he couldn't have been more eager to share them. It was impossible to drive on. He pulled the van over in the shade, and, turning to look at his three shocked companions, he spilled his guts.

When Samuel finally faltered and stopped Zulfikar didn't so much stare at him as glare, with that unsettling, laser focus. He knew what the old man was thinking: *We've been together for two days, and you're only now telling me you were here the whole time? You saw me. You probably saw Bhisma, too. Yet you stayed quiet. Just what kind of person are you?*

Samuel turned away from his accuser's eyes. He'd said his piece. Zulfikar and Amba could do with that information as they wished. He drove on, the road becoming increasingly winding as it rose up into more mountainous country. It wasn't until after Jacko asked him to stop that Samuel realized Amba was crying in the backseat.

14

The Healer

They walked into the engulfing sonority of the mountains, following Jacko's lead. *Trust,* Samuel kept mouthing to himself. He wasn't sure why he felt he needed to convince himself, perhaps because Julius— *his* guy!—had taken the cake on matters of duplicity. As they walked Samuel could see in the glinting valley below not just Lake Rana, but also the roofs of houses, the locals working among the fruits and vegetables in their gardens, farmers tending to their rice fields. The greenness and the expanse of things pleased him.

As they climbed higher they saw fewer houses, and then none, but Jacko was confident of his direction. "When I was in this area two years ago, a local whispered to me there was a house on the hill, a house belonging to a healer. A healer who used to be a prisoner. It must be our guy."

And then, just like that, a hut appeared before them. It sat at the edge of a steep drop into the valley, with the sea green of Lake Rana spreading out below. It was a stand-alone structure made of driftwood and stringy bark, not the usual *gaba-gaba*. A decomposing chair stood near the entrance, an inflatable Doraemon doll with a wide, cartoon-ish grin sitting in it. They found the healer nearby, poking at the soil beneath a sickly-looking plant. He was grizzled and sun browned, dressed in a pair of tattered shorts and looking a hundred years old. He seemed oblivious to the rocks he knelt on as he poked and prodded at the plant.

"A girl gave that to me," he said without preamble, proudly indicating the Doraemon.

Samuel saw Amba shudder, apparently taken aback by the toy's idiotic face.

"And why not?" he said. "Perhaps it will help keep away the thieves."

"I know this man," Zulfikar whispered to the others. "Unit XV, if I'm not mistaken."

The moment seemed to demand a certain curtness and economy. He stepped forward. Extended a hand toward the old man. Introduced himself and his old unit at the prison camp.

"Ha! I know what you're thinking," the healer roared with a friendly laugh, halting Zulfikar in his tracks. "You think I'm trouble!"

He rose unsteadily with the aid of his stick and hobbled toward Zulfikar. Samuel had to suppress his laughter. Trouble? No, more like black magic. Devil's rock. Fertility. Failure. How spectacular it was that this man, who looked as though he hadn't bathed for years, perhaps since his release from the penal colony, still seemed connected to the outside world.

He watched the ancient figure sweep his gaze over the odd group. It seemed a gaze accustomed to assigning people to boxes. What did he see? Zulfikar as a Sumatran, Jacko as either a Buru native or an Alfuru, Samuel himself perhaps as a funny hybrid, and Amba, ah, surely he would see her as a pleasing specimen of Javanese. But there was a strong sense that despite it all they were no different from a pack of dogs, or goats, or ducks, and of no concern to him.

The old man was waving his stick now, animatedly. Maybe he hadn't seen so many people for a long time. Then he squinted. Looked Zulfikar up and down. "Do I know you?"

"I'm a friend of Bhisma Rashad from Unit XVI. My name is Zulfikar." As they finally shook hands, Zulfikar's voice turned a little wavery. "So happy to meet you again, bung. If I'm not mistaken, your name is Rukmanda, yes?"

The next hour passed slowly. The old man tipped the Doraemon off his chair and invited Amba to sit there; the men found places on the floor. Samuel, sitting on the edge of the porch, felt the house sway, as if it had no foundation. The healer offered them no nourishment, not even water. He just perched himself on the damp edge of the raised platform made of split slabs of wood. Jacko sat fidgeting until, finally unable to contain himself, he stood and volunteered to put a blanket of soil over the areas Rukmanda had disturbed with his stick.

But the healer waved away the offer. "There will always be thieves, even at this height," the healer said with a laugh. "No use hiding my treasures anymore."

There was a subtle shift in the air, like a gathering of breath. Zulfikar must have sensed it, too, because his next question changed from the small talk and reminiscences of the last hour into something much more direct.

"You gave Bhisma your powers, yes?"

The healer smiled, forming further wrinkles on his already over-creased face. "You knew him well?"

"Yes. We were close."

"Have you been in touch since you left the island?"

"No."

"Wait. Let me make sure I've understood," the healer said, suddenly gathering focus. "You were close, and yet this is the first time you've tried to find out what became of him?"

"I can explain. I always knew Bhisma was meant to be alone. I had the sense that if he knew too much, about anyone, anything, he would someday be compelled to do"—Zulfikar's voice began to falter—"well, to do something heroic. There was no news about his whereabouts, not until recently."

"That's why you never tried to find out about him?"

"Pak Rukmanda," Amba suddenly interjected. Her voice seemed hardened by new resolve. "I'm the one looking for Bhisma. It's because of me we're all here today. I needed to find out if Bhisma is dead or alive."

"So you are she."

Amba let his reply breathe. Then she said, perhaps deliberately, "You see, Pak. Someone I don't know recently sent me an e-mail. It was sometime in January. He or she told me Bhisma had died."

The old man leaned back and with a gentle toss of the head he said, "All right. Let me tell you something about Bhisma."

ꝏ

The healer had first noticed Bhisma when the tall man and some other prisoners joined his work crew for a meranti logging project. Rukmanda's unit hadn't had the manpower to do the job themselves, and because in such a project there was always a risk of accidents, the young doctor was exactly the insurance they needed. Like getting a two-for-one deal. This young doctor certainly was worth it. In fact, he was something else. His reserve, his elegance, and his impossibly fine features were hard to miss. As was his extraordinary endurance.

That first day of working with Rukmanda's team, for instance. He worked all day in the blazing sun, worked as though the strength of a dozen men had been crammed into him.

"Before an hour had passed," the healer said, "I knew that he was special. The work was punishing. There were not enough sickles, shovels, and *parang*s to go around, and we often had to pull grass six feet high with our bare hands.

"On the eighteenth day of that hell, after the crew had nearly completed clearing a four-mile stretch of road, I was called to inspect a small dike to the west. I wasn't well, so Bhisma and two other tapols were dispatched along with me. The sun was low by the time we began our return. I remember dawdling a bit. Suddenly something cold slithered across my bare feet. It was a mud snake. Not your typical *sanca*, but a black brute, about four feet long. *This is it,* I thought to myself. *This is how I will meet my end.* My mind raced, turning over all the advice I'd ever heard about dealing with snakes: don't run, wait until the snake moves on and walk away quietly. But I froze. I was in shock. Afterward, all I could remember was the sight of the back of the head of the man who was ahead of me, thinking how funny it looked, the hair caked with a thick layer of mud, how helmetlike and bald, and how this would be my last vision on earth.

"Then Bhisma ran up and there was the sick sound of something tearing the air, and the next thing I knew the snake's head was chopped off. Bhisma was staring at it, dumbfounded, fresh blood dripping from his parang.

"'Whatever made you do that, get so close to its head?' I asked when I recovered my breath.

"'I don't know,' Bhisma said. 'I had to take the risk.'

"Together we stared at the carcass of the mangled reptile. The man in front, Helmet Head, came back to take a closer look, but I pushed him back, saying, 'Don't. Sometimes dead snakes bite.'

"'That's life,' Bhisma said suddenly. It was such an unexpected thing to hear that I spun around.

"What?"

"'To kill a snake you've got to chop off its head, not hack at its tail,' he said with a hard but vacant look.

"That's when I first realized that Bhisma's essence was that kind of wisdom, at once impulsive and measured. He'd do this kind of stupid, surprising, artless thing one moment and the next he'd exercise the utmost control. Everyone cleared the way when he walked because they all saw the light that emanated from him, and they never doubted his intentions were just."

After the incident with the snake, the healer said, he knew Bhisma would be the one to receive his powers. His were neither the powers to perform magic, nor were they the powers to heal, to kill, to vanish at will. They were the powers of self-preservation.

"Once I conferred those powers no one would be able to touch Bhisma, alter his physical self, or harm him without his consent. He'd be able to choose the moment of his death."

"But did that happen? Did he choose that moment, my Bhisma?" Amba asked with that quiver Samuel had come, absurdly, to know so well.

The healer looked at her tenderly. "My own powers do not extend to knowing such things, Bu," he said, sounding genuinely regretful. "In fact, I am quite certain that my own abilities diminished the day I gave Bhisma those powers."

"How will I know, then?" she said, her eyes starting to water. "How will I know if he has truly died?"

The healer was silent. "Buru is full of spirits," he finally consented to saying. "Good spirits that will lead you to him."

This seemed their cue to leave.

After meeting the healer, Amba seemed momentarily appeased. There was an easy accord between her, Samuel, and Zulfikar as they dropped Jacko back at his soa and moved away from the hinterland. When they arrived in Namlea, they immediately checked in at the hotel near the port.

At dinner that evening, at a restaurant near the hotel, Amba mentioned the possibility of going back to Jakarta. Maybe it was Zulfikar's obvious fatigue that compelled her. Perhaps she just didn't want to be a burden to them any longer. Or perhaps she was so sick and tired of them—of him—she just wanted to up and disappear.

At this point she still hadn't spoken of her personal life. He had no idea if she had children, a husband, parents who were still alive. He mistrusted her look of defeat a little. She seemed resigned; the man she loved had certainly died, and finding the cause, or his grave, would be too long and harrowing a process. She looked like someone who was ready to close a book. But who was she kidding?

And what would closing the book mean to him, Samuel Lawerissa from Ambon? Would she still need him, or had this journey with her been for naught and he meant nothing at all to her? He desperately wanted time alone with her, to ask those questions about her life, just to be with her. Fatigue might have softened Zulfikar somewhat, making him more benign, but he was still always in the way.

So Samuel did what all men in thrall to a woman do: he began, quietly but actively, to court Amba. He offered, out of a mix of chivalry, responsibility, and grief over the prospect of losing her soon, to gladly escort her and Zulfikar back to Jakarta, should that be their plan. He told her he could arrange the boat ride back to Ambon—on a fast boat if she preferred it rather than that shitheap of a ship—and a flight to Jakarta.

"I know a nice hotel near the market in Ambon where we could stay," he said. "The fruit and vegetable stalls look wonderful this time of year. You'll be able to glimpse them from the balcony of the hotel when you're having breakfast."

But Zulfikar, as usual, took over and ruined everything. "Thank you, my boy," he said while laughing dismissively, "but we already know that same hotel in Ambon. We stayed there for the night before board-ing our ship to Buru. We'll probably stay there again. But you're most welcome to travel back with us."

Samuel decided he couldn't take any more of the older man's near-psychotic need to be in control. Later, he told himself, he would catch Amba alone.

❧

The opportunity came sooner than Samuel anticipated, after dinner, on their walk back to the hotel. Zulfikar had unexpectedly met an acquain-tance, an attractive local businesswoman wearing a headscarf. She was accompanied by her brother. The woman was once a manager with quite a prominent state-owned bank, Zulfikar told them with a wink. "She's almost like a younger sister to me. By the way, she was quite a looker in her day." Obviously he found enough traces of how she once looked to feel the urgent need to disappear with her for a while.

Amba suggested to Samuel that they go somewhere for a beer. She didn't seem to miss Zulfikar's presence. In fact she seemed happier, more relaxed. Samuel liked the way she drank her beer, at the bar, with none of the bourgeois unease all too often encountered among her kind. He felt himself uncoil, too.

"So what did the e-mail actually say?" So easily, so painlessly he asked it.

"A single line: 'Bhisma is dead. He who began and ended in Buru.'"

"There was no way to identify who sent it?"

"The address was savana.jayamahe0903@gmail.com. Go figure."

"Sounds fake to me."

"Hmm, yes, I thought so myself. I sent a reply. No surprise, it bounced back."

"So, pretty much a dead-end street?"

"Yes. And it was funny, really. Funny in that it was so effective. It looked like a combination of words I'd read somewhere a long time ago, something important, something that didn't have anything to do with grasslands or plains, or a certain porn star, or even with '*Jalesveva Jayamahe*,' which I remembered from my daughter's history lessons as the Sanskrit motto of the Indonesian Navy: 'In the seas we triumph.' But I did connect the dots: Savanajaya, the sea, the savanna, and so forth. I knew whoever wrote it was legit."

"Strikes me as rather poetic, though, that line."

"I suppose."

"Do you think it might be deliberate? For effect, I mean."

"It might be. Have you seen some of those widely distributed Ramadhan good wishes and Eid Fitri greetings? All those tedious, long-winded *pantun*s. Ridiculous. But there are types of poetry that take a long time to write, trudgingly, heavily, heart achingly, with all your soul, with all the weight of your pain and longing, and every time you finish writing such a poem you feel the same tiny death you feel after you've just given birth. Believe me, I know."

"Which particular part do you know?"

"Both. I like writing poetry and I have given birth."

"Do you have more than the one daughter you just mentioned?"

"No. Just the one."

"How old is she?"

"You know, you're really quite cute," Amba said, laughing as though to remind him that they weren't exactly strangers. "Sweet and cute. You ask as though I were a mere child myself. My daughter is nearly forty. She is a conceptual artist. She's tough and wily, gets to travel the world."

"Oh. And her father . . . ?"

"She looks exactly like her father."

"Ah. I'm sorry. Your husband—Zulfikar told me that he passed away quite recently, at the end of last year."

"He told you that?"

Samuel nodded.

"Yes, my husband did pass away. But my daughter—she looks very much like her father."

What Amba was trying to say, or not, slowly dawned on Samuel. He said hesitantly, "Do you suppose—is it possible that Zulfikar sent you that e-mail?"

"Zulfikar? I know what you're thinking, that he's capable of such a thing, that there is something in his nature that latches on to such tricks. But somehow I don't think so. Why not make himself known to me directly?"

"Deep down, do you believe Bhisma is dead?"

She paused to consider it, then said: "Let's say I don't yet believe he's not dead."

In the morning, Zulfikar was gone. Samuel and Amba had seen him before, scurrying back into the hotel close to midnight, so flustered that he hadn't seen the two of them talking at the bar over a nightcap. Samuel tried not to think about what the old codger had been up to but couldn't help wondering how it was arranged: was it the woman joining him in his room later, upon a text message signal from him, or would it be him sneaking out of the hotel later to join the woman?

To Samuel, Zulfikar's absence at breakfast the next day felt like no more than a slight shrinking of the air.

15

The Truth and the Grotesque

Daytime has a way of dancing without a care on Buru Island. It was the first of March, and Samuel felt a sense of accomplishment in the air. He still couldn't believe it had only been a few days since he'd first met Amba on the *Lambelu*. How quickly she had become part of his life and had seeped into his being.

Now, having just finished breakfast and with a blank slate of a day, they agreed to meet in an hour for a stroll around the port and the beach area.

Samuel went back to his room to smoke and gaze out the big window of their hotel, an unabashedly nouveau riche stucco construction of loud salmon hue. Amba had said something rather sweet at breakfast. Something about her mornings here with him giving her a surprising lightness, exactly what she needed in order to be in touch with her own wellspring.

Yet how close were they really to the truth she was seeking? Was it possible for Bhisma to still be alive? From Samuel's perspective it would be so much easier if he weren't. Though who knew how long it would take for them just to establish that fact? As with many figures of myth, the more Samuel heard about Bhisma the less he felt he had existed at all.

So he was this demigod, a creature for burning and exaltation. As epic as the woman who loved him. But from what Samuel had gleaned from Amba and Zulfikar, he was also reluctant and unreliable, deceptive in his anchor-like stillness and veneer of worldliness. Yet he touched people like no one else, it seemed, even if he had the tendency to let go what passed through his healing hands. After all, this man, Bhisma, had abandoned Amba. And with him no longer by her side, this woman, so remarkable in her own right, had had to sew her life shut in order to keep him intact.

Now she seemed to have given up hope, and in light of that he felt he was tasked to shepherd her to safety. He felt blessed as his gaze strolled along the coastline below, buoyant breezes driving away the smattering of clouds to reveal an expanse of blue that mirrored the aqua beneath. It was almost impossible not to feel magnanimous before such beauty.

But an hour later, when they took that walk by the water, Amba's mood had darkened. They hadn't yet agreed on a plan to leave for Ambon and continue on to Jakarta. It was clear that she was now torn between staying and leaving. Around them the port teemed with pedestrians, motorcycles, vans, and taxi drivers peddling their wares all the way to the shoreline. There were more men with hints of a crew cut beneath caps than women with headscarves. This only confirmed what he'd been thinking for some time now: all things considered, Namlea was a modern city, a veritable unisex scene of cell phones and tight jeans, and something about this warmed his heart. He wanted to point this out to her as they walked along the waterfront toward the military headquarters, which used to be the central command of the penal colony.

All around them were satellite dishes and neat cement roads.

"What a blow for Communism, eh?" he said.

Despite her weak smile, Amba hadn't snapped out of her desolation. Gone were her wit, that laser gaze.

"Look," he said, perhaps a little too desperately, "I know one man who might help us. I know you might not trust me after the Julius debacle, but this man is a policeman, a good one. He won't turn us in. So let's go back to the hotel now. And give me an hour or two to find him. I'll bring him to meet you."

He would never forget the look on Amba's face the moment she first laid eyes on Sabarudin, the Grotesque.

They met over lunch in a restaurant. First Lieutenant Sabarudin didn't look like a policeman. He looked like his features had been thrown together from random bits of wood and rock, as if in some troglodytic battle. His mouth was not so much a mouth as a terrible red gash. Everything about him was gross: the size of his body, his feet, his hands, the way he dribbled oil all the way to his chin like a rich fat brat and didn't even bother to wipe it off. Very early in their acquaintance he appeared to have decided not to look at Amba, even when addressing her. While this was by no means a rare occurrence in Indonesia—many men are taught not to look at unmarried women, or young women, or attractive women at any rate, perhaps because there is always something of the monstrous in them—Samuel could feel Amba's distaste.

"What is his value to us?" she said almost hysterically when the policeman had gone out of the restaurant to take a call.

"Mobility," Samuel shot back. "Without informers or intelligence agents on our back."

"Where has he gone now—with that phone? What is he saying now, about us? Where is all this coming from? Have you sold your soul?"

Samuel felt his heart empty out. Why was she so angry? He wanted to shout back at her, *I'd do anything for you, anything to reunite you and your lover, dead or alive. I'd do this three thousand times over even if I think Bhisma is an ungrateful, unworthy idiot to have abandoned you like this.* But he didn't.

"We may have to go to Kepala Air," Sabarudin announced as he lumbered back into the dining room. He wolfed down the last of the fried tempeh and then leaned back in his chair. "So. Here are the facts," he said. "Kepala Air is farther inland, near the headwaters of the Waeapo. The wellspring. There's a major village there, but it avoided most of the religious conflict. Many survivors went up there to hide. Folks say that it's either the safest or the most perilous place on this island, depending on which spirit you've traded your soul with. There's also a hospital there, and that's where people are bound to end up. I have a feeling that's where we have to go."

"Why, again, do we have to go specifically to this place?" Amba's voice was hard.

"I believe this man you're looking for, Bhisma Rashad, eventually settled there. Rumor has it that over the years of the Transmigration Era—as the locals call it to distinguish it from the Tapol Era of the penal colony—Bhisma cultivated himself as not only a healer but something of a sage, a shaman. He was called the Wise Man of Waeapo."

Samuel tried to absorb this information objectively, like a history student. Over the time he'd spent with Amba and the others he'd formed an image of how Bhisma must have looked. If the man was so godlike, it was easy to understand how he could have earned such a reputation.

Then followed the rest of Sabarudin's account. "In August 1999, after the fighting that broke out in North Maluku spread to the islands, something in Bhisma must have snapped because, according to my informant, he packed his bags, closed his house, left his goats, chickens, cows, and his beautiful green gardens of *turi* and *mahoni*, *puspa* and *rasamala* in the care of neighbors, and went away."

The Grotesque went on to explain that the next thing the Burunese knew, the rage of religions that had begun in Ambon started to bear down on them, too. In the middle of the night a fire fiercer than any they'd seen gutted a church near the coast in a little over half an hour. The Christian community retaliated, followed by more and more retaliations from both sides. It lasted through the year, the violence uncontrollable. It was hard to distinguish between those who wronged and those who were wronged; neighbors who saw each other as enemies searched in the rubble for neighbors who had been friends. Soon dawn and dusk were interchangeable as violence's preferred aperture. People did unto others what they felt they had to while closing their eyes.

I too have an account of those days, Samuel thought. He would share it with Amba inside of a minute if he could. But while he felt for Bhisma, slinking in and out of that black-and-red time that he, too, so vividly remembered, he continued his silence on this matter, the boy having grown into a man.

When Sabarudin finally finished his meal they formulated a plan, agreeing to head to Kepala Air. They would leave the hotel very early in the morning so as not to waste time.

After the Grotesque left, something in Amba seemed to come undone. She told Samuel that Sabarudin was right. She needed to go back to her room. She would come to his door in the evening, when she was ready. Then maybe they could have another stroll, or a meal, or whatever it is that people do when chained to waiting.

Samuel sat on the bed in his hotel room, unable to stop his legs from shaking. He kept hearing footsteps in the corridor, pacing and hesitating, but when he rushed to the door and opened it he found only damp carpet, a trail of clove cigarette, and silence. He did not see her for afternoon tea, or for another walk, or for dinner.

Sometime before midnight, when he thought he was losing his mind, he went back out into the corridor and stood in front of her room, two doors down from his. He stood a moment, trembling, irresolute. And then knocked.

In his derangement, Samuel had forgotten that he had removed his shirt. He saw her cast her eyes over the ribbed flesh of his long torso as he stood in her doorway, towering above her in the dim overhead light, his chest heavy with expectation. She had been crying; her face was pinched and red.

A gust of air conditioning from her room wrapped him in chill, then she was in his arms, her warmth pressing against him. Just like that, in the corridor of a hotel, at the end of the world, in the middle of the night. The light quivered, as though he was on the threshold of a new intimacy. Was she finally about to allow him to be happy? Allow herself to be happy?

But it was her cry that suddenly penetrated the air.

"My God, Samuel! To be left in this state! In this *god-awful* state! Have you any idea how bad it has been? This forsaken island, this hellhole of a hotel! After all I've been through! The fridge in my room doesn't work, there's no hot water, the dust's waist deep, and the sink is full of peeled paint. I can't even get a phone signal. Do you even care? Do you even care about how I feel in this room by myself, too afraid to read? Would you give a shit if I died in my bed not knowing whether he was dead or alive?"

How could he even begin to tell Amba that it was he, and not Zulfikar, who had paid for her room? He who had very little money, who always had to work several jobs at a time to make ends meet? That he'd in fact paid an extra two hundred thousand rupiah to ensure her comfort, and that consequently he ended up with the last room in the entire hotel, its creaking bed so bug infested he'd have been better off spending the night on the damp and slashed vinyl sofa by the pay phones in the lobby.

It couldn't be avoided. He had to put it into words. But before he managed to say anything, she pulled back dramatically from his arms.

And there it was: the snap in his chest. He'd held on for too long. He was like a driver sensing the rear wheels of his car slipping away from him each time he steered into a curve, and now he'd crashed. He was a hell of a driver but he'd lost it. He'd crashed.

Still, the words didn't come out. Meanwhile, she folded her arms across her chest and hissed, "You have deceived me. I understand if you couldn't tell Zulfikar, or Jacko, or that shithead Julius. But how could you not have told me you were a police informer? You lived here as a child, and you could have told me earlier that you might have recognized Zulfikar, and you might even have seen my Bhisma. I understand that your childhood may be a part of your life you don't really want to talk about. But to lie about the reason you've been helping me, letting me think you were just being kind and considerate, even a godsend? Did you really think I hadn't the right to know?"

Had it been so obvious? When had she realized?

"You're a goddamn snitch. Yes or no? You brought that treacherous bastard Julius into my affairs!"

Samuel still couldn't find his voice.

"You know, I'm not some rich bourgeois bitch who came here looking to *understand* something about how the other half lives."

What to say? He might have spent his life with gunshots and cries splitting the winds around him, but he would never understand anger.

"You *knew* what I was about. I've opened up as much as anyone could under my circumstances. After years of waiting for Bhisma, of not knowing why he disappeared, of not knowing what happened the day I lost him, where the hell he'd gone, whether he was dead or alive, why he didn't come back to me as soon as he could have, in '79. Forty-one years of loving a ghost—"

He turned away.

"Look at me," Amba said. "Damn you. Look at me."

When he finally spoke, he didn't recognize his own cold voice. "What do you want from me? Yes, I am a police informant. *A goddamn snitch.* If I'd wanted to, I could have turned you and Zulfikar in on day one. But I didn't, which is why you're here with me now, and not at the mercy of those men who'd do things to you, things so unspeakable you'd wish you were dead. That's the plain truth. Deal with it as you will."

Morning only piled up the cruelties. Minutes before he was to meet Amba in the lobby, not having slept a wink, he received a text message from Sabarudin. *Sorry, duty calls. Can't make it with you and Ibu to Kepala Air.* Samuel called the policeman, frantically pleaded with him. But the outcome stayed the same: the Grotesque wasn't coming.

Conveying the news to a sullen Amba wasn't easy. "Sabarudin's been held up. Some guy has been detained for nearly killing his wife, and he's been left with the case file."

"Maybe that monster was talking about himself," Amba said. "Wife beater? Pimp? Sounds about right. He looks as though he's diving for scraps. He'll probably feed his own daughter to the sharks."

She turned and walked toward the elevator. "There is no need for us to stay any longer. I will go back to my room to pack. I understand there is a fast boat that leaves Buru for Ambon today, after lunch. I want to be on it. And I want to be on the earliest plane out to Jakarta. I will take care of my plane reservations myself through the hotel. I suggest you do the same with yours. But," she said, coolly, "I'd appreciate it if you could help me with the fast boat ticket, and the Ambon hotel reservation, whatever hotel you think might suit."

With that she left.

Samuel knew there was no use asking her why she wanted to book her plane ticket to Jakarta herself. He walked outside. He needed to breathe. He needed to smoke.

Afterward, he called a friend who was a travel agent and booked the tickets. Then he walked aimlessly through the streets of Namlea. He couldn't bear the thought of bumping into Amba anywhere in the vicinity of the hotel.

In these strange hours, it felt like a thick line had been drawn between them.

✺

When they reached Ambon, after a tense and mostly uncommunicative fast boat journey from Buru, that line was still there, hard, sardonic, unkind. Samuel took a long solitary walk in the evening, revisiting the charred ruins of familiar buildings whispering the names of dead relatives, remembering the time before the violence, those long sweet nights, so thick, so red-blooded you could taste them.

In the morning, from the hotel balcony where guests were directed to take their breakfast, they could glimpse the market's unison of colors. Amba had emerged from her room still remote, but the view was too tempting. She announced that she had to see it up close.

When Samuel said, "I'll come with you," Amba nodded as if he'd offered a careless apology and she was big-hearted enough to accept it.

But then again, they were in a relationship, of sorts, were they not? It was a painful but necessary lesson: she would come around, eventually, when she was ready. And he was in love. He waited.

When they reached the market, the colors did not disappoint.

He followed along, taking care to keep his distance, give her some space. He caught up with her when he saw her looking at rows of tempeh. She picked up a piece from a stall. Even tempeh wrapped in paper had a different sheen in her hand, a hint of an inner life. For a moment the image seduced him, but then he felt a sharp pang in his chest as he remembered what had allegedly started the cycle of violence in this city: rumors that pieces of tempeh had been wrapped in torn pages of the

Qur'an. He focused again on Amba, watching her touch the rows of tempeh, pronouncing them cool and smooth and compact, telling the stallholder they were very different from what she was used to in Java. Samuel sensed a burden lifting.

"Tempeh." He tried to laugh. "Do you even like it?"

"Of course. Who doesn't?" She seemed genuinely amused.

He didn't reply, savoring this glimpse of reconciliation.

"You remember how Sukarno used to tell us not to become a nation of tempeh, a weak people? But now people all over the world love tempeh—it's eco-friendly, it's gourmet, it's protein packed. And best of all: it's remarkably unfussy. In this it is so unlike its brother, tofu. And that's quite a virtue in the age of the confessional."

Amba, too, seemed happy with the change of mood. She began to comment on the produce that had the tables around them groaning— purple stacks of eggplants, baskets of hot red chilis and papery garlic, plump twists of turmeric—comparing hue and smell, suggesting how to cook this, what best to pair with that.

Samuel didn't try to push their conversation, but in the few hours that followed he knew whatever had divided them before had begun to melt away.

That evening they went to the seafood restaurant next to Firma Abdulalie, the purveyor of the island's best melaleuca oil, the same restaurant Zulfikar had mentioned to distract the thugs who had barged in at Julius's house. The food was brilliant, their order of mantis prawns tasting like soft, billowy gold. They talked about mundane but relaxing things, about fat Maluku breadfruits, about the deliciousness of *komu asar* fish and smoked tuna, about what the local papers were saying about the new mayor of Ambon, about the Chinese family who owned

Abdulalie and had for five generations been Muslim, about Bugis people Samuel knew who had settled as far away as the interior of Papua.

Afterward Samuel suggested they go to another restaurant up in the hills, famed for its views and ready supply of alcohol. They went outside to hail a taxi. It had started drizzling and there were raindrops in Amba's hair. He kept wanting to touch her and for a while her eyes lowered, like a schoolgirl. But when they got to the restaurant, all natural vista and hardly any lighting or patrons, she had regained her composure. She asked for a glass of rum; he ordered beer. For a moment, the air stilled around them. Samuel felt another shift in mood, another change coming: they were like two people poised on the edge of two worlds.

16

Revelations

For the first time in days Samuel retired to his room feeling grateful for his own space. After their drinks at the bar on the hill, he and Amba had parted almost formally in the hotel lobby, muttering about the logistics of leaving for the airport the next morning to board a plane to Jakarta.

He opened his window, smoked some more, showered. Then he fetched a can of beer he'd left on the table all night and drank it at room temperature, facing the dimming lights of the port. His mind wandered back to the restaurant on the mountain above Ambon, when Amba had looked so relaxed. He still wasn't sure what had triggered her anger and lingering resentment over his deception just before they left Buru, or her sudden about-face at the market. Was it relief at his having finally revealed his utmost secret?

At one point in the market, she even asked whether he had a girl-friend. The question came out just like that, so raw, almost girlish. It took him a while to decide how to answer. It was hard to recall all the disastrous half lives he had left trailing in his wake.

Then he told her about his latest, the woman he had left when he'd taken the flight from Jakarta to Ambon. How dewy she had looked at 5:00 a.m. with a touch of flu and her own frail beauty, and how he had not replied when she asked how long he would be gone. She asked again, would it only be a while or should she pack up and turn the page? This last lover, who was named, fittingly, after a flower, had seemed different from the others. When he had refused to commit to her she had said, "What special powers do you think are invested in you, that you can just come and go with impunity?" These words had seared like salt in a wound. The look she gave before he closed the door behind him was neither shock nor reprimand. It was, rather, like the look on the face of an actress realizing that her rival had remembered the line she herself had forgotten.

"I've spent a lot of time musing about that moment," Samuel told Amba. "Impunity? What had she meant by that? Special powers—what did she mean to imply?" He had thought of the special powers that people spoke of, the ability to control and communicate with animals or to see distant people and things, to touch an object and perceive its history or see another person's aura, the ability to stretch, deform, expand, and contract, to generate heat, to alter people's minds.

"Maybe impunity is, like all kinds of manipulation and omission, a special power as well." He finally said, "In any case, when I left I felt she was the last woman I could love."

Samuel opened another beer. There were so many things he hadn't gotten around to asking Amba. *Did you manipulate your husband? Have you manipulated your own daughter? Does Srikandi know who her real father is? Shouldn't it matter that she knows?*

There is still time to ask these questions, he thought. In less than eight hours they would meet downstairs to check out from the hotel. There would be time in the taxi to the airport, there would be time at the airport, there would be time on the plane because he would make sure they sat together. *Of course* they would sit together. Hadn't they been together all this time? Hadn't *together* been their modus operandi for the past week? Maybe he would even tell her about more of the women in his life, those whom he had desired and those whom he had used, those who had used him. Maybe he could tell her he was in love with her, and leave it at that.

The air in the room was damp despite the outside breeze. It had the dark blue smell of bark and iron and cheap carpet. He drank the last drop of his beer, hoping he would sleep now.

Samuel woke with a start. The morning was unusually gray and blustery. He had overslept by half an hour, which was ominous, considering the many things that could go wrong with this day.

When he reached the lobby, hoisting his backpack, there was no sign of Amba. He sat on one of the lounge chairs, waiting. It wasn't exactly a colorless vigil; a large bus had just disgorged a flock of delegates for a local beauty pageant, and while they fluttered around the lobby his eyes were temporarily appeased. But not for long. Every time he heard the elevator ping his heart jumped, hers the only face he sought.

After thirty minutes he went to the counter and asked the receptionist whether he had seen the handsome older woman who was always with him. The receptionist replied that madam had checked out and left for the airport earlier, but had left a little bag for him. She had said he should take it to the airport for her.

It felt like a slap in the face. It was too early in the morning for that. He tried to keep his voice steady.

"Did she tell you why she left so early? Did she look nervous?"

"She didn't look particularly nervous, no. She seemed in a hurry, though. She kept looking at her watch."

"Why didn't you call my room?"

"I didn't think there was any need. And she didn't ask me to."

"You said she kept looking at her watch."

"I thought it natural because she didn't want to miss her flight."

Samuel looked at the bag Amba had left him—a small tote as shapeless and inconsequential as an afterthought. It didn't seem to contain much, but she'd asked him to take it to the airport. It didn't occur to him to check the contents, having been raised that way.

How could she have nursed her anxieties alone and—worse—impulsively made a decision that did not involve him? If this was her way of getting back at him for his earlier duplicity, so be it. But there was no time to lose.

He checked out, rushed outside, and hailed a taxi.

At the check-in counter at the airport there was no sign of Amba. With time running out he checked in, anxiously scanning the crowd for her. He realized he didn't have her phone number. In fact he had nothing of hers except the bag she'd left, a small artifact that felt so valuable he didn't even shove it into his backpack for fear of damaging it.

Time was unkind. Too soon he heard the last call for boarding. He scanned every café and shop he passed in his dash to the boarding gate and survived the reprimand of the crew member who was just leaving the counter. But as he walked down the aisle, the last passenger to board, he knew without a doubt she would not be on the plane. At the first groan of the engines panic began to engulf him. Miraculously, the plane was leaving with no delay, meaning everything was going well for the whole fucking universe except for him.

As the plane taxied to the runway, Samuel realized that Amba had left the hotel well before she could have known he had woken up late. The plane gathered speed, then with a lurch it took off. Samuel listened to the sound of the wheels retracting. *She planned this all along*, he thought. *She never intended to leave with me. I was never part of her plan.*

ॐ

Somewhere over the Java Sea four hours later, Samuel was still trying to make a mental list of everything he should and should not have done, everything that he *could* have done in order not to have lost her. But his time as savior was up. How did it go again, that line every sad soul seemed to recite after being cruelly wrested away from someone beloved? *There is a season for everything and a time for every purpose under heaven . . .*

He was stuck at the back against the toilets, with a row all to himself, at least. But it was that time during a flight when most passengers, until now either sated or sedated, would find their bladders full and make a mad scramble before landing. On balance Samuel preferred trains to planes, but right now it felt like there was no difference: train stations, transit lounges, moving walkways, boarding areas—they were all the in-between places that were his true home.

To distract himself he looked at the faces around him and tried to imagine the circumstances of other lives: lovebirds enjoying trysts, doting new parents, people who had just met and hit a common note and wanted the freshness of a new acquaintance and conversation before life on the ground took hold. He remembered conversations he'd had with strangers that had lodged in his mind: with a prison warden from a prison just outside of Nusakambangan, who had found inner peace in his daily encounters with total fuckups; with a broken-down bank executive who was going home to tell his wife he'd fathered another woman's child; with an Ambonese he'd met, a man so damaged for not being allowed to marry his Muslim sweetheart he joined a militant group and started burning down mosques.

What had he done? He'd gone on the path of desire and arrived nowhere. The woman he had followed so helplessly had gone back to Buru; he felt it in his gut. Of course she couldn't give up her search for the man with whom she was so obsessed. Why would she? Perhaps telling him about her daughter had spurred her into that realization. Perhaps tiptoeing her way for so long through his neediness had finally made her snap.

Suddenly he remembered he still had her bag. He pulled it onto his lap, staring at it. It looked like an invitation to further disaster.

Strangely, he felt calm when his fingers met the letter, folded so neatly it nearly felt like part of the bag's lining.

He was still serene as he began to read.

March 1, 2006

Dear Samuel,

It feels strange to be writing the things I could have told you when we were together in Buru. There were many moments that availed themselves. But I didn't seize upon them.

Some say that happiness writes white; it doesn't show up on the page. But here I am, writing, soiling this whiteness, because I know I must explain my decision to return to Buru. The simple truth is this was my plan all along.

Yes, Bhisma Rashad was my lover. But he was not just my lover. He was the love of my life. You must have guessed as much, though you had learned things in snippets. Yet you seemed to take it in your stride, as we tend to do in this country.

We were together in 1965, in Yogyakarta, directly before and after the political unrest of September 30. I don't have to tell you how dangerous those days were. Even though we had less than a month in total, we were together in a way that cemented my life's path. We were oblivious, we were in love, and we stared those dangerous days in the face because that's what lovers do.

On the night of October 19, 1965, we were together at Res Publica University, at a memorial service for an activist friend, when the Army stormed in. They opened fire, and we lost each other. In a split second Bhisma was gone. It was the last time I saw him.

I was bereft. The loss and grief were devastating. I searched for him, but no one could tell me what had become of him. It was like finding myself suddenly Godless and orphaned in one go, for I could not go near my family in Kadipura, partly because I feared for their safety, and partly because of the shock I knew they would feel once they found I had broken off with my fiancé, a man they chose for me and whom they adored. I knew I couldn't go back. I loved a man who was a friend of Communists. I'd been with him at that wake for a Communist agitator. The risk was too great. I had to abandon my friends and stay away from my aunt and uncle.

Samuel, you didn't live through those days, you were in another world entirely, but I think you understand when I say that I, and many others, lived in fear and paranoia at that time. I trusted no one and soon went into hiding. Later I began to wonder if Bhisma had gone through the same thing. And to realize that even if he had not been captured, if he had later tried to find me, he wouldn't have been able to.

Then I found out that he'd left something behind, after all. Something that lived inside me, something that, despite everything, he might have wanted me to look after. There was only one solution for me and that was to leave Yogyakarta. I had convinced myself by then that he had disappeared from my life because he wasn't sure of me, because there were other women better than me. I talked myself into believing he had loved me only because he had momentarily taken leave of his senses—because, like any man, he couldn't resist a novelty and challenge, the excitement of an underground love.

I vowed to take care of myself, no matter what, and to make a life for myself in Jakarta. So I married the man who agreed to make this life, my life, and the life growing inside me, his own. That man was a German-American scientist whom I met at the university only weeks after the October massacre. His name was Adalhard Eilers.

I can't even begin to explain the pain of keeping this secret from my daughter, who has always believed Adalhard was her father. But how could I tell her? Adalhard was a good man who loved Srikandi as a true father should, and I had no idea if Bhisma was dead or alive.

Then, sometime in 1976, I heard from an acquaintance that her relative, a doctor, had just come back from a field assignment on Buru Island. He told my friend about meeting a certain Dr. Rashad, a man who had greatly impressed him. Rashad is not an uncommon name, but how could I not hope, with all my heart, that man was Bhisma?

After President Suharto ordered the termination of the prison camps on Buru, I waited and waited for news of Bhisma's release. I dreamed that somehow I could become part of his homecoming, of his return to Jakarta, to his family home in Menteng. Even though I was married to another man I thought every day I might see Bhisma again. But his name never appeared on the lists of prisoners returning home.

After a long time I resigned myself to the fact that if he'd been on Buru he was not ever coming home. And during all this time I waited and hoped, it was with an unclear conscience—for I knew that by marrying Adalhard, yet still loving Bhisma, I'd betrayed both men.

After I received that anonymous e-mail less than two months ago, the one claiming Bhisma was dead, I set off to find someone among the former political prisoners who had known him on Buru. Someone told me a man named Zulfikar had been Bhisma's friend. Once I had his name it was not difficult to track him down.

I found him in an office in Central Jakarta, where he served on a company board. He said his position was a way to keep him away from home and his memories. When he told me that Bhisma had indeed been on Buru and he had been Bhisma's friend, I told him about the e-mail I'd received, hoping their past friendship was strong enough to lure him back to Buru to help me. I appealed to both the duty of his memory and his common sense, and I succeeded.

When I first met Zulfikar I found him difficult—as you undoubtedly did. He had that look of calculating patience, and he talked so much of his own lost world— you saw it on the ship, that strange way he had of going back into the past. I know how you feel about Zulfikar. I've seen the half resentment and half awe cross your face so many times. But, as I've said before, nothing changes the fact that Zulfikar was the only person I could find *who'd known my Bhisma, or rather, the man Bhisma had become after I lost him.*

Had you told me earlier that you once knew him, too, that you had met both Zulfikar and Bhisma, in fact, when you were an imp of a child with no business to be hanging around a prison camp, I would have clung to you, kept you close for as long as it would take me to believe. But by the time you sprang that surprise on us, I had made up my mind to let you go.

The worst part of my grief, up to that glimpse in 1976 of a possibility he had survived, was more than not knowing whether he'd been captured or killed, in Yogyakarta or elsewhere later. It was the huge question mark surrounding the circumstances of that fateful night at Res Publica University. What had torn us apart that day when the Army opened fire? What was it that had happened in the commotion that ensued to alter our fates? Why was he suddenly not beside me?

When my mind began to function again I allowed myself to believe the unbelievable: that he had been playing me all along, that he was cheating on me, that that moment of blood and chaos had given him the opportunity to escape from me. It felt like such a betrayal, the love that had bound us instantly broken. And that's the thought I held on to for so long, even though time did its duty of forgiveness, but when the prison camp was dismantled I had nothing but longing for him.

The thing is, Samuel, I've always been a very jealous person. I didn't know this about myself until I had Siri. Up to that point in my life I'd worked hard to be better than the people I knew. I wanted to be better than

everyone, my beautiful twin sisters, my virtuous parents,
my fiercely independent grandmother, my noble fiancé.

It was when I met Bhisma that I realized I was noth-
ing, that I knew so little of anything. But he also made
me feel good about myself, even about what little I knew,
such that it was unbearable to me when I started to real-
ize that others felt the same way about him. If those others
knew so much more than I did to begin with, why should
he stick with me?

I thought there was another woman, you see. A
woman who was both formidable and beautiful. But
now I wonder if I was wrong about her. Perhaps she
meant nothing to Bhisma, not even as a passing thought.
But the fact remains she was with us when all hell broke
loose that day, and for many years I convinced myself
that Bhisma followed her, disappeared with her. Because
I felt inadequate, I thought that he somehow deserved
my being gone from his life. I let my jealousy overrule
my heart.

But now I realize many things could have hap-
pened in that mayhem. He could have been injured
and dragged away by a friend. He could have pan-
icked and followed someone else thinking it was me.
But because this woman was everything I wasn't, and so
seductive at that, I allowed myself to believe, right from
the moment she introduced herself to Bhisma up to that
explosive moment of separation, that she already knew
Bhisma and was trying to steal him away from me. I
convinced myself that his love was fickle, that he would
be prepared to abandon me, that he had followed her
instead of me.

Believing in Bhisma's betrayal helped justify marrying Adalhard, even though I didn't love him the way I did my one true love. It also helped me loathe myself less for using someone so blatantly. And for needing someone to save me, for I felt I needed an Adalhard to marry me, to intervene in my fate and prove that I was not the spurned woman of The Mahabharata. I needed to defy the legend and show that I was capable of finding a man who loved me, that I would not live my life as a fallen woman.

But over the years I have felt increasingly ashamed—and I cannot stress this enough—for not being able to go it alone, for not being able to rewrite my story without involving a man.

I am telling you this because I want you to know that my daughter is capable of the same degree of passion. She was the one who opened my eyes to what I could be, given half the chance.

Please indulge me, and let me tell you about her.

My daughter Siri—Srikandi—is not just beautiful; she is both vengeful and vulnerable. Those two qualities, you will know, are interchangeable. She can be self-righteous and full of herself, but also surly, diffident, sometimes completely done in by her own insecurity. This is my private take on my daughter. I would never tell her I think this.

The aunt and uncle I once lived with in Yogyakarta came to Jakarta to witness her birth. They promised they wouldn't tell my parents, and I was grateful to them. But they did try to warn me that it was unfair to impose on a child a name she might not be cut out for. "Keberatan nama," my aunt whispered, but then again, she's Javanese.

It was clear to me from the moment of my daughter's birth that there was no other name for such a lovely, wicked, impossibly bouncy creature. She was so beautiful I knew I could only allow the purest hands to touch her.

Several days after Siri was born, I was in her room in our old Jakarta home. She was contented in her crib, about to fall asleep. Every now and then I would bend over her, this baby, this splendid stranger, with her unusual liquid green eyes. Her crib was near the window, which had pale yellow curtains. It was sunny outside, and the room was filled with a golden glow. Suddenly a breeze parted the curtains, and a shaft of light fell on my daughter's face. Her eyes opened, and that was when I saw it.

Siri's face had changed. Not docile nor soft nor sweet, and with no sign of that quality of tameness young mothers sometimes fancy. In that moment, in that pinprick on the time map, I saw my Siri's beautiful soft girl face turn into a boy's. As I watched, the two faces flickered, half female, half male, so absolute was the transformation.

The spell was broken when I heard her cry, a sort of low wail that I hadn't heard from her before. I reached into the crib and picked her up. I just stood there holding her, stunned, oblivious to any other thought or sensation, almost shamed into incomprehension by my mental sprint to a premature conclusion. And then another cry, sharper this time, a little impatient, after which my baby was once more a girl.

That was how I knew I had given her the right name. Srikandi. As she grew, her face was a constant reminder to me that her soul was never only meant for her mother. She is her father's daughter, and she is the one who will close the chapter in my life that needs closing. Yes, her soul has never been mine. Not even in childhood, when she was happiest in my hands, snug and warm in my protection. I tried, always, to make sure she was learning in the light, never in the dark as owls and other night creatures are fated to; that she would learn the world always on the side of right, like a sum well done, not given to acid and rust. But I have always known there is a dark side to my daughter.

Siri is, and always will be, entirely her own person. I've called her many different names—Siri, Sikan, Sindi, Didi—anything that might wash away the fate-tempting blatancy of the name I felt compelled to give her. But she is Srikandi. Who else could she be?

When she was growing up and brought friends home from school I saw that none of them would ever be her equal; she would surpass them all. And so it was. The reason why I became a late bloomer was because she was born a star. The reason why I succeeded as a professional translator was because she was always the better writer. My daughter was always better at the things I should be better at and so, to my surprise, the jealousy I've told you of, that so shattered my life, was changed. I wasn't jealous of Siri. She challenged me. Challenged me to make more of myself.

Even as a small child I could see that my daughter was curious, insatiably so. She stared at things, stared at them until they became something else. She would tell me about the tremors of paper, the fish scales of someone's eyes, the lost love in leg cramps. As she grew older she would describe to me more complex things, an aftertaste, the particular slant of an eye, the exact interval between the smell of bile in someone's breath and the time the breath would be stripped of smell altogether—the moment of surreal emptying out, the way the air is suddenly odorless after hours of hard rain. She would poke into things for the red rimmed, the glassy, the soft, and the blind; she would ponder wrinkles, brown spots, what the flare of nostrils might actually mean when shaped this way instead of that. Told of the death of a relative, she would wonder which came first: the maggots or the vultures. I began to understand that she saw inside and behind. Instead of just seeing an object she saw the eddying, the scurrying, the vanishing— a crowd thinning to rivulets, or night's ingress, glib but full of doubt, veiled by buildings, lamps, tears.

She also loved my husband, Adalhard Eilers, like no other. As far as Siri is concerned, it is Adalhard's tide that runs in her veins. He is the only father, the only Bapak, she's ever known.

After his death she refused to see me for many months. She blamed me for his death and she was right: I deserved the blame. She was right in accusing me of not loving him throughout the years we were together, for being cold and distant, things I had become because I loved someone else. So I was punished. Witnessing Adalhard die his slow death in the prison of my making became a screen through which I saw the pain of Bhisma, whom I never saw in his physical suffering, and whose pain I couldn't even begin to imagine.

My husband Adalhard died of the cancer I know I planted in him, the seeds of which I sowed and watered each day with my callous indifference. Siri believed I *had killed him. She told me that every word, every little defense that came out of my mouth was a nudge forward to the disintegration of our family, including everything that was once good about it. She said that with my cold indifference I ruined her father's life and his memory of his life in this world.*

Samuel, I confess that not only did I reserve the love I should have given my husband, but I also withdrew the love I owed, and felt, for my loving father and mother, my aunt and uncle, my two sisters. I could have removed the wall I erected between myself and my family. I could have loved my husband for his kindness, his selflessness, for giving up his right to be loved, for my sake and for my daughter's. But I chose not to. In my own way I became the Amba I didn't want to be, and I inflicted on my entire family my worst spell, far worse than the Amba of myth could have ever inflicted. Did I ever deserve to be with Bhisma? I still ask myself this. For I am a cruel person, am I not—cruel and jealous and wrong.

If there is one person in the world who deserves to bury me for this it is Siri. At the same time I had to protect her from my sins.

I hope you have come to understand why for so long I have kept the knowledge of her true father from my daughter. I feared she would not have survived what she would have made out of our story. About how she was born into this world. About the only man I had ever loved and who he was to her.

I'm not sure you know the significance of our names, Amba and Srikandi, especially in relation to each other. I felt that if my daughter knew that there was a real Bhisma in my life, she, with her different way of looking at things, would have understood immediately why she carried the name I gave her. She would have spun a yarn greater than our story, to say nothing of the epic itself, and that would have been her ruination. No amount of protective mothering could have equaled the force of that single determination of her subsequent life.

Now I hope you understand why I left the hotel without telling you. Why I had to go back to Buru to finish what I set out to do. I know that nothing I can now do will make things right. There can be no miraculous salvage because Adalhard remains dead and, in all likelihood, Bhisma is dead, too.

I need to get to the bottom of what happened, to learn the true story of my lover so that my daughter can know our story and do with the facts what she wishes. I cannot believe how much of my life I have wasted on this perpetual treadmill.

But now, after my long suffering, I know I have earned these hours or days. Whatever it takes I owe it to myself to go back to where my daughter and I began.

Yours,

Amba Kinanti

After reading the letter a second time, Samuel folded it and put it back in the bag. *Even in correspondence Amba is proud*, he thought. Despite her remorse, she remained proud of her history and the choices she'd made. Proud and distant and stubborn. There was no apology for the way she had treated him—trusting, trustworthy, pushover Samuel. And no word of thanks.

For a fleeting moment he felt an affinity for Adalhard Eilers, the man who had let his life wither away for love. He also felt a deepened sense of serenity.

The serenity didn't leave him as the plane landed in Jakarta, or even later, when he found himself being reabsorbed into the madness of that city, fully realizing that he was irrevocably somewhere else, somewhere not where she was. He felt the joy of knowing. It was the same kind of knowing, perhaps, that had led Amba to accept Adalhard's solution those many, many years ago.

It was a knowing that allowed him to understand how Adalhard's hand would have clung tightly to Amba's as she went into labor, and how it firmly signed the form under "Father" on the newly-born daughter's birth certificate. How Adalhard must have felt when he returned to the hospital to hold "his" daughter for the first time.

Samuel envisaged this man as a graying foreigner set against the gray screen of his life: a man who would always be somewhat out of focus, more spirit than flesh, supportive but distant, hovering above and beyond the vivid colors of the lives he was nurturing.

This became the one strand out of this new knowledge that Samuel felt he completely understood: he would be like Adalhard, never knowing how it was to have the life he imagined within him merge with his own blood and grow out of his own tissues, but aching for love all the same.

BOOK 5

Bhisma

1965–2006 (The Missing Years)

Prologue

A year after Bhisma Rashad disappeared his sister Paramita Rashad managed to gather various conflicting pieces of information regarding his fate. Most were no more substantial than rumors.

One report suggested that Bhisma was murdered in a violent clash in the Ngadiredjo sugar factory in Kediri, although the head of Sono Walujo Hospital, Dr. Suhadi Projo, said he very much doubted this information. Another claimed he was injured during the right-wing attack on Res Publica University, Yogyakarta, and while undergoing treatment managed to escape to Boyolali and then to Blitar, where he went into hiding. Yet another suggested that Bhisma was detained in Fort Vredeburg, along with several Bumi Tarung artists, where he was tortured and died.

Even when his family finally learned of his true fate, the circumstances of his arrest were never clarified, and again the rumor mill ground on.

Some said he was arrested in 1970 during a meeting of the Association of Indonesian Scholars in Surabaya and was taken to Salemba Prison; others claimed that when he was visiting the Faculty of Medicine of the University of Indonesia he was scooped up by members of KAMI, the right-wing Indonesian Student Association, on charges of being a CGMI member. It seemed particularly strange to Paramita that a non-CGMI member could be arrested by KAMI, an organization that was already banned and had no authority to detain anyone, especially on charges of being a member of CGMI, an organization that was also banned. *Somewhere up there*—Paramita must have thought, for she was that sort of person—*the gods must be having a hissy fit.*

Three years before the first batch of prisoners was released from the Buru penal colony in December 1977, Miriam Rashad died from heart disease. She was sixty-six. Her husband, Asrul Rashad, turned over all his company affairs to Paramita, his most able and trusted daughter, and spent most of his twilight years in the family's holiday house in Megamendung.

His eldest daughter, Rosida, left Jakarta for Sweden and later became the first woman to be made chargé d'affaires of the Indonesian embassy, while his youngest, Maya, married a ceramics businessman, lived in Bali, and became a well-known travel writer.

On December 5, 2006, the day Bhisma would have turned seventy-four, Paramita collected everything she could find that her brother had left behind. This included three photo albums of his life in Leiden and Leipzig. To her regret she found that most of his letters to the family, including the ones from when he'd worked at the hospital in Kediri, had been accidentally, or deliberately, misplaced by their mother, who had been crushed by her son's unknown fate.

17

The Buru Letters

Like a bereft widow Amba glanced through all the letters, but there was too much to absorb all at once. But like a bereft lover, she singled some out to return to from time to time. After all, the heart uses what it can.

***

Buru Island, December 5, 1973

My dearest Amba,

One day I may wake up and know with certainty that you will never read this letter. Or the next letter, or the one after that. But I will keep writing to you, hoping that even if I never find you perhaps my words will. Here, hope is the one thing we have to keep us going, and isn't it in the nature of hope to seek the impossible? Hoping against hope can be a kind of healing.

Besides, it's been so long, too long. I no longer know how things work outside this system, whether letters are even sent after they're censored, whether some, such as this one, may have the power to escape authority and travel by osmosis. But miracles do happen, and strange as it may sound, they even happen in this place.

I try to imagine your face as you finally read this, which I know will not be this decade, or even the next. Perhaps you have become old and sad, older and sadder than you imagined your parents would become when you once thought of fleeing with me—this worthless, spineless thief. I remember when you lay awake on our damp mattress in Kediri, weeping as if you could hear your parents astir in their bedroom and misting the air with their sorrow. When you rose ahead of the new day you asked me, "What if the news of me leaving with you breaks them, and their bodies, that last ballast, give way? My sisters and I would be orphaned, lost without them."

But I believe you are just as beautiful as when I last held you.

I suppose you will already know, by the time you read this letter, much of what has happened to me, and the vagaries that led me to this place: those difficult months in Salemba Prison following my arrest, the harder three months in the prison on the island of Nusakambangan. They weren't pretty, those places, but folks endured. Turned their prisons into something else. Which is what I did.

Here, in Buru, things, as in a long twilight, are never black or white. It is a place of perpetual gray, which makes it a better place than the Buru that exists in the collective imagination, and certainly better than the other prisons I've been to. Here, even if life boils down to one thing—unpaid labor—at least we still see the sky, feel the breeze, breathe the air, hunt, enjoy the taste of sago and local fruits, and catch fish in the lake. While this doesn't make it ideal as a final resting place, somehow I know I may never leave this island.

Who are you, as you read this? Are you single? Are you with someone? Are you married? I can see you married. You may have been married for many years. You may be beholden to your children, weighted down by your relatives, cheered up by your grandchildren. I'd like to think you happy, surrounded by family, thriving in their company. At the same time I'd like to think you independent and free, doing things you love.

Forgive my rambling. Were it possible for my thoughts to sidle off the page and reappear in the flesh, of course there would be no need for questions. Or for letters, for that matter: one look at you and I would know. I suppose I just need to believe that you're happy, and that you haven't settled for a life you don't deserve. But the truth is I don't know enough of the real world anymore to understand, much less accept, what makes it hard for people to go against the grain. Maybe I never knew enough in the first place.

I would like to think I still know certain things about you. That you love reading, that you love lingering over images, that you love the bee sting and birdsong of poetry. And that you will not lose those loves whatever shape your life takes, whomever you love or don't love. It is for that reason that I find myself, lately, ever more deeply thrust into the world of verse. It makes me feel closer to you, to your will and beauty.

I wish we could have read each other more poetry when we were still together. I wish things were other than they are. You understood how little people really knew of me. They thought me distant, solitary, closed off. I wonder if to some extent you thought the same of me? That something about me made me at once a lover and an eternal stranger to you.

Eight years ago, I gave my heart to you for safekeeping. If my heart now still beats for the love of you and I want for nothing else, it is because I know my heart is safe, my heart is home.

Bhisma

December 6, 1973

Mein Liebling,

It's been two years since I got here, and so many things have happened since. Let me tell you about this place, known to us as Tefaat Buru.

First: the physical facts. It is by any standard a huge, sprawling camp, divided into twenty-two units around the Waeapo Valley. Each unit comprises a main building, places of worship, an art center, a warehouse, and a medical center. The rest is barracks, where we prisoners live.

Each unit may hold as many as a thousand prisoners divided into as few as fourteen and as many as twenty-three barracks. Each barracks averages fifty prisoners. This makes Tefaat Buru much more humane than most prisons in Java, which are built for twenty people but crammed with sixty.

Now the human elements: Each barracks is guarded by *tonwal*, and the commander of each of those groups of soldiers is known as the *dan tonwal*. He in turn reports to the unit commander, known as *dan unit*. In each barracks we vote for a *kabrak*, our own supervisor. He's called the head prisoner and he gets to choose a work coordinator to keep the prisoners in order.

Then there's us, the inmates. Right now I'm sitting under the stars with a group of fellow sufferers. There is a lovely scent in the air, something familiar to me. On this island beauty always comes forewarned, like the birds that are taught not to linger, and perhaps just as well.

Unlike my comrades, I'm tuning in and out, but in front of us, on the stage of our new art center, is our main band, Bandko, belting out tune after (out of) tune. Bandko is short for Band Mako, and mako is our term for HQ. Most of the players are terrible musicians, some are not musicians at all. But they act as if they are.

For isn't that the point, that we shouldn't care whether we're crappy or not, as long as we get our entertainment? So long as we can get our fill of laughter, enjoy the narcotic effect of art? At the end of the day, isn't that all we want—entertainment? Because laughter suspends disbelief, and we don't want to forget that we are human? "*Mensch sein ist von allem die Hauptsache,*" Yes, Rosa Luxemburg again. To be joyous is a necessary part of life, no matter what happens. "*Heiter sein, ja heiter trotz alledem.*"

Tonight must be special. There's a lot of "black tobacco" going around, instead of those pathetic blends usually found at the barracks. And this can only mean one thing: even the people who chain us must be in a magnanimous mood tonight. It's good to know that occasionally the people at the top are willing to feed the rats, even if most of the time they'd rather step on them and crush them because they are all Communists. Ha ha.

Ah, now the men from Unit I are up on the stage. Which means the same old boring diet of "Mexican Rose" and "Words Get in the Way." Those guys are way too Westernized and often they get booed off the stage because most of the folks hate those songs.

I guess my point is that each year there is some progress. For all it's worth, every unit now has received musical instruments from the government. "Modern" instruments, to be precise, as per the official description on the inventory of the Ministry of Social Affairs I once glimpsed in my unit commander's office. They may not be top-quality instruments but they do hold and make music, and are an improvement over what used to pass in our pathetic self-made arsenal as "drums," "violins," "maracas."

Recently the basic gamelan sets and puppets that came with every unit were dug out from their forgotten tombs. Not only were they in danger of decaying, but if the sounds of modern instruments are to start filling the air, so the thinking goes—and it is good thinking—the traditional instruments had better be put somewhere they will be, if not necessarily enjoyed, at least seen and admired. And remembered.

The music's been going on for two hours now. I don't remember having been this happy for a while, and those guys up on that stage are not bad at all, all things considered. They forget the lyrics, bungle the tunes, and don't so much sing as shout their lines. Some are as tone-deaf as I am color-blind. But at this moment they are happy, laughing hard, filling their lungs with joy. It is a lovely and not insignificant thing.

Still, there are diehards among us who are only too happy to mock these bands for reasons other than aesthetics. To them, it isn't so much about the music as about providing fun for the oppressors. Yet I look around me and every single face is split by a smile a mile wide.

Oh darling, I sense your doubt. I know the things I tell you are no laughing matter. But you must know how to laugh in this place, or you perish.

Bhisma

December 12, 1973

Mein Liebling,

Here folks don't recognize irony other than as some kind of dark humor.

1st irony: Those among us who fancy themselves Marxist-Leninists have generally not read a single word of Lenin's, let alone Das Kapital.

2nd irony: While we are incarcerated here for being Communists, the economics of this place are organized along centralistic, collective lines—in other words, the exact opposite of the so-called new ideology of the Suharto

regime. Behold: a penal colony dedicated to the reforma-
tion of Communists, but which is itself a giant copy of the
Chinese commune system.

To wit: every activity in this place, from plant-
ing and harvest to rice field management, is orga-
nized according to groups. The warehouse only accepts
unhulled rice in the amount predetermined by the unit
commander. It's almost expected, however, that the com-
manders will find an excuse to extract more than they
should. Meanwhile supply at any given time depends on
many factors that have nothing to do with diligence and
hard work. So, whether we like it or not, it is imperative
that each group creates its own unhulled rice reserves
for the survival of its members. Especially for when the
going gets tough.

Most units have their own illegal storerooms, namely
obvious covered-up spaces behind the staircases, which
must have been inspired by children's detective stories.

Mercifully, my unit has become expert in storing
unhulled rice, hiding some in the main warehouse when
it is taken to be weighed, and siphoning out the rest when
no one's looking to our own storage spaces in the trunks
of certain trees. Yes, my love, just one of the reasons I love
trees.

But there are certain "mutual interests" that have
brought about some improvements in the system. Every
now and then there comes along a unit commander with
a smidgen of a brain. He might say, "Okay, let's reactivate
those old, unused, so-called terra-cotta kilns," and all of
a sudden we will get a much better cement platform. It
will also mean we have to produce some fifteen thousand
terra-cotta blocks a week. But this is nothing compared to

the anticipation of the feast the commander will probably throw every time we meet our quota.

It's easy to be cynical about everything, I admit. Why throw a celebration? Why create happiness? What are the motives hiding behind such gestures? You soon realize, though, that they—the prison camp lords and their min-ions—are as needy as we, the prisoners. They are just as desperate for respite, for some fun, and perhaps even for a measure of salvation. When that time arises, sharing with us doesn't seem to be a burden for them. You of all people would understand this, you who shun the black-and-whitenesses of life.

Some of our jailers are painfully young. Sometimes, when the night loosens up, or when there is music or ciga-rettes or whatever it is that momentarily unknots people, they ask us for advice. They ask us about sex and fertility and black magic and how to make radios out of nothing (which we happen to do extremely well). Such things may seem trivial, but they are not. They are important because they are about the depths of us—about how we feel and respond to the power game that defines us in this hellhole.

Sometimes I don't know how to behave. It's difficult, when you don't know what it is exactly that differentiates Us from Them, other than boots and rifles.

Bhisma

December 13, 1973

Darling, an important question: What does this word summon for most people? I think I know. Guards. Savages. Heartless killing machines.

They are not wrong.

As I write, someone in Unit VII is being beaten and kicked by the guards to within an inch of his life because the timber planks he'd sent to the port of Namlea as part of the target quota have disappeared. Every prisoner in that unit is required to send two meranti wood planks a day via the River Apo to the port, where the timber will be shipped by the Tefaat rulers to Ambon or Makassar. But occasionally one or two of these wooden planks are sold by the prisoner to the guards, who pay 3,000 rupiah a cubic yard, only to be sold by the guards' bosses to the market outside Buru for 15,000 rupiah per cubic yard. Then a few prisoners are selected randomly to have the life nearly beaten out of them for "not filling their quota."

There are hundreds of stories like this every day. So yes, folks are not wrong when they think the worst of this place.

From my perspective there are three options for the people incarcerated here. Some choose to live their days in a cancerous silence, or in rancor and rage, hating unequivocally everybody and everything that represents the penal colony.

Some, including me, think not all the guards are savages or heartless killing machines (admittedly we think in terms of the individuals who are exceptions to the rule, not in terms of the larger system), and we learn to focus on these exceptions.

Then there are those who genuinely believe we've entered better times. Among them folks who were recently mocked by some visiting journalists who thought them delusional or in denial. Those outsiders suggested those inmates refused to see how bad things really were so that they could feel better about themselves.

But even those journalists had mixed feelings about what they saw here. One I happened to meet, who kindly gave me pen and paper, thought that the bitter ones among us were so burdened by the weight of what they'd had to endure in the past years that they couldn't see the light, even if it was glaring in their faces.

But really, how can any one person speak for the rest of humanity? I have long stopped, and perhaps rightly so, presuming that we all think alike. Yet in my heart of hearts I believe in this: give humans darkness and most will see the light.

The more optimistic among us attribute this light solely to the new commander here, Samsi. I'm not sure what to think of him yet. As soon as he arrived he wanted to let us know that he is building some kind of legacy. I have to give it to the man: he is certainly different from his predecessors. He has some understanding of a very basic law of human nature: that domination only breeds resistance. He also understands that art is key, and now we have these concerts. Most of all he is a good manager.

Yet it's not just him. The times have also changed, it seems. There is now international pressure from human rights groups, and it is getting louder. People may deride Sukarno for the hubris and perceived debauchery of his later years, but Suharto—well, he has to think of the consequences of being placed in history alongside such delightful characters as Hitler, Chiang Kai-Shek, and others. (Don't you laugh—I still can't bring myself to write Stalin's name on that list!)

What I find hard to imagine is how the history of this place will be taught in Indonesian schools in the future.

By the way, the paper I have isn't the best quality. That is reserved for the real writers among us. Especially Bung Pram! I was elated to have the chance to talk with him yesterday—the great Pramoedya Ananta Toer, the man who seems destined to bear, and so courageously, the burden of our collective memory on his slender shoulders. It's touching to see how his unit comrades willingly and selflessly take over some of his workload so that he can continue writing. Although I am not what they call a "real" writer, still I have paper: even if it is only made of bark it will be a long-lasting thing, and it reminds me of the love I have for you.

Bhisma

December 17, 1973

There is something far too quiet here at the barracks— certainly not how most folks would picture this place.

The thing is, my darling, you'll be surprised at how little ideological talk there is. It's almost scandalous. You'd think every day there'd be plenty of raised voices and raucous debate about politics. The air full of spleen and splinters and exchanges of perspectives on history. Fists banging on tables, mugs flying, indoor bickering, and confrontations taken outdoors turning into physical altercations. But, no. There's nothing of the sort. Or very rarely is there anything of the sort.

And it is quite astonishing. The first batch of prisoners has been here four years. For my batch, the third, it has only been two. Yet already we feel, for lack of a better term, this terrible ideological exhaustion.

When I first arrived at the end of 1971, the main conflict was between the diehards and the moderates. (The disillusioned cowered in a corner and kept quiet.) It never became out-and-out war—impossible when the size and magnitude of our new fascist regime is our common enemy. Instead, it was a kind of infantile hostility, woefully shorn of imagination.

The old fogeys, a vociferous lot, would insist the Party was always right and that the youth should learn from them, while the youth responded with "fuck off," reasonably politely, and seemed to have little more to say. Poor bastards, most of them are members of CGMI, like our friends in Yogyakarta. Some told me that they too knew Untarto and are still saddened about his death.

On the whole the younger men weren't prepared to believe in anything else other than that China was always right; they held up Mao and the Revolution as the only models of rectitude. There is little of such talk now.

Once anyone arrives in this place the focus is on survival. But also, subconsciously, we must prepare ourselves to die on this island, and accept we may never see another place on earth.

At first I must say I was quite vexed by the lack of, how should I say it, fight. But I could also sense the resignation, which became anger in some. Because we who have ended up here have been defeated, defeated politically—and for most of us this is the worst fate imaginable. There is nothing worse than to be defeated politically; it means the end of everything.

But I have also noticed in many of us a deep, abiding need to restore some kind of personal dignity—a need that arises from a sense of pride, or nostalgia, whatever. The loss I'm talking about doesn't just wrest loved ones away from you, it also strips you of your sense of being in this world. But because our grasp of Marxism is minimal at best and because we have been defeated after all, what some of us do, instead of strengthening our theoretical knowledge, is to indulge in the baser aspect of ideology. And we do this by turning our focus to power. And by this I mean erecting the Communist Party structure in every unit.

So, do you see now what's happening? Instead of engaging intellectually in order to rise above our daft circumstances and what got us here in the first place, we resort to childish playacting.

I know what you're thinking. Such make-believe, of course, is a puerile stab at self-appeasement, and, as such, it is shallow and false. It must sound like something willed into being in spite of, and precisely because of, its improbability. Yet—and here's the funny thing—such false structures don't only exist in some dark, subversive corner of this place, but in ALL of the twenty-two units of the penal colony bar none. In this sense, it is almost impressive.

And what is more surprising is that it seems to help folks get by. After all, tragedy has to have a whiff of the comic to be bearable.

Let me try to explain how it works. Each unit has created a committee, with a clear and detailed structure. Each has an impressive arm of eager couriers, mostly drawn from the excitable youth in this fetid pool of obsessions.

These guys, I must say, are very handy to have around, and we build our self-justifications upon their very existence. We send them to talk to the unit supervisor: "Oh, so-and-so just received word that his uncle in Unit X is in a bad way. He just has to see him, so can he go? I promise in return to do double kitchen duty and bend over backwards for you," etc. etc.

Then the unit supervisor will nod and say, "Okay, okay, you'll get it within the hour. Now fuck off," and in no time you find yourself with a permission slip. After making a big production of looking grave and concerned before you exit your barracks, you are out and sitting in some spot in the ungovernable woods for a couple of hours. Or meeting your "uncles" from the other units to chew the fat, to "consolidate," to babble about ensuring the Party's efficacy. For we know that for posterity's sake we must do everything in our power to keep Marxist thinking alive.

It's amazing how language can be deployed to do man's dirty work. Idea becomes doctrine, doctrine becomes slogan, slogan becomes the seal of loyalty.

There are many among my fellow prisoners who actually remember, line by line, Party strongman Sudisman's document of auto-critique. You must know it as well, my love. The difference being, though, that you understand it not just with your heart, but also with your head, unlike some of these fools, who are too used to memorizing words without analyzing them. Yet so many of them use their memory like a badge and still manage to miss the point.

I mean, why do they never seem to learn new and useful things about their condition? Is that why creating this miniature pseudo-Party soothes and sustains? Is it exciting because it is a caricature? Does it feel real because it is not?

In any case there is a tacit understanding that in the matter of the September 30th Movement the Communist Party might have been in the wrong. And there is no end to the vehemence used to express this point. At the same time everybody seems to agree that it was "adventurism" that unwittingly led us to this place, and that Chairman Aidit ought to be held responsible.

Maybe that, too, is part of accepting defeat—accepting reality without apportioning any blame for ourselves.

Bhisma

December 22, 1973

My love,

This morning, after an emergency visit to another unit, I went out to the river to bathe. The guard who went with me was kind; he didn't supervise me as much as share stories about his childhood and offer me drags off his cigarette. The river cuts through at least four villages. In this place the heat can spike up to over 95 degrees Fahrenheit, and the dry season can last for eight months. Then the river is totally desiccated. But not today.

Anyway, I'd forgotten my shoes, and there was broken glass on the shortcut I took. Perhaps it was the detritus of some altercation that happened the previous night, or some fool on "indoor" corvée perhaps tripped and crashed with a tray of glasses on his mad rush from the central kitchen to the barracks. But when you've walked barefoot as much as we have, before too long you cease to feel anything.

I remember the walk mainly because of a peculiar smell hanging in the air. I notice smell a lot. This was an iron smell, a blood smell, the smell I associate with the color red, the color that has occupied my mind for the past few years.

I thought at first the smell was from the cuts on my feet, but then I noticed it hung most forcefully around a strange tree. It looked very much like a strangler fig, a banyan, the way it was all grandly wound up. But it wasn't. It seemed older but more alive than anything else around it. I could sense its roots pushing beneath my feet. And no one I asked could tell me its name.

I was instantly captive to that tree. When I reached the river I bathed in the most perfunctory way because I had to return to it, and as soon I did, I remained awestruck under its spreading canopy. The guard, bless him, gave me my space.

I fell asleep there, until the guard woke me up. He interrupted a dream in which I was reliving how I lost you that day—October 19, 1965—at Res Publica University.

I was reaching for you after that horrible moment that sounded like a thousand bombs exploding. My one thought was to make sure I didn't lose you. How could I lose you when we had a life to live together?

I saw you running ahead, I recognized your blouse— the red blouse you so sweetly told me you wore out of

*respect for Untarto and our CGMI friends. But red was
my undoing as I discovered too late.*

*In all that commotion, I had followed the wrong
woman, some random, middle-aged woman, and when I
realized that, and was gabbling something about the red
blouse, she said, as if I was a madman, "What are you
on about? I'm wearing green!"*

*I think I told you, in Kediri, that I am color-blind.
Perhaps I didn't explain, and I must do so now. I only
confuse red and green. It's not a severe or debilitating condition, mostly a minor inconvenience for those afflicted.
But for me as a student, certainly in the beginning, I had
to bluff my way through medical school without letting
my peers know of this weakness. And it was no easy thing
when so much of diagnosis relates to color. But I learned
to develop other markers to go by—the smell, warmth,
and slippery texture of blood, for instance.*

*How could I have known that my flawed vision, the
fault in myself I had spent my life concealing from others,
would be the reason I lost you?*

Bhisma

December 23, 1973

My love,

*The strangest thing today. Someone's lifeless body was
dredged from the swamp near Unit XV, Indrapura. I
was there, watching, when suddenly I heard strains of
"Ummah, Sallih" in the background. A friend told me
later it was an interpretation of the Al-Araf, chapter 7
of the Qur'an. It's not the first time I've heard this song*

sung since I arrived in Buru, and although it won't do to appear touched by such things, it kills me each time I hear it.

These days I am so easily moved. By the tiniest, darnedest things. A tree, a bird, the river. Things we know as lovely become magnified, almost God-like, as you come close to them. It feels melodramatic writing this, but it's true. And you know I've never been religious; I even used to make a point about not being religious, to avoid being thought of that way by my peers. But I've discovered that learning to rest in solitude is in itself a religious experience.

Bhisma

December 24, 1973

Today we buried a man called Ruli. I couldn't save his life, and this makes me very sad.

I was not in the barracks when it happened, because when it's not time to sleep, I try to avoid being there. It's too depressing. In this dark and damp space barely six by thirty yards, many fights have occurred between prisoners, between the young and the old, between ex-inmates from different prisons in Jakarta, between the so-called edu-cated urbanites and the self-professed "masses." So much useless blood has been spilled that the less time we spend there the better.

So anyhow, I was outside with a few inmates after the afternoon drill when I heard screaming from inside. Then the sick sound of someone writhing in intense pain, followed by the sound of someone being dragged out of the room. Despite my doctor's instincts I couldn't move my legs.

The bare torso of the man brought out from the barracks by two other prisoners was covered in blood. For a moment I wasn't sure if he was the victim or the attacker, or if I should step in or if I should wait. Then something fell from the bloodied man's hand.

There was a collective jolt among those of us already gathered outside the barracks. We heard the heavy footsteps of the guards who came toward us yelling and waving their rifles. They were ready to beat the shit out of us. As the guards took away the blood-covered man, shaking and slapping him while they were at it, I realized with horror that I couldn't take my eyes off what had fallen to the ground—a knife. I was transfixed.

You know very well from our time at the hospital in Kediri that I've seen and treated too many stabbing victims. But the sight of that bloodied knife was so overpowering, so nauseating and awful, it still haunts me to this day.

All of a sudden I heard people calling, "Bhisma! Where's Bhisma?" Someone pushed me toward the barracks and inside I found a man who was barely a man. He was lying there in a river of blood, he was in pieces. I went to him, propped his head on my lap. I asked for a rag, anything, to hold over his chest and abdomen and continued to cradle him. There was nothing I could do; life was seeping out of him, and there was nothing I could do.

When I looked down at his face I remembered him as Ruli. He was a LEKRA member from Lamongan, a young man who was uncommonly fetching and curiously feminine, quite a dancer. He was a seasoned ludruk performer, used to playing women's roles in ketoprak shows. I saw him perform two female roles during the last Independence Day celebration: once as a queen and another time as some proud princess. Little did I know you could get killed for such things.

The guard hovering over me muttered, "So many wounds. How many, Mas?"

"A dozen or more," I said.

A shudder ran through the crowd that was pressing in around me. There is a perverse excitement at the elucidation of suffering—it is kind of exciting as long as it happens to someone else.

I closed Ruli's eyes and tried to block from my mind the sound of his last horrific scream. The guards were impatient to claim the victim's body. I spoke to their leader, the most reasonable among them.

"It's dark now, Pak. You can't give him a proper Islamic burial today. Let me bathe and shroud the body and lay him down somewhere decent. Then you can bury him tomorrow morning at dawn like anybody else."

I knew that too often the bodies of dead prisoners were unceremoniously dumped into a hole and covered over by earth to become maggot feed, without the proper observances.

The head guard snorted that the commander would decide what to do. This morning I was informed that the commander granted my wish. Ruli was given a burial of sorts. With prayers. The prisoner who presided over the ceremony later whispered to me, "You do know that man was gay."

Ruli's murderer, a man named Yazid, was a union guy from Belitung. According to some, they'd been lovers, but for three months Yazid suspected Ruli of two-timing him. In this purgatory three months can feel like forever, and it must have been hard enough being the way they were. Yazid has been transferred to Namlea, to Jikukecil Prison, where I am sure he will be beaten senseless for being both a murderer and a homosexual. I doubt he will survive.

Bhisma

December 27, 1973

And now, my darling, I've come to this most vexing of topics. You guessed it.

Sex is a big deal here, as you would imagine. The men always seem to find ways of ensuring they get enough, if not with each other then often with local women who are only too eager to offer themselves. Occasionally someone will be crazy enough to try and seduce a comrade's wife or teenage daughter, at great personal cost.

Do you wonder whether I ever get tempted? Oh, I do. I do get tempted. But something always holds me back.

There's a recurrent dream, one I should tell you about. It's about a child, a little girl, our child. Deep down I probably willed that child to exist. But ever since we were in Kediri, I've always felt I must have planted my seed in your womb. This is something I cannot know, yet the dreams come anyway. And I don't want any other child brought into the world—my child—that is not yours, too. So yes, I hold back.

I met a local warrior here. Huge, powerful, impressive. His name is Manalisa. I don't know how to describe him to you, but I can tell you that we meet occasionally and we talk.

He told me that male energy flows like nature's energy and will never cease as long as nature remains. He has taught me how to be at one with this energy—walking the entire span of the island, learning to communicate with the waves, living at peace with the cold. He has taught me to have faith in my dreams.

Bhisma

December 28, 1973

Tonight I think of you like a certain star above me in the sky, one that twinkles and fades but reappears at the point of forgetting.

I imagine you weeping, surrounded by pearly blue.

Bhisma

December 31, 1973

Mein Liebling,

The year draws to a close, and I am once again cushioned at the base of an overgrown tree, watching yet another ketoprak performance. My fellows are spread out, huddled in unprepossessing bunches. Extension cords from the giant speakers not far from where I am sitting snake through the grass all the way to the stage. Amazing, how much electricity we're using today!

The night sky looks like a canvas on which the doodling gods have stopped painting to take a little time out with us mortals. For some reason there is a lightness in the air. The place suddenly feels like an oasis of moonlit optimism, its occupants suspended in a haze of laissez-faire. We almost do not recognize ourselves.

I have mentioned before that our minders seem to have become more compassionate. This is our third staged performance in one year. A positive sign, even though these ketopraks can be quite tedious and the repertoire ranges from the shamelessly banal to the overly creative.

Most of tonight's performers came from Unit XIV, Bantalareja. I have few friends there.

On the whole they are a fun lot. They point out repeatedly that they have at least half a dozen performing groups, each with a particularly unparalleled skill for reviving the sounds of old Djakarta: one for lenong, one for a keroncong orchestra, one for irama Melayu. Bantala-this, Bantala-that, Bantala-the other. A group of youth from Tangerang, an area outside Jakarta, are the leaders, and they look down on wayang performances. Maybe this is why they can always be counted on for political fervor, if not aesthetics, and why they always insist on performing folk stories.

In fact, that's what they are offering now: fairly palatable stuff, more than a touch tedious. Moral of the story: down with feudalism. As though life is only about heroes and patriots.

As you doubtless know from your mother's experience, it's the behind-the-stage stories that are more exciting. They always are. Fresh love declared, new allegiances made, old friendships broken. And always, this sense of deepened reality in the air.

But by tomorrow all will be depleted, and everybody will be slightly depressed.

Bhisma

February–March, 1974

It's been a while since I've written, my love. But things have been a bit difficult here.

For one there has been a spate of sickness here, mostly relating to food. Or the lack thereof.

Most of the time, the circumstances are hard to avoid. Many prisoners on rice-field duty look forward to getting their extra protein from catching orong-orongs. These insects come out and float haplessly in the water when soil is crushed into it. Lizards are common, and there are kelabangs, too, a kind of crab-like spider.

Now, the kelabang is a tricky bastard. If it comes in contact with fire it releases a bluish substance and gives those who consume it the most debilitating case of the runs. One has to admire the fortitude of the inmates here: as far as human beings go, they are as hardy as they come. Still, some do manage to become so sick they need to be transferred to the hospital in Namlea, where there are better facilities.

Today, a man was brought to me who had recently sought medication for kelabang poisoning. But this time he was dead; he'd been knocked unconscious, and there were three stab wounds in his abdomen. I asked the people who carried him in what happened. They said the man had such severe diarrhea that he accidentally emptied his bowels into the River Bini. In his haste he'd forgotten a new rule in the penal colony: no one should crap in the river because we all rely on it as our only source of clean water.

So of course the people who saw him do this beat him up. He must have fought back, which was why they finished him off with the knife. I felt awful. He had previously sought treatment from me, but he must have mistrusted either me or the tablets I'd given him. Or both. Perversely he had gone to the river, which is supposed to give life, only to have his life taken away from him.

Bhisma

April 1974

There is a man from Banten I visit from time to time, usually on my way to the farthest units. His name is Rukmanda, and he believes I have special powers. When he first tried to tell me this I dismissed the idea immediately. I said, "I don't want to hear it. I bet you think it's something about my name being Bhisma. If it is, I already know. I don't need a sage from Black Magic Land to tell me that I will only die when I choose to."

But gradually I've come to wonder if Rukmanda could be right. I've told you about the occasional beatings. Most of us, including myself, do not escape them. Yet—and this is the darnedest thing—when it happens to me I don't feel any physical pain.

I don't feel it during interrogation either, which is really another word for torture. I read somewhere, once, that intense physical pain mimics death. Each time intense pain is inflicted upon the body it is a kind of mock execution. I try to conjure in my mind the tonal sensation of pain, if there is indeed such a thing, but I simply can't. I see what pain does to my body, the gashes, the swelling and inflammation, the festering pus. I can see what inflicting pain is about, the wanting to hurt, the naked show of brute force, the power game. But I can't summon the sensation of pain, even if only to confirm that I am mortal.

This has been an idle hour, acquired through sly machinations. Now it is getting dark.

I have to take leave of you once more. What I'd give to be able to hold you again in my arms.

Bhisma

April 1974

I've learned to love the ocean because unlike the mountains I rarely see it. I often think of sailing out instead of coming in to shore. I imagine the tremendous reefs under the water and the anemones that, a blind friend once told me, are glued to the coral like jeweled mouths. Color and poison, he said, are two sides of the same coin.

Imagine, then, this island. Precariously small, yet refusing to be leveled by anything—not even by the sweeping blue and fickle waves.

I've learned so much from people who live on the coast. The three villages nearest to us are full of such people. They are Butonese, and therefore they are not from around here. These people are happiest at sea. Every night they say to themselves, "Tomorrow we might live another day." Yet even if they feel a threat in the sky, or detect the ocean's panic, they still sleep noiselessly and rise early as though racing dawn to another beginning.

Bhisma

—, 1974

Is it possible, my love, to compare suffering?

A comrade with a chronic stomach problem asked me this question when I came to check on him this morning. Yesterday he'd come to me for treatment. He told me he nearly beat up a guy last night at Unit I. "That man Zakir. You know him, the one who never stops complaining. Who always says how much he suffers. I want to kill him," he said, with no remorse in his eyes. "If I do I won't feel sorry."

We all suffer here. For me it is losing you, losing my family. Yet how can I even begin to compare what I've lost with what others in the units have lost? Some have nothing left, not even their skills, their hopes for a future, their purpose in life. So I told him: "Suffering can't be compared. Here are your meds, and please stay away from Zakir."

But perhaps I'm oversimplifying. If you can't compare suffering then what is the meaning of sacrifice?

Still. This guy Zakir is a real piece of work. I've heard how he talks to our fellow prisoners.

He came before most of us, in the First Batch. This makes him annoying as hell. Loud, self-righteous, a little deranged. Sounds like a broken record too. "I built this place!" he would bleat, and when somebody says, "We all did!" he would bark, "It was I who built this unit! It was I who measured the land, cut down trees, cleared the groves, came crashing down while putting sago palm leaves on your goddamn roof!"

One day one of my friends challenged him. He said, "The guards said army troops cleared the land." This friend had come with me in the Third Batch so he did not witness what had happened.

"You really believe they did all the dirty work?" Zakir scoffed. "What they had were the drawings, that's all. The rest of the time they were too busy ordering us around and kicking us even if we didn't make mistakes. Look at this scar on my forehead!"

Zakir was greeted with silence but he went on, pointing to the tools on the ground. "We had nothing. None of these." He spat, then said, "The machetes they gave us had blades that were damn useless, and still we did more than you."

Then he went on and on about the soil being too hard, the days too long, the food too meager; about pouring his sweat, and only his, into the building of roads, dams, bridges, buildings, irrigation canals; about breaking his back opening, filling, cutting, harrowing, mapping, leveling, and slashing; and about getting mugged by the guards. About being forced to eat snakes and baby mice and cicak lizards and locusts because what other fucking food was there, while our batch does nothing but build shitty collapsible structures, sing stupid songs, make up stupid plays, and go to Christmas Mass, even if we're Muslims, so we can get wine from the pastor.

Then one of us couldn't stand it anymore and told him to shut up. "You think you're the only one who suffered?"

Okay, so what he said was true enough. The First Batchers did clear the land, build the road from Sanleko Beach to the interior, and build the first units. But the work didn't stop. We, too, had to barefoot it through stretches of grasses higher than even the tallest of us, the blades cutting through our skin and mud snakes biting our legs. We, too, know what it's like to eat ungodly stuff and carry weight on our shoulder more than we can bear while surviving humiliation of all kinds.

Last night I heard that my patient with the stomach problem saw Zakir spitting on one of the plates stacked for his comrades to use at dinner. Something about this made him snap. He grabbed Zakir by the neck and nearly beat the bejesus out of him.

That was why I went over, this morning, to see my patient. I wanted to find out exactly what had happened. He said to me, "I know Zakir suffers. I know he feels he has given his all to the Party. That's what makes him mad. But suffering, especially on behalf of the Party, doesn't make you nobler than the rest of us. If I didn't give him that beating someone else would have done worse."

My patient may be right. But perhaps every suffering needs some salve at some point. And for Zakir, feeling noble in the name of sacrifice, sad as it is, may just be part of his way of surviving.

Bhisma

—, 1974

Darling, more depressing news.

Last night, a sergeant named Panita Umar was ambushed near the rice fields while making the rounds on his bike between Unit XV and XVI. He was hammered to death.

They say he was killed by guys from Unit V. So today Unit V prisoners were butchered in reprisal. We'll never know how many, but there were many. In the minds of the executioners, the murderers of Sergeant Panita Umar were from Unit V, so all of Unit V was responsible.

Zulfikar tells me the sergeant who was killed was quite the model guard. He wasn't cruel like many others, in fact he was quite popular. He liked to share the occasional cigarette and swig of arak with the prisoners, was fun and casual in his ways. Joked a lot.

And so here we are, here I am, pondering the same feelings again, how violence and its aftermath reside in us, too, in all of us. The crazy trajectory of it. The panic, the bile rising, the inexplicable rage, the yielding, the numbness, the dumb settling-back-into-place.

Asking the same old question again: what is it, exactly, that accounts for bloodlust such as yesterday and today, when so many of us are also capable of appreciation, of the little improvements we see around this place, of unexpected kindness?

For there is plenty of kindness around, too. The guards of my unit, Unit XVI Indrakarya, for instance, they are from the Hassanudin Military Command. The name Hassanudin itself may evoke fear, but those guys, they are not fierce at all. In fact many of them are so much more humane than those Pattimura pigs who murdered so many innocents to avenge the death of one of their own.

But Samsi, our commander, mostly has his heart in the right place. I don't say this lightly. I mentioned he's a good guy. I'm sure he won't let anything on this scale happen again. Besides, from the government's point of view it would be too humiliating.

As for the lot of us, what can I say? We're shaken, battered, depressed, sure. Soon we'll probably be dead, too. But—again, forgive my mawkishness—we can also be stronger. Kinder. Help others. Remind ourselves that music is a gift. Know that something is beautiful.

Bhisma

—, *1974*

My love,

A friend in Leipzig once likened history to the footsteps of a heartless giant. At first I thought he was just straining to sound brilliant, and that his words were in fact hollow. But then he qualified this by saying: "History knocks ordinary folks off the record. It makes them disappear by not putting their names down on Posterity's list."

That friend went on to introduce me to a poem by Brecht, and these lines live in my memory: "On every page a victory is listed, but who is going to cook for the party? 'Wer kochte den Siegesschmaus?' Every ten years a great man is born, but who is going to pay the price?"

These lines come back to me every time I remember a boy I once knew. I won't name him. Let me just call him the boy.

The boy was all of seventeen when he died. I first met him on our way to Buru, on that foul ghost ship, when he was only fourteen. His was a sad story.

Prior to ending up in Buru, the boy was sent by his mother all over Java, from prison to prison, in search of his father. When he finally found his father at Wates Prison, the boy declared he wanted to stay there, in the prison, for fear of losing his father again. The prison warden granted his wish because the boy made no trouble and even proved himself handy. Perhaps the man was secretly touched by the boy's love for his father, but it wouldn't do to show too much compassion. So in no time the boy found himself doing petty errands in the prison as a way to pay his dues. He was allowed to stay in the storage room next to the lavatories, and nobody ever heard him complain.

It turned out that the boy's father didn't have to stay in prison for long: his mistake was considered minor; he was released after a year, and soon enough his name appeared on the list of the new recruits to the Office of Post and Telecommunication Services. But he was not allowed to take his son with him. The boy's status in the prison wasn't clear, and since the prison warden who'd admitted the boy no longer worked there it took some time to sort out the boy's release papers.

Months passed. Suddenly every inmate in the prison suspected to be involved in the September 30th Movement was moved to Nusakambangan Prison. Through some bureaucratic mix-up the boy went to Nusakambangan, too. A few months later he was shipped off to Buru. As I said, he was in my batch.

In Buru the sadness of losing his father again, with no chance of his father finding him, clearly ate the boy up inside. Because I liked and trusted him, once my medical privileges began to grow I enlisted his help.

He was an able and diligent worker. He looked after what medical equipment I had, he kept the clinic clean, and he also cleaned the "office" of Zulfikar, our revered unit coordinator.

But the boy wasn't well. He started to have dizzy spells, fainted a couple of times. I sent him back to his unit hoping he wouldn't be burdened with extra work there.

A few months later his fellow prisoners in Unit III took it upon themselves to call me. The boy, they said, needed medical assistance. Zulfikar wanted to come along so we put in our request for permission, and the unit commander, ever enthralled by Zulfikar, gave us the go-ahead. The way to the boy's unit involved a pleasant walk through Wai Babi Forest, in the direction of Wanareja, and then a few more miles farther toward the river.

At the time, political prisoners who had been taken ill were usually treated in barracks wards or unit medical centers. When an outbreak occurred, such as dysentery or malaria, a handful of doctors and officers from the Ministry of Health were sent to set up an isolation ward until the outbreak was controlled—sometimes this took up to a year.

Pragmatically, the Ministry also employed prisoners with medical backgrounds, such as students and male nurses, and this freed up the qualified doctors among us, such as myself, to be "distributed" around the units. Because there were so few of us the ratio was sometimes as low as one doctor to five units. This is one of the reasons the unit commander gave me permission to treat the boy right away. So you see, not just Zulfikar had his usefulness!

It was immediately clear that the boy's condition was far too serious to leave him at his unit's medical center; nearly all the centers were sad affairs with poor equipment and ill-prepared staff. The sorry bastards who manned them haplessly clung to their random medical wisdom, which too often involved bare fists, tough love, and bubble-brained diagnoses.

The headquarters hospital, the one we call Mako Hospital, wasn't yet up and running, so I had no choice but to request the boy be taken to the hospital in Namlea. I wouldn't be able to go with him, but he would be better off there. But as soon as my request was approved we learned that there was no vehicle to transport him to Namlea. The boy's unit commander promised the loan of an army vehicle, due to arrive in a few days, and was kind enough to let me stay to look after the boy. Zulfikar was to leave the next day.

By this time, Zulfikar and I were so worried about the boy's condition that we agreed to turn over eight months of our medical stipends, four hundred rupiah *each, to pay for extra medication. I don't know what made us do that; God knows we need all the money we can get for our own survival, but my friend's words were ringing clear in my mind: history is a heartless giant. The heartless giant that separated the boy from his family and threw him instead to this godforsaken place, along with the sick twist of fate that knocked him off the list of people who "count."*

If he were to die who was there to care that he had existed, this boy whose only mistake had been to live? "So viele Berichte, so viele Fragen . . ." Brecht again, and yes, so many questions.

Unexpectedly, during the days we waited for the damn vehicle, the boy absolutely blossomed in my care. In no time I began to love him. He was thoughtful and sensitive, vulnerable, and like anyone schooled in long suffering, he'd learned to keep his sadness under wraps. But every so often he would wake up in the night and cry out "Bapak!" or "Simbok!", calling for his lost and grieving parents. To soothe him I would read him stories and poems—poems I have now lost.

Once he asked me whether the poems I read were mine. When I told him some were he asked me how it was possible that I wrote them if the prisoners weren't allowed pen and paper. "Oh, but I owe Zulfikar this luxury of writing," I said. "The unit commander appointed him the ghostwriter of his official speeches, those to be read out loud in front of the prisoners. So sometimes he gives me a "spare" pen, or paper. But being Zulfikar, he has warned me to only write after work, and only out of everybody's sight."

"How do you hide what you write from the guards?" the boy asked.

I told him how I stuffed all my scribbling into small bamboo tubes and buried them under a meranti tree not far from the barracks. I told the boy that I wrote a lot of letters to myself (and these letters to you, my love).

Then the boy looked up at me and said, "Will someone be able to find those letters if you die?"

"Maybe you will find those letters one day," I told him. "I can show you where the tree is."

The boy didn't get to see the tree. That was the last evening I spent with him. The next morning the Army vehicle arrived to take him to Namlea Hospital, and he was out of my hands.

Three days later I heard he had died. He had become nonexistent: his cause of death didn't even make it onto Posterity's list.

History, indeed, is a heartless giant.

Bhisma

—, 1974–75 (?)

Night is falling, my love, and the tree is gathering the last of today's light.

Two geckos have been peering at me from a branch above my head. Now they are making babies.

I can't remember how long it's been since I last wrote. I have been so busy tending to the sick. But things do continue to improve around here. More music, more laughter, more cigarettes. Tape recorders are now allowed—but still no radios—and now there is also a television: 20 inches, black and white, sitting prettily in the Mako auditorium. Of course we all want a piece of it, despite tight restrictions on viewing. We are allowed to watch the 5:00 p.m. and 9:00 p.m. news, though at times the sound is turned off.

There have also been more visitors—people from far away who tell us, "This is horrible, this is wrong, this won't be forever, we won't stand still, we will go back and spread the word, we will fight for your freedom." They make no difference to us—these, surely, are just words—but it's nice, all that fussing. Nice and fuzzy.

Improbably, there are also more girls. Girls, pure and simple.

I mentioned how things changed with the opening of Savanajaya to families. Lately teenagers and children from the village have been invited to take part in the performances at Mako. Mostly girls, of course.

Don't get me wrong. There is no ulterior motive here. True, we are twelve thousand mostly red-blooded men cloistered on a remote island, and because of the way so many of us lose our wits around women this change has the potential to stand the whole island on its head. But these young women are so remarkably self-possessed, so remarkably hard to crack, being rightly cautious and hardened, I suppose, to the strangeness of their situation in the first place.

Correspondingly, we were warned, under pain of torture, to keep our hands off the visiting angels when they stayed a few days in the Mako complex. There were a thousand and one ways of glimpsing them as they bathed, or as they slept, and yet we were the perfect gentlemen.

It was a kind of fealty, in other words. But to what, to whom, none of us is sure.

Perhaps to our doom.

Bhisma

P.S. Whereas with me, I can only set my heart and sight on you. Corny, but true.

——, 1975 (?)

Mein Liebling,

Today I saw strange markings around the spot where I've been burying these notes. But I didn't dare check, much less risk raking them up. So I left them there. I will find another tree. It is not easy to leave a tree. It may not have seen all of a person's landscape, but it has seen most of what it's done to him. And holds its breath, provided it escapes the greed of man and remains unscathed, until the moment the man's children see those very things he'd seen.

Bhisma

——, 1975 (?)

My love,

Remember I wrote to you about the boy I loved like a son? The boy who should not have been here on this island, who shouldn't have been ill, who shouldn't have died here? Remember how I'd traveled to see him and ended up staying longer than I should? I have learned that as I was caring for him, folks here saw me in another light for the first time.

Strangely, it was another boy, a rather handsome boy, who pointed this out to me. A boy who, like me, has greenish, gold-speckled eyes. He looks as though he might belong to this land, yet something about him is also foreign. He must live nearby and he likes to hang around us, particularly near our main warehouse in Namlea. He came to me like an omen. I asked him his name but now I've forgotten it. A Christian name. It begins with an S.

He told me the men here respect me, not because I am a doctor, but because I care about people. Then just like that, he said, "You must be a father."

He said the word father as though he saw a side of me even I didn't know. After he'd gone, the word stayed with me. "Father." For the first time I knew I might die in this place happy, as if I had found my resting place.

Bhisma

—, *1977–78 (?)*

My beloved,

Men are going home. There is something to watching the back of a ship disappear into that elusive line in the farthest distance, a line that for years has seemed to me to be your mouth. There is a lovely finality to this, men who have been imprisoned here for years, separated from their families, their real lives, now at last returning home.

Some things still surprise. Years of imprisonment, including in Salemba and Nusakambangan, have taught me that in the worst predicaments it is often the most delicate things that survive. I saw this in the faces of those men sailing home. Even the seemingly meek ones, guys hardly seen or heard, the so-called little 'uns, who seemed to lack the will to survive, looked very much alive and well.

How would it be for us, for you and me, had I been one of those men going back? Would I have the courage to seek you out? Beg you for a second chance?

But I am staying behind.

Almost every night during the past few weeks I have been wakened by the night itself. I have learned to love the rain, and for the past few months, at Mako Hospital, where I have bunked in one of the rooms, it has poured down the windowpanes, emptying me of thought and desire. The night rain has made seeing familiar faces depart somewhat easier.

Bhisma

—, 1977–78 (?)

Every four years, it seems, Buru succumbs to a long drought. The melaleuca trees burn as though in self-purification, and the fires at night conjure images of Rome buckling under Nero's wrath. The local people believe the fires are nature's way of reforestation because, after four years, the oil content of the trees is severely depleted.

Have I told you about the cold? At the height of the dry season nights can dip down to 57 degrees Fahrenheit. I know for sure because I once took out the thermometer and held it against the wind. We are often roused against our will during such evenings, as most of us don't have blankets to keep us warm. Then someone will light a fire in the kitchen, and we gather around it.

In the morning, even though we come out of the barracks to witness how the drought is killing our corn and shallots, it is still possible to smile.

Bhisma

—, *1977–78 (?)*

Mein Liebling,

Last night I dreamed of waking up in an unfamiliar room. Being both in the dream and outside looking in, I could see that the room was like a room in a dollhouse, something of the sort illicit lovers dream they will be happy in forever.

Then I saw her. A little girl sitting at the foot of my bed.

Before I could speak she said, "Don't think I am here because I am soul searching, and you are somehow part of that. We are here as equals."

She had a big voice for her size, an adult voice.

Blinking away sleep I told her, "Okay, I understand." But I didn't.

She insisted I walk with her to the living room. I silently obliged. She was bare legged, and there was a quiet intensity about her, her young face wearing the ravages of a time not her own.

After I sat myself down she sat, too, quite a distance away from me. It was then I saw that she had your way of tilting her chin. Even though it was the dead of night, the curtains were parted, and a strange bright light was streaming into the room. An otherworldly light.

Still I said nothing. She looked about eight years old, but her mind was clearly older. She let out a chuckle, though her eyes remained guarded.

"You really think I'm going to actually do it?" she asked, with no mockery in her voice.

"I don't know what you mean," I told her.

The little girl laughed. "But I think you do."

Slowly, like waves contained in a current, a realization washed over me, something I was supposed to have known all along but had deliberately forgotten. Then I pictured you, and I thought, So, this is the assassin you have sent to finish me off. This is the angel of death who will help me repay my debt to you. And in the dream I laughed and said to myself, "Amba, you crazy, cheeky, wonderful woman. Only you would have thought of sending me a little girl."

Death. Not that I haven't thought of finishing myself off; many of us here have entertained that possibility. The thought of suicide has snaked through me, always. Sometimes it felt like the only way out. But even in the dream I reminded myself that there must be a reason why I am urged on by life. Images of Rukmanda, the healer from Banten I've told you about, flashed through my mind. Also Manalisa, another man believed to have special powers. I remembered my early bravado toward them, saying things to them like, "Do you really think I can escape fate? Do you think I even want to?" and I shuddered at the memory of my cockiness. But the little girl held me in her stare.

She said, rather menacingly, "I find them tedious, those clichés of destiny. I would like to think you have other ways of dealing with this moment."

I was awestruck. The little assassin could even read my mind. "What a wonderful creation she is, Amba," I remember telling myself. "How smart of you to have brought her into the world."

"Tell me where you live," I asked the girl.

She seemed slightly perplexed by this question, but quickly regained her composure. She stood up, and it seemed she was the sort who felt sturdier with two feet planted firmly on the ground. I could see that she was still restless. On the one hand she wore the look of someone who'd just stumbled into the wrong house and was thinking of bolting; on the other she looked so determined to do whatever it was she had been sent to do. What unnerved me was her resemblance to you. It was uncanny. In her very erect, proud bearing she was most like you.

She made it clear she was not there to answer pointless questions.

"Tell me about your mother."

"I don't want to talk about her. I want to talk about myself."

For a moment she looked like any child her age, petulant and a touch mischievous. But that impression vanished when she spoke. Her words were those of a far older person.

"My mother is a difficult, proud woman, yet I always try to accommodate her. You should know this, even if you haven't been there to see it. I try to be the model child. I am neither vengeful nor dramatic. I apologize to those who owe me the apology. I am the best kind of only child. And yet, my mother talks about me to others, and also in her journals, which I sometimes read, as though I'm not my own person."

"But all stories are made up," I offered. "All telling is retelling, and therefore it is fiction. Everybody knows that."

There was no change in the girl's face, no pause in her thought for something she might have missed or overlooked.

"My mother has a good heart, but she loves words too much," she continued as though she didn't hear what I said. "I think that is why she keeps me at arm's length. I excel in language. I write pieces of such profundity that my peers choose to stay away from me. It is she who is jealous of me, not the other way around, as you"—and here she gave me a piercing glance—"might expect. I think she has been jealous all her life, jealous of the life around her. She has an overwhelming sorrow for the world. That's why her husband is a great blessing to her even though I've always suspected her of not loving him the way he should have been loved."

Deciding not to antagonize her I did not offer solace.

"I never wanted that sorrow," she said. "I have my own life to live."

"So what will you do?" I asked, not really expecting an answer.

She laughed. "I will become an artist. I want to explore the disconnect between word and matter."

I was intrigued but kept silent.

"I will live it up. I will live it up the way my mother didn't. Because for all her wit and intelligence my mother has very little courage to really live. She has chosen words as her companion, and at the very least she should let them help her live grandly, have a public life, where she can be a commercial success, a celebrity. A life where she *can allow herself to travel, to have lovers on different continents and cities, to dance on a table in a negligee, with her breasts spilling out, for instance. But because of what she went through bringing me into the world, because she lost her courage, she chose to write virulent fiction to appease her inner demons. After the death of her husband she will resign herself to the life of a widow."*

"And you. How will you live it up?"

"I'll party hard." She grinned. "I'll travel, accumulate friends, do shocking things, both bourgeois and bohemian, that will make my mother's life seem as dull as an accountant's."

Her words were certainly cocky, but sadness seemed to wash over her as she tried to rein in her thoughts. For a minute she sat gazing down, the way you often did, my love, when you were angry or wanted to conceal your true feelings.

"What will your art achieve?" I asked carefully.

The question caused this strange child to look up, tilting her chin again.

"I know how to take two, three ordinary things and put them together in the same space in such a way that you see something else, something that subverts ordinary naming. You may see fear, anger, doubt, but not what causes it."

This woman-child moved me. I was about to tell her as much when she suddenly said, "And so we've come to this."

The handgun was almost too dainty; it could have been her finger. The ringing shot didn't seem real. For a glorious, immortal second, I thought I had escaped it, but then I felt myself shatter and scatter like a star.

Bhisma

—, *1978*

Amba, mein Liebling,

I've written you so much and also so little, it seems. My heart is still heavy. There is one important thing that I have not yet told you. Now is the time.

Back when I was still in Jakarta, in Salemba Prison, on a typical day when my mates and I had nothing to do but count the cockroaches on the wall of our dimly lit cell, Salwa came to see me. Yes, your Salwa. I have no idea how he found me or even came to be there; he must have pulled some strings at the attorney general's office.

I knew who he was even before he introduced himself, and I was shocked by his thinness—he was skinnier than a wishbone. Because of my training I could see that his body type was not a matter of genetics; it came from something deep and dark and pulverizing. How could I not guess it was sorrow?

"Isn't this fitting," I said. "Two adversaries who have never met but who have both paid dearly for the love they shared."

In so many ways Salwa defied my expectations. He had an elegance that seemed to have come from an ancient place and a face whose features were marred by the wilted petals of waiting.

"Why have you come to find me?" I asked, although what I wanted to say was, What do you really know?

Yet I didn't expect him to be so straightforward. He said calmly, "You must be wondering how I knew, but when two people are in love they often don't realize what the world can see. I'm surprised that you, of all people, a man of the world, a man of such extensive knowledge and experience, would not know this."

I waited, knowing he needed this, his chance to get even.

"The head of the hospital in Kediri," he went on. "He could see that the two of you were in love. That man was a good person. Perhaps at the time he did not seem to care, but he did. He caught every flutter, every tremor, everything the two of you tried to hide from him. Like me, he is Javanese." Here Salwa stopped, as if by offering a crude stereotype he was trying to provoke a reaction from brash, unrefined, Sumatran me. Perhaps he was also dismissing me for being only half-Javanese, and therefore never enough.

"When I asked that good doctor where my fiancée had gone, he broke down because his shame, for not preventing what happened, was unbearable. It was as if he needed to divulge everything he knew about the two of you."

I will never forget the sight of your betrothed, standing there outside my cell, like a drowning man who at last had reached the surface. And then he said, his voice flat and expressionless, "I won't ask you where she is. I doubt you will give me an answer. But because I am suffering, you will do this one thing for me." He paused as if to muster his courage. "You will tell me whether you deflowered Amba."

His toneless register when saying "deflowered"—such an ancient word—was as if he felt it was the word he must use, while also wanting distance from it. Memories of the two of us together came flooding in: my hand cupping your breast; the way your eyes closed when I told you that you were beautiful, before you glanced up at me again through your lashes, wanting to hear it again; how I obliged, gladly, willingly, catastrophically—How beautiful you are, my darling, how beautiful you are.

I looked up at Salwa, and his face was smug and triumphant. He knew exactly what was in my mind. I nearly blurted out, Yes, my dear man, and will you ever know this about a woman? She will always want to be told she is beautiful, every little part of her, because by that time she is already in love, already undone, and because of that she will do the sorriest things.

No sooner had I thought that than I felt guilty. For Salwa—so long a phantom, the man I wished so many times would just perish, disappear forever, the name that had finally acquired a face and a voice—was outside my cell, tall, regal, and possessing all the power. I didn't wish to strike back. I didn't want to make him suffer another instant of my wretched existence. I found myself delaying my answer, as if I still needed to understand deeply, ethically, the question.

But Salwa understood my silence.

"So she made her choice," he said. "Is that what I'm given to understand?"

"It isn't that simple," I offered.

"Oh? You didn't even give her a choice?"

"The real issue—"

"No, spare me. I've heard enough. My issue—the only real issue—is how to live with betrayal. Betrayal by the woman I loved and trusted most in this entire world. There is no deeper wound. It is finished. I cannot have her back. From now on she is your problem."

I wanted to say: I don't even know where she is. That's the plain truth of it. We were separated from one another. I've searched for her everywhere. At least accept that about me. I searched everywhere, but then I was arrested.

But how could I tell him that? I could see that this man, the man I had wronged, was at the end of his journey. Having buried the only light he knew in the deepest trough, from now on he had only two choices: being buried along with it, or finding himself a new set of eyes. He looked at me one last time, then left without a word.

And so, my love. For the first time since October 19, 1965, the date tattooed upon my heart, for the first time since that exploding pinprick of a moment when our lives turned upside down, I finally knew why I lost sight of you. Why I allowed fate's spirits to let me follow that woman who wasn't you in the blouse that wasn't red.

It was because I loved you, plain and simple, because you had told me you were wearing a red blouse, because I had painted my entire world red, the color of my love for you.

Am I right in thinking this way? Did I lose you because our love was already too extraordinary, larger than life? How many people will ever experience such a love? But did I, in winning the object of my love, create injustice? What else can we call something that is built upon another person's suffering?

The gods have been right all along. Our fates are already written in the stars. We can rewrite only so much.

Bhisma

18

The Question of Red

Namlea, Buru Island, April 2006

Night has tipped into day. Amba and Samuel have been in the empty hotel coffee shop for more than six hours. With the droll pictures on the wall and the beverages from a vending machine.

All that time it is Amba's voice, and only her voice, that fills the silence around them. It is the only thing about her that is unchanged, now that there is color in her cheeks, a new charge in her eyes.

She is not of this world, Samuel thinks. *A lost star.*

The letters, of course, are not the end of it. Letters never are. After reading them, after learning the truth, people have to go on living. For Amba, reading Bhisma's letters means knowing that Bhisma had really loved her and had not run after Rinjani on that fateful day over four decades before. For Samuel, it is the revelation, at once startling and serene, that Bhisma had remembered him, out of so many strangers he could have remembered, because he had unwittingly said the right thing, evoked the right thing, read him the right way.

Samuel thinks of the two dizzy days it took, after he landed back in Jakarta, after that initial curious calm, to realize he must return to Buru to find her.

His mind replays his frantic calls to Sabarudin, who finally owned up to his part in the subterfuge. The scramble to get a ticket for the half-day plane ride back to Ambon. That ghastly ferry ride to Buru: sitting on the deck, rain drenched, bladder at the bursting point, hungry as hell. Fending off Hasan's questions, that stupid son of a bitch: how much he had to pay him the second time for his van, plus bribing him to shut him up and losing their friendship, most likely. The crazy journey inland to the hospital in Waeapo he'd rather not remember. Finding Amba there in the state she was in.

And, once back in her presence, the days of agony waiting for her to come around. The confession of Mukaburung. The ceremony at the grave of the Wise Man. Hasan storming in on them at the mauweng's house. Those cretinous hours of being investigated by the idiot in uniform. The magical Manalisa bearing down on them as though a character from an old sacred book.

"It's funny," she says, "how in the end it simply comes to this. That everybody has a story to tell. You have your story, Zulfikar has his, my dead husband Adalhard had his. No journey is ever about one person alone."

He waited.

"And now I'll tell you how he died."

❧

With the letters, Amba explains, are scraps of notes Bhisma had written privately to Manalisa, plus some documents originally given to him for safekeeping. The most difficult to read, she says, are police reports and the transcripts of witness interrogations.

"Sorry if you've heard some of this before. But telling it again will help *me*. Make things clearer in my head, you know."

It's only seven o'clock. He has all the time in the world.

"So here we go." She draws a deep breath. "We knew Bhisma chose to stay in Buru after the penal colony was dissolved. I looked through the documents and his letters for something to explain his decision. It seems he thought that he owed it to me not to return home.

"Like everybody else who stayed, he was given a plot of land to work. For several years he made do with the plot that was given to him and, as Manalisa told us, he would have attended to those who sought his medical help with the same infinite patience and care he gave to his trees."

Her degree of circumspection is, of course, to be expected. This retelling, after all, is part reading, part experience, part fact, and part fiction; she has to construct a few things along the way. And love is a powerful engine.

"Around three years after the prison camp was dismantled, he left the Transmigration Area for the estuary of the River Apo. There he swiftly made himself indispensable. So indispensable"—Amba pauses, and Samuel sees her face cloud—"he was given a wife by a grateful chieftain. A common practice, still, among the people of Buru, but you of course know that.

"We also know this: the woman, Mukaburung, had been adopted by the chieftain as a daughter after she had come down alone from the mountains. She had been banished from her own soa. I imagine this woman would have been grateful for this new turn of fate. Perhaps for the first time in her life she felt the world could be just.

"I found three of Bhisma's notes to Manalisa in the pile of things he gave me, although I very much doubt the old man can read. In one of them, he said her previous husband, the one she ran away from, had been a brute who beat her. Bhisma told Manalisa that she was a fragile thing, and he took care to treat her gently.

"Even in his new life, Bhisma would still disappear to the mountains for months, accompanied occasionally by Manalisa. He would return with medicinal leaves and sacks full of breadfruits to share with his neighbors. Sometimes his longing for the ocean would be great and he would spend time wandering around a place called Air Buaya (Crocodile's Tears). Sometimes he would sleep on the beach. I wonder if it was the same beach you mentioned on the *Lambelu*, after we first met, Jikumerasa.

"Anyway, he went there to catch the sunrise, then swim and walk. He mentioned in another note to Manalisa that he had let his hair and his beard grow long. He would have been tanned, and that must have set off his golden eyes." Amba's voice grows dreamy. "He'd have had the aura of a rock-star sage."

She suddenly stops, as if trying to remember something.

"Samuel, something Bhisma wrote referred to the violence that started here in the Maluku Islands in early 1999. Do you remember, on the ship, when I asked if you had ever killed?"

"Those years of religious violence," Samuel replies after a momentary hesitation. "What can I say? It was shaming and incomprehensible to say the least. It completely ripped us apart. I was here when that group of Muslims murdered the Christians in the plywood factory, scores of them retaliating for the burning of a Muslim house by Christians the day before. It was a god-awful time."

And it was. He has a poor memory for stats, but these are imprinted in his mind like a birthmark: more than 170 homes and buildings destroyed by Muslim youths, some forty to fifty people killed, and scores injured. Some people escaping inland, seeking refuge in the woods and mountains. Others fleeing Buru, over eight hundred refugees. The chain of violence between Muslims and Christians continuing in Ambon, at least another forty dead.

He realizes he has not answered Amba's original question. How many people has he killed? Two, he once told her, when he first met her on the *Lambelu*. Why does he need to go over it again?

"Bhisma apparently moved into the woods, too, sometime in August or September," says Amba, sensing his reluctance. "More than thirteen hundred people had died there since the start of the fighting, and he was sure many of the refugees would need medical help. So he bade farewell to his wife and the village and set off.

"He found a place to settle not far from a melaleuca oil refinery, in the region where the bloody clash had occurred in the plywood factory. When he arrived there he was told of the escalating brawls between youths in the streets. As soon as he had set himself up he went to see if he could help treat the injured, perhaps take some victims back with him to the safety of his place.

"I know all this," Amba explains, gazing earnestly at Samuel as if seeking validation, "because he wrote a report of what he witnessed, and it was among the papers Manalisa gave me. He described how, as the body count climbed, he plunged himself into work. He must have decided to stay long-term because he acquired the lease for a small tract of land from the local soa chief and started a vegetable and medicinal garden. In addition to the refugees from the plywood factory massacre, after an outbreak of cholera he treated over a hundred people from the village in less than a month in his makeshift infirmary. He must have tried to be everything to everyone. People paid him with produce if they could, but some gave money—then he would hitch a ride with the distillery truck all the way to Namlea to buy medicine.

"It seems people liked him enough, but they found him hard to figure out. He was fingered for an *Obed* (a Christian) as well as an *Acang* (a Muslim). From what I've read he was attacked, held at gunpoint, received death threats. But somehow, miraculously, he managed to cheat death at every turn. At least, he did for a long time.

"He worked hard, and alone," Amba says, clearing her throat. "He told Manalisa that he needed no flesh on his bones, no one to protect him, no one in whom to place his trust. He knew how to deal with people and communities of every kind, understood that folks have a way of protecting their own, long after the beliefs that fired and molded them have been whittled away. And it's true—people started referring to him as the Wise Man of Waeapo.

"If anyone knew his state of mind, or where he occasionally disappeared, it would have been Manalisa. In the police report there was a transcript of the interview they recorded with Manalisa after Bhisma died. He said, 'It's true. Something changed in my brother Bhisma during those last months. It seemed that he was losing hope. He kept saying things like *My work is finished* and *I'm done.* Then suddenly he escaped me.' The police report detailed what happened, the day he died. It could have been any day, but it was just after New Year's, 2000.

"Bhisma was apparently walking home alone when he saw or heard something that drew him into the bush. Perhaps he heard shouting or pleading. Then he saw two men. One man was wounded in his stomach. He seemed to have been shot by the other man. With the police report there were mug shots of the attacker. He looked tall and lanky, with wild eyes and greasy, long hair. Perhaps when Bhisma rushed to help the victim he didn't see that the other man had a gun. Perhaps he didn't care; the official police report wasn't clear on this, but a conversation apparently ensued between the tall man and Bhisma, which ended in the tall guy tailing him deeper into the woods and shooting at him again and again, like prey. Then shooting him one final time, point-blank, in the back of the head."

Tears spill down Amba's cheeks. "You see—and this is where it is so *galling*, so truly terrible—I already knew, deeply, instinctively, what happened to Bhisma. I felt his death, back then, at the beginning of this new millennium. Long before coming here I knew his end was violent.

I saw that scene in a dream. A red dream, red, the color he was blind to—the color of his blood, the color from which our daughter sprang."

❧

The rest of it was hard to stomach.

The man who killed Bhisma gave his name as Sabas. He was twenty-six years old, a Christian, and had been an oceanography student at Pattimura University in Ambon. Before moving to Buru, he had been involved in several bloody clashes against Muslims in Ambon, Tobelo, and Halmahera. But he didn't kill the "bloody Acang"—his description of the man he'd dispatched before shooting Bhisma—because of his religion. He killed him because the man had cheated him out of money—money they'd collected from campaigning for the Golkar Party in Buru and had planned on splitting.

In the matter of Bhisma's murder, he had shown a similar lack of remorse. He was remanded twelve hours after Bhisma's body was discovered by two villagers, fittingly men whom Bhisma had once treated. Bhisma was facedown in a pool of his own blood at the base of a tree. It was the killer's brashness that did him in, for he lost no time in boasting that he had killed the man who local idiots thought was some god, and that he'd proven to everyone that he was no god because now he was dead as a doornail.

Some of the locals asked him what the dead man looked like. The killer's description must have been pretty accurate—because the people listening realized at once who the bastard had killed and promptly took matters into their own hands. They were people whose lives Bhisma had saved, and thus they were prepared to pound the murderer to a pulp when the police interfered, thanks to Manalisa, whose embodiment of the Buru spirit also included pragmatism: he understood the value of getting the murderer to trial.

When Amba hands a sheaf of papers to Samuel she says, "Take this away. It's a photocopy of the killer's confession. Don't read it here; you'll need time. And I can't bear to watch."

Back in his room Samuel reads the criminal's handwritten statement:

What the hell do you people know about anything? Why did I kill that freak? Because he started lecturing me. He told me the man I just killed, that sonofabitch Udin, might have had a wife and children, innocent souls I'd robbed of a husband and father. This annoyed the hell out of me. I knew he had no wife or children. He was Udin, for Christ's sake, that loser Udin who had been living off his old mother for ages, the loser who had cheated me out of my money. When the scumbag refused to return it I killed him.

So that's it, the freak annoyed me. I told him to fuck off but instead he went over to Udin to see if the lying bastard was still alive. When he saw Udin was dead he started to preach at me. Yep, he should have minded his own business, but the fool started to preach. He said he'd been to the plywood factory before it was torched and how it was once a peaceful place where the only arguments were over soccer and everyone, the Acangs and the Obeds, used to play together as one team. He told me this as though I was a moron and didn't know these things.

And then they were hacking women and children, he said. As though that was my fault. Then he started raving about these goddamn islands, how people had lived with difference all their lives. He went on and on about the beauty of children, saying that children were a blessing.

I didn't want to be hearing all that stuff. I mean, what a fucking asshole!

So I asked him whether he believed in God. He didn't give an answer. Then I asked him whether he believed in religion. He started raving again, saying crazy stuff like man makes religion, and religion multiplies the hatred of man, and what happened in the plywood factory showed how horrible human beings can be in the name of religion.

Okay, fine, I said, human beings are rotten, but what is the role of religion then? He looked as though he was thinking really hard, and he kept stroking that stupid long beard he had, the one he must have thought made him look like fucking Jesus or something. He said religions historically came about as a retreat from violence, and they were supposed to guide the weak and powerless. Yes, but not Islam, I quickly said. But he disagreed.

Something about this got me all interested. The thing is, before he ranted and carried on, I didn't think he was a Muslim. His eyes had me fooled. They were kind of golden. He looked almost foreign. I thought he was a Christian, like me, so why the fuck was he disagreeing with me?

Then he said that Islam began as a peacemaker among warring Arab tribes, and the problem with Muslims is that they have forgotten their initial empathy. That Islam is now used as a call for truth and victory, not of humility and fraternity among men. I was confused, so I asked him what his religion was and something about him saying Islam caught me by surprise.

Do you love your God? I asked him. I do, but not right now, he said. So you don't believe in your God? I asked. Not when he's not doing his job, he replied. What would you do, I asked him, if I killed you now? Would you ask your God for his help?

Then, for some reason, the stupid shit looked at me and said he could not die if he didn't wish it himself. I couldn't believe my ears. I thought, whoa, here's a jerk who needs to die. So I said, Okay, I'll make it easy on you then. You will start running, and I will give you some time before I shoot my first bullet. You will run into the forest. I will be close on your heels but I will pace myself. I want to see how much greater you are than your God. Maybe you can even join my faith, ha ha ha.

He must have recognized what my gun—an HK VP70 semiautomatic I got from an army guy in East Timor—could do. I thought he was going to chicken out but he just stood there, smiling. He nodded.

So there we were, him in front and me behind, shooting. A couple of times I thought I had hit him. There was a thump, and I would see his head sway as though he'd taken a hit, but he kept going. For the longest time there was no blood trail. This freaked me out. I started to wonder if he really meant what he said.

So I picked up the pace but he stayed ahead of me. I just wanted to kill the bastard. Suddenly it was raining and the whole earth looked like a world of haze, a new world altogether. If there was a blood trail the rain washed it away, which made it harder for me to track down the shithead. I called him all sorts of things. I cursed his God, told him his God was a sick sonofabitch, and that he was even sicker than his God. I shouted that I would blow so many holes into him and into his smug face nobody would know what he'd looked like.

Finally, I saw him beneath a tree. He was facing me. I could see blood on him, though not as much as I expected. He had a strange light about him. You know how in movies the bad guy and the good guy always talk before they kill each other? Well, I didn't want to waste any time talking so I just started raining bullets on him. All the while I thought to myself I wouldn't want to die this way, but this bastard's a Muslim and I am a good Christian who deserves to live.

By the time I was finished he should have been punched full of holes, but he still looked intact and refused to buckle. He was on his knees though, and I knew then that he had it wrong about being able to die only when he wished it, and that made me laugh. I asked him, So what is it that you want now? What is it that you are asking of your God? I am ready, he said. You can take away my life now. I've atoned for my sins. It's time to let other people live.

Then I walked around behind him and I fired the last bullet into the back of his head. He fell facedown and died. It was that simple.

Later Amba finds a note she's missed in the pile of letters and paperwork Manalisa gave her. It is Bhisma's own account of what happened the day he went to the plywood factory. The villagers, including Manalisa, had urged him not to go. But Bhisma hardly needed a lesson in the limits of human tolerance; he was a doctor above all else.

I arrived on site at noon on December 24, 1999. I did not see a single corpse. The survivors of the carnage, all Christians, told me the bodies had been removed from the scene by local Muslims and their military friends. When I asked which military group, no one could say because they weren't from that region. Someone suggested they were reinforcements, most probably from Ambon. All the people I spoke to believed the military sided with the Muslims.

This is what I have pieced together from the accounts of the survivors.

When the threats of violence against the Christians began, on December 22, the factory owners promised a truck to take them to safety. But the truck arrived only after they'd barricaded themselves in the factory for more than twelve hours. Then only a handful of people, just the foreign workers, were allowed on the truck. The Christians were denied their rescue.

Around four hours later, the killing started. From what I heard, the violence seemed premeditated. There is no denying it was revenge for the action of the group of Christians who burned a Muslim house the day before, following an argument between a Christian and a Muslim worker at the factory. The Christian worker took his anger back to his village, and there his neighbors took up his cause, setting fire to the house. Of course, then the Muslims, too, took up arms.

By early afternoon, scores of Muslims had arrived at the factory searching for Christians. Although the factory was guarded by police and soldiers, there to protect the Christians, they clearly failed in getting them out of the facility or driving away the Muslims. Survivors told me

*the first thing they heard were shots fired and the clang-
ing of metal, followed by shouts and screams and cries of
"Allahu Akbar."*

*After the carnage the Muslim mob began to search
for survivors. They found some Christians hiding on
the second floor. Most of them were killed. One badly
wounded man I tended told me he saw a Muslim youth
scream at a woman holding a baby to tell him if she was
an Obed or an Acang. When she answered "Obed" he
struck her and the baby down with his machete.*

*When I arrived at the burnt factory things seemed
to have calmed down, and the last of the survivors had
come out of hiding. They had not eaten for nearly forty-
eight hours; they were severely distressed. I, along with
other people who'd come to help, made sure they were fed
and clothed properly. Most were in shock, but some could
talk about the experience. One or two even seemed blasé.*

*In my life I have learned something about human
endurance: there is no end to it. But when one survivor
asked me, "What happened here? We used to live side by
side," I was so stricken with grief that I couldn't hold in
my tears. I had to go outside to cry. For the first time I felt
I had been outside the cage of humanity, peering through
the bars, trying to get an understanding of what life was
about, and I'd gotten it all wrong. Perhaps I was lucky to
have been spared this insight for so long.*

*It is clear to me that the religious conflict in Maluku
has not ended; it may never end. The words "Obed" for
Christians and "Acang" for Muslims that seem to prevail
since the Ambon conflict sound as though they were taken
from the language of children, not unlike silly nicknames.
But here those two words can kill.*

For years I have lived with words and terms that divide people, words that mark who is to be exterminated and who is to be spared. When I lived in Leipzig I saw how people's lives were destroyed because they were labeled "counterrevolutionary." During my time in Javanese prisons I both witnessed and experienced the way language was twisted to become a weapon.

I once believed one must be prepared to sacrifice oneself to prevent the triumph of hatred. Even amid all the violence of 1965, when I was in Kediri, I was still hopeful there was something stronger than hatred, something precious to help us survive.

But hatred doesn't go away, I realize now. It lingers even in the hearts of the bravest fighters, and even in the hearts of friends.

And now I've come to understand how hatred can also become an instrument of survival. But in the face of what I've witnessed over the past few months, it won't be the case with me. Something seems to have died inside me. Perhaps that thing is hope. At the age of sixty-seven, what I feel is hopelessness.

I write this on the night of December 24, 1999, and I feel the end is near. I wish my brother Manalisa could be sitting here, next to me, for he knows that if I leave it is because I want to go.

Bhisma Rashad

BOOK 6

Srikandi and Samuel

Jakarta, 2011

19

A Falling into Place

In Jakarta not many afternoons follow a design. When Samuel sees Amba leaving the DVD kiosks at Ratu Plaza he calls her from afar. She turns and sees him, smiles. When he catches up with her, she lets out a cry and kisses him on both cheeks.

They sit down at a café, order tea. He has sworn off coffee—too much acid in the stomach—and she is pleased to hear this. She only drinks green tea now, she tells him. It's also good for the brain. Especially for the kind of work she does, translating literary novels and writing the odd corporate profile. In between she moonlights as a private English language tutor and still publishes a poem or two.

He tells her, in turn, about his new job at a mining company, which has seen him shuttling back and forth between Ambon, Waimena, and Jakarta for the past year. How he recently returned to Buru since gold was rumored to have been found in Wamsaid, Waeapo.

There's too much to catch up on, and the sun is going down. So they jump into a cab and find a restaurant nearby.

࿓

Memories flood in: their journey on the *Lambelu*, their first greasy meal at Warung R. M., the morning the military intel guys ambushed them at Julius's house. And all those first sights: of Marko and his bile, the healer Rukmanda and his unlikely love, Doraemon, the one and only Manalisa, and of other things Buru: Bhisma's meranti tree, Lake Rana, the postcard-pretty school in Walgan. And, of course, Zulfikar, who, Amba informs Samuel, moved to Bandung a year ago after a heart operation.

When Samuel mentions Mukaburung, something in Amba's expression changes.

"It's funny, you know," she says. "I've been thinking about her a lot. I feel that in a way we are even, she and I. Married, both of us, to men we weren't able to love. She to her first husband, who beat her, and to Bhisma, who didn't allow her to love him, and me to Adalhard."

She touches his hand lightly. "I never said this," she says, giving it a squeeze. "Not in the way I should have, at any rate. But I don't think she ever held a grudge against Bhisma—for loving someone else, I mean."

"You know, I actually liked her," Samuel says. He takes a long drag on his cigarette and leans on his chair. "I know I should have hated her for nearly taking your life, but she had a big heart. And she was funny. I remember when I went to see her the second time, only an hour after my first visit. She looked like a changed person. She not only lit up at seeing me again, but boy did she know how to talk. With wild hand gestures, with squeals of delight, with this, this . . . zest for life. She was hilarious. Tried to sit up and dance and nearly knocked the glass of water from her bed stand. I remember she had the most comical range of expressions, a village-elder seriousness, childlike joy, many different grins. It was impossible not to like her."

Amba nods, no sign of resentment on her face.

"I don't remember all the details, of course," Samuel continues. "But she did tell me she was jealous of you, without knowing why. She understood, though, why you had to come. To Waeapo, I mean. She said, 'That's what people do when they love someone, and only people who love can understand this feeling inside.' I was so moved I laid my hand on her arm to stop her beating her own chest. But she went on, pointing at her chest, pressing it. 'I still have this big feeling inside for him.' Okay, so she had this curious body odor, and it made me a bit woozy. It really was the most extraordinary smell. But as I was sitting there, listening to her, she made me think of all the women in my life. How I used and discarded many of them. And I was ashamed. So I told her she was lovely, that her husband was lucky, and he must have felt the same way."

Amba is quiet for a moment.

"You said before that you thought you and she were similar," says Samuel, shifting the focus.

She hesitates, as though struggling for precision. Then says: "I suppose. In that we are both capable of great acts of jealousy."

Jealousy. There it is again. Some topics resist the entry of men, even if they are invited. And Samuel knows too well not to probe. He's learned that from Adalhard's story—a man whose quiet suffering brings a familiar pang to his heart.

"Perhaps her love was more like Adalhard's," he says. "She loved Bhisma the way Adalhard loved you. She must have known he was in love with someone else. She just didn't know who."

She nods.

"So when you planted that photograph of Srikandi on his grave . . . It was Srikandi, wasn't it?"

"Samuel," says Amba softly, ignoring his question, "do you remember when we parted at Jakarta airport? Before we went our separate ways? You asked me what I would tell my daughter?"

Samuel hesitates. Takes another long drag.

"It was just an instant," says Amba, "But I swear in that moment I saw you about to faint from pure pain. You could have been Prometheus with the eagle gnawing at your liver."

He doesn't quite remember the question, but he remembers that she had not let go of his hand when he squeezed hers. If they'd been in a movie the camera would have panned back and forth between their two faces, rapt and tragic, doomed from the start. He'd had a surge of hope that she loved him, and that she might tell him that. But with time he understood that her feelings for him were akin to what she'd first felt for Adalhard—that she loved him because he'd saved her.

Aah, love, he thinks. *What a fickle, arduous thing. It is the one thing that makes you both the hunted and the hunter, the riddle and the prize, suburbia and the universe—but it is never just the one love.* He tells her he doesn't remember a thing.

The light outside the restaurant has changed.

"You know, I think I know who sent me that e-mail," says Amba, smiling.

"Tell me."

"I'm pretty sure it was Salwa."

"Why?"

"It should have been obvious," she says. "No one else loved me like he did, and no one had a reason to resent me more. I read in one of Bhisma's last letters, the letters in the tubes that Manalisa gave me, that Salwa had visited him in Salemba Prison. Bhisma thought he must have had a contact in the attorney general's office, someone who was able to locate Bhisma in the prison system. It stands to reason that Salwa could have kept track of when Bhisma was sent to Nusakambangan and Buru. He would have also been able to keep tabs on Bhisma's movements ever since, and, finally, learn of his death from the police."

Samuel considers this. Salwa, who always did the right thing, always rose to the occasion. Did he think, in some weird way, he was helping Amba by making sure his rival stayed out of the way by being dead?

"You know, I think I understand him a little," he offers. "Salwa, I mean. After all, I happen to know a thing or two about obsession. But something doesn't add up. If he was still angry after all these years, how did it help to tell you that Bhisma had died? And why did he wait six years?"

"Maybe it was his way of forgiving me. Maybe he was trying to say, *Now you're free, free from not knowing, free to stop loving someone out of reach. He's at peace now, and maybe you should be, too*," says Amba. She catches her breath. "But why did he take so long? I thought about this many times. Then decided it must have been because of Adalhard. Salwa is so proper, I'm sure he wouldn't think it appropriate to tell me while I still had a husband. He must have heard that Adalhard had died. Knowing the way Salwa thought back in those days—and still thinks, I am sure—perhaps he was somehow grateful to the man who rescued me and my daughter from a life of indignity. Besides, what could I have done if I learned of Bhisma's death when Adalhard was still alive? I couldn't possibly have gone to Buru the way I did."

"He sounds to me like a complex man, more complex than you painted him all this time."

"A few years after I moved to Jakarta—Siri was around three, I think—I received a letter from Ambika. I'd written to my father, after my daughter's birth. An apology of sorts, wanting the news of his grand-daughter's birth to help repair something of the mess I'd created. But he and my mother found it hard to reconcile with me. While they acknowledged my letter, the distance was too great. I never heard from them again. Or from my other sister, Ambalika, though that was no great loss as we'd never been close. Anyway, Ambika, in her letter, told me she was married. Not exactly to an 'Arjuna' she said, but to a man with money, a businessman of some kind, *a really successful guy.* That made me laugh. Aaah . . . my darling sister. We certainly had our differences, but she's the only member of my family who writes to me and visits me and Siri from time to time. I'm convinced she was once in love with Salwa. At one point I was even certain that she was planning to steal him from me."

"You're so crazy that way," Samuel says, remembering Amba's senseless jealousy of the woman named Rinjani. "For someone with so much you are strangely loath to enjoy your gifts."

"I was wrong about Ambika." Another deflection. "In the end I saw how loyal she is. So I reciprocated by trusting her with my story, telling her about Bhisma, telling her Siri isn't Adalhard's child. And, bless her soul, she kept this secret from my parents. She told me in her letter that Salwa paid my family in Kadipura a final visit. He didn't stay long, no doubt aware of their embarrassment and shame, not wishing to compound it further. I think, from what I read in Bhisma's letter, Salwa's visit took place after he located Bhisma in jail, but he apparently didn't mention anything to them about him. He only told them that he had heard I ran away to Jakarta because of my involvement with CGMI. That I was accompanied by a Western social scientist, that we got married, had a daughter. That's it, the measure of how honorable Salwa is. I gave him every reason to hate me, yet . . . yet he does this."

Has she ever considered it might have been because of her, that men do what they do?

"He stayed in touch with my family for a few more years, Ambika told me. He got married in '73 and moved to Makassar. Maybe there was a job for him there, I don't know."

Samuel wonders if Salwa moved so far away because he couldn't stand the thought of returning to Yogyakarta.

"You think Salwa is a complex man," says Amba, touching his hand again. "On one level I think that's true. But on another level, all his decisions and actions boiled down to one thing: duty. In the end, like Mukaburung and me, he and I have ended up even, in a strange way. We've both learned what it feels like to have lost a love. And still we don't know how to bear a grudge, even if we tried."

She is laughing now, but with such tenderness in her eyes. "He's certainly not the Salwa of the wayang," she said. "This Salwa is a deeply human and ethical man."

On a traffic-choked Friday evening Samuel arrives at Galeri Pittoria on Sam Ratulangi Street, where Siri has an exhibition opening. Amba has invited him to join her there, but before he reaches the door he receives her text: *Sorry. Stuck in traffic.* He has arrived too early and feels like a fish out of water. He thinks of finding Siri and introducing himself, but instead he decides to absorb the space, to learn about her work.

He wanders for twenty minutes while the gallery fills, forcing himself to look closely at her art. It is like nothing he has seen before, and soon he finds himself standing for minutes on end before this or that painting, just drinking it in. After a while, his mind begins to ponder different aspects of the works: their balance, or their lack thereof. The juxtapositions of color, image, texture, shape. And miraculously the pieces respond to him, telling him he is neither liberated nor trapped. Just here, now, in the present.

He suspects he is not the only visitor to the gallery who feels this way. Obviously there is something powerful in the air; its aura seems to brush over him, opening his mind even more.

He moves to the edge of the crowd that has formed around the artist. He still can't see her, but he hears her response to the question:

"Can you tell me why there is so much red in this work, especially in the last four plates?"

"Well, how shall I explain?" Her voice is surprisingly deep and weighty. With an innate sweetness, like the sound of ripe plum. "I grew up with red, you see. It's been the key color of my life. I learned at school, of course, that red meant one thing, I think you all know what it is, and I understood how that was supposed to have made us all fear it. But I never bought it, this lie, because, wherever we are, red is inescapable: the red of apples and tomatoes, of the blood of the chicken you cut up for food, and for us women, of our own menstrual blood."

The voice breaks into laughter as some members of her audience titter, then continues, "Any of us could be hit by a car and end up drowning in our own blood. And of course there is war. But deep down, I was never scared of red, despite Suharto's brainwashing, despite that stupid propaganda film we schoolchildren had to watch each year. I'm happy that the red has caught your eye tonight. Over and above any other aspect of these engravings. I think, perhaps, this says something."

The voice pauses for a moment, then says, "At home as a child I grew up with the most glorious shades of red. Ruby, scarlet, vermilion, puce, carmine, claret, burgundy, crimson, magenta, damask, garnet, maroon. I knew the power of each of those names. For that I have one person to thank, and that person is my mother. She was a warrior, someone who was not afraid of anything."

Samuel smiles. Srikandi has such a clear, confident voice, suggesting someone who is at peace with her world. It is almost too much for Samuel, the relief that Amba's life hasn't come to naught, not when through her trials and tribulations she has raised such a solid child.

He feels a tug in his heart. Should he leave? Is the soul designed to bear so much?

Suddenly a voice rings from behind him, followed by a light tap on the shoulder. "Surely you can't leave just yet."

It comes as a surprise to him when he turns back to find that the crowd of admirers has parted, and he is looking at the artist, a young woman who looks like Amba, but is not Amba. She is not a replica of her mother but is clearly molded from the same stuff: same height, same proud bearing, beautiful clear skin and golden-green eyes that, as she advances toward him, become a mirror image of his.

"I know you, Samuel," she says in her strong but limpid voice. "Ibu told me you were coming. You are the man who saved my mother, twice."

"Is that what she told you?" he hears himself saying. He has never thought of himself in that way.

Like her mother, she dithers a bit, doesn't reply immediately. Instead she watches him for a while, as if deciding whether his reality fits her vision of him. Her gaze is voluptuous, as if she is undressing him with her eyes. He looks away.

Then she comes close, close enough to say so that only he can hear, "You know, I've seen you before, Samuel, or someone very like you. In a dream."

Siri keeps Samuel close to her, despite having to devote much of her time to her admirers, the gallery owner, eager collectors. When he suggests he should leave she says, "No, Samuel, stay. Ibu still isn't here." Later, when Amba has called to say she can't get there—*Was almost there, but then felt unwell, a sudden stomach bug, you kids just carry on without me*—Siri says, "Stay. Please. This will be over soon. There's so much to talk about."

When the artist's gift has been celebrated, the crowd has thinned, and the gallery owner has been thanked, she pulls Samuel by the hand and says, almost instructs him: "Come, there's a bar nearby. It's private enough and I want to tell you about my dream."

The dream, she later tells him, is recurrent. "It first came to me five years ago, when I found out my mother had disappeared. This was when she went to Buru. She had told me nothing. I was exhausted from a big project, and I'd stopped at a restaurant near the grand mosque. I must have fallen asleep because the next thing I knew a waiter was shaking my shoulder. 'You were screaming,' he said. 'It sounded like you were being murdered.' He was joking, of course, but I did feel like I'd been murdered. I had seen in my sleep a man that I recognized from other dreams. A man who, strangely, looked a little like you. He lay at the base of a strange tree, in a pool of his own blood. But when I turned him over, I was staring at my own face. That was when I'd screamed."

Samuel looks down—*Those eyes are too much, those cheeks, that mouth*—he can't bear it, and starts to mumble, partly because he finds her overwhelming, and partly because he knows he could explain that dream to her but can't. For surely that explanation should be her mother's to give?

He can hear the voices of other patrons in the bar, but they seem very distant. The woman's focus is entirely on him, her stillness and concentration uncanny. She has the gaze of a woman in charge of her own world, a woman who will not allow herself to be compromised, to be sullied. *Aren't artists supposed to be at the mercy of shifting realities?* he wonders. *How is it possible, then, for this woman to be this focused, this certain?*

Something in the room changes. A beam of light catches the pendant that sits in the creamy hollow at the base of her throat. It is similar to the pendant Amba wore when she and Samuel were together in Buru. Siri draws a deep breath. Her chest heaves, the pendant ripples.

Suddenly he doesn't want to avert his gaze anymore. His hands reach for hers; their fingers meet and lock. When she smiles, it all feels right, an inevitable falling into place.

Three months later, Siri is nursing a stiff drink with Samuel at some bar. It's become a bit of a habit between them. *Meet my drinking buddy,* she would say to anyone who stops to say hello. He still doesn't know much about her personal life, who she sees, where she actually lives, how long she will be gone when she says she's leaving again.

"The dreams still come," she says. "I don't know why. But it's odd. Now that I know the truth, the details keep changing. It's becoming like an unending story—or variations on a story. The one thing that remains constant is the color—the red of his blood and the white of his clothes."

"The sound of white," Samuel says, shamelessly paraphrasing some poet whose name he doesn't even know, "is the night. It is not the sun that guides you to white. It is moonlight on stone. Everybody in the penal colony knew this."

He might even have gotten the lines wrong. But as usual, she takes this in her stride, telling Samuel that when she thinks of her mother and father these days the images are clear and abiding: beneath a banyan tree contemplating the color of an eggplant, or breathless in the corridor of a small hospital. Sometimes she sees her mother counting the stars with a tall man beside her, the pale light sifting down from the heavens to illuminate their faces, both holding the sadness of a city.

The calm in which she envelops herself when talking about Amba, or Bhisma, or Adalhard is quite a thing to behold. Samuel, who for his part has learned what it means for a woman to love two men at the same time, now understands deeply that it is possible for a man to love two women simultaneously.

Acknowledgments

I am eternally beholden to Amarzan Loebis and Tedjabayu Sudjojono, survivors of the Buru penal colony and other prisons in Suharto's Indonesia, for having shared with me so much of their time, their memories, and their personal experiences, which have made their way onto these pages. I can never thank them enough for their trust and for their generosity. To me, they are living symbols of the fortitude of the human spirit.

I am also indebted to the patient and nurturing members of the Buru Seven (excluding myself): Alif Alim, Arif Zulkifli, Goenawan Mohamad, Ian White, Teguh Ostenrik, and, again, Amarzan, for saving me so many times during our 2006 trip to Buru, while still finding me great seafood and karaoke, and the bluest, bluest sea.

I owe special thanks to Dr. Aru Sudoyo, my family doctor for many years, for sharing the story of his fieldwork in Buru in the '70s, and to Wolfgang Oey, who shared the inspiring story of his late father, the surgeon Dr. Tjong Hian Oei, who in the '50s returned to Indonesia from Stuttgart, and who for many years dedicated his life to the people of Papua (then West Irian).

Among published sources, my greatest debt is to the indispensable memoirs of those who courageously bore their lives on Buru Island: Hersri Setiawan's *Memoar Pulau Buru* (Magelang: IndonesiaTera, 2004); Kresno Saroso's *Dari Salemba ke Pulau Buru* (Jakarta: ISAI & Pustaka Utan Kayu, 2002); and the late Pramoedya Ananta Toer's *Nyanyi Sunyi Seorang Bisu* (Jakarta: Lentera, 1995). I. G. Krisnadi's excellent study of the Buru Penal Colony, *Tahanan Politik Pulau Buru (1969–1979)* (Jakarta: LP3ES, 2001), is also a fount of much information and insight. I have drawn several invaluable real-life stories, such as the story of the fourteen-year-old boy who went in search of his father but ended up being carted off to Buru and several others, from these sources, especially for use in the chapter on the Buru letters, and given them my own spin.

I am also grateful to the following authors and their work, which has informed my own: Hermawan Sulistyo, *Palu Arit di Ladang Tebu: Sejarah Pembantaian Massal yang Terlupakan: 1965–1966* (Jakarta: Kepustakaan Populer Gramedia, 2000); Robert Cribb (Ed.), *Pembantaian PKI di Jawa Tengah dan Bali 1965–1966* (Jakarta: MataBangsa, 2000); John Roosa, *Dalih Pembunuhan Massal: Gerakan 30 September dan Kudeta Suharto* (Jakarta: Institut Sejarah Sosial Indonesia & Hasta Mitra, 2008); Mary S. Zurbuchen (Ed.), *Beginning to Remember: The Past in the Indonesian Present* (Singapore: Singapore University Press, 2005); Ariel Heryanto, *State Terrorism and Political Identity in Indonesia; Fatally Belonging* (London: Routledge, 2006); Suyatno Prayitno, Astaman Hasibuan & Buntoro (Eds.), *Kesaksian Tapol Orde Baru* (Jakarta: ISAI & Pustaka Utan Kayu, 2003); Rex Mortimer, *Indonesian Communism under Sukarno: Ideology and Politics: 1959–1965* (Jakarta: Solstice Publishing, 2006); Ken Conboy, *Kopassus: Inside Indonesia's Special Forces* (Jakarta: Equinox Publishing, 2003); Pipit Rochijat, "Am I PKI or non-PKI?," *Indonesia*, 40, 1985, pp. 37–52; Ben Abel's interview with

Pipit Rochijat on the mailing list KdPNet, 22–31 October 1996, under the title *Pipit Rochijat dan Pembunuhan Massal 1965*; and the testimony of the late Syu'bah Asa about the tense days in Yogyakarta following Lieutenant Colonel Untung's national radio broadcast on the morning of October 1, 1965.

The story of the attack on Res Publica University on October 19, 1965, with some modifications on my part, came from Tedjabayu Sudjojono's real life account of the event, for which I am grateful.

On Indonesian fine arts in the '50s and '60s, I am indebted to Misbach Thamrin, *Amrus Natalsya dan Bumi Tarung* (Bogor: Amnat Studio, 2008); Aminudin T.H. Siregar, *Sang Ahli Gambar: Sketsa, Gambar & Pemikiran S. Sudjojono* (S. Sudjojono Center & Galeri Canna: Jakarta, 2010); and the late Mia Bustam, *Sudjojono dan Aku* (Jakarta: Pustaka Utan Kayu, 2006). On old Javanese texts, Elizabeth Inandiak, *Centhini: Kekasih yang Tersembunyi* (Yogyakarta: Babad Alas, Yayasan Lokaloka, 2008); Andjar Any, *Rahasia Ramalan Jayabaya, Ronggawarsita & Sabda Palon* (Semarang: Aneka Ilmu, 1990); and Prof. Drs. I Ketut Riana, S. U., *Kakawin desa Warnnana Uthawi Nagara Krtagama: Masa Keemasan Majapahit* (Jakarta: Kompas, 2009).

During the many years it took me to write *The Question of Red* I devoured scores of newspaper articles and historical documents, both print and online versions. I acknowledge my debt to accounts of events at Gadjah Mada University in the '50s and '60s and Res Publica University in 1965, to descriptions of Leipzig and Leiden in the '50s, and to accounts of the religious conflict in the Maluku Islands and on Buru Island, which lasted from 1999 until early 2002. I also referred to stories from *The Mahabharata* and *The Book of Centhini*, as well as *The Book of Wedhatama*.

I am indebted to Aamer Hussein, Tash Aw, Rana Dasgupta, Johanna Lederer, Sylvia Dornseiffer, Amitav Ghosh, José Eduardo

Agualusa, Uzodinma Iweala, Mark Danner, Chris Keulemans, James Norcliffe, Sean Whelan, and the late Lim Chee-Seng, for all manner of help and advice.

I am deeply grateful to Victoria Holmes, Tânia Ganho, and Yu-Mei Balasingamchow, who offered their help in editing the earlier versions of this novel, and whose deep, enriching influence are to be found on these pages. To Joy Harris and Caroline Upcher, for their support and hard work on my behalf. And to the gracious and tireless Dael Allison, who helped me edit the first published version of the novel, to Peter Milne and Irfan Kortschak, who proofread said version at the last minute, and kept their good cheer throughout.

My boundless thanks to Nung Atasana, without whom my manuscript would have not traveled far, to my agents, Kirby Kim and Cecile Barendsma, who have been so patient and supportive throughout, and to the wonderful people on different continents who have published my work: Siti Gretiani, Kristine Kress, and Sander Knol. And, most especially, to the soulful Gabriella Page-Fort of Amazon Crossing, for her friendship and for her faith in me.

I couldn't have written this book without Kurnya Roesad, who kept me firmly in the German-Austrian mold and gave me Bhisma. Or without the love and support of my friends around the world, who have fed me and given me a roof over my head, nourished me with their critical insights and rousing conversations, and supplied me with music, images, wine, and poetry. I am grateful to the following friends, allies, and journey mates: Paul, Peter, Winfred, Lenah, Sadiah, Willemijn, Chris, Aamer, Yenni, Adinda, Nesya, Maya, Lies, Lucy, Panuksmi, Linawati, Margaret, Martina, Wim, Tash, Gary, Tim, Sitok, Nezar, Christian, Stephanie, John, Albert, Amit, and Anthony. And to those who held me aloft during the critical final phase of this current version—you know who you are.

Finally, my eternal thanks to my parents, for so many beginnings, and to my daughter, Nadia Larasati Djohan, for her immense strength and wisdom, and for being the source of all light and laughter. This book is dedicated to them as much as it is to the brave victims and survivors of Buru.

Notes

Book 1

1. I have relied on Pramoedya Ananta Toer, *Perawan Remaja dalam Cengkeraman Militer* (Jakarta: KPG, 2001) for the part on *jugun ianfu*.

Book 3

2. The fragment of Lady Tambangraras's letter to her parents in *Serat Centhini*, quoted by Amba in her letter to her father, comes from Song #136 in Elizabeth D. Inandiak, *Centhini: Kekasih yang Tersembunyi* (Yogyakarta: Babad Alas, Yayasan Lokaloka, 2008), p. 476.

Book 4

3. The quote from the Bible comes from the King James Version, Ecclesiastes 3:1.

Book 5

4. The poem Sudarminto explained to his student is from Song #117 from *Serat Centhini*, in Elizabeth D. Inandiak,

Centhini: Kekasih yang Tersembunyi (Yogyakarta: Babad Alas, Yayasan Lokaloka, 2008), pp. 301–302.

5. For the insight into poetry on page 163, I am indebted to Stanley Kunitz's translation notes to Anna Akhmatova, *Poems of Akhmatova*, selected by Stanley Kunitz with Max Hayward (Boston: Houghton Mifflin Company, 1967).

6. Subagio Sastrowardojo's lines ". . . a line of poetry / rather than promise-choked formulae / that got me thrown out so far / from the earth I happen to love." comes from "Manusia Pertama di Angkasa Luar" (1962). The English translation is the author's.

7. The two lines from *Serat Centhini* that Amba recalled during her train journey to Kediri come from Song #107 in Elizabeth D. Inandiak, *Centhini: Kekasih yang Tersembunyi* (Yogyakarta: Babad Alas, Yayasan Lokaloka, 2008), p. 280.

8. The full version of Rosa Luxemburg's partly quoted sentence is *"Ich fuhle mich in der ganzen Welt zu hause, wo es Wolken und Vögel und Menschentränen gibt."*

9. Paramita Rashad's notes on *geschicktheid* are drawn from Ann Laura Stoler, "A sentimental education; Native servants and the cultivation of European children in the Netherlands Indies," in Laurie J. Sears (Ed.), *Fantasizing the Feminine in Indonesia,* pp. 77–91 (Durham/London: Duke University Press, 1996).

10. T. S. Eliot's lines, ". . . to be conscious is not to be in time" and "Only through time time is conquered" come from "Burnt Norton" in *Four Quartets* © Estate of T. S. Eliot and reprinted by permission of Faber & Faber Ltd.

11. The lines Bhisma read to Amba, "I love you as certain dark things are to be loved, / In secret, between the shadow

and the soul," are from "Sonnet XVII," from *100 Love Sonnets: Cien Sonetos De Amor* by Pablo Neruda, translated by Stephen Tapscott, Copyright © Pablo Neruda 1959 and Fundacion Pablo Neruda, Copyright © 1986 by the University of Texas Press. Courtesy of the University of Texas Press.

12. Philip Larkin's lines "This is the first thing / I have understood: / Time is the echo of an axe / Within a wood." come from the XXVI poem in "The North Ship," taken from *Philip Larkin: Collected Poems* © Estate of Philip Larkin and reprinted by permission of Faber & Faber Ltd.

13. The lines ". . . stays as it was left, / Shaped to the comfort of the last to go / As if to win them back . . ." come from "Home is so Sad," taken from *Philip Larkin: Collected Poems* © Estate of Philip Larkin and reprinted by permission of Faber & Faber Ltd.

14. The lines quoted in the scene at Res Publica University, ". . . let us endure this separation, for I am forging the days, clearing forests, and walking in night's wake, all in the name of our children, children to be raised, children browned by the sun . . ." come from the poem "Memilih Djalan" by Amarzan Ismail Hamid, which appeared in *Kepada Partai (To the Party)*, a journal of the Indonesian Communist Party. The English translation is the author's.

15. Rosa Luxemburg's words, "*Mensch sein ist von allem die Hauptsache . . . Heiter sein, ja heiter, trotz alledem,*" are from one of the letters she wrote in Breslau Prison, 1917.

16. "*So viele Berichte, so viele Fragen . . .*" comes from Bertolt Brecht's poem, "*Fragen Eines Lesenden Arbeiters*" (1935).

Book 6

17. Srikandi's series of engravings was inspired by Louise Bourgeois's *He Disappeared into Complete Silence 1947*, and the indelible impression left on me after viewing, almost back-to-back, two magnificent Bourgeois retrospectives, at the Tate Modern in November 2007, and at the Centre Pompidou in May 2008.

About the Author

Laksmi Pamuntjak is one of Indonesia's most versatile bilingual authors. She is a bilingual journalist and an award-winning food writer as well as a poet, translator, and novelist. *The Question of Red*, her bestselling first novel, was short-listed for the Khatulistiwa Literary Award, appeared on the *Frankfurter Allgemeine Zeitung*'s Top 8 list of the best books of the Frankfurt Book Fair 2015, and was named #1 on Germany's Weltempfaenger (Receivers of the World) list of the best works of fiction translated into German. Pamuntjak was selected as the Indonesian representative for Poetry Parnassus at the 2012 London Olympics. She works as an art and food consultant, writes opinion articles on culture and politics for the *Guardian*, and divides her time between Berlin and Jakarta.